MORNINGSTAR'S HEIR

BY
MELINDA M. SNODGRASS

Credits
Cover Design: by Fakel Barros

Malignant creatures from alternate universes engulf the world in chaos, converging to feast on humanity's worst instincts.

The only person standing against this invasion is the unlikely hero, Albuquerque police detective, Richard Oort. One of the few humans capable of wielding an ancient weapon with the power to destroy both magic and monsters, he's become a Paladin, fighting for the ancient order of the Lumina.

And if saving the world wasn't enough of a challenge, Richard has become the CEO of Lumina Enterprise, a secretive, worldwide operation devoted to spreading knowledge and technology to battle the evils of ignorance, superstition, magic and religious fundamentalism.

As Richard struggles to lead a gang of unlikely allies in this desperate battle, he must conceal the damaging secrets that will cost him the respect and love of his cold, judgmental, and distant father—and try to hide his love for Damon Weber.

Will Richard collapse under the pressure or can he learn to accept and stop hiding that he is gay, saving both himself and all of humanity?

THE CAROLINGIAN BOOK 2

MORNINGSTAR'S HEIR

NEW YORK TIMES BESTSELLING AUTHOR
MELINDA M. SNODGRASS

CHAPTER ONE

WHO IS THIS GUY?

D R. EDDIE TANAKA dug his elbows into the mud, releasing the sweet and sickening smell of rotting vegetation. He wriggled frantically toward the river. It was monsoon season, and the leaves of the bushes, disturbed by his passage, sent water pattering along the length of his body. Some trickled down his collar and joined the sweat bathing him. His sweat wasn't due entirely to the tropical heat. Most of it was because of gut-trembling, bowel-loosening terror.

What were those things?

Behind him he heard screams of pain and terror from his colleagues, maddened, triumphant screams from the attackers, and, over everything, the keening wail of the things. Eddie pressed his belly against the muck, reached out for a tree root coiling up from the earth like an exposed rib, and pulled himself forward. Ahead was the soft gurgle and slap of running water. Not much farther now.

He wondered if anyone else had made it out of the lab, and even as he crawled, he hated himself for not going back. To look for any other survivors. To help them escape. But the only reason he was alive and outside was because he had been on the catwalk suspended high over the accelerator. There was a narrow access tube used to replenish the hyper-

1

pure oil surrounding and shielding the rest of the building from the massive, though brief, release of atomic particles created by their experiments. Experiments that tried to approximate conditions nanoseconds after the Big Bang. Though Eddie was tall, he was also thin, and he had been able to squeeze through the pipe.

The men who attacked the lab offered no mystery. Brandishing knives and machetes, faces obscured behind headcloths, they had extolled their god in voices made shrill by nerves and euphoria. It was what was with them that froze the throat with pure, blind terror.

Things like whirling dervishes constructed of slivered glass. The sound as they spun was a mind-numbing howl. When they swept across a person their passage ripped away clothes and flesh.

Eddie pushed up on his elbows and vomited. He had seen Anne just before he entered the pipe. Clothing and skin flayed off, screaming, still standing, not dead. He retched again and brought up only bile. It wasn't just water and sweat bathing his face now. He tasted tears. Anne had liked him. After they got past him following her into the bathroom that one time. They had been discussing the results of that day's experiment, and Eddie just hadn't noticed. *She liked me. She had told me so. And I didn't do anything to help her.*

Tears blinded him, and he found the edge of the river without meaning to. Arms flailing, he rolled down the bank and into the water. The current took him. The pockets of his lab coat filled with water, but despite the added drag Eddie waited until the water had carried him perhaps a mile downstream from the lab before kicking off his tennis shoes and shrugging out of the coat. He didn't want the things realizing that someone had survived and escaped.

He had to find a phone. Call the emergency number he'd been given. Tell the man who ran Lumina Enterprises what had happened. Hope he didn't get committed as a madman.

✧   ✧   ✧

THE LOW HUM from the big jet's engines and the under-oxygenated air of the cabin conspired to send her to sleep. Dagmar Reitlingen blinked hard, removed her wire rim glasses, rubbed her eyes, and pinched the bridge of her nose. Another five hours and they would arrive in Dallas. A three-hour layover, then the two-hour flight to Albuquerque. Add to that the hours she had already spent sitting in the first-class lounge at London's Heathrow airport. The ground crew kept saying there were *phenomena* which were keeping them from departing, but they never said what *phenomena* meant. Dagmar did the calculation and realized she had left her house twenty hours ago. *Only ten more to go,* she thought glumly, *assuming there aren't more phenomena.*

She had tried to take the Lumina jet, but discovered that Brook was in jail in Baltimore, and the Gulfstream V was parked in a hangar in Maryland. Since she had a new boss, she didn't feel comfortable just hiring another pilot. It was a quirk of her charming, though secretive, CEO that Lumina Enterprises owned only one plane and employed only one full-time pilot. When she'd complained to Kenntnis after one particularly daunting journey back from Singapore, he'd given that rollicking, fixture-shaking laugh and told her he didn't want his chief officers becoming too distant from the average run of humanity. He'd then added that it wasn't like he made them fly coach. So she only got to travel on the GV when Kenntnis was aboard. She had spent a lot of hours on the private jet, but compared to how many she spent flying, it wasn't nearly enough, and she'd tell him so next time. The thought choked and shifted to a worse thought. Maybe there would never be a next time.

The call had come from George Gold, chief counsel for the company, on Christmas Day, informing Dagmar that certain criteria had been met which set in motion the transfer of control of the company into the hands of—

Dagmar pulled a copy of the *Washington Post* from her briefcase and studied the face of the man who now controlled a vast corporate empire more valuable than Microsoft and far less visible.

Despite the grainy quality of the photo the young man's extraordinary beauty came through, although his face was marred by what looked like dark bruises. He was flanked by two older men, one whose severe features showed kinship. It was clear from the relative heights that Richard Oort was not a tall man. His expression was tense and haunted, and he held out a hand as if to ward off the photographer. The headline shouted out BOMB PLOT UNCOVERED. In smaller type was *American evangelist sought to bring about Armageddon in nuclear fire.*

All of Dagmar's instincts screamed out *fraud*, and she said as much to George. The lawyer had disabused her of that notion.

"No, the documents were carefully drawn. Mr. Kenntnis

was very specific in his instructions. Oort is to have total control of the company up to and including liquidating all the assets."

As the COO of the company, Dagmar was left shaken and sickened by that bit of news.

"When did this happen?" Dagmar had demanded.

"December second."

"As if Kenntnis knew something might happen."

"I couldn't say."

"Is he dead?"

"I couldn't say."

She had wanted to scream and curse him for the legalistic caution and cold precision. *Tell me if Kenntnis is alive or dead!* But perhaps George didn't know that either.

"What do we know about this Oort?"

"He's a policeman. From a well-to-do and respected Rhode Island family. Father's a federal court judge."

So, Richard Oort was not a con artist, but he was certainly heedless and indifferent to the welfare of his employees. Why hadn't he obtained Brook's release? Well, she would find out in a few hours. She hoped that Oort was bright as well as beautiful.

The paper crackled as Dagmar lifted it from her lap and studied that face again. She wondered if this insane action by Kenntnis was due to passion, although she hadn't thought Kenntnis had been inclined that way. But why else would you leave a multibillion-dollar company in the hands of a young cop in a nondescript city in a nondescript state?

✧ ✧ ✧

THE REVEREND MARK Grenier stood on the verge at the edge of the westbound I-81 freeway trying to thumb a ride. It wasn't easy to do when your right hand was missing. Overhead, the moon struggled among the heavy clouds, occasionally breaking free and touching the ice-clad branches of the trees with silver. There had been an ice storm two nights ago, and the cold was so intense none of it had melted.

He couldn't keep standing still. Grenier began to walk along the shoulder. His thin-soled Italian loafers offered little protection against the cold, and the buttons of his shirt and coat barely closed over his burgeoning paunch, allowing fingers of cold to lick at his skin. He was losing sensation in his feet, and he stumbled on tussocks of winter-brown grass.

He had made bail yesterday and rushed to his Washington apartment, the apartment he'd maintained so he could be close at hand when a president had need of a little midnight counseling. He was desperate for a shower in privacy, the thick lather of verbena soap, the crackle of a starched Egyptian cotton shirt, and the caress of a cashmere sweater to drive away the memory of that polyester prison jumpsuit. But he'd found the locks changed. He rushed to the bank and discovered his accounts had vanished. He had always been a subtle man; he didn't need a skywriter to get the message. He had failed his overlords, and they had jettisoned him.

Resentment burned in his gut. He had given his life to the study and attainment of power, but not just the power of wealth and influence. Through long and arduous study, he had become a sorcerer. Magic flowed through his hands and sang in his blood. He had worked hard to open the gates between the dimensions and allow the Old Ones to return, and *they had fucking succeeded.*

Then, because of one *tiny* miscalculation, because he underestimated the strength of will of one Richard Noel Oort, he had forever lost his ability to do magic. He remembered that space black blade with a nimbus of stars surrounding it swinging through the air, and the glitter of Richard's pale blue eyes seen over the sword, and then Grenier's hand was gone, the stump pumping a jet of blood into the air. There was a twinge of pain, and the memory of movement from his missing right hand. Grenier laid his remaining hand over the stump. It was as sore as his emotions.

Headlights swept around a broad curve in the road. Grenier stepped onto the edge of the pavement and frantically waved at the car. It was an older model Chevy; two doors, its white paint peeling in leprous gray patches. Grenier had an instant to see the driver's reaction, an upthrust middle finger, before the car swept past. The wind from its passage blew his coat hard against his body, and a blast of exhaust set his eyes to watering. He *hated* pollution. Well, the Old Ones' arrival would eventually put a stop to that. Unless they were thwarted, and that didn't seem likely with Prometheus bound and all hope resting on one slender young man.

He plodded on for another mile or so before another pair of headlights swept across the verge. Light shattered against the ice-encased boles of the leafless trees lining the roadway. It was a big, tan RV. To Grenier's surprise it didn't rush past, but instead pulled onto the shoulder.

The passenger side window lowered. Grenier could barely hear the man's voice over the dull rumble of the RV's diesel engine.

"How far you going?"

"As far as you'll take me."

"Hop in."

Grabbing the handhold beside the door with his left hand, Grenier hauled himself onto the running board and into the RV. He tucked his stump under his coat, a protective if useless gesture. Grenier settled into the passenger seat and studied his rescuer. Late fifties, unusually fit for that age. Grenier noted the military haircut, short and tight over the ears, and the way the man canted slightly to the right. Grenier leaned forward slightly and spotted the holstered pistol on the man's left hip. Cop or soldier. He was suddenly acutely aware that he was jumping bail.

He glanced back through the door leading into the body of the RV.

A woman sat at the small table. She cradled a long rifle the way another woman might hold a child, or a child might hold a teddy bear. The woman looked to be in her twenties, with brown hair that brushed at her chin, a chin too square for real beauty. Straight, thick eyebrows frowned over brown eyes that welled with tears. Grenier checked, worried that the barrel might soon be facing him.

The man seemed to read Grenier's concern. "It's not loaded," he said in a low voice. "She really freaks out if she's not holding it, so I let her be." The man put the RV back in gear, and they went bumping off the shoulder and back onto the freeway.

The man held out his hand. "Syd Marten."

Grenier slid his arm from beneath the concealing coat and held up the bandaged stump. Marten jerked back his hand. "Consider your hand duly shaken," Grenier said, stalling for time while he thought what name to offer.

Grenier had been a famous man. Preaching on the Christian cable networks, lending his support to various "culture of life" issues, leading prayer breakfasts at the White House, attacking scientists on the twenty-four-hour news channels, spouting his nonsense without pushback from the national media. He had been written up in various magazines and newspapers as the most powerful voice of America's evangelical movement. Would he be recognized? While in jail he had grown a beard and mustache and being assigned by a sympathetic guard to kitchen detail had enabled him to eat constantly as he alternately cursed at and wept for his lost power. He decided to offer a false name.

"Mark Jenkins," Grenier said, using his mother's maiden name.

"Where are you headed?" Marten asked.

"West." It seemed a safe, if vague, response.

"Us, too," Marten said. He gestured at the eastbound side of the freeway with its steady line of cars, their headlights like a chain of diamonds. "If they were smart, they'd be hightailing it the other way, too, but their government isn't leveling with them."

"About what?" Grenier probed gently.

Beads of moisture popped out on Marten's forehead, and a trembling shook his body. He wiped away sweat and sucked in a quick, deep breath. "What's happening in

Virginia," came the choked reply.

He's been to my compound. He's seen. What a strange coincidence.

Grenier wondered if some vestige of his magic was still working. Or perhaps it was one of those flukes of quantum coincidence that scientists struggled to explain. Whatever the reason, Grenier would have to be careful. He thanked the cautious instinct that had led him to give a false name.

"What's happening to our world?" Grenier asked.

"Damned if I know. Whatever it is, it ain't good. I've seen this thing, and I went nuts. Ended up locked up in the booby hatch. Look at her." He gestured back toward the woman. "That's my daughter, Samantha. The girl who had to out-jock every jock in the FBI. Prove to me it's okay that she's a girl and not a son ... like I care, I'd love her no matter what, but she just won't accept that."

It was a gift, Grenier thought. He'd always had this ability to engender trust in people and elicit their confidences. His career choices had been obvious, politician or preacher. Preacher had paid better.

"Anyway, she volunteered to go out there. She's in the FBI, just like me. She's a trained sniper, and since she went there all she does is sit and cry. I think this thing, this effect ... whatever it is, is going to spread. So, I loaded up the RV and we left." The man fell silent, but Grenier could tell he was eager to talk more. Grenier inclined his torso forward, softened his expression, begged to receive the confidence. Marten obliged.

"I didn't give notice or anything. The last guy who tried to leave got locked up. Jacobson. They say it's because he refused to go out there, but I can't help but wonder if he got locked up because he's a Jew. Next, it'll be the blacks. All the old hates and distrusts are coming to the surface. The world's gone a different kind of nuts."

No, just the same old nuts, Grenier thought, but what he said was, "You seem very sane."

"Yeah, now."

"What did they do for you?"

"Who?"

"The doctors."

"Not a damn thing."

For Grenier a certainty began to grow. It was all too perfect. If his instinct was correct, he was going to have an opportunity to fuck over his former masters.

"It wasn't the doctors who fixed me, but this young guy, Richard Oort. I don't remember much about him, but there was this sword."

"With a blade as black as space, shot through with glittering points of light like the swirl of stars, and when it's drawn you feel the bass tones growling and reverberating in your chest like the notes of a massive organ," Grenier said softly as he remembered.

"You know him," Marten said.

"Oh, yes." Grenier softly stroked the bandage over his stump.

"I've got to reach him. Have him help my Sam like he helped me," Marten said.

"I'd like to find him, too." And Grenier clenched his left fist and felt his phantom right hand also close. "For a lot of reasons."

✧ ✧ ✧

THE BAR WASN'T nice enough for Bourbon Street. It was a few blocks and a universe away from the French Quarter, especially the new Disneyfied version of the French Quarter after the devastation of Hurricane Katrina. It was dark and, even in January, hot, and it stank of spilled booze, cigarettes, mold, and infrequently washed bodies.

Doug Andresson couldn't pay for the shot and the beer that stood on the bar in front of him. He'd used what remained of his money on the last round. He watched the head of the beer go sliding down the side of the glass, and for some reason it reminded him of the white foam that would run out of the horses' mouths when his uncle broke the new broncos. Sometimes the fat old bastard would apply the bit so hard that the foam would turn red with blood. He was just as mean of a bastard as his brother, Doug's father.

The memory brought other memories, of a belt laid hard across his back and thighs. It was after his father's beatings that his mother would send him off to Uncle Frank's ranch, separating the father and son. Doug had vowed he'd kill the man. Cancer had done it first.

Doug fumbled in his pants pocket for the can of tobacco. Pulling off the lid, he pinched off a plug and thrust it between lip and gum. The bottom of the can showed silver through the rich mahogany of the tobacco. He was almost out of that, too. He needed money, and he needed it fast. He weighed the pros and cons between a B&E in the Garden District or a mugging on Bourbon Street. Big, fancy houses often had dogs and alarms, and private security. Drunks were usually easy. He'd make up his mind after he finished his drink.

It wasn't supposed to have been like this. He was supposed to be on easy street. Grenier had promised him power, respect, and money, but those dickheads couldn't find their asses with both hands, and when the FBI had shown up, they'd either dithered or fought. Only Doug had had the brains to head for the property line the minute that big helicopter had come roaring in. All those promises about how he was going to be taken care of, looked after—it was just more crap. He was broke in New Orleans, Grenier was in jail, and eventually the cops would come after him again. They always did.

There was always a level of rage that bubbled along all his nerve endings, but now a new emotion twined around that life-sustaining feeling—melancholy and loss. He studied the fading bruises on his knuckles, legacies of the blows he'd delivered to the cop's face. Grenier had said Doug was special, but because of that little faggot Doug had never found out if he actually *was* special.

It was time to drink. He spat out the plug. It hit the stained wood of the floor between his feet with a wet splat and formed a starburst pattern. It was kinda pretty. He picked up the whiskey and downed it with one quick swallow. The heat from the alcohol burned the hot place on his gum where the plug had rested, and it felt like he'd swallowed smoke. He chased away the fire with the cold of the beer, draining the mug in five long swallows. He then pushed back from the bar and started for the door.

"Hey!" The bartender's basso shout almost hurt Doug's ears. "You haven't paid for that." The Cajun accent made musical mush of the words.

Doug turned slowly back to face the man. The bartender was big, red-faced, and fat, with a sweat stain at the neck of his T-shirt. The sandy hairs on his forearms stood up like the bristles on a pig and blurred the anchors and mermaid tattoos that adorned the freckled skin.

"Not going to." He patted his pockets. "No money," Doug said.

And then he smiled. His *special* smile.

The big man's glare faded into nervous confusion, and he lost some of his color. Suddenly he seemed like a flaccid balloon. "Well … well, you get on out of here. Now. Don't want deadbeats. You just go on now."

With a jaunty little half wave, half salute, Doug left the bar. Maybe he was special. He had a special kind of crazy that made people afraid. And someday he'd use it again on Richard Oort.

CHAPTER TWO

POOR BASTARD

R HIANA DAVINOVITCH NERVOUSLY touched the earrings running from the tops of her ears down to the lobes. Where once they had been cheap Walmart junk, they were now real diamonds, emeralds, and pearls. She walked over to the hotel window, reveling in the play of muscles and tendons in her legs.

In her father's dimension she wore a different form, and it wasn't a comfortable one. She was glad to be back in the universe that housed the Earth. Maybe it was because this world had birthed her. Her mother had been human.

Rhiana looked over to where her father, Madoc, sat watching CNN. He was anything but.

Madoc wore his human form, but with the impossibly narrow face, upswept brows, and glittering eyes, he still didn't look human, not really.

Rhiana looked back out the window at a sunny California day.

Droplets of water from the sprinklers glittered on the leaves on the avocado tree that offered privacy to their cabana at the Beverly Hills Hotel. It seemed weird to be back in California. Her foster parents were only a few miles away, sitting in their tiny 1940s tract house in Van Nuys. Years ago, they had driven onto the grounds of the famous hotel just off Sunset Boulevard, and hotel security had reacted to her dad's built-up pickup truck. Her father had blustered, but ultimately, they had left without ever crossing the portals of the lobby. Now she was staying here.

There was a knock. Rhiana opened the door. The warm air blew into the over-air-conditioned cabana, carrying the scent of clipped grass and star jasmine and the heavy aftershave of the man at the door. Jack Rendell wasn't what she had expected. Since he had been presented as the replacement for Mark Grenier, she had been expecting another unctuous, older man. Someone to play the role of reverend-as-daddy. But Rendell was young, early thirties at most. He topped six feet by several inches, and the tall frame supported an athlete's musculature. His features were regular and handsome in that corn-fed, all-American way that you expected to see in a war movie from the 1940s. But there was an expression deep in his hazel eyes that belied that impression. Something cold and hungry and calculating lived beneath the pleasant exterior.

Rendell was a wildly popular spiritualist with a cable show, the occasional special on network television, and lucrative speaking tours where he put grieving people in touch with the "beloved departed." Unlike many of that ilk, he was not a fraud. Instead, he was a major magical talent. Even as introductions were made and handshakes exchanged, Rhiana could feel the power coming off him in waves. It was to be her task to teach him control of his magical ability.

Rendell held her hand an instant too long, stood a fraction too close, and allowed his gaze to drop lasciviously to her bosom. Rhiana longed to be older, more sophisticated, and know how to handle this. Instead, she jerked her hand away and retreated.

Madoc began the meeting. "Grenier is gone. He made bail yesterday and vanished."

"And this matters how?" Rendell asked. "Isn't he useless now? I don't see any way for him to fuck us up."

The slow pullback of Madoc's lips revealed sharply pointed teeth. Rendell sucked in a quick breath. "I agree, but it would have been so pleasant to punish him for his failures." The tip of his tongue flicked out, and Madoc licked his bottom lip as if tasting that punishment. "So, are you ready to approach the Cardinal of Washington, DC, with your 'visions'?"

"Are you ready to back them up with a miracle?" Rendell countered. Madoc nodded. "I have a question," Rendell added.

"You may ask it," Madoc replied.

"Why aren't you using one of the other heavy hitters from the Religious Right to inoculate the gate? Why come to me and the Catholic Church?"

"Because of the involvement first of the FBI and now the military." Madoc shot Rhiana a sideways glance.

And that was her fault. She had offered Richard's rescuers a piece of information that brought in the cavalry. Despite being his child, despite his seeming forgiveness, she still had a fluttering in the pit of her stomach.

Because he never misses an opportunity to remind me of my transgression. Which probably makes his "forgiveness" not all that sincere.

"Word has filtered out that there are demons there," Madoc continued. "The Catholics are perceived as the go-to guys on demons and exorcisms." He gave a thin smile. "And once the Virginia compound has been rehabilitated, it will give us a nice rallying cry for the fundamentalists: that the Papists have taken control of the place where the Lord will arrive for his Second Coming."

Rendell absorbed this, nodded slowly. "Anything else?"

"Yes. When you address your followers, I want you to strongly suggest that science and scientists are evil, and that they will block the efforts to bring back the age of magic and miracles. We need the scientific community neutralized and eventually destroyed."

"I don't understand."

"We don't want any dissenting voices," Madoc said smoothly.

And we also don't want anyone looking too closely at how I bound Kenntnis. For while Rhiana had used magic to summon the power, it was physics that held the creature trapped. It was possible that physics could offer a means to free him, and Kenntnis/Prometheus/Lucifer unbound would put an end to their conquest of this world.

"... and we especially need an interdiction of nuclear weapons."

Madoc's words penetrated Rhiana's wandering thoughts. "As hostilities increase, we want to make certain that the violence is planned, limited, and carefully directed."

Rendell looked up from where he was taking notes on his phone. "I thought you guys fed on death."

Madoc turned his head slowly and regarded the human. Rhiana saw the black spikes flaring from his human form, anger made manifest. Rendell seemed unaware. "You are mistaken," Madoc said. "Death itself is like eating ash. It's fear, hate, grief, despair, and agony that offer the most nourishment. We would rather have a thousand Rwandas than one Hiroshima."

"Got it," said Rendell. "Oh, I put out the word to my viewers about that guy you wanted to find, and we got—"

Madoc held up a minatory finger. "We are done for now. Let me walk you to your car."

Rhiana frowned at the door that closed behind them. *What was it that he didn't want her to hear?*

She pulled a penny out of her pocket. Set it to spinning and glowing, summoned the power, and sent a tendril undulating among the trees and bushes lining the stone walkway. She took out her cell phone. The spell reached out and touched the phone in Rendell's pocket, turned it on, and linked it to her cell. Their voices came through clearly.

"He's in New Orleans," Rendell was saying.

"And I've got someone in New Mexico. He's going to kill the Paladin, and get the sword for us," Madoc said.

Shock at Madoc's words caused her to drop the phone; the link shattered, and her phone fused into blackened metal and melted plastic, destroyed by the flow of magic through material never meant to contain that alien power.

Rhiana had tried not to think of him since their parting in a dell in Virginia, but now Richard Oort's chiseled features filled her mind. She wanted him; to love and to punish, to torment and impress, and now Madoc was going to let him die.

"You promised! You promised I could have him!" Rhiana whispered. Her throat was tight and small.

The moment the words were uttered she felt foolish and naive. What were Madoc's promises really worth? Richard was just a human, albeit a unique one, and Madoc and his kind were here to conquer and enslave humans.

Rhiana swept up the destroyed phone and thrust it deep into a pocket. She had to warn Richard. She came up short, picturing how that beautiful face would freeze in aristocratic disdain, how cold those pale blue eyes would become. She had betrayed him. It was foolish to think Richard would ever trust her again. But she had to try. She picked up the hotel phone.

Dr. Angela Armandariz, Albuquerque's chief medical examiner, walked past body-filled gurneys that lined the hallway. She took this as a clue that there was no more room in the drawers in the actual morgue. She sighed and gave up any hope of dinner at a reasonable hour. It was a New Mexico tradition to celebrate New Year's Eve with gunfire. This year it seemed that everyone had decided to shoot not into the sky but at each other. Except New Year's had been a week and a half ago, and she didn't understand why they were still buried in bodies. Granted, she had been out on medical leave for several weeks, *after the vines in a carpet were magicked so they would attack me and try to kill me.* She shuddered as she remembered those writhing vines thrusting up her nose, and past her lips, filling her lungs and her belly, but she wasn't the only coroner in Albuquerque.

Pallid feet, the big toes adorned by tags, thrust from beneath sheets like displays on a butcher's counter. Her eye was caught by the title on one toe. Dr. Kenneth Wilson. The body on the next gurney was also a doctor. She counted seven before she reached the double metal doors of the morgue.

Angela wrapped her arms around herself, trying to banish the sudden chill that wasn't entirely due to the big coolers and fans in the morgue. She would need to tell Richard about the dead scientists. She hit play on the cheap boom box, and U2 throbbed through the morgue. Angela slipped the strap of the big rubber apron over her head, snapped on her surgical gloves, and flexed her fingers.

She walked to the stainless-steel autopsy table. It held the naked body of a young Hispanic man. Bruises covered his chest and face, as if a mad tattoo artist had lost control of the needle. The head was caved in on one side. To her practiced eye the groove looked like a baseball bat. The waxy skin depressed under the scalpel's blade. She drew it down the length of his chest. A red line, formed by muscle tissue and a bit of sluggish blood, followed the path of the cut. She wondered why she was bothering; cause of death seemed pretty fucking obvious.

She was distracted by the bang and squeak as the double doors were thrust open. "Put 'em in the hall. There's no room in here," she called over U2, not bothering to look up.

The music cut off abruptly. Angela whirled, ready to rip someone a new asshole. She relaxed when she saw Lieutenant Damon Weber. His square-jawed face sagged with fatigue, and the dark bags hanging beneath his eyes made him look like a raccoon.

He swiveled his head from side to side, counting the gurneys, but it was a slow and careful movement, as if his neck were made of glass and would snap if he moved too quickly.

"Yes, I am up to my ass in dead people," Angela said.

"At least you don't hear them," Weber said with the briefest of smiles.

"In this wonderful new year, I wouldn't put that beyond the realm of possibility. What do you need? And please don't say a report."

Weber shook his head, grimaced. Angela pulled off her gloves and tossed them in the trash. "Here," she said, indicating a wheeled metal stool. The big cop sat down, and she set to work massaging his neck. It felt less like muscles than like metal bands shifting beneath the skin. He groaned and allowed his chin to fall onto his chest.

"I need Richard to come in. How do you think that's going to go over?" The words were muffled, trapped by the tucked chin.

"Like you don't know the answer to that," she said, recalling the discussion at the Lumina offices five days before.

Judge Robert Oort had harangued his son for forty-three minutes.

Angela knew; she had kept time. In this he had been ably and brutally assisted by his daughter, and Richard's sister, Pamela. Pamela had arrived in Albuquerque the day before, been given a crash course in the World According to Lumina, been touched by the sword, and had instantly assumed a position of authority.

There were facial similarities between the siblings. They both had high cheekbones, pointed chins, and translucently fair skin, but Pamela's eyes were dark gray rather than pale silver blue and were sharp and judgmental. By contrast, Richard's eyes held a sweetness and a vulnerability. Pamela was attractive, with soft light brown hair. Richard was gorgeous with silver/gilt hair. Angela wondered if that cosmic unfairness had added to Pamela's seemingly constant irritation with her brother. Angela found the young lawyer insufferable, and she said so now.

"Actually, you're a lot alike," Weber said. "Which is probably why she bugs you so much."

"We are not. I would never berate Richard like that." Angela moderated her tone and shook her head. "Not that they aren't right. He probably does need to quit."

"Yeah … maybe … but not right now. I need him. Ortiz called in last night …" His voice trailed away, and Weber scrubbed at his face with a hand.

The rasp of skin on stubble was a reassuringly male sound, and Angela wished she wasn't standing in a morgue, but at her condo fixing breakfast, and hearing that sound as Richard wandered into the kitchen wearing only … She shook off the daydream.

"Yeah, and?"

"It was weird shit. About how he wasn't coming back because he had to go up to Truchas Peak, and wrestle with demons the way his granddad used to."

Fear rippled down Angela's back. Captain Ortiz was a hard-nosed cop with twenty-one years of service. What he lacked in imagination he made up for in tenacity. He would never be fanciful or insane.

"It's because of the gates."

"No!" Weber came off the stool with such force that it went squeaking and skittering away across the concrete floor. "Do *not* say that! This shit cannot have spread this far or this fast. We've gotta have more time, to plan … to prepare."

"Prepare for what? To do what?"

"Richard has to tell us that," Weber said.

"Yeah, and you want him to work as a homicide detective, and his dad and sister want him to be Bill Gates, and—"

"And what do you want him to do?" Weber asked.

"I want him to keep me safe." She hugged herself; her fingers dug into her upper arms, and her throat ached with unshed tears. "Because I'm scared, and he's the only person who can do that."

"Poor bastard," Weber said softly.

They stood silently for a few moments. "So, what are you going to do?" Angela asked.

"Tell him I need him and let him decide."

✧   ✧   ✧

ALL THAT REMAINED of her brother's presence in the grand office at the Lumina building was the faint scent of his aftershave. Richard had listened, eyes veiled by his long lashes, two spots of hectic color high on his cheeks, while she and their father had once again carefully detailed why he had to resign from the Albuquerque Police Department.

"Well," she said with satisfaction. "We finally won."

"Yes, Richard can be made to see sense." Judge Robert Oort bent and picked up several papers that had gone skittering off the large multicolored granite desk, swept up by the speed of his son's departure.

"So now he can concentrate on *saving the world*." She laid sarcastic emphasis on the last three words, only to have her father round on her with fury glittering in his dark blue eyes.

"Don't take that scornful, doubting tone with me. Do you doubt your brother's and my word? And if you do … if you think this is all hyperbole and hysteria, perhaps you ought to return to Rhode Island."

"To what?" she asked. "Somebody burned down our house."

"The same somebodies who killed your mother," Robert said quietly. Pain edged the words.

"She committed suicide."

"Richard was right. She was encouraged to do so." Robert slid his glasses back on and picked up another document.

"Maybe if I had experienced some of this instead of just hearing about gates and Old Ones who masquerade as gods and feed on human misery, I might not think this is some kind of hallucination all of you are sharing."

"You've seen the sword, and felt its effect," the judge said.

That was true, but despite the twisting pain that had seemed to reach down into her very cells when her brother had laid the blade on her shoulder, she couldn't really tell what was supposed to have happened. Supposedly she could no longer do magic. Well, she had never been able to do magic, so this seemed like a bizzarly pointless exercise.

She said as much to Robert, and then added, "It's a specious and circular argument, like saying 'I painted an elephant on my barn to ward off lightning, and, by God, my barn has *never* been struck by lightning.'" She shut the cabinet doors with a bang. "And there is nothing on the news about gates and monsters. Let me see a monster, and then maybe this wouldn't feel so crazy and surreal."

"You have. You've seen Cross," her father said.

"Who lives in a crate behind the building. Not exactly filling me with dread."

"He's the weakest of his kind." Robert shook his head. "Which is rather sad when you consider that he represents the loving, forgiving, and merciful brand of Christianity."

"So, bring on the monsters," she said lightly.

Her father's head jerked up and he stared at her. His jaw worked for a moment. "No. I hope you never have to face them." He paused and stared out the window toward the distant snowcapped peak of a mountain far to the west. "Bad enough that Richard has to. I just hope he's strong enough."

Pamela heard the thread of doubt in her father's voice.

CHAPTER THREE
UNSEEN THINGS

W EBER TAPPED A cigarette out the pack, stuck it between his lips, then with a growl returned it to the pack. He needed a smoke desperately, something to do with his hands, something to help center his tumultuous thoughts. He also didn't want to have to head downstairs and out into the parking lot or climb the stairs to the roof to get his nicotine jolt. And there would probably be other addicts in either place, and he didn't want to have to make small talk as if the world was normal, which it was *fucking not*.

His mind returned to the quiet, woeful voice of Richard Oort as he told Weber he was driving into work but not to help, instead to resign from the police force. Damon's explosive reaction had elicited a frightened gasp from the younger man and a very long silence before Richard's voice had returned, sounding very young, to say, *"I just couldn't take anymore haranguing."* There had then been a long pause with some convulsive swallowing before Richard had continued. *"My father's hard enough to resist, but when I've got two of them ganging up on me ... And they're probably right ... I guess."*

That quick gasp kept returning to haunt Damon. He realized he had scared Richard, and that—

Like a needle skipping on an old-style vinyl LP, Damon jerked his thoughts into a new groove. The old man. The judge. The tough old bastard. Since their return from Virginia, Damon had had plenty of opportunity to observe the dynamic between the father and son and it left him with an ache at the hinge of his jaw as he fought to stay quiet. Over the weeks Robert Oort had vacillated between occasionally showing affection toward and approval of his only son and abruptly withdrawing into a distant, austere figure constantly finding fault as Richard tried to cope with the reality that a multibillion-dollar company had just been dumped in his lap. On top of the fact that monsters ... aliens ... from other multiverses were pouring through dimensional gates all over the planet.

And the guy who was supposed to hold back the invasion and close the gates with this woo-woo sword thing was a five-foot-four twenty-eight-year-old who had just come off being tortured and sometimes looked like a strong breeze would knock him over.

Damon just wanted to—

Another needle jump. He needed to go tell the acting captain to expect Richard's resignation. Since he'd be out of his office for that maybe he'd go get that smoke. As he stepped out of his office and into the controlled chaos of the bullpen, he saw Lucile from dispatch beckoning wildly.

"We've got a bad one, Lieutenant," she said, and patched him into the 911 call she was monitoring.

The 911 operator kept his voice low and steady. *"So, where are you now, honey?"*

"In the bedroom." A little girl's voice, shaking with terror.

"Are you alone?"

"I've got the baby and Matt."

"Have you locked the door?"

"Daddy hurt Valerie. There's blood everywhere."

Damon's phone rang with the music he'd assigned to Richard.

"Damon, I've been monitoring on the radio. I'm only a quarter of a mile away. Heading there now."

"Wait for backup. We're on our way," he shouted into the phone as behind him he could hear Torres alerting SWAT, and Lucile calling for EMTs.

"We may not have that long."

"Damn it, Richard—"

"They're children. Frightened children." The call was disconnected.

Like you, Weber thought, as fear made a vise around his heart.

RICHARD ROLLED DOWN the window and clamped his siren to the roof of his car. He then floored the POS used Volvo, managed to get it up to eighty as he tore down the quiet residential streets. He really wished he was driving the Ferrari, or the Lamborghini parked beneath the Lumina building. *But if you'd been driving either of them, you wouldn't have had the police radio. Wouldn't have known you were so close, couldn't have responded.*

Still monitoring the 911 call, Richard killed the siren and made the turn onto Quincy.

"Julie, have you locked the door?"

"Yes ... but he's got Toby."

Then the screaming started. Even filtered through two phones and the radio the sound was ghastly, a child's agonized cries. Richard's hands jerked on the steering wheel, sending the car bouncing up onto the sidewalk and nearly taking out a mailbox. He got the car back under control and turned into one of the alleys that ran behind the houses in this older neighborhood.

From the radio came the sound of panting breaths, each holding a shuddering sob. It took every ounce of control Richard possessed not to floor the gas pedal again so he could get there faster.

There was a sudden silence. Then Julie's voice whispered, *"He's coming."*

Damon's voice cut in. *"Richard, it'll be at least twenty minutes before we get there."*

"Copy. Damon, is there anybody in the area? Any backup at all?"

"Snyder's coming."

Richard wanted to curse. In his opinion Dale Snyder was a lazy cop just marking time until he had in his twenty years. They had a strained and antagonistic relationship because he resented Richard, viewing him as a rich East Coast dilettante playing at being a cop. He also believed Richard made detective because somebody pulled strings. *He probably wasn't wrong, on either count,* Richard thought rather wryly, but personal rivalries became irrelevant when faced with a crisis of this magnitude.

"Tell him I'm going in through the alley and backyard."

"Copy that."

Richard stopped the car and jumped out. The January sun was warm enough that the garbage cans in their little pens filled the air with that sickeningly sweet scent of rotting food. Nausea gripped his gut. Some of it was the smell. Some of it was fear. It was never fun walking into a domestic situation. It was when most cops got killed.

Opening the trunk, Richard ripped off his suit coat and donned his vest. The barrel of the shotgun glinted in the sunlight and the wood of the stock felt silky beneath his hands. Richard hesitated. It was a hostage situation; he couldn't really use such a weapon. Instead, he drew the Heckler and Koch.

Okay, so I guess I'm resigning later.

The back wall was a low cinder block affair only four feet tall. Set in it was a wooden gate so old that the wood had weathered until it looked like frozen smoke. It rested on a concrete path, and Richard knew it would shriek like a scalded cat if he tried to open it. He braced his free hand on top of the block wall and vaulted over. The winter-dry grass, faded like an old man's hair, crackled beneath his feet.

The yard would have been lovely if it were summer. There were arched trellises supporting the skeletal branches of climbing rosebushes. Water fell with a gentle tinkling down a small stone waterfall and into a fishpond. Gold flashed and flickered beneath the water.

Richard ran as lightly as he could for the back door, past an incredibly expensive swing, slide, and jungle gym set and a hand-built playhouse designed like a Victorian Painted Lady. The air was deathly still, but suddenly the swings rocked, and the chains creaked. Richard whirled, thinking the father had come through the side yard, but there was nothing there. To his left the manes of five plastic horses on springs, frozen in a wild gallop, formed waves of palomino, chestnut, gray, and black.

Richard frowned. The backyard was a child's paradise. It didn't jibe with a man murdering his own children. There was a flutter of movement past the window of the playhouse. Richard jumped, drew down on it. Again nothing. His neck hairs felt like they were heading toward the top of his head.

It was like that elusive movement sometimes caught at the border between darkness and headlights, or the shadow one sees out of the corner of an eye just before sleep takes you. In the past Richard would have dismissed it as his eyes playing tricks on him. Now he knew differently. Three months ago, Richard had learned there were unseen worlds on the borders of reality. Dimensions filled with horrific, nightmare creatures. Things that viewed humans as food. Things that drove people to acts of unspeakable violence. And Richard sensed they were here with him now.

There was one sure way to tell. Unlimbering his cell phone, Richard watched the glow beginning to fade. There was also only one way to prevent what was happening from happening. A way to keep electronics functioning and guncotton from being warped and changed on the atomic level. Snyder or no Snyder, Richard had no choice; he had to draw the sword.

Richard had reached the kitchen door. Now that he was at the house, he could faintly hear drumming, rhythmical kicks from inside. The back door was pierced by a medium-sized dog door, and Richard wondered if the dog had also fallen victim to the madman inside.

Drawing in a deep breath, he dropped the phone back into his pocket, and reached for the sword hilt that he carried in a holster at the small of his back. His finger slipped through the Escher-like curves as he drew the hilt, the twisting gray glass was cool against his palm and fingers. Richard placed his right hand against the base of the hilt and pulled it away. A space black blade filled with swirling silver motes like stars seemed to appear from his hand. Richard had discovered that whenever he was in the presence of powerful magic, the lights would emerge from the blade and form a spinning nimbus of light around the sword and even around him. It was happening now, proving his paranoia was justified. When the sword was drawn there was also a sound as if a cosmic organ had played a chord whose bass tones and overtones extended far beyond the range of human hearing. It echoed in the backyard.

At the same moment and setting a jarring counterpoint there was the shriek of wood on concrete as Dale Snyder pushed through the back gate.

"Jesus shit!" Snyder yelped; his eyes were locked on the sword. Richard braced himself for the questions and the mocking, but oddly none were forthcoming. Instead, the other detective joined him at the back door, though his eyes kept sliding to the sword. There was no sign from inside the house that the various noises outside had been noticed.

"Tried it yet?" Snyder asked in a whisper.

"About to."

It was too much to hope that it would have been unlocked. Richard sighed, and he and Snyder exchanged a glance. "Wanna try that pigsticker on it?" Snyder asked with a jerk of his chin toward the sword.

Since the sword was an alien weapon created by a man … creature … alien that was no longer able to make a replacement, Richard was more than a little reluctant to make the experiment. He shook his head.

Snyder rolled his eyes, and they pressed their shoulders against the door, but it was sturdy and well hung. It barely quivered. There were windows to the left and right but wrought iron bars covered the glass. Seconds, precious seconds, were ticking away. How much longer could that fragile bedroom door withstand the onslaught, Richard wondered? He was trying to breathe. Trying to think.

The dog door.

"I think I can wriggle through that," Richard whispered to the larger man.

Snyder nodded. Richard laid down on his back, sword hilt pressed against his chest with both hands, the blade running the length of his body. He had a sudden vivid memory of the effigies of dead knights on their tombs in the crypt at Westminster Abby, and he pushed back a shudder.

Years of gymnastics had made him flexible; they had also given him rather broad shoulders for his height and build. He wriggled first one shoulder and then the other through the narrow opening while Snyder held the flap out of Richard's way. He felt the sill of the dog door catch on his back pants pocket and the material rip loose. Something wet and sticky began soaking into his hair now that his torso was inside the kitchen. The sweet coppery scent of blood hung in the air, overlaying the spicy scent of cooking tomato sauce. Richard choked briefly on bile.

Now that he was partly inside Richard could hear a man's voice muttering in an almost unintelligible monologue, a *basso continuo* beneath the crash of the kicks and the splinter of wood.

"Iknowwhatyouare.   Openyouupletthemonstersout. Wheredidyoutakethem?"

Bracing one hand against the floor, Richard felt the sluggishly congealing blood well up around his fingers. He sprang to his feet. The cell phone in his pants pocket vibrated, but Richard ignored it and unlocked the door. Snyder stepped in, and his eyes widened. Richard mentally braced himself and turned to face the source of the blood which had his clothing sticking to his body.

A woman lay in a pool of blood in the middle of the kitchen floor. Wounds like red mouths puckered the material of her white sweater. Her throat was partially cut. A large white Le Creuset pot sat on the stove. The burner was turned on, and there was an occasional wet *plop* as spaghetti sauce roiled in a slow boil.

There was the rending sound of wood tearing, a crash, and Julie's shrill screams. Stealth no longer served any purpose, and they were out of time.

THEY HAD WALKED the dimensions back to the gate in Virginia. Madoc had told her to wait for him in the public rooms of the great stone-and-log house that had once been both the headquarters for the Worldwide Christian Alliance and Mark Grenier's palatial home. She didn't know why she was being left like a piece of luggage to be called for later. Maybe he was up to something. Maybe he was angry. It was hard to read her father. He placed human emotions on his face like a Mardi Gras attendee changing masks.

Eventually she became restless. She hated the white carpet underfoot and the blue velvet upholstered furniture and what passed for art. There were a few framed studio photographs of Grenier, and some too-bright, too-colorful pictures of Jesus suffering the little children to come to him, doling out the loaves and fishes, praying in Gethsemane. The girl growing up in Van Nuys would have been impressed with the cushy carpet underfoot and the plush velvet beneath her fingertips. But the weeks she had spent living in Kenntnis's penthouse had taught her enough to know that this was kitsch masquerading as elegance.

She pushed open the door leading to Grenier's private quarters.

Partway down the hall there was a smear of blood down a panel wall. The FBI had seen that the bodies were removed, but no actual cleanup had occurred. Once the dimensional gate had opened, the humans had retreated. Each day the perimeter of soldiers moved back another mile or so from the compound.

Rhiana wandered into the office. A number of panes in the bay window which cupped the desk were missing. Plywood had been nailed up, but it had been a hurried job, so they were crooked. A hot wind gusted through the gaps. It carried a strange scent. Burnt cinnamon and oil was the only way she could describe it. The edges of Madoc's dimension were pushing deeper into the Virginia valley, and within the confines of that bulge, where one universe extruded into another, living things died. Rhiana assumed the Old Ones would eventually stop the creep. They would have to if they wanted humans to feast on.

The carpet had undulating rents In the fabric. At the extreme edges she could see a pattern of vines. There was a large brown stain on an intact piece of carpet. *Blood.* She wondered if that was where Richard had cut off Grenier's hand. She pictured the scene; Richard slim and quick, a frown of concentration between his brows as he fought, magic against sword.

Would he have used the sword on me if he'd reached me before I bound Kenntnis?

She sat down in the Tempur-Pedic foam chair behind the desk, rested her toes on the floor, and swung back and forth. She noticed a notepad off to the side. In bold print, she read: *Drew Sandringham = Richard.*

Richard had been underscored three times. A green-gray mist spilled out of one of the dulled and grayed mirrors. She swiftly tore off the page and thrust it into her pocket. The mist resolved into Madoc.

"You seem determined to annoy me today," he said without preamble. "I told you to wait in the public rooms."

"I got bored. And what have I done?" Rhiana asked.

"Do you think I can't tell when magic is being done?" Madoc demanded. The edges of his human form frayed. Tendrils of oily green mist leaked from his eyes. Rhiana clasped her hands tightly together and thrust them beneath the desk to hide their trembling. "Don't you *ever* spy on me again. You are told what you need to know. Do you understand me?"

"Yes, Da ..." Her voice choked on the word. "Sir," she amended.

"Did you warn him?" Madoc asked. Rhiana lifted a shoulder; it was both an answer and a dismissal. "Did you warn him?" Madoc repeated more forcefully.

"Don't you know? I thought you'd know," Rhiana said, and added, "Since *you're* spying on *me*."

Madoc stared at her. His human features were back in place, and he had the same expression she'd seen on her adopted mother's and father's faces at various points during the past few years. With a sudden insight beyond her eighteen years, Rhiana realized that teenagers were baffling and inexplicable whether the parent was human or a formless horror. The thought made her giggle.

"This is not a laughing matter."

That was just what they always said. The giggle became a laugh.

Then her lungs stopped working, and her tendons seemed to be dissolving. Her arms clasped protectively across her breast, but then a dark red light flowed out of her and into Madoc's gaping maw. He was no longer human.

"Don't, please, stop," Rhiana whimpered, though she couldn't tell if her mouth had managed to form the words.

The sucking pressure stopped. The light snapped back to her, and her body reknit. "Lesson learned?" Madoc asked, and he sounded smug.

With a trembling hand Rhiana swept back her hair. It felt

wonderful, warm, and smooth against the skin of her palm. Rage took her.

"How could you do that to me? You were *feeding* on *me*! Well, here's a little lesson for you. If I die, I'm pretty damn sure that Kenntnis will be freed!"

That wiped the self-satisfied expression off Madoc's face. "What?"

"I wove my essence, every part of my being, into that spell, and the gate. So, you better keep me safe." Madoc took a step toward her, threat implicit in every line of his once more human body. "And don't think you can make me alter the spell!" Rhiana's throat was tight with tension and fear. It squeezed the words into a harpy's shriek. "If anyone hurts me, I'll use my last breath to shred the bonds holding him! So, you better treat me right!"

It hadn't been a conscious or even calculated thought. She had drawn her own strength into the binding spell because she had needed a little extra boost of power. But what she'd learned since that day, made her glad she had taken the action.

Rhiana had naively believed that the Old Ones all shared the same goals. She hadn't understood that they occupied different multiverses, they were different creatures, they had different goals. *And they were all equally greedy.* Since the gates had opened, Madoc had been involved in a few rather vicious turf wars with other Old Ones. Rhiana had come to realize that she might well be in danger. She just hadn't thought the threat would come from her sire.

"So, when you die, we once again lose this world?" Madoc demanded.

"No. Let me live a long and happy life … and I mean a *really* happy life, and I'll alter the spell. But only when I'm a lot older. A *whole* lot older." Rhiana waited tensely for his reply.

"Give you whatever you want, is that it?" Madoc asked.

"Yes."

"And does that include the Paladin?"

"Yes."

"You don't really want him. You want the fantasy of him," Madoc complained.

"Maybe, but I want the chance to find out for myself," Rhiana answered.

Madoc shook his head. "Once this is known, everyone is going to focus on recasting the spell. Then they'll kill you for your temerity."

It was said matter-of-factly. Rhiana gaped at him. "Wouldn't you try to stop them? Do something to help me? I've done so much for you."

"I, too, am just a servant of the great ones."

Rhiana's surprise and sense of betrayal deepened. "I thought you were, like, really important."

"Sorry. No." It seemed like no matter where she lived, she was doomed to the lower class. He seemed to read her emotions. "You're still more important than a human."

"What can I do to … to …"

"Fix this?" She nodded. "Recover the sword, capture, or kill the paladin—I don't care which—and destroy the nascent Lumina. That would help buy you some forgiveness."

"And how fast do I have to do all this?" Rhiana asked. A weight had settled into the pit of her gut, a leaden ball of despair and loss.

"Quicker would be better." He steepled his fingers in front of his mouth. His expression was reflective. "You know, this might actually prove to be helpful. We have located the dark Paladin and have been trying to figure out what to do with him until we acquire the sword. Go to him. He can be your responsibility. See to it you keep him happy."

CHAPTER FOUR

MADNESS AND MURDER

T HE TWO MEN ran out of the kitchen and through a small
dining nook which opened into the living room. A
young girl lay curled on the hardwood floor, her hands in
front of her face. Her palms were slashed and punctured,
testament to her desperate attempt to protect herself. Every
part of her body bore a wound. Adrenaline sang along
Richard's nerves.

In the short hallway they found the body of a little boy.
His throat was cut, and his body also punctured in multiple
places. At the end of the hall Richard saw a man lunge
through the door on the left. Even in that brief glance
Richard saw the man, presumably the father, was soaked in
blood. Richard signaled Snyder that he would go low and left.
Snyder nodded and they raced to the bedroom door. Richard
knelt on one knee, his shoulder pressed against the door-
jamb, point of the sword resting hard against the wood floor
to try and keep himself steady. Richard could feel a deep
trembling in his muscles as he tried to hold back both fear
and horror. Taking a deep breath, he moved the sword into
his right hand so he could draw his pistol with his left hand.

Snyder was standing on the other side of the door, drawing down on the tableau in the center of the bedroom. A

kneeling man held a little girl pressed against his chest.

"Police!" Richard shouted over the screaming of a toddler standing on one of the twin beds. Not for the first time he wished he wasn't a tenor. Damon's deep baritone carried far more—Richard yanked his thoughts away from Damon, but he hoped the man was close. *Please be close.*

The little girl was dressed in denim overalls and Richard found his attention drawn to the daisies embroidered on the yoke. Her brown hair was in pigtails. She was a picture of innocence gripped by a hellish figure. Blood spattered her father's face like macabre measles, and his hands and arms were stained red up to the elbows. The steel of the large kitchen knife was occluded with blood, and its point rested against her breastbone.

Julie's mouth was stretched open in a rictus of terror, but only grunting breaths emerged. In her arms she held a bundle wrapped in a soft white blanket. At first Richard thought it was a doll, but then the blanket moved, a small, waving fist appeared, and Richard heard a high-pitched mewling. It was an infant. If they took a shot and their aim wasn't perfect it would most likely tear through one of the children, if not both. Richard wanted to pray, but he knew better. Praying would draw *them* closer, and they were already here. Only the sword was holding them at bay.

His mind felt like it was spinning, grasping at plans, and feeling them slip away. Richard frantically scanned the room, trying to locate anything that might be used to break the standoff. A fantastic mural of mountains and castles and unicorns and fairies stretched across every wall. A bookshelf loaded with children's hardcover books stood beneath the one window. The top of the case was covered with dolls and stuffed animals. Their plastic eyes glittered at Richard as if they were watching him, and damning him for his failures, all of his failures ... *Kenntnis trapped because Richard had failed with Rhiana, a company left in his inadequate hands because of that first failure, his father's disappointment—*

No! Stop it! Think! Think! Think!

In the father's eyes he suddenly saw madness and determination flare to an even higher level. The muscles and tendons in the man's right hand tensed and flexed on the hilt of the knife.

Richard could almost hear Kenntnis's rich basso tones as he spoke about the sword. *Among its many other attributes, the sword has the ability to restore reason and sanity.*

I just have to get close enough to touch him with it, Richard thought. *Because drawing it sure hasn't been enough.*

Richard knew he would only have a split second, and if the gamble failed it would be up to Snyder to take the shot. The safety slid beneath his thumb. He didn't bother to holster the pistol; he just dropped the Heckler and Koch onto the floor. The heavy *thunk* as it hit the wood had the desired effect. The father's eyes flickered down to the pistol.

Richard flowed to his feet. As he took one step forward, the father's eyes widened in shock as he looked toward Snyder and then back to Richard.

It was instinct more than conscious thought. Richard threw himself onto the floor in a long dive. He landed on his knees and the heels of his hands, and his chin hit the floor hard enough to set dark spots dancing in front of his eyes. He kept a desperate grip on the sword as he was deafened by the crashing report of Snyder's .38. Richard glanced back over his shoulder. There was a ragged hole gouged into the wood of the doorframe. His *head* had been there only seconds before.

"*Snyder! What the fuck?*" Could the madness that had affected the father have somehow been transferred to Snyder?

The barrel of the .38 was swinging toward him. Snyder's face suddenly seemed very small and distant when compared with the cannon-sized hole at the end of the pistol. Frantically Richard rolled to the side, but not nearly fast enough. It felt like a burning fist slammed into his right thigh. For several heartbeats the leg just felt numb; then the pain came crashing down, sharp, and hot, as if an electric wire had been thrust through his flesh. Richard screamed and clutched at the wound with one hand. The blood was hot against his skin, his slacks were now soaked with blood on both the back and the front, but it wasn't the gush of a severed artery. Richard realized he wasn't dead ... yet.

But he soon would be if he didn't do something, and quickly. Snyder was walking toward him with a grim expression. The older cop's face was tight with concentration and grim determination. This time he wasn't going to miss.

He thinks I'm disarmed. Whoops.

Okay, Training Officer Gertz, maybe you weren't wrong to force me to have a backup weapon.

Richard had resisted because all too often the so-called *drop gun* was used to justify a shooting, usually of a person of color, after the fact. Now it might very well save his life. Gasping with pain, Richard coiled into a fetal position, clawed at the cuff of his left pant leg, and pulled it up enough to reach the ankle holster and the tiny Taurus Curve that rested there.

He yanked the gun free, swung it up, and double tapped. There was no real time to aim, but Snyder was only two feet away. The recoil sent the pistol sliding in Richard's blood-slicked hand. The first round got sucked by Snyder's vest, but it affected his aim, so his third shot buried itself in the floor next to Richard's head. Smoke trailed like ghostly hair, and the biting smell of cordite filled the room from all the gunfire.

Richard's second round took Snyder in the cheek. Shattered teeth, bone, blood, and flesh seemed to hang in the air as half his face ripped away. Snyder tipped sideways and fell to the floor. The vibration of his fall shivered through the length of his body and black spots danced in front of Richard's eyes. More than anything he wanted to rest his head on the floor and slide away into unconsciousness. But there were three children and a madman in the room.

Managing to lift his head, Richard assessed the situation. The little girl had at some point pulled away from her father. Currently he was gaping at Snyder's body. The Taurus was still in Richard's hand, but shudders were sweeping through his body as he started to go into shock. There was too great a risk he would miss if he tried to shoot the father, or, worse, the errant shot might hit one of the children. He dropped the weapon.

Using only his left hand and elbow while his right hand still desperately gripped the hilt of the sword, Richard dragged himself toward the man. Each move pulled a strangled moan from between his tightly clenched teeth.

The father seemed to recover his murderous focus, only now Richard was the target. Rising to his feet, the man headed for Richard, knife clutched in his hand. They would probably come within range of each other at the same time, and Richard doubted he would be able to strike first. Then the little girl, braids flying, baby clutched tight to her chest, ran up behind her father and kicked him *hard* in the back of the knee. He stumbled a bit, and he swung around to face the child. Desperately Richard jammed his elbow on the floor and flung himself forward, sliding the point of the blade into the man's ankle. The father fell back screaming. His back arched as if he were trying to break himself in half and he collapsed on the floor, heels drumming as a violent seizure gripped him.

Richard's hands seemed to belong to a stranger. They seemed very, very far away, and they shook like a person afflicted with palsy. With the last of his strength, Richard released the hilt. The blade vanished, and he tucked the hilt beneath his body before the advancing wave of darkness washed over him.

✧　✧　✧

AT 3:00 AM. Bourbon Street was rocking. Music poured out of the doors of bars and dives—the sob of a saxophone, the husky voice of a blues singer, the clear blare of a Dixieland clarinet, even the rollicking rhythms of a Celtic band. The moisture-laden air reeked of booze, grease, the pungent scent of seafood, humidity, and humanity.

Neon signs blinked and flared, throwing garish multicolored light across the cheap T-shirts that hung in every store window demanding SHUCK ME, SUCK ME, EAT ME RAW. Signs screamed out ALL NAKED, ALL THE TIME!!! A big-bellied white man, his face beet red and moisture-slick with sweat, shouted at her.

"Come on in, darlin'. You could win a hundred bucks! Mud wrestlin' contest. You'd be a natural." Rhiana froze him with a look.

Dazed people brushed past her, clutching brightly colored plastic cups adorned with umbrellas. No doubt they contained New Orleans's infamous Hurricanes. There was a tingling along her nerve endings, which weren't entirely human. This was a place where the membranes between the dimensions were tissue thin. Were the membranes thin because of Catholicism, a legacy of slavery, voodoo, or had belief in magic taken root here because of the lack of separation?

They had stashed the man at the Inn on Bourbon. She reached the hotel and ran gratefully up the steps and into the air-conditioned lobby. Bellmen, all of them African American, catfooted past her, looking like officers in an operetta with their red uniforms and gold epaulets. The staff behind the front desk were all white. Rhiana wondered if this was how New Orleans had always been, or if it was a small symptom of what was happening with the opening of the gates.

There was a pressure on her chest as if the city were breathing, focusing on her. It forced her to lean against the wall of the elevator. She stepped off and got her bearings.

Down the hallway to the corner room. A room service tray piled with dirty dishes lay on the floor outside. The door was flung open after only a single knock.

The man was of medium height and whip thin. He wore only a pair of black jeans. There was the white line of an old knife wound across his ribs; his toenails were long and yellowed. The stink of cigarette smoke hung in his clothes and hair, and he needed a shower. Doug Andresson reared back and raked her with a hot look.

"Now that's more what I'm talkin' about. Some serious booty." He grabbed Rhiana's wrist and yanked her into the room. "Now get those clothes off and get your ass in the bed." Whiskey breath gusted into her face.

Rhiana reached out to her power, ready to freeze the breath in his chest, choke him on the offensive words, but she met an implacable wall. *Oh, shit, I forgot, he's a Paladin. Magic won't work on him.* She felt a flash of all too human female fear.

Time for a human solution. She swung her purse and hit him in the temple while at the same time she drove the high heel of her shoe into his instep, managing to puncture the skin. He howled, clutched at his bleeding bare foot, and hopped. While he was off-balance she shoved him hard in the chest. He crashed down on the unmade bed.

"First, I am Madoc's daughter. Second, I'm in charge of you now. Third, I'm going to get the sword for you."

As she watched, the furious glare faded from the dark eyes, and calculation took its place. He wasn't smart, but she bet he was cunning.

"Now get dressed. I'm taking you back to the compound."

"No." He folded his arms behind his head and stared up at her. "I like it here just fine. There's shit to do in New Orleans."

"Oh, really?" She looked ostentatiously around the room. "It's pretty clear from the stink that you haven't let a maid in here in days. I saw the room service tray outside the door. The women are coming here." She forced herself to look at the crusted stains on the sheet. "And you don't look like a music lover."

For the briefest flash she saw Richard's profile, eyes half-closed, head thrown back as his hands swept across the keyboard of the piano. She pushed the memory aside.

"I'll keep you supplied with whatever you want, but you need to be where I can find you fast." Rhiana had a sudden inspiration. "And I need to keep you safe. You're very important."

His dark eyes flared with delight, and he sat up, almost preening.

Oh, you liked that, didn't you, you disgusting creep.

✧ ✧ ✧

SMELLS—DISINFECTANT, OVERCOOKED VEGETABLES, bedpans, and the sweet-rotten scent of cut flowers left to stand too long in water—identified the location. *Hospital.* Not all that many years ago Richard had spent way too much time in a hospital, and hospitals made him remember the events that had put him there, and that was never a good thing. He hated hospitals.

Through the door Richard could hear male voices shouting at each other.

"*... hadn't responded we'd have had three* more *dead kids, and SWAT would have shot and killed the father.*"

"*That would have been preferable.*" It was his father's voice.

Damon's outraged baritone cut in. "*Which part? The dead kids or the dead dad?*"

"*Obviously the father. The greater horror would be to live knowing you have massacred your family.*"

A new voice cut in. "*Gentlemen! Please! We have other patients to consider.*"

The voices dropped to a murmur and moved away until Richard could no longer hear them. He stirred, and pain lanced down his leg, pulling a hiss from between his dry, cracked lips. Sweat beaded his forehead and went trickling away into his sideburns with a feeling like ants crawling across his skin. The inside of his mouth was sticky and tasted like a compost heap. He moaned.

"Here." A drug dispenser was thrust into his hand. "You'll want this."

The words sang with the lyric cadences of Spain filtered through four hundred years in the mountains of northern New Mexico. *Angela.* Richard looked over, and the little coroner held a plastic cup to his lips. It was filled with ice chips. He managed to croak out, "Water."

"In a minute. Suck on the ice first, otherwise you might throw up." He obediently took a few chips into his mouth. They did taste good and began to relieve the gummy feeling.

Angela smiled and gently brushed the sweat soaked hair.

Richard became aware of the sheets, damp and twisted against his bare backside, the way the skin under his arms stuck to his sides, and his own smell. He was suddenly desperate for a shower.

"Pain slows the healing process. Use it," Angela ordered. Once again, he obeyed, depressing the button, and started counting the seconds until the chemical relief arrived. While he waited, he noticed the spill of city lights through the slats and around the edges of the blinds.

"What time is it?"

"Little after ten."

"At night?"

"Yes, that's why it's dark," she said with a teasing smile.

Slowly the events of the afternoon stuttered into focus. "Snyder?"

Angela shook her head. "Died in route."

He killed someone.

Again.

But not a perp this time. A fellow officer. Bile clawed at the back of his throat, and Angela quickly got a basin to catch the thin thread of vomit. This time she did give him water so he could rinse out his mouth.

"What happened with him?"

"He tried to kill me. It was self-defense," Richard whispered, testing out what would be his defense at the inevitable board of inquiry. It didn't sound very compelling.

A new concern intruded; but for the morphine washing through his system, it would probably have been full-blown panic. Richard levered himself up on one elbow and scanned the surface of the small rolling table next to the bed. The movement sent agony shooting out of his thigh and into his groin. "Sword! The sword," he groaned. "Where—"

Angela grabbed his hands, trying to steady him. "Damon secured it before the ambulance arrived. Your dad's got it now. It's okay. It's all okay."

The pillows folded up around his ears. He just laid there feeling his heart rate slow, drowsiness creeping over him.

"Everybody's here. In the waiting room," Angela said. "Damon wanted to watch the local news. See how the whole thing is playing."

"And how bad is it?"

"Well, on the one hand you saved three kids. On the other hand, you shot and killed a fellow officer. Are you a hero or a villain?" Her voice took on that breathless singsong of the news whore trying to gin up interest in a story.

"Neither. Both. Confused," he said, trying to match her levity.

"Are you up to talking?" Richard nodded, and she started for the door.

"Wait." She turned back. He touched the sheet covering his right leg. "How bad?"

"Not very. In and out. You were damn lucky. At such close range the expanding gases bruised the bone in addition to putting a really big hole in your leg. It's going to hurt like hell for a while." A humorous light danced in the velvet brown eyes, and her teeth flashed white against her cocoa-hued skin. "You'll be on crutches for a few weeks. Or if that's too déclassé you can accessorize with a really bitchin' cane and suffer."

She didn't miss the hot rush of blood into his cheeks.

Richard had, in fact, just been considering brass versus silver handles. Angela correctly interpreted the blush and laughed.

"It's okay. Your sartorial splendor makes up for the rest of us slobs." This time she made it to the door before turning back. "Oh, one more thing. Your dad is really, really pissed. Just wanted to warn you."

The door fell closed behind her, and even the morphine couldn't calm the sudden flutter deep in Richard's gut that her words had triggered. *When he's one hundred and I'm seventy-two he will* still *have the power to make me feel five,* Richard thought, and he wondered if every parent had that power or if it was just his fearsome sire? A deep longing for his mother washed over him followed by the knowledge that she was dead. They had buried her only a few weeks before. Tears prickled at his eyelids. Then the door opened and what seemed like a torrent of people crowded into the room.

CHAPTER FIVE

MAYBE I WAS ADOPTED?

WEBER GRABBED THE ugly green armchair and dragged it over to the side of the bed and sat down. Studied the wan face against the pillow. The dark shadows beneath Richard's eyes washed out the already pale blue eyes. Weber stared at the bruise blooming against the white skin of Richard's hand where the IV needle was inserted. He gave the younger man's fingers a gentle squeeze and felt a frenzied grip in response. Suddenly uncomfortable, Damon pulled his hand away. Richard looked away, biting at his lower lip.

Angela, busy on the other side of the bed untangling the tubes from the IV drips and checking the monitors, had missed the interplay. Weber was relieved. He also realized he and the little coroner seemed more like guards than concerned friends. Which was a hell of a thing when the other two people in the room were Richard's family.

The sister, Pamela, carried a bouquet of flowers. She quickly crossed to the sink, filled a vase, and began arranging the yellow calla lilies with elaborate care. Richard was staring tensely at his father, who stood by the window. Disapproval was radiating off the old man, making the small room seem even smaller. Occasionally the judge parted the blinds and looked out. Damon wondered if he ought to be the guy keeping watch, but he couldn't quite bring himself to abandon Richard.

Angela transferred her fidgeting from the tubes to Richard. Picking up his wrist, she took his pulse. "Must be a pleasant change from most of your clientele," Richard said in a feeble attempt at a joke, and it was totally swallowed by the tension that hung like a suffocating miasma in the room.

"You wanna sit up a little?" Weber asked.

Richard gave him a look of heart-melting gratitude, hardly merited by the meagerness of the offer, but Damon busied himself with locating the controls for the hospital bed and elevating the back.

Richard looked to Damon. "What's going to happen to me?" he asked.

Pamela spoke up. "Well, hopefully you'll get fired. Since you didn't quit like you were supposed to. You told us you were going to quit." It seemed the sister was taking it as a personal affront.

"The call went out. I was close and in that moment, I was still a police officer," Richard said softly, looking down at his hands folded in his lap.

Damon swallowed his anger, shook his head, and tried to match Richard's quiet tone. "No, he's not going to get fired. I think he's …" He transferred his gaze back to the young officer under his command. "You're going to come out of this okay." Damon glared over his shoulder at the sister. "And why the fuck does he have to quit?"

Agonized blue eyes were raised to his. "Are … are you angry with me? I really couldn't wait for SWAT. I wish I'd told you to have Snyder stay away, then I wouldn't have …

wouldn't have … Maybe I could have aimed for the leg and not killed—"

Weber realized the glare he'd intended for Richard's sister had ended up getting directed at Richard. "No, no, no, kid, you didn't do anything wrong. That piece of shit tried to kill you. He fucking deserved to die. And here's another reason you're going to be just fine. You've got one hell of a witness in that little girl. She seemed to want to talk more about how the one policeman tried to kill the other policeman, instead of talking about her daddy."

"And who can blame her," said Angela. "I get to autopsy these babies." Her glance toward Richard's sister and father was challenging. "At least three of them are alive thanks to Richard." She reached down and gave Richard's hand a squeeze. The old man's profile didn't alter, but the sister's back stiffened.

"Thank you, Angela, for the kindly impulse, but protective justification doesn't play well with my family," Richard said. If it was another attempt at humor, this one really fell flat because Damon could hear the undercurrent of hurt and anger roiling beneath the words. Richard looked back to him. "Any idea why Snyder wanted to kill me?" he asked.

"Well, putting aside the hating your guts part," Damon said with a snort. "I convinced Judge Cole to give me a warrant, and I had a little peek at Snyder's bank account. On January seventh he deposited twenty-five thousand dollars," Weber said.

The blue eyes went wide, and Richard sat bolt upright followed by a hiss of pain and a grab at his thigh. He blinked rapidly several times. "It … it was a hit?"

"Seems like," Damon said.

Richard fell back against the pillows with a sigh. "I should have paid more attention when I drew the sword. He had an initial reaction and then nothing. No demands for answers...." His voice trailed away.

"Implying he knew about the sword," Damon said grimly.

"Which means somebody told him about it. Gee ... three guesses as to who that might have been," Angela added, and smiled. If it was meant to be an ironic smile it failed, presenting instead like an angry grimace.

The long lashes lowered to shroud Richard's eyes. "She's a child," he murmured, turning his face away.

"She betrayed us. Imprisoned Kenntnis," Angela spat. Hectic color bloomed in Richard's cheeks.

Weber threw out a hand in a placating gesture. "Hey, hey, Angie, slow your roll." Damon hoped the Oort clan would assume Angela's fury was solely related to Rhiana's betrayal of Kenntnis, but he knew it had a whole lot more to do with Richard. For an instant he wondered if Richard's extraordinary good looks and the ease with which he attracted both passion and vitriol was more than he could bear.

Might have been better if Kenntnis had arranged Lumina as an order of warrior monks, or celibate Amazons, Weber thought, and it was only partly a joke.

Damon studied the way the light glinted in the faint golden stubble on Oort's jaw and chin, wondered how he'd look with a beard. Probably couldn't grow one. He gave his head a shake. He was clearly getting punchy. It had been a long fucking day. He stood and rested a hand on Richard's shoulder.

"Look, you rest now. If I bring by a laptop tomorrow, do you think you could write up a report?"

Richard forced a smile, and infused energy into the words. "You bet."

The blinds snapping together with a metallic clink brought Damon's attention back to the senior Oort. The judge walked to the door and Damon realized that the man hadn't said a single word.

He opened the door and raked them all with a look. "I'd like a few words in private with my son."

To Weber's ears it sounded more like a threat than an innocuous comment. He looked back at Richard. Apparently, the son had interpreted it in the same way. He had gone even whiter, and his throat worked as he swallowed convulsively. Weber briefly considered objecting, but he'd grown up in a hardscrabble mining town in the Iron Range of Minnesota. He was familiar with men like the judge, dour, silent men who ruled their families with force of will and an iron hand. His own father had been just such a man. Arguing earned you the fist or the belt, though Weber had a feeling Judge Oort didn't resort to that; words would probably be his weapons. Bottom line it would probably only make things worse for Richard if Damon objected. He headed for the door. He could almost feel those wistful, desperate blue eyes piercing his back.

✧   ✧   ✧

RICHARD HAD HEARD those words too many times in his life

not to know what they portended. Bile climbed up the back of his throat. He wanted to beg Damon to stay, but that would just make whatever was coming worse, and Richard also knew the judge brooked no disobedience. Even Weber, a nineteen-year veteran of the police force, was suddenly in motion heading for the door. But not Angela, she was made of sterner stuff.

"I think Richard has had enough conversation. He needs to rest." Angela folded her arms across her chest, shifted her feet as if she planned on taking root in the linoleum floor, and stared defiantly up at Robert Oort.

"He can tolerate one more," the judge said, and the level of ice in the words told Richard that this was a fight even Angela could not win despite her reputation as the World's Meanest Chicana. She had met her match in the World's Toughest Man.

"Angela, please, it'll be okay," he whispered.

At Richard's words she deflated. She leaned down and pressed her lips against his cheek, catching the edge of his mouth. There was a sharp burst of chocolate and coffee and wistful yearning. Nausea roiled his gut. Richard wanted to blame it on the taste of coffee but knew it was really guilt.

"I'll be back in the morning. You get some sleep. Don't stress."

Angela walked to the door, then looked back at Pamela, who leaned against the wall, arms folded across her breasts, clearly intending to stay. His sister's face held an odd mix of disapproval, pleasure, and contempt. Angela's eyes narrowed, and Richard realized Angela had decided that while she might not be up to his father's weight, she was *definitely* up to Pamela's.

"Either *everyone* or *no one* gets to hang around for the ass-kicking," Angela said.

"*This* is a family matter," Pamela flared back.

The judge walked to the door and yanked it open. "All of you, *out.*"

"Papa, I think—" Pamela began.

"Out!" It was the voice that had issued from the bench for sixteen years, and mobsters, drug dealers, and murderers had quailed before it.

No wonder I never had a chance to resist him, Richard thought.

Until you did. His father had opposed him becoming a policeman, but Richard had defied him and done it anyway.

But now I guess he's going to get his way, came the defeated thought.

The door closed, and the father and son regarded each other. Only a few weeks ago he had come to Richard's rescue. After days of beatings and torture Richard had been at the end of his strength and bravery. Robert had run into Grenier's office and gathered Richard in his arms, and Richard had never felt that safe and loved before. Now he was hurt again, but there was none of the warmth and love he'd felt in Virginia. A faint shivering invaded his gut, and a tightness filled his chest. This was going to be an ugly one.

"This must stop." His father removed the hilt from his pocket and laid it on the bed next to Richard's uninjured leg. "*This* is your life now. This and nothing else. Accept that. Because of a fluke of genetics, you are the only one who can use this weapon. Had there been a more well-ordered manner of selection, I'm sure you would not have been anyone's first choice …"

He lost track of his father's words. Instead, his thoughts were filled with a mental wail. *But I did well in Virginia. I was clever.*

What could I have done differently?

I didn't break. I took it.

I'm not a coward.

How could I have done things better, Papa?

The judge's words came back into the focus. "The madness that infected that father today is symptomatic of events occurring across the country and around the globe."

"And because I had the sword I saved three kids," Richard said.

"Yes, and that was admirable, but we have far bigger problems than the fate of three children in Albuquerque, New Mexico. It's fallen to you to lead the defense of our world. You're hesitating and regretting and postponing making hard decisions instead of accepting your responsibilities. That has always been your problem, Richard. Always. This weapon"—he gestured at the hilt—"is the only defense we have against these creatures."

"I don't know how to save the world, Papa," he whispered through lips that felt numb. "I knew how to save those kids."

An ember of anger was starting to flicker deep in Richard's chest. It was an odd feeling; normally all he felt when his father berated him was trembling self-doubt. He lifted his gaze and then they were matching stares. There was a flicker of surprise in Robert's face.

"Can you look me in the eye and seriously tell me that I should have done nothing? Just driven on down to headquarters and resigned? Let those children die?" Richard asked.

The judge hesitated, then said, "Yes."

Richard stared at him and wondered who he was, and wondered how he could possibly share blood with this man. At some point every kid secretly suspects they were adopted. In Richard's case he figured he was a stepchild. It was clear he was his mother's child. It was written in his face, and the emotional bond they had shared, but he was so different from his older sisters and father that he figured they couldn't share any genes. Rather than offer comfort, it had been a source of grief for Richard because he so wanted to be Robert's. Now Richard was grown, and he knew the judge was his father.

And in this moment, he didn't want to be his son.

"You don't get the life you wished for, Richard. You get the life you have. Now it's past time you got on with it." The words were cold, clipped, and precise. "You will resign from the force immediately."

Richard couldn't look at his father's face, pinched with anger and disappointment, any longer. He closed his eyes while remembered faces pushed their way forward. Faces of victims as their fear turned to relief at learning of an arrest. The blank surprise and anger that crossed a perp's face at the moment of capture. That sense of enormous satisfaction he felt when his testimony had resulted in a guilty verdict and taken another animal in human skin off the street.

And the face of every criminal he had arrested held a

shadow of the face of the man who had hurt him, disrupted his life, and led him to attempt suicide. That assault had brought Officer McGowan into Richard's life, and with his help Richard had regained his strength, the will to live, and found his life's work. Work that he now had to abandon.

"Have you anything to say?"

Richard opened his eyes and looked at him. "I'm going to be on leave anyway because I shot a fellow officer and because I've been hurt. We don't have to deal with this right now." The judge opened his mouth to continue the argument. Richard cut him off. "Now, I'd appreciate it if you got me a wheelchair." He picked up the phone and started dialing.

"What nonsense is this?"

"They hired someone to kill me. I don't really want to stay in an unsecured hospital. I'll be safer at Lumina. The limo is big, so I won't hurt my leg ... too much."

The expression on his father's face was hard to interpret. "You need medical care."

"Angela can look out for me."

"She's a coroner, for God's sake. She cuts up dead people." The words were explosive with fury.

"Yes, and I'm trying to keep from becoming one of her customers."

✧　✧　✧

DESPITE BEING NEARLY eleven there were still some lights on in the big house on Rio Grande Boulevard. Angela knew it would be either her mom or her grandmother, or maybe both. Even though the holidays were past there would still be various members of the extended Armandariz family hanging about. Which meant there were people needing to be fed which meant the women would be cooking and cooking and cooking.

She figured her dad, known to the family as the Major, would have gone to bed. Twenty years in the Air Force meant you could set your watch by the man—in bed at 10:30 PM, up at 5:00 AM. Which meant it wouldn't make her feel too guilty to wake him. That was the other infuriating thing about the man. His head hit the pillow and he was asleep.

She keyed open the driveway gate and drove past the pasture. The few horses they kept at the Rio Grande property were looming shadows against the stars. The large, rambling house sat in the center of the property with the barn, arena, and another pasture out back. The back of the property abutted the acequia from which they drew their irrigation water in the summer.

The crunch of the tires on the gravel had the front door opening even before she had turned off the car. Her mother stood framed in the doorway, the light spilling around her lush body. Josefina Armandariz towered over her middle child. Long black hair touched by silver curled and foamed onto her shoulders. She gathered Angela into a warm embrace. Angela noted the dusting of flour on her muscular forearms.

"You're baking—"

"What's wrong?" her mother said over her statement.

"Nothing. Well, everything actually, but nothing specific to me. Just the world going to shit."

"You know your father doesn't like to hear a girl curse," Josefina said as she pulled Angela inside and closed the door.

"Then it's a good thing he doesn't come by my work," Angela muttered as she followed her mom into the big farm-style kitchen.

"Or in here when we're cooking Thanksgiving dinner," said Angela's grandmother, Marisol. She was tiny, wiry, white-haired, and had dark eyes that seemed to dance with amusement almost all the time.

"This isn't a very feminist household," Angela said as she snagged a fruit-filled empanada off the rack where they were cooling.

Josefina rolled her eyes. "No, I clearly failed. Let's see, among my four daughters we have a doctor,—"

"Not a real one," Marisol muttered, and both Angela and Josefina glared at her.

"An accountant, a research chemist, and an aide to the governor."

"Yeah, the boys really have fallen down on the job," Angela said as she poured herself a glass of milk and grabbed another empanada.

"Two of your brothers followed their father into the military and Gadiel has time yet to figure it out."

Angela rolled her eyes. "*Another* gap year?"

"It's all right," Marisol said placidly, "Our little *patito* will be amazing once he finds his way. When he gets back—"

Angela straightened from where she had been leaning on the table. "Where is he?"

"Hitchhiking in—"

"Never mind. Doesn't matter. Wherever he is, he has to

come back. Right now. Everybody needs to go to the ranch. Mom, please wake Dad, I've got a lot to tell you all."

Her mother gave her a piercing stare, and then her father's bass voice rolled out from the doorway. "I take it you didn't have a really bad flu over the holidays."

Angela turned. Even in a bathrobe and pajamas he was an imposing figure. Graying hair against ebony skin. His powerful physique had softened into a thrusting gut, but he stood with the steadiness and authority of an Easter Island statue or the monolith from *2001*.

Heels clattering, Angela raced across the kitchen and buried her face against his chest as his arms closed around her.

"Oh, Daddy," she whispered. "I'm so scared."

CHAPTER SIX

TESTAMENT TO GENIUS

THE CLINK OF silverware on china had Richard jerking from a light doze, and the abrupt movement set his thigh to throbbing. The bedside lamp, a tall glass column, switched on, momentarily blinding him. Richard threw an arm across his eyes, but in that brief moment before spots exploded across his vision, he had seen Cross, soup bowl clutched in one hand.

"Oh, sorry," the creature muttered. The light was dimmed, and Richard opened his eyes.

Cross dragged over a chair with one hand while with the other he tried to control the bowl. The effort was not notably successful. Soup sloshed across his hand, then the spoon shipped overboard and rang and clattered on the polished slate floor. Cross picked it up, blew across it, sat down, and began slurping. Noodles clung to his lower lip like a walrus's bristles, then were quickly sucked in. Broth dribbled into his beard. Watching the homeless god eat was a stomach-churning experience. Richard swallowed hard a few times until his stomach retreated back where it belonged.

He found himself staring at the Old One. In the weeks before Kenntnis's capture, their enemies had kept up a constant assault on Cross to keep him splintered into fragmentary pieces. He had been reduced to a fragile stick figure barely able to muster up the strength to "see" magic, which was his primary use to the Lumina. But now that sickly creature was gone. Color shone in his cheeks. His eyes were clear. The envelope in which he wrapped his alien form looked strong and virile. Richard said as much and got back Cross's usual tactless response.

"Thanks. *You*, however, look like shit."

"I got shot. What's your excuse for being so chipper? I thought you'd be almost permanently splintered with all the crap that's going on in the world," Richard countered.

"Yeah, things are getting rough out there, but when bad shit happens, good people, I mean truly good people, tend to get even better. They help their neighbors, they donate to charity, they feed the hungry. In short, they're worshiping me *hard* right now, so I got a little reserve built up against my asshole brethren. And don't forget, the chaos feeds me, too."

Well, that was an alarming thought. "Help me up," Richard ordered. He did not want to face what that remark might portend while flat on his back.

Cross set aside his soup bowl, grabbed Richard by the forearms, and helped him sit up. He snatched up the pillow and revealed the pistol and the sword hilt that had been hidden beneath it.

"Little paranoid?" Cross asked. He plumped up the pillow and leaned it against the curving steel-and-glass headboard. Thrusting his hands beneath Richard's arms, he effortlessly slid him back until Richard could rest his back against the headboard. The pressure of his hands both tickled and hurt the muscles and tendons in Richard's armpits, and he was struck by the extraordinary strength of the creature.

Moving also changed the throb in his thigh to a white-hot line of pain. Richard clamped his teeth together so hard that his jaw ached, and he still couldn't hold back the strangled moan.

When Richard could talk again, he snapped, "Can you blame me?"

"Nah. Your dad told me what happened. Talk about a coworker going fucking postal." Cross paused and cocked his head, considering. The flippant expression faded. "You know, you should probably make sure no one in this building gets similar ideas."

"And just how do I do that?"

"Well, duh, use the fucking sword."

"Snyder tried to kill me out of greed, not because of all the craziness."

"Yeah, but as our dimensions push deeper into your universe, your reality is going to get really fucked up. People are going to believe crazy, crazy shit—"

"Like that isn't a thing *now*," Richard grumbled.

"Here's the major diff; get enough people believing and the crazy shit's going to *start happening*. You've gotta at least protect the people around you."

Richard reset the pillows supporting his injured leg while he chewed on that. "Great, I can just picture how well that's going to go over. Hi, I'm your new boss. I know you don't know me yet, but if you want to keep your job you've got to let me touch you with this *sword*."

"Tell 'em to think of it as your version of a drug test."

Richard wasn't buying it. He shook his head and then

asked, "Will the madness affect your worshipers?"

"Richard, hello." He bopped the human on the forehead with the palm of his hand. "Remember, believing in *me* is crazy, too." It was said with that patient gentleness you reserve for the old and senile, or the very young.

With an irritable wave of his hand, Richard brushed off the condescension. "But you appeal to the *best* of our natures. Even if the underlying belief is irrational, I'll settle for the good result."

"Problem is, once *my* worshipers get organized, and agree to power sharing, *their* worshipers are going to come and kill *my* worshipers, and they've got a lot more warm, crazy bodies than I have."

The silken black duvet cover snagged on a hangnail as Richard began to pleat it between his fingers. "That's sad."

"Which part? The killing or the fact that charity, love, forgiveness, and mercy are way less fun than righteous vengeance and punishing the infidels and the sinners?"

"Both, and what does that say about us as a species?" Richard asked.

"That you suck, but you sure are tasty." Cross lifted the bowl to his lips and slurped down the last of the soup.

Perhaps it was the pain making him testy, but Richard wasn't finding Cross's shtick at all amusing at—he peered at the Bose clock radio—2:17 AM. "Kenntnis thought we were worth the trouble. He believed in our ability to grow and change. To do good."

"Yeah, but do *you*?" And the creature's brown eyes were suddenly swallowed by his expanding pupils until they were just stone black. Richard had seen it happen a couple of times before, and it still had the hairs on the nape of his neck trying to climb up his scalp. A million years of evolution were screaming at him that this thing was evil, it was a predator, and it would kill him, and Richard needed to run like a ... a ... he tried not to use the profanity, but nothing else would serve. *A motherfucker.*

Papa can't read my mind. He can't know that I'm cursing like a sailor.

But you'll slip and say it out loud sometime. Stop it! Focus. Answer the question.

What was the question?

Are humans perfectible? Can we rise above our baser impulses?

Richard thought back on the violence he'd witnessed in four years of police work. There was the toddler killed when his angry father had thrust a hose up his rectum and turned on the water as punishment for a full diaper. A woman beaten by her boyfriend until her face was just pulp, knifings at a party, drivers shooting each other because they got cut off in traffic. And beyond Richard's small and petty personal experiences, there was all of history rolling out dark, and violent, and terrifying. The destruction of the Cathars. Auschwitz. Pol Pot's killing fields. The body-choked rivers of Rwanda and Iraq. Richard lay there unable to muster a single argument for why in the hell mankind deserved to survive, and he hated Cross for making him face how evil humans really were.

Maybe we do deserve to be cattle for the Old Ones.

Then his eye was caught by the Impressionist paintings hanging on the walls to either side of the gigantic bed.

Shimmering water, flowers in dreamlike colors, misty landscapes. Twining through Richard's errant thoughts were the haunting strains of "Il mio tesoro intanto" from Mozart's *Don Giovanni*, and then the music modulated in the final movement of Beethoven's Emperor Concerto. He could almost feel the keys of the piano beneath his fingers.

Next, he looked at the enormous LED television hanging on the far wall, and thought about the scientists, inventors, engineers, and machinists who had created that wonder of technology, who had placed a machine the size of a compact car on Mars. He remembered thunder shaking the ground and vibrating in his chest that time Papa had taken Richard to Cape Canaveral to witness a space shot. He had been nine. It was supposed to be a lesson on why math was important, and that Richard had to do better, but the ship lifting skyward on a pillar of fire had been blurry because of the tears that filled his eyes and Richard had felt his very soul longing to join with the rocket and *slip the surly bonds of Earth*. All of these were testaments to mankind's genius, to the value they added to the universe.

If you follow my path, I will give you the stars. It was one of the first things Kenntnis had ever said to Richard.

But is it enough?

It wasn't rational, but a certainty that all these things *were* enough to justify human existence filled Richard. The tension headache pounding in his temples eased.

"Yes. Yes, I do." Cross must have heard that certainty in Richard's voice, because he straightened in the chair and his eyes became human again. "Now get back out there. Walk on water. Turn water into wine. You may be a fraud, but at least you're *my* fraud, and you're a fraud that appeals to what's best about people. Give them hope. Help them hang on. We need them and we need *you*."

Cross stood and looked down at him. "You're taking an awful risk. I'm one of the monsters. I just happen to be on your side … for now. If I feed and use magic, I get stronger. There's a chance I'll revert to my essential nature, and then you're *really* fucked."

"And I don't think that will happen."

"And why is that?" Demanding, pugnacious.

"Because I believe in you. In your ability to grow and change." Richard smiled up at him. "We're not that unalike."

AFTERNOON AT THE Round Robin Bar in the Willard Hotel was fairly subdued. The after-work rush of lobbyists, lawmakers, bureaucrats, lawyers, and hookers hadn't yet arrived, and the luncheon crowd had gone. Rhiana paused just inside the door and surveyed the room. She knew it was a famous Washington, DC watering hole, and this was the place Jack Rendell had suggested after she'd called him and asked to meet, but she'd never been here before. It was pretty, with wide expanses of rich green watered-silk wallpaper bisected with narrow vertical wood panels. It smelled of aftershave and liquor, money, and power.

Jack Rendell leaned on the circular mahogany bar, one foot resting on the brass rail. A wide-mouthed martini glass was held negligently between his fingers, and the light through the red glass stem stained his fingers like blood.

There were only a few patrons in the bar, all of them were male, and they all reacted to Rhiana's entrance. The hem of her long black wool coat swung at her knees and brushed at the tops of the stiletto-heeled black boots worn over formfitting pants. She finished off the ensemble with a cashmere sweater and a scarf pinned on her shoulder with a large amethyst brooch. There was a rattle like dry leaves in a high wind as *Wall Street Journals* and *Washington Posts* were hurriedly lowered, and Rendell, sensing the tide of male attention flowing toward a single point, turned. The attention ebbed when it became apparent where Rhiana was heading.

"Hey," Rendell said, saluting her with his glass.

"Hi."

The young bartender hustled their way. His eyes were alight with interest and pleasure as he looked at Rhiana.

"Get you a drink, miss?"

"A Dubonnet on the rocks."

Jack drained his martini and waved the glass at the bartender.

"And I'll take another."

"So, how did things go with the archbishop?" Rhiana asked.

"He's conferring with Rome. I expect we'll get some action in a few days."

"Good."

The bartender deposited the drink in front of her. She took a sip and couldn't control the corners of her mouth.

Jack laughed. "You really are a baby, aren't you? Would you rather have a Coke?"

Rhiana nodded and swallowed past the lump in her throat. She was feeling too depressed and humbled to respond with haughty rage to Jack's familiarity. And she had asked him to meet her. The Coke arrived, and Rhiana gratefully cleared her tongue of the sharp alcohol taste.

"Why did you order it?" Jack asked. "The Dubonnet, I mean? It's not a very common drink anymore."

"My grandmother ... adopted grandmother. She just loved Jackie Kennedy ... all the Kennedys, really. She talked all the time about how beautiful and sophisticated Jackie was, and how she drank Dubonnet on the rocks."

Jack looked down at her, and some of the sharp calculation faded, replaced by a gentler emotion. "That's kind of sweet. But stick with me, kid, and I'll teach you how to drink." He threw back his head and laughed. "That's a hell of a trade. You teach me magic and I teach you how to booze."

"*Shhh*. Not so loud," Rhiana said.

Jack looked around the historic old bar. "Why not? All of this ... this bullshit." He swept an arm around. "Is going to be gone soon."

"Yeah, but we don't want them waking up and panicking."

"Really? I thought the whole point was panic. Well, never mind that. You called me, and I assume it wasn't just for an update, since I've been reporting to your dad."

Rhiana pulled the piece of notepaper from her handbag and laid it on the bar. Jack read the notation and quirked an eyebrow inquiringly at her. "I found this in Grenier's office," Rhiana explained. "Since Grenier thought this Sandringham guy was important, I think we need to find him, and I want you to help me."

"That seems to be all I ever do for you guys. I find people for you," Jack complained. "When do I ever get to be part of the big game?"

"When I do," Rhiana said. "And before that can happen, I have to capture Richard." She laid a finger on Richard's name where it was scrawled on the paper.

Her nail resembled a blood-tipped talon. Rhiana stared for a moment at the long acrylic nail. Thought about the optical illusion that had turned Jack's fingers red. Thought about the news coverage of women and children trampled to death during a religious procession in Mexico when word had come that miraculous cures were happening inside the tiny shrine. Thought about the Druidic group that had decided to resurrect human sacrifice as a way to tap the power. The normally unflappable British had been shaken by that event. And these were isolated incidents. More would follow in frequency and intensity. She felt a moment of doubt, but when she weakened the bonds that held her physical body she could feel the power, flamelike, licking at the edges of thought and emotion. It was enthralling, heady, far more intoxicating than the Dubonnet she'd tried.

"Richard is this other paladin, right?" Jack asked.

"Yes."

"Do you know anything about ..." Jack glanced back down at the paper. "Sandringham?"

"I did an internet search. He owns a boutique brokerage firm in New York."

"So, if you've already found him, you don't need me," Jack said.

"I want you to go with me when I talk to him. There's a connection to Richard. I just don't know what it is."

"Why me?"

"I'm young and a woman, so people don't take me seriously." Rhiana gave a humorless little smile. "At least not yet. But you're a man. You're famous, or at least infamous. People will talk to you."

"Aren't you the Queen of the Night, or the Princess of Air and Fire, or the King of Elfland's daughter, or some other damn thing? Take one of ..." He hesitated and nervously licked his lips. "One of *them* with you. The guy will talk, trust me."

Rhiana studied him and couldn't control her amusement. "So, I guess you got a gander at my dad when he's not in his human form."

"And some others." Jack drew a hand across an upper lip suddenly shining with sweat.

Rhiana shook her head. "I don't want the Old Ones knowing what I'm doing until I've finished the job."

"And *I* don't want to piss them off," Jack said.

"If we succeed, they'll be very, very happy with me ... and anyone who helped me."

"What if we don't succeed?"

"I'll take all the blame," Rhiana said.

"Yeah, like I can take that to the bank," Jack said.

"I trust you," Rhiana said simply.

"Why?" Jack asked.

"Because you're smart enough not to totally trust the Old Ones. Because I have something you want, and because you're the only human I know who doesn't hate me."

The words just came tumbling out. Rhiana gasped, lifted a hand to her mouth. Her stomach clenched down tight, and her mind began whirling, playing the *I didn't say it. Why did I say that? What if I'd said something else?* game. She wanted to cry.

He missed the center of the cocktail coaster. The martini glass teetered between cork and wood, then fell. Rhiana watched the tendrils of gin catch the light. Small rainbows raced across the top of the bar.

It was Jack's arms sliding gently around her shoulders that brought her back. "Why not? I like New York. Maybe we can catch a show while we're up there."

✧   ✧   ✧

"… MUST HAVE some protein." Pamela followed her father's voice into the big granite-and-steel kitchen.

The judge was seated next to Richard in the bay window breakfast nook, pushing a plate closer to her brother. Richard looked ghastly. His hair was tousled, and dark circles hung under his eyes and pale skin was tinged with grey.

"I'll throw up. Pain medicine always makes me nauseous," Richard said, and looked up as Pamela entered.

She laid the letter down on the table next to his elbow. "I got this ready for you." She watched as his eyes flicked across the brief and terse lines of text. She knew it by heart.

Dear Sir,

This letter is to inform you of my decision to tender my resignation from the Albuquerque Police Department, effective immediately.

Richard N. Oort

When he looked up at her, she almost took a step back at the bitter fury that twisted his face. "We haven't discussed this. I would prefer to wait until the inquiry is over and I've been cleared."

Their father didn't respond. He just pulled out a pen and held it out to Richard. There was a look of desperate pleading on her brother's face, but he lowered his lashes, veiling his eyes, and his face was suddenly as cold and as expressionless as a statue's. Pamela stiffened; when Richard closed down, there was usually something going on behind the frozen facade. But there was no way he could get out of this. She had made damn sure of that. He took the pen and scrawled his name, threw the pen onto the table like a toddler.

The childish behavior irritated her, so she took more than a little pleasure in adding, "It's customary, is it not, to turn in the badge and the gun?" Pamela smirked down at him. "So where are they?"

He stared at her, struggled to his feet, and pulled the pistol out of the pocket of his royal blue bathrobe.

"That is just pathetic," she said as she took the gun. The metal was cold and heavy against her palm. "The badge?"

He grabbed up his crutches and swung out of the kitchen. Pamela followed him across the living room, down the hall, and into the master suite. He hobbled into the enormous walk-in closet. His bare heels were a flash of white in the gloom of that vast space. They moved past mahogany shoe racks, sock drawers, cedar-lined sweater drawers, and electric tie holders.

Pamela had always thought Richard had a lot of clothes, but his wardrobe barely made an impression in the closet. In fact, his suits looked like huddled little men overawed by their surroundings. He moved to where a line of sports jackets hung. One was hanging apart, and Pamela suddenly realized the dark stains on the navy blazer were dried blood. It was mesmerizing and horrifying, and she just kept staring at it as Richard dug into the inside breast pocket. He threw a leather wallet toward her, and the badge flashed gold as the top flap fell back. Another petty gesture on his part. She wasn't all that coordinated, and he knew it. Sure enough, the wallet grazed her fingers, she grabbed for it with a jerky motion, and it hit the floor at her feet.

"There. Happy now?" he spat.

She picked it up, glared at him, and then forced her glare into a smile.

"Ecstatic." She gestured at the coat. "Why are you keeping that thing? It's disgusting."

"Maybe to remember."

"Remember what?"

"What I used to be. What it meant to me. The difference I made."

"Oh, please, don't be so dramatic. It was just a job. And you've got a new one now."

CHAPTER SEVEN

PRIORITIES, KID

P AMELA LEFT WITH his life tucked away in a cloth tote bag. Richard's father got him settled in a recliner with the rolling computer desk and laptop close to hand, a stack of reports about the various subsidiary companies Lumina owned, and a glass of milk.

"I'll just be downstairs in the office if you need anything."

Once the hum of the elevator faded away, Richard grabbed his crutches and headed back to the bedroom. Pain raced up and down his thigh each time he planted the crutches and swung through. Gritting his teeth against it, Richard wished he'd grabbed the cell phone out of the coat pocket while he had been in there. But Pamela would have asked why he needed it, and he wouldn't have had an answer she would have believed. She'd always been suspicious of him. Probably with good reason.

And though the thought filled him with guilt, while he loved her, Richard had always rather disliked her. *With some reason,* he thought defensively. Memories from childhood went stuttering through his head—Pamela humiliating him when he was seven by telling a tableful of guests that he sang along whenever he watched *Mary Poppins.* Pamela, pompous at twelve, declaring that she had thrown away his Transformers because they were silly. Richard had raced to the curb and pushed over the garbage cans, but the truck had already gone by. His mother had offered to replace them, but Richard had refused. There were some things which once broken and hurt could never be repaired or replaced.

Once in the bedroom he hesitated in front of the closet, dreading having to touch the blood-stained coat again. It probably couldn't be salvaged, and despite his bravado to his sister she was right, it just needed to be thrown away. *And it was his only blue blazer, and his credit cards were already maxed out.* Then the phone was in hand, and Richard stopped worrying about his wardrobe or his wallet. What he was about to do would *really* give him something to worry about. *But only if they find out.* That thought was immediately followed by another—

I really should have the courage to just discuss this with my father.

His thumb depressed the speed dial button.

The lieutenant picked up on the second ring. *"Weber."*

"Hey, it's me."

"Hey, Rhode Island, how you doin'?"

"Crappy. It hurts. My blazer's ruined."

"Priorities, kid, and as for your leg … consider the alternative." Weber paused, then added, *"Hey, we got the shooter in the Mora case."*

Richard recalled the facts of the case—Edward Mora, age fifteen, dead on New Year's Eve after a street drag race went bad. His mother had been nearly mad with grief. "Oh, good. Have you told Mrs. Mora?"

"Yeah, and she turned up at booking with an antique

cannon of a pistol ready to kill the perp."

"Oh, shoot."

"*Fortunately, not. I called in a psych team, and they took her off for observation.*"

The phone clutched in his sweating hand gave a faint beep. "Damn, my battery's running down. Let me get to the point. My sister's going to be turning up with a letter of resignation, my gun, and my badge."

"*Shit, I thought we'd put that bullshit to rest.*"

"Well, we didn't, but I want you to throw away the letter and bring me back my stuff."

"*Your father is going to fucking kill you.*"

"Only if he finds out." A smile curved his lips, and Richard couldn't resist adding, "And if he *does* find out I can always blame *you* for intercepting it."

"*Gee, thanks, you're a real pal. But why defy him like this?*"

"Because in a weird way being a cop gives me some cred I wouldn't have otherwise. People will be less likely to think I'm a nut."

"*What are you planning?*"

"I haven't gotten as far as a plan. I just know I want my badge, and I *especially* want my gun. They're going to try again."

"*You've got security.*"

"Would you depend on that alone?"

"*Oh, hell, no.*"

"I rest my case."

There was silence for a long moment. The phone bleeped again. Richard propped his shoulder against the full-length mirror at the back of the closet. He needed to get off his feet soon.

"Okay, I'll do it. If for no other reason than it will really piss off your sister." They shared a laugh.

"I've got to go."

Richard hung up, and that's when he noticed the message icon on the screen. He called the voicemail center and waited through the announcement of *"One call, received on January 16th at 1:55 PM."* That was right when he had been in the kitchen of the Quincy house. The memory brought back the phantom smell of blood, and a sticky feeling on the back of his head, and he swallowed hard, forcing down the rising bile.

"Richard," came Rhiana's voice. She sounded frightened; she was almost whispering.

The sound of her voice sent Richard swinging wildly between conflicting emotions. Regret that he hadn't handled her better, fury over her betrayal, and guilt that his behavior had helped lead to the betrayal.

"Richard," she said again, as if repeating his name forged a link. *"They've got someone to kill you. Someone in Albuquerque. I don't want you dead. Be careful."*

She couldn't have called the day before, he thought somewhat bitterly.

"End of message. To delete press seven …," came the robotic voice. He pressed nine and saved the message. And then he saved the number. He might find an occasion to need it.

✧ ✧ ✧

PAMELA HAD PULLED a chair around behind the broad granite desk so she could sit next to her father. They were studying the webs of interlocking contracts between Lumina Enterprises and a surprising variety of subsidiary companies. Pamela's specialty was criminal procedure and constitutional law, so she wasn't all that familiar with contract law—at least as played at this level—but even lacking the background she was impressed. It was almost impossible for someone to use a subsidiary and reach through to Lumina proper.

After a glance at her father's profile, Pamela realized her instincts were correct. Her father's expression held grudging respect, and it wasn't easy to earn that. He had been a partner at one of Rhode Island's most prestigious white-shoe law firms, and Pamela had hoped to join him there when she finished law school.

But by the time she was done and had passed the bar, he had been appointed to the federal bench. She opted not to court the inevitable comparison, and whispers of favoritism in hiring, and so had turned down an offer from the firm. Instead, she'd gone to the prosecutor's office. She liked litigating, and she had earned a fearsome reputation as the DA most public defenders wanted to avoid. Her father had been pleased and proud.

She knew that Richard was, supposedly, studying the same information upstairs, though someone would probably have to explain it to him. He had been a rather indifferent student. It was probably wrong of her, but it gave her an odd shiver of pleasure that *she* had been the one to take the accouterments of his life as a policeman down to APD headquarters. She had ignored Weber's coldness; she and her father were right.

She wasn't sure why she had such a visceral reaction to her only brother becoming a cop. She worked with cops all the time. Respected them, but they just weren't ... She shied away from where her thoughts were taking her, but then faced it; she was a snob. There, she had admitted it.

Her contradictory thoughts both prideful and self-flagellating were interrupted when the elaborately carved double doors swung open and Jeannette stepped into the office. The judge looked up and pulled off his glasses inquiringly. Pamela resented the woman's intrusion without buzzing first to see if it was convenient.

"Our company's COO has arrived, sir. Since Mr. Oort ... Richard, is upstairs, shall—"

"No," her father said. "I want to talk to him first. Give me a minute and then send him in."

"I'm a her, actually," said a woman, who stepped around Jeannette and walked toward the desk. She was dressed in a rather wrinkled rose wool skirt, an eighteenth-century-inspired matching coat, an ivory cashmere sweater with a coral necklace, and high-heeled brown boots. She carried an expensive briefcase in one hand and a newspaper in the other. She paused to glance down at the picture on the front page, then looked up and studied the judge critically.

"No, you are not, in fact, the man who runs this company." She had a German accent, and she sounded snotty. She turned back to Jeannette. Pamela noted that her shoulder-length brown hair had been expertly highlighted. "So, I would like to see my employer now."

Pamela could feel her face going stiff.

"Judge Oort is Richard's father. I'd start with him." There was a pause, and then Jeannette added, "If I were you." Pamela caught the significant look the two women exchanged.

Richard needs to fire this woman. She acts like she runs the company.

"Fine. *Gut.*"

Jeannette withdrew and closed the doors behind her.

Her father stood and extended his hand. "Perhaps I was out of line, but my son is convalescing."

"Convalescing? Why? What has happened?" She looked again at the paper that showed the bruising on Richard's face. "Is it this? Was he hurt more badly than reports indicated?"

Pamela couldn't help but smile at the little throat-clearing sound her father made, and the way it had the COO's attention instantly focused on him.

"You are?" her father asked.

The woman hurried to the desk and reached across. As they shook hands she said, "Dagmar Reitlingen." Something niggled at the back of Pamela's mind, but when she reached for the elusive memory, it went skittering away.

"And I am Robert Oort, and this is my daughter, Pamela."

"Pleased to meet you."

Dagmar next took Pamela's hand. Pamela noticed the woman's short-clipped nails, very out of character with the expensive clothing, and the width across the back of Dagmar's hands. It was the mark of a horsewoman. Pamela had it, too.

"I would have been here two days ago, but I had the journey from hell," Reitlingen was saying. "We were late leaving Gatwick, and instead of three hours in Dallas it became eight." Her mouth worked as if she were chewing on something. "And *mein Gott*, how absurdly dry it is in this place. Normally, Mr. Kenntnis and I would meet in London. I've only been here once before, just after the building was completed. The heat was shimmering on the pavement if you can believe it. The sky is still that impossible blue, but at least this time the temperature is bearable."

Pamela felt like she was being pelted by the nonstop words, but her father was faintly smiling.

"Is this a long way of asking for a drink?" he asked.

"Why, yes, exactly," Dagmar said, and smiled.

"Water or something a little stronger?" the judge asked.

"Oh, don't tempt me. But as tired as I am, I'd best be cautious. Water, please."

At a look from her father, Pamela moved to the hidden bar and filled a glass with water and ice cubes from the small refrigerator. The polished red metal of the professional espresso machine gave her a distorted view of the COO. She realized the woman was assessing her with equally sharp and calculating eyes. Pamela brought her the water.

The judge settled back into his chair and indicated the chair on the other side of the desk from him. An offended look, quickly masked, flashed across the older woman's face. *What is she worried about?* Pamela thought.

"Are you here to brief my son or evaluate if the company is in trouble because of this queer turn of events?" the judge asked, and Pamela felt both stupid and enlightened for not realizing the source of Reitlingen's discomfort sooner.

Once she found out a gaggle of relatives had arrived, she probably thought we were a gang of rapacious hillbillies. Well, she's been set straight now.

"You are very direct," Dagmar answered. "But I think these discussions should best be held with my employer, and not with *you* … no matter how close your relationship. Which brings me back to the convalescing. What does convalescing mean? Exactly. If you please."

"My son was shot yesterday."

"*Mein Gott.* How did this happen?"

"He was responding to a … er … domestic disturbance call," the judge said.

Pamela watched the color flee from Dagmar's face. "He is *still* working as a policeman."

"No," said Pamela. "He finally listened to Papa. He quit today." Pamela caught the flicker in Dagmar's brown eyes, and wished she could have trained herself out of pronouncing *Papa* in the French manner. It was such an affectation, and it was *so* like her mother to have stuck her children with it.

"In my experience that career is either very easy or very hard to leave," Dagmar said.

It was so rude, but Pamela couldn't control herself. "Oh, God, please, not another one! I am so sick of cops."

"Well, let me make you feel better. I was never a policeman. My father, however, he was a policeman, and after watching his life I had no interest in pursuing that career." The older woman paused and gave a wry smile. "But damn, I wish I could have had the uniform."

"Why?" her father asked.

"My country has always loved a uniform." Dagmar paused, and the smile she gave them was a study in irony. "Often to Germany's detriment. But because I didn't have a uniform, it made it harder for me to achieve my goals."

Suddenly it all clicked into place for Pamela. "My God, you're *that* Reitlingen. I thought I recognized the name. You won the gold medal in dressage with the highest overall score ever posted."

"Ah, I was right, you are a horsewoman. I spotted your hands immediately, and your thighs. So many American woman are ..." She made a gesture that indicated bulges. "How do you call them? Saddlebags, yes? But not ladies who ride, at least not those who ride well."

Her father frowned again. Pamela knew this discussion of horses was not to his taste. "I don't know. When we were taking Pamela to horse shows I saw a good many ladies who would qualify as ... er ... large."

"Ah, but they are not *riding*. They were just riding," Dagmar said with a smile. Pamela saw her father's frown of confusion, as she nodded in agreement. The COO clapped her hands together with delight. "Yes, you know exactly what I mean. So, do you still ride?"

Pamela shook her head. "Not anymore. I quit when I started college. I checked out a few universities that offered horsemanship programs, but Papa pointed out that selecting a college based on whether it had a barn was spectacularly foolish." Pamela wondered why in the hell she had added all of that. She slid a glance at her father. He was not looking happy. "He was absolutely right, of course."

"You are very young now, and it is never too late to return to the sport," Dagmar said, her tone kind.

"Why is it that women have this obsession with horses? And apparently none of you outgrow it," Robert grumbled.

Dagmar gave the judge her shoulder and turned to face Pamela straight on. "Does your brother share your father's disdain?"

"No, he rode, but he decided to focus on gymnastics, and they're not exactly complementary sports."

"I'll take you to Richard," her father said, his tone making it clear that there was to be no more discussion of horses.

✧   ✧   ✧

THE CARDS FILLED the computer screen like signal flags on a mast, but the message they spelled out was *you lose*. Richard guided the cursor to the red button and depressed the mouse. The cards vanished from the screen. He decided that whoever invented Spider needed to die. Talk about a time sink, and it was totally addictive. Just mindlessly clicking on the cards, trying to get used to the Mac mouse. It felt weird not to have the right and left buttons.

He should have been doing something useful, but mostly Richard was fighting nausea brought on by overheated air and Vicodin and worrying about what he'd just done to circumvent his father's command. The fact that it felt like a sauna in the penthouse was another strike against his sister. Pamela hated the cold. She had probably hiked the thermostat sometime during the night. Richard plucked at his pajama top and pulled it away from his damp skin. His scalp prickled with sweat, and he gave his head a vigorous scratching. He wanted a shower, but Angela had said he had to wait a couple of days and then protect his thigh with plastic wrap when he did bathe. It all felt overwhelming, but God he wanted a shower.

Gritting his teeth, he told himself he had to get to work. No doubt his father would be quizzing him once he returned upstairs and telling the judge he'd done nothing all afternoon was not happening. *Well, I did disobey him.* Not *helping.*

Richard virtuously guided the cursor over to the folder titled LUMINA BOOKS. Then, almost like it was a maddened guide on a Ouija board, the cursor circled the file several times, then darted back to the dock at the bottom of the screen. But of course, the cursor didn't really have a life of its own; Richard was just stalling. He set the arrow on the folder and firmly depressed the mouse. The subfolders, each one titled with a year, filled the screen. How many years was he expected to go back? Richard opened one at random and was faced with a P&L statement.

The numbers marched like lines of toy soldiers. It took him back to that seven months he had spent working at Drew's brokerage house. Which took him to other memories of Drew. To the smell and taste of semen and blood. A weight seemed to be pressing down on Richard's chest. Usually when he felt one of the panic attacks coming on, he would go swim laps or run or take a hike or go to the gym.

But all of those coping mechanisms weren't available right now.

He needed … no, he *had* to find another distraction. Eyes

flicking about the room, his gaze fell upon the Steinway grand piano under the large picture window. Through the glass Richard had a view of the hunched boulders that littered the foothills of the Sandia Mountains. It had been kind of Kenntnis to buy the Steinway, but Richard preferred the touch on his Bösendorfer. He wondered if he could have Jeannette arrange to get his piano out of his old apartment and over to the penthouse. But was he really going to stay here? He felt like an utter imposter and interloper in the elegant space.

The geometric pattern of the Oriental rug, picked out in rich reds, blues, and creams, offered another distraction. Richard thought about the women in Turkey and the various "stans" knotting these treasures. Well, for their buyers elsewhere in the world they were treasures; for their creators they represented a small amount of money and a large amount of drudgery. What would happen if workers around the world finally achieved a living wage: Would this art be lost? But maybe that was a good thing. A machine couldn't go blind.

Richard lifted his eyes and surveyed the beautiful objets d'art that filled every available surface. There was a tiny Roman marble sculpture of Diana, her features carved in exquisite detail. A Mughal dagger. Egyptian tomb figures. Did the value of the objects keep this room from being a cluttered mess? Richard's uncle's house in Vermont was also filled with collectables, but the only word that came to mind was *tchotchkes*. Was this any different? Yes, because he suspected that Kenntnis had collected them as memories of other times and other places. *And perhaps other Paladins?*

On the wall to his left stood two tall bookcases crammed with books. They flanked a Caravaggio painting of the Madonna. *Wonder which Old One she'll turn out to be,* Richard thought. *Or maybe she had been a creation of Kenntnis's? A loving, comforting mother to offset the vengeful, "damn you all to hell" males? Mothers didn't scare you like fathers did.*

It was an uncomfortable moment as Richard realized his errant thoughts had turned out to have a psychological agenda. Richard didn't want to dwell on where that thought had come from. He opened another file. The spreadsheet lay before him, numbers centered precisely between the grid lines. There were lots of them. With large amounts. No, make that *huge* amounts. Correction, *unfathomable* amounts. And Richard was supposed to juggle, manage, invest, and ultimately decide how to spend the money represented by those numbers. He closed the file and pushed away the rolling table holding the laptop.

He grabbed up a report from a subsidiary company and started reading. *Nonrefundable fees received at the initiation of collaborative agreements for which we have an ongoing research and development commitment are deferred and recognized ratably over the period of ongoing research ...* A pounding settled behind Richard's eyes. It felt like his brain was trying to hammer its way out of his skull. He set that report aside and tried another. *Intangible assets are the singular source of differentiation in a postindustrial economy.*

The pages flapped like a gooney bird attempting takeoff as Richard threw it back toward the pile, but the slick paper sent it skidding off the other side. It overbalanced the entire dead-tree tower, and all the reports went tumbling to the floor.

Fuck it.

He would try music; play for a while, maybe sing a little. That might clear his head, and he could come back to the reports refreshed and able to concentrate.

Yeah, right. You have no idea what you are doing. You'll never have any idea.

CHAPTER EIGHT

FERVENT HOPES & ACTUAL FACTS

THE ELEVATOR RIDE was conducted in total silence. Pamela could feel her father's eyes boring into her back. She probably shouldn't have come along, but she was hoping for a chance to talk to Dagmar Reitlingen and find out what happened to that amazing gray mare she had ridden in the Olympics. Was Mist still alive? Had she been bred? How many foals? Were they competing? She pressed a hand against her forehead. *God, she was being as flighty as Richard.*

They stepped off the elevator into the foyer. Piano music and Richard's rich tenor met them. The liquid runs reminded Pamela of children laughing, but the gaiety of the music didn't mollify her father. His lips tightened into a thin line.

"Damn the boy," Robert muttered half under his breath.

Pamela and Dagmar had to hurry to keep pace with the judge. Their heels made a discordant syncopation that shattered the purity of the music. Then they were through the archway and into the living room.

Richard sat at the concert grand piano. His crutches leaned against the side of the instrument. His body swayed in time to the music, and a lock of silver/gilt hair flopped against his forehead.

The judge stood between the two women, and Pamela felt

her father gather himself. She was startled when Dagmar laid a restraining hand on his arm and held up a finger in a shushing gesture. The older woman then turned back to Richard and watched him intently. Pamela wondered what she was seeing, and really hoped the woman wasn't going to prove to be like every other woman and be swayed by her brother's looks.

As an experiment she tried to look at Richard dispassionately, as an outsider might. Richard's eyes were closed, his concentration was total, and his entire body was immersed in the effort of drawing music from the piano and his body.

Pamela found it disturbing to look at the fading bruises that trickled down from his eye, across his cheek, and along the line of his jaw. For some reason the physical beating made this seem more real and more frightening than the gunshot wound he'd sustained the day before. It wasn't rational, but that's how she felt. *Maybe because cops and guns go together. Maybe it felt strange because it was a cop getting beat up.*

She focused on his hands with their long, slender fingers, and listened to the deep hiss of an indrawn breath followed by the floating ring of his voice, and wondered why she hadn't been granted even a modicum of his musical talent.

Richard opened his eyes and, as if sensing the scrutiny, turned his head to look at them. Dagmar drew in a steadying breath.

Maybe outsiders can't be dispassionate, Pamela thought with bitter irony.

Dagmar began applauding. "That was absolutely exquisite. 'Im Haine,' 'In the Woods,' poem by Franz von

Bruchmann, music by Franz Schubert." Then she leaned in close to Pamela and the judge and added in an undertone, "Well, I'd wondered why Kenntnis gave the company to an unknown. Now I think I understand. I'll just keep reminding myself that I'm a married woman and the mother of two lest I succumb as well." Dagmar's tone was bantering, but the judge took it badly.

In a hissing undertone he said, "I'll thank you not to even *suggest* such a thing."

The COO gave him a startled look. "My apologies."

Richard rested a hand on the piano and, wincing, levered himself to his feet. He nodded to Dagmar. "Thank you, but it wasn't that good. By the way, who are you?"

"I'm Dagmar Reit—" Dagmar began, but the judge ran over her.

"What are you doing wandering about?" he demanded as he walked to Richard and handed him the crutches with the air of a drill sergeant offering a recruit a rifle. "Angela will flay me alive if you break open that wound."

"I couldn't think anymore," Richard answered. "I thought music might clear my head."

"Well, we've brought you someone who might help," Pamela said as she moved to stand next to the judge. "This is Dagmar Reitlingen, the COO of the company." She indicated Dagmar with a sweep of the hand.

Richard got the crutches tucked under his arms and went swinging toward Dagmar. He stopped, rested on the supports, and held out his hand. "Richard Oort. Pleased to meet you, ma'am." Richard gave Dagmar a sharp look. "And I just said something that offended you. What did I do?"

Pamela looked from one to the other in confusion. Her father had an expression that she bet was similar to hers.

"Maybe you ought to loan me one of those crutches now that I'm in my dotage," Dagmar said in faltering accents. "Ma'am? When did I become a ma'am?" But then she threw back her head and laughed, and Richard relaxed and also smiled.

It was one of the things Pamela had always hated about her brother. He was always hyperaware of the people around him, always able to read their moods and respond in a way that set them immediately at ease.

Pamela thought it was a way to garner attention, being so sensitive and so attentive to people. A ploy so that people would always talk about how *nice* he was. *As opposed to you,* came a little voice that partook a bit of her older sister, Amelia, and her now-dead mother. Pamela pushed the thought aside.

Richard's smile blazed out. "Actually ... *Dagmar,* pleased doesn't begin to cover it. I'm ecstatic to meet you. Thrilled. Delirious with joy."

"Don't be so silly," the judge said sharply. Dagmar gave him a startled, disapproving look, and Robert added with his rather ponderous attempt at humor, "You sound like you've swallowed a thesaurus."

Richard ducked his head. "Sorry, sir." He focused again on Dagmar. "But I really am in over my head here, and I desperately need help."

"And I'm happy to do that, but before we get started could I get something to eat? I've been in the air or sitting in airports for the past thirty-one hours, and the food in either place is not of the best," Dagmar said.

"Oh, I'm sorry. That was thoughtless of me," Richard said. "Please, let's go into the kitchen. I don't think Franz has cleared the lunch buffet yet."

They all followed Richard as he hobbled through the formal dining room with its cut crystal chandelier like a frozen waterfall over the polished cherrywood table. Dagmar didn't spare a glance at the china and crystal in the buffet, or the magnificent silver centerpiece that featured winged horses and women in diaphanous gowns.

Probably just old hat to her, Pamela thought. When she had first arrived in New Mexico she'd inspected the living quarters very closely on the theory that you could tell a lot about a person by the items he owned, and she was highly suspicious of a man who would leave *anything* to her brother. Given the rarity of the other objects in the penthouse, Pamela could only assume that the champagne flutes etched with bees and an elaborate N had belonged to the Emperor Napoleon. The china was Royal Crown Derby, and it was an antique pattern. She had found other china in a storeroom off the kitchen, not all of it European design. Her best guess, as she held the almost translucent plate with its pale willow pattern, was that it was Chinese and very old. She glanced back at the living room. The sunlight seemed to be haloing the priceless objects on the tables and drawing the colors from the paintings.

Who had he been, this man who had stormed into her brother's life and changed everything?

And not just Richard's life. The unknown Kenntnis had turned Pamela's and her father's lives upside down. Maybe the COO could tell her who this Kenntnis had been, answer her questions and lay her doubts and concerns to rest. She brought her attention back to Dagmar in time to see her father almost tread on the woman's heels because he was walking so closely behind her. The way the judge crowded in on her made Pamela think of stalking predators. Dagmar abruptly stopped, and the judge actually bumped into her.

"I won't hurt him. I promise," the woman said. Richard also stopped and looked back inquiringly. Her father and Dagmar measured looks for a long moment; then the judge gave a sharp nod.

No, Pamela corrected herself, *not a predator. A protective parent guarding its young,* and the realization gave her a strange little jolt. The reaction was gone before Pamela could fully grasp the fleeting emotion.

They entered the kitchen, where the sunlight poured in like honey through bay windows surrounding the breakfast nook and sent searchlight beams down through the skylights to dance on the lids of the silver chafing dishes lined up on the center island and drew blue fire from the opals embedded in the chocolate brown granite of the countertops. Vases filled with large sunflowers were strategically placed so they would reflect in the brushed chrome surfaces of the appliances and add to the genial air of the big room.

Richard gestured toward the chafing dishes while Franz came bustling out from behind the counter carrying a plate and silverware wrapped in a linen napkin. *"Guten nachmittag, Frau Reitlingen."*

"Grüß gott, Franz. Wie geht es Ihnen?" Dagmar said as she accepted the plate and flatware.

There were a few more flurries of German between the two of which Pamela understood about half and her brother clearly followed it all. Her brother had always had a facility for languages. At last count he spoke four in addition to his native English.

"It's been sitting for a couple of hours," the chef warned.

Dagmar gave the Swiss chef a wink and a smirk. "I'm certain it will surpass the McDonald's in DFW." The man pressed a hand to his chest in feigned outrage and devastation and retreated behind the counters.

Her father pulled out a chair for Richard and, once he was situated, made sure the crutches were within easy reach. Pamela's attention was split between watching her father fuss and Dagmar pile her plate high with a Monte Cristo sandwich, a handful of potato puffs, fruit, and a wedge of cheese.

"You should have a little something," the judge said. "You didn't eat much at breakfast. Pamela, get him something."

Pamela felt her spine going stiff. Richard shot her a nervous glance. "I'd really rather not. I'm still nauseated from the Vicodin," Richard said, and this time he split the nervous glance between Pamela and their father.

Dagmar set down the full plate, remarking brightly, "My husband, Peter, is very high-strung and nervy, too. He is also a musician. A violinist. Professional, though." Dagmar returned to the buffet, filled a cup with coffee, and poured in a large dollop of cream. "Although I think you are good enough to have performed professionally," she continued. "Did you ever consider it?"

Now it was her father's turn to go rigid, and for Richard

to go red.

Dagmar returned to the table, sat down, and gave them all a bright smile. Pamela was surprised when Richard was the first to respond.

"You play the role very well," her brother said softly. "But I've seen the books, and I sincerely doubt someone as disingenuous and ditzy as you're *pretending* to be would actually have become the COO of Lumina, so why don't you cut the crap."

Pamela watched her father's brows twitch together in a sharp frown. He hated profanity, and the Oort children rarely cursed. Obviously, that was something else Richard had learned as a cop.

"*Bitte?*"

"Just ask your questions and stop trying to stir the pot," Richard answered.

"All right," Dagmar said, and her tone was suddenly less jocular. "But let me fortify myself a bit first."

Pamela found that her leg was vibrating with anticipation. To occupy herself she began nervously rearranging the sunflowers in the vase on the table. Richard sat perfectly still. The judge, seated next to him, was equally composed, and for the first time Pamela saw the resemblance between the two men. Before she had only seen her mother reflected in her brother's features.

"So." Dagmar pushed the now empty plate aside. "Why in the hell *did* Kenntnis put you in charge of Lumina?"

"Well, it's certainly not for my business acumen." Richard paused; head cocked slightly to the side. "I suppose to protect it," he said slowly and thoughtfully, almost as if he were answering a question for himself.

"Protect it from whom?"

"Maybe from *you*," the judge said, suddenly entering the conversation.

"Me? Do I look like an untrustworthy person?" Dagmar said. She sounded more surprised and puzzled than angry.

The judge was not disarmed. In that precise, dry way of his he said, "We haven't had a very good run with CEOs, COOs and CFOs over the past few years, madam—Enron, Global Crossing, Madoff, Tyco, ERCOT."

"Actually, I think it more likely that *you* are the crook," Dagmar replied. "Your son is given control of a fantastically valuable company, and suddenly we have the whole family descending upon us."

I was right, Pamela thought. *She does think we're carpetbaggers.*

Then she noticed how the edges of her father's nostrils went white, and his spine became even stiffer. *And it didn't occur to Papa.* For some reason his lack of acuity bothered her. She quickly pushed aside the thought. Of course, it wouldn't occur to him. He was the most honest and just man she knew.

"We are not opportunists or thieves. I resent the implication."

"And I resent your accusation. I'm not the female version of Dennis Kozlowski except with dancing boys."

Pamela saw the woman steal a glance at the indentation at the base of Richard's throat.

Oh, not you, too.

Richard laid the tips of his fingers lightly on the judge's

wrist. "Papa. I may not have known Kenntnis long, but I got a good sense of him in that time. He read people very well. If he hired Ms. Reitlingen, then I have every confidence in his decision."

"With one glaring exception," the judge said.

Her brother's long golden lashes fluttered down to cover the pale blue eyes; the fair head bowed. For a moment Richard seemed discomfited. Then he looked up. "Are you talking about me or Rhiana?"

"Rhiana, of course," the judge snapped a little too quickly.

"She was a unique circumstance, Papa."

"And who in heaven might Rhiana be?" Dagmar asked.

"Who in *Hell* is the better question," her father said as he pushed back his chair and stood. He moved to the buffet and prepared a plate for Richard. "Well, I've had my say." He looked back at Dagmar. "Just know that Richard has resources beyond you. We will be keeping an eye on things." He returned to the table and set the plate down in front of Richard. "Eat. Pamela, shall we finish what we were working on?"

The order was heard and understood. Pamela followed him out of the kitchen. She looked back once to see Dagmar staring at her father's back. The older woman's expression was not warm.

❖ ❖ ❖

THEY WERE DOWN to a Costco carton of peanut butter and cheese crackers and had eaten two-thirds of the carton.

Grenier's belly felt like an empty sack, and he was past being embarrassed by his stomach's angry rumbles. The trip west had taken much longer than anticipated since they had abandoned the interstate system just inside the borders of Oklahoma because of the crowds of people converging on Oral Roberts University. The plan had been to ride I-44 into Oklahoma City and then transfer to I-40 for the drive to Albuquerque, but the interstate heading into Tulsa was like LA on a bad day, and Syd had feared the wild, exalted expressions on the faces of the people.

Grenier couldn't blame him. He'd seen those faces in Serbia and Lebanon, India, and Poland, and during government-mandated purges against the Uighurs in China. The Old Ones used religious hatred as fuel for killing because it worked so very, very well, but any kind of fervent, irrational belief that brooked no challenge would also do. Star Wars and even video games were useful, he thought as he contemplated Gamergate. Grenier sighed fondly as he recalled how they had taken Pizzagate and spun it up into Qanon. That had been one of their most effective conspiracies ever. Bottom line, as long as the outcome was lots of hate, fear, and death, his former masters were indifferent to how he had sparked the conflicts.

To avoid the maddened faithful, they had bailed out onto local roads, some no better than farm tracks, and headed south. The vast emptiness of Texas had been a challenge because gasoline was scarce, and the shelves in the groceries of the small towns through which they passed had been very bare. Eventually they quit stopping because of the covetous looks the RV received.

They had driven into the next wave of wild-eyed worshipers around the New Mexico town of Roswell, site of the supposed saucer crash in 1947. A tent city had sprung up in the desert, and everyone was watching the skies. The saucer nuts seemed less prepared than the religious nuts, and they were in a particularly hostile environment. It might be January and colder than a witch's tit, but it was still the desert. As they drove past the seething crowds, Grenier could hear the low thunder of drums. It seemed some members of the Harmonic Convergence also believed in aliens. A group of young women were whirling in an elaborate dance at the side of the highway. Multicolored scarves, sparkling with sequins, trailed around them, and they sang in eerie high-pitched voices. The only other sounds that penetrated the windows of the RV were the piercing wails of young children and babies. Too young to be true believers, they just knew they were hungry, thirsty, and cold.

Syd had pressed his foot down on the gas. "What the hell is wrong with them?"

Because Grenier was tired and hungry and scared, he forgot himself and answered. "The gates are opening. It makes it harder for people to separate a fervent hope from an actual fact. And it's likely they'll get their wish. Something may come for them." He swallowed hard, remembering the faces and that now he had to fear them too. "It just won't be what they expect."

"How to Serve Man shit, huh?" Syd asked, though he had neither expected nor wanted an answer.

They hadn't stopped in Roswell either.

Now they were driving up a long street lined with strip

malls and cheap apartment buildings toward the towering gray granite face of the mountain. High up among the tumbled boulders was a seven-story office building. The western side glittered and sparkled, and it wasn't just the windows. Grenier realized the wall between the glass was lined with solar panels.

They left the last of the buildings behind and went winding up a curving driveway toward the building. *Lumina.* He had seen the building many times in photos. This was the first time in person. The only time Grenier had led a crusade in New Mexico, he'd stayed well south of Albuquerque and Kenntnis. Grenier had been a true sorcerer, and it was rumored that Kenntnis could sense magic. In fact, it had been Cross, but the humans serving the Old Ones hadn't known that until Rhiana had been placed on the inside, close to Kenntnis.

A few short months ago Grenier had launched a devastating attack on the place in an attempt to kill Richard before he could be armed. His stump flared with pain, and Grenier gripped it tightly, trying to remember that he was supposed to be glad he had failed.

CHAPTER NINE

ARE ALL OF YOU MAD?

R ICHARD LISTENED TO his father's retreating footsteps, but he waited until he heard the faint whine of the elevator before turning back to this woman who was now his employee. If it had been hard to give an order to Kenntnis's personal secretary, Jeannette, Richard couldn't image giving Dagmar Reitlingen an order.

He was startled by her expression when he met her gaze. She looked like she wanted to give him a hug. Richard felt like he should offer her one instead. "Look, don't worry. I know that might have seemed rude—"

"Seemed?"

"Okay, it *was* rude, but we've all been under a lot of stress. My father really is a remarkable man."

"I'll agree that having all the cards on the table is better than not. And always say something to my face, Mr. Oort. I can tell your father is a ..." Richard watched as she paused and seemed to search for a word. "A stern fellow."

"Looking for your English or looking for something more diplomatic?" Richard gave her a smile and got one back. One front tooth was slightly crooked, giving her an impish quality. She had a nice face that was framed by light brown hair with blonde streaks, and he liked her eyes. They were sort of sherry-colored. "I know he's tough, but he never expects more of others than he expects of himself," Richard added.

He didn't want to face the rather ironic look in her eyes, so he looked out the window. What Richard had just said brought a cascade of memories. *Huddled at the top of the stairs and gazing down through the banister rails as Papa put on his overcoat. He could hear the rain thundering at the windows of the house and the wind moaning under the eaves. Alannis Oort's soft pleadings.*

"Please, Robert, you're sick. Call Judge Manley. He'll understand."

His father's firm headshake. "No, we have the momentum now. I can win this."

Later Richard learned his father been running a hundred and two fever, but he was fighting against a large developer and the city in defense of a man protecting his pharmacy. He had won, and it had become part of the family's oral history. It meant he expected the same dedication from his kids. Richard couldn't count how many times he'd delivered newspapers when he had been sick or played Little League with a sprained wrist or ankle. There was one unbreakable rule for Robert Oort—you didn't let people down who were counting on you.

Richard turned back from the window after briefly noting how the rabbit bush and dried, seared ragweed were starting to twitch in a rising wind.

He took a deep breath and said, "Look, you said you liked getting things out front, so I want to be completely honest about the Herculean task you're about to undertake."

Richard gave Dagmar a smile, and he had a feeling it was singularly shit-eating and apologetic. "I ..." He coughed and took a sip of water. It was so hard to say this. "I never balance my checkbook. I just check my bank balance online," he mumbled.

Dagmar's voice caught on a laugh. "Well, that *is* shocking."

Richard held up a hand, but he couldn't help smiling because he was so relieved. "It gets worse. I've got *five* credit cards, and *they're all maxed out.*"

Richard had steeled himself for the reaction, but all she said was, "Well, those we should probably clear. It wouldn't do for the CEO of Lumina Enterprises to carry such a *small* amount of debt. When we carry debt, we carry a *magnificent* amount of it. Mr. Oort ... Richard ... May I call you Richard?"

"I'd prefer it. And it would be great if you didn't tell ..." He bit back the rest of the sentence and felt himself blushing.

"What?"

Richard shook his head. "No, nothing."

Dagmar leaned back in her chair and regarded him. "I think I know what you were going to say, and I can assure you that whatever we discuss will remain strictly between us."

"Thank you. And by the way, I speak German fluently." She looked surprised at that.

"Not at all common for Americans."

He heard that touch of European arrogance in her voice, so he added, "I also speak Spanish, Italian, and French."

Dagmar regarded him for a long moment. "A very useful

skill for the head of Lumina. I know Mr. Kenntnis was fluent in a great many languages."

"I'd bet all of them," Richard muttered under his breath.

"Pardon?"

"Nothing."

Dagmar resumed, "As for balancing your checkbook—you're not going to be a bookkeeper. You have a CFO, chief financial officer, for that."

"I do know the differences between CEOs, COOs, and CFOs. I worked for a few months in a brokerage firm." Richard hated even mentioning it, and he quickly dropped his eyes. This woman saw a little too much for his comfort.

"Good, then we're not starting from nowhere. Anyway, you have Mr. Fujasaki and his staff in Tokyo. Your task is to make the large decisions. You set our course, and it's my job as the chief operating officer to see that those decisions are carried out. So, now it's time for your questions."

"Okay. I looked for an annual report so I could get some sense of the company, I mean what it does. But I couldn't find one. So, I dipped briefly into the books." Just remembering those lines of numbers made his head hurt. Richard pressed a hand against his forehead and pushed back his hair. "Uh ... wow."

"A lot of money, no?"

"A lot of money, yes."

"And you wouldn't find a report. Lumina Enterprises is that very rare beast, a privately held company. It has controlling interests in companies that are public companies, but the core company is required to report to no one. Our only contact with the wider public is that we pay taxes. As for what we do ... Mr. Kenntnis's interests were in cutting-edge technology: biotech, high tech, private space ventures, open-source code, alternate energy sources. Education. We fund pure science projects such as CERN, endow university science departments. And alleviating poverty, which Kenntnis considered to be the source of many of the world's ills—war, terrorism, overpopulation, pollution. One-third of our annual income is spent on various charitable efforts—building wells in sub-Saharan Africa, Doctors Without Borders, providing medicines to impoverished nations. It takes a lot of money to do good."

Richard had known all this for weeks. Cross had given him some of the highlights when Richard had first met him and Kenntnis, but it hadn't really registered because it didn't affect him. Now it sure as hell affected him, and he was the guy who couldn't balance his checkbook. Richard had sometimes wondered what it would be like to be an Elon Musk, or a Bill Gates, or a Jeff Bezos with the power to literally change lives. Now he had it. Except to keep doing it, this company had to keep making money, and Richard was the person in charge.

We're doomed.

Richard picked up a strawberry and brought it toward his mouth, but the smell was nauseating. He pulled it away and started spinning it by the stem. "Now I'm even more intimidated."

The stem suddenly broke. The strawberry hit the edge of the plate, bounced, and left a smear of red on the etched metal top of the table. Richard scrubbed away the stain with the tip of his forefinger, contemplated the red-tinged skin, and suddenly saw the blood in the Quincy house again. He jerked his thoughts away and crashed against the crushing responsibility of Lumina that had been dropped onto his shoulders.

"There are real consequences if I screw up," he whispered, and gave her a sickly smile.

"So, don't screw up." But Dagmar softened the blunt words with a smile and then added, "What you told your father about Kenntnis can also be applied to *you*. He picked you for a reason. He must have had faith in your good sense and your integrity. Listen, you have smart, good people to help you." She scooted her chair in closer to the table and leaned across, taking one of his hands in hers. "Richard, the secret to running a company is both simple and hard to do. You find people smarter than you and give them space to do their work."

"And how do I know if they're good people who I can trust?" It was the million-dollar question.

"You make decisions, and judge from people's reactions to those decisions if you want to keep that person working for you."

Dagmar released Richard's hand, leaned back in her chair, and cut off a forkful of carrot cake before popping the bite into her mouth. She reminded Richard of a cat, comfortable, secure, and maybe a little bit complacent. Richard realized she had him pegged as young and insecure. He wondered if that would change when he pulled out the sword. Or would she just add *nut* to the equation?

"Okay, I'm going to take your advice."

"Excellent."

"Starting with you."

"All right," but she sounded uneasy, and Richard wondered what she was reading in his face.

"So, it's pretty clear to me that you don't actually know the *true* purpose of the Lumina."

A rather amused smile curved her lips. "And I take it you do?"

"Yes."

She leaned back and opened her arms in an expansive gesture. "Enlighten me, please."

The gentle sarcasm was drilling onto Richard's already stretched nerves, but he gritted his teeth and plowed on. "The company's just a front."

She laughed. "A front. Well, that's an interesting theory. What was Kenntnis doing that I didn't know about? Something *naughty*, I hope."

He hated that humoring tone, and how she was turning something deadly serious into a joke. Richard used the edge of the table to help lever himself to his feet. The laugh stuttered to a stop in the back of her throat as he stared down at her.

"No. Something dangerous. Lumina was founded to combat magic, religion, superstition, and ignorance. And Kenntnis dedicated his life to it."

"Magic," Reitlingen said in an amused tone. "Well, it looks like he won that one."

"I'm going to let that go because you don't understand, not yet, but you will in a few minutes. One of my ... associates said that I need to be certain of all my employees. I don't care about their honesty, or yours, for that matter. You can all rob me blind, but I have to be sure that none of you will become a conduit for magic, or that you'll be ensorcelled and turned against me, try to kill me."

"All right, this has become silly and annoying—" Her voice had lost its jocularity.

"I am serious," Richard snapped. "Deadly serious."

Richard decided it was time for showing and not telling, so he pulled the hilt of the sword out of the pocket of his bathrobe. The sunlight was beating on his back and head, and he felt sweat, born out of heat and nerves and annoyance, beginning to trickle down over his ribs with that horrible crawling sensation as if small insects were on his skin.

The chair shrieked across the stained concrete floor as Dagmar thrust it back and jumped to her feet. Fear tightened her features. "You will sit back down, and I am going to call your father," she began in a tone of voice that reminded Richard of animal trainers.

"Fine. Go ahead. He'll back me up. He's already submitted himself to this. All of my family and friends have. Now I'm asking ... no, *demanding*, that you do so as well." Richard thought—*hoped*—he had matched her tone of snapped command, but rather doubted it.

"What happens if I refuse?" Dagmar asked.

Best to keep it simple, he decided. "I'll fire you."

Shock flickered across her face, followed by alarm, and then rage.

She finally got a smile pasted back into place and said with forced lightness, "Maybe I'd better find out what you're going to do before I refuse. It might be quite painless, although I'm guessing it's eccentric."

"It's not painless, but I can't predict how much pain you'll feel. The amount of pain seems dependent on how much magic you possess," Richard said, and immediately wished he hadn't added the last sentence. *Keep it simple. Keep it simple.*

Dagmar stood dithering. Richard could see her trying to decide if she'd humor him or carry out her threat to send for his father.

Or just call for commitment papers right now, Richard thought grimly. *Well, sometimes a demonstration can save a thousand words.*

Richard swept his hand away from the base of the hilt. There was the strange basso *thrum* that shook deep in the chest and laid a pressure against the back of the eyes. Dagmar pressed a hand against her chest and took several gasping breaths.

"You're not having a heart attack," Richard said gently.

She looked up, and her eyes widened at the sight of the sword he was now holding. Richard took an instant to contemplate the long black blade filled with distant glittering silver lights like the fire of ancient galaxies that flowed up and down its length.

"And no, you're not hallucinating. I really am holding a sword."

He felt like an idiot just saying it. For, like, the millionth time Richard wished that Kenntnis could have recast his weapon into something less silly, archaic, and cliched. *But maybe it was a good thing he hadn't turned it into a gun or a taser,* Richard reflected. Then he would have been saying, *I'm going to shoot you with this gun or tase you.* Instead of saying, as he now did, "I'm going to touch you with the sword." Her eyes widened, and Richard rushed to add, "Just with the flat side of the blade."

She started backing away. "No, no, I don't think you are." Suddenly she turned and went running out of the kitchen and through the dining room. Richard dropped his head, berating himself for handling things so badly. He let the blade vanish, stuffed the hilt back in his pocket, grabbed the crutches, and started in limping pursuit. This was the first time he'd really tried to move fast, and it hurt. Richard felt stitches beginning to tear and the slow warm trickle of blood down his thigh. Yeah, this was going great.

He nearly caught up to her in the living room. Her high heel had twisted on the edge of the Oriental rug, and she stumbled into an Italian inlaid table. Yelping, Dagmar clutched at her knee, looked back at Richard, terror filling her eyes. She limped frantically through the foyer and began punching the elevator button.

Maybe mad pursuit wasn't the best plan. Richard stopped under the archway. "Please, wait," he said in the gentlest, sanest tone he could muster. "Obviously I didn't explain things very well. Let me try—"

Dagmar's eyes were darting around the foyer. She spotted the door to the stairs, ran to it, yanked it open, and vanished down the stairwell. Richard listened to her footfalls clattering and fading away down the steps and he really hoped she'd pull off the high-heeled boots before she broke her neck. The elevator gave a gentle *ding* and arrived. Richard hobbled onto it and dithered between the button for the office and the button for the lobby. He really didn't want his father to know how badly he had screwed things up. He'd try one more time to convince the COO that he was neither mad nor dangerous. Richard punched the button for the lobby.

◆　◆　◆

THERE WERE CARS in the parking lot, all of them fully electric, but it was relatively few cars when compared to the size of the Lumina building. As Syd eased them into a couple of parking spaces, Grenier, staring avidly at the building, saw the front door of the building burst open. A woman came running out.

She was frantically hopping and hobbling, and he realized she'd broken the heel on one of her boots. She stopped at the bottom of the steps that led up to the building's entrance, unzipped and yanked off her boots. She focused on the still rolling RV and came running toward them, waving her arms over her head, and cried in German, *"Du musst mir helfen, bitte!"*

Grenier and Syd exchanged glances. The FBI agent eased the RV to a stop and opened his door. The woman jumped onto the first step and hung on to the hand grip, gasping for air.

"Please ... I need ... a ride ... please!"

She had apparently recovered her grasp of English.

"Okay, ma'am, just calm down—" Syd began, but the woman interrupted.

"No time. I must get away!"

Syd stood up, the woman retreated down the step, and

Syd jumped down onto the pavement of the parking lot and caught her by the shoulders. "Whoa, whoa, why do you have to get away? What have you done?" His tone was sharp and suspicious.

It must be the nature of cops of every stripe to assume everyone is a criminal until proven innocent, Grenier thought as he moved to get out of the RV. His belly gave a monstrous growl, and he belched. The gust of air across the back of his tongue carried the scent and faint taste of his last packet of peanut butter and cheese crackers.

The woman leaned back, trying to pull free. She looked angry. "I haven't done a damn thing. It's my boss ... former boss. He's quite mad. He's got a sword—"

Syd's expression cleared and he smiled with relief. He squeezed past Grenier, who was exiting the RV, and called toward the back, "Honey, Sam, he's here. Come on, you've gotta come out now."

Sam crept to the opening between the cab and the cabin and peeked around with the air of a timid deer gazing fearfully into an open meadow. The rifle was still clutched in her hands. Tears welled up in her brown eyes and slowly spilled down her cheeks. "Come on, sweetie. You're going to be okay now," Syd said, ever so gently. "And you can keep the gun if it makes you feel better. But everything's gonna be better real soon now."

The woman standing barefoot on the cold asphalt was frowning up at the father and daughter. "Pardon me," Grenier said. She hurriedly stepped aside, and he stepped down with a grunt.

Syd had his arm around his daughter's waist now and

was gently urging her down the steps of the RV. The German woman's eyes widened when she saw the large rifle that Sam cradled in her arms. She slumped and shook her head.

"First swords and now guns. Are all you Americans mad? Would someone please tell me what the hell is going on?"

But Syd ignored the question. Instead, he was hurriedly walking Sam toward the building. His head was bent solicitously over hers, and Grenier heard the soothing murmur of endearments and encouragement. "It's okay, honey. We're almost there. You're going to be fine now."

The German stared in bemusement after them. Grenier cleared his throat. She turned to face him. "So, it looks like Richard didn't do a very good job of show-and-tell with the sword."

"Does everybody know about this fucking sword but *me*?" she burst out.

"A select few, and some of us have a more intimate knowledge than others." Grenier lifted his maimed arm, and smiled as he watched the woman move to the logical conclusion—he had lost his hand to that sword.

"Okay, I am definitely out of here," the woman said and started to walk away.

It suddenly dawned on Grenier that if Richard had wanted to touch this woman with the sword, she must have some importance. He grabbed her by the upper arm, digging his fingers deep into her biceps.

"Four months ago, I would have done everything in my power to hurry you on your way, but now, well, let's just say that if you give Richard an advantage in the coming battles, then you are going to stay." Grenier dropped his maimed arm over her shoulders and frog-marched her back toward the front doors.

✧ ✧ ✧

PAMELA HUNG UP the phone and looked over at her father. "That was the front desk. Dagmar went running through like the hounds of Hell were after her. It looks like Richard made a mess of things."

Her father stood up from behind the desk, ripped off his reading glasses, and tossed them down on the piles of papers. "Come along."

When they stepped off the elevator into the front lobby, a man's voice was echoing off the black marble and steel panels of the room.

"She went down to Virginia while I was in the hospital."

Richard was there, leaning on his crutches. There was a bloodstain at thigh height on his bathrobe. Her brother's entire focus was on the face of the older man who was pouring out words so quickly that it was hard to distinguish between them.

"By the time I figured out what was wrong with her you were gone."

The *her* appeared to be a young woman with chin-length brown hair and wild brown eyes. The man was holding her by the wrist. She bucked and struggled like a hooked fish trying to break the line. In her free hand she held a rifle, and that rifle was waving wildly.

"Sir, we need to secure that gun," said Estevan, one of the security guards. Pamela totally agreed.

"I told you it's not loaded," the man snapped. He turned back to Richard. "I really need you to do the thing ... with the sword. You'll do it, won't you?"

At that moment Dagmar and a fat man entered. The man had amazing hazel eyes, and it looked like he'd once had good features, though they were now blurred under a layer of fat. His belly strained at the buttons of an expensive dress shirt. He looked vaguely familiar, but Pamela couldn't place him.

Her brother's reaction left no doubt that *he* knew the identity of the man. "You!" he said, and the single word was filled with loathing and an undercurrent of fear.

Pamela looked over at her father, but he was also staring at the man with hatred, at least equal to Richard's if not greater.

Richard spun on his good leg, putting himself within reach of the bemused security guard, and yanked Estevan's pistol out of its holster.

A lot of things happened all at once. Dagmar hit the floor. The man with the terrified, rifle-toting woman said, "Huh?" Rifle Girl began to scream. The receptionist joined in. Richard pointed the gun at the fat man.

Estevan said in agonized tones as he shifted nervously from foot to foot, "Sir! Sir! That one *is* loaded, sir!"

"I sincerely hope so," Richard gritted out. "Otherwise, I'm going to have a hard time killing this bastard."

"Richard!" Pamela shrieked out her brother's name. "*What* are you *doing*?"

The fat man was speaking, the words both furious and contemptuous. "Good God, what do you think I could do, here in your own stronghold? Assault you? I'm here to offer you, my *help*."

"How dare you come here, sir! Leave at once!" Pamela's father commanded.

Pamela heard the clack of the front door's bar being depressed. A new voice, a rich contralto, joined the cacophony, "Richard, what are you doing? You've opened your wound."

Angela began to rush to Richard's side only to stop, confused by the sight of the guns. Her eyes followed the barrel of the pistol being held by Richard to the fat man. "Oh, shit, Grenier!"

Now Pamela realized who he was. At that point everyone started talking at once and Pamela couldn't untangle a single sentence.

"Everyone! Please! Shut up!"

It was Richard. His voice carried above the screaming, crying, and talking. *Guess all those singing lessons were good for something,* Pamela thought.

And, amazingly, everyone did.

CHAPTER TEN

TAKING THE RISK

THE FURNISHINGS AND art in the penthouse were stunning and made Grenier's possessions look like cheap Walmart crap in comparison. He'd loved the big stone-and-timber building on his estate in Virginia. The public rooms had been trailer park chic—blue velvet upholstered furniture and thick, white pile carpet with bad modern religious art; but his private quarters, that was where he could be his true self, a man of taste and refinement. Where he could revel in beautiful things away from the gaze of the credulous rubes he had bled for all those years.

Grenier had collected eighteenth-century English furniture, silver, and paintings. He'd loved the hunting still lifes, the way each feather on a dead bird had been so perfectly rendered, but his antiques paled in comparison with the objects in this room. Resentment clawed at the back of his throat.

Of course, I'm just a man, a mortal, and had only a few years to amass my fortune and collection. Kenntnis had eons.

He found himself mourning his lost home, his power, his money, and hating virtually every individual gathered in this exquisite room. Grenier moved away from the central fireplace and took up a position against a bookcase. He watched the people swirling, clotting, and breaking apart, like balls on a billiard table. Conversations flared and jumped from person to person without any connection or logic. He hoped Lumina wasn't always this disorganized. Perhaps it was his arrival that had thrown them into such total disarray, and perversely the thought made him feel better.

"*Was ist* this sword?" the barefoot woman was asking, continuing to jumble German and English.

Pamela, referring to the still screaming, weeping Sam, said, "Can't somebody *please* shut her up?" Grenier felt like he knew the sister. He'd studied her photo, her education, her cases in the DA's office in Newport, her boyfriends, and lovers, in his effort to understand Richard and find the key to breaking him.

"Who are you?" Judge Oort was demanding of Syd.

"You will help her, right?" Syd was yelling into Richard's left ear while Armandariz yelled into his right ear, "We need to redress your leg."

Grenier studied the coroner curiously. He had never actually met the woman. *Just nearly killed her when she came between Richard and one of my spells.*

Richard waved Armandariz off. "It can wait. We need to deal with …" Richard put a hand in the center of Syd's chest and pushed him back a step to get the former FBI agent out of his personal space. "What's her name?" he asked, nodding at the whimpering Sam.

"Sam," Syd provided.

"Short for Samantha?" Pamela Oort said, and Grenier couldn't tell if she was correcting the father or just testing out the name.

Syd didn't take offense, just babbled as he nervously patted his wailing daughter on the back. "Yeah, but never call her that. She hates it. The whole *Bewitched* thing."

Pamela sniffed and took herself off to sit on the piano bench. Richard pulled the hilt out of the pocket of his bathrobe, swept his hand away from it, and the blade appeared. There was a flare of intense pain from Grenier's stump as he remembered that blade shearing through his wrist. Rage and tears beat at the back of his throat.

As it was drawn, musical overtones went echoing away into infinity. Sam stopped crying, lifted her head from her father's shoulder, and turned to face Richard. Richard said something to the young agent, but it was so low that Grenier couldn't hear the words. Then Richard touched her lightly on the shoulder with the blade. She cried out, shivered, and would have collapsed to the floor except for her father's supporting arms.

Once the convulsions stopped, Sam lifted her head from her father's shoulders. *It really was remarkable, the power of the thing,* Grenier thought as he studied her eyes now cleared of the madness, her expression calm, if more than a little defensive. The young agent furiously brushed the last of the tears from her cheeks.

The German woman who'd tried to commandeer a ride dropped into an armchair. She looked shell-shocked.

Grenier was surprised when Richard limped over to confront him. Grenier had pegged the young Paladin as a person who avoided confrontation at all cost.

"Why are you here? What do you want?" There was nothing soft in the delivery, and Richard stared defiantly up at him.

"Sanctuary ... since we're in a medieval frame of mind," Grenier said, with a gesture from the sword in Richard's hand back toward Sam. "My former ... associates take a dim view of failure."

"What failure?" Richard asked. "You bound Kenntnis." Bitterness lay over the words, but Grenier also heard the deeply buried fear and loss.

"Ah, yes." He cleared his throat. "But I failed to deliver the sword. And in trying to deliver the sword I also never got around to killing *you*." The young man before him blanched. It probably wasn't easy to hear someone so matter-of-factly discussing your death. "So, here I am. Throwing myself on your mercy because you're the only person who can protect me. And if the milk of human kindness doesn't work for you, you can try enlightened self-interest. You might find me useful."

"Tough! Get the fuck out of here, and I hope they *do* kill you," Armandariz spat out. Anger blazed in her brown eyes.

"Angela." The way Richard said her name demanded silence.

The coroner subsided, and Grenier realized that the young man actually had a commanding presence but seemed totally unaware of it.

"Taking him in makes a certain degree of sense," the judge said in his dry, precise way from his position on the sofa. "But only if you can trust him. Do you think you can trust him, Richard?"

"Probably not, sir." Richard turned back to Grenier. "Still, he has knowledge and information that we need. I think we must take the risk."

The timid fawn look was back in the blue eyes, as if Richard were already second-guessing his decision. The coroner kept silent, but she still managed to make her feelings known. She let out a snort, threw her hands in the air and stalked away.

Across the room, Sam shook off her father's embrace saying to him, "I'm fine. I'm fine now. Really." Her tone and expression radiated embarrassed defiance.

The judge stood. "Richard needs to have that wound dressed again. Many of you have been traveling. We can reconvene after you've all had something to eat and perhaps a wash?"

The plan was met with universal approval. Grenier joined the move toward the arch separating dining room and living room. The judge caught him by the sleeve, holding him back.

"Your Honor, *so* good to see you again," Grenier said.

The last time they had met, they had been in Grenier's office at his compound and Grenier had been trying to kill the elder Oort with a series of magical spells. But the remark didn't elicit a rise. The judge's control was better than his son's.

"I've had the chance to observe you over the years," Oort said, referring to political events in Washington they had both attended. "My impression was that you were an opportunist. So, I expect you can be trusted, at least until someone makes you a better offer. Just be aware that I will never allow you accept that new offer."

"Bald threats, Judge? And here I thought you were a great Constitutional conservative defending the rule of law,"

Grenier drawled.

"You shattered those rules when you joined forces with those *things*. And on a very personal level—your people drove my wife to suicide. *You* imprisoned and tortured my son. I won't allow you to betray us. Have I made myself clear?"

"Crystal."

✧   ✧   ✧

RICHARD WISHED HE could feel more naughty than embarrassed and vulnerable as he lay on his side on his bed. His pajama pants had been eased off his right leg, leaving his thigh and part of his ass bare to the world. He pressed his flaming face into the pillow, hands tightly gripping the corners of the pillowcase as Angela probed the entrance and exit wounds. He hissed softly as she wiped away the blood with a disinfectant wipe, but when her latex-sheathed fingers began to pluck away the torn stitches Richard yelped and jumped.

"Please, try to hold still. I knew I should have packed lidocaine. I just didn't expect you to go galivanting all over the building."

Richard bit the corner of the pillow to avoid objecting, and to prevent any more embarrassing outbursts. The fabric tasted faintly of detergent, and his mouth was already Sahara dry because of tension and pain. Chewing on a flannel pillowcase wasn't helping.

Grenier.

Richard wished he had kept thinking about the taste of

the pillow and his desperate thirst. Instead, his mind went skipping back to Virginia. He could hear the *spark* as Grenier had brushed those stripped electrical wires together. His muscles tightened as if he were once again struggling against the thin cords that had bound him in that straight-backed chair. The cords had cut so deep that blood had trickled along the sides of his hands. Maybe in time he could have used that slick blood to help him worm out of the knots, but he had been far too distracted by the application of those wires to his balls. Just the memory had his scrotum tightening, and his testicles trying to retreat deep into his belly.

So why are you letting him stay?

He's worked among them. Served the Old Ones. He might be able to help.

But we've already nurtured one traitor. Rhiana had been planted on us. What if Grenier is the same?

But they wouldn't try the same thing twice. *They would know that the members of the Lumina would never* fall for *that again.*

Oh, really? You're falling for it right now.

Angela's voice along with the firm pressure and pain as she pressed an antiseptic pad onto the hole left by the bullet's exit pulled him out of his spiraling thoughts.

"The sutures have cut into the edges of the skin," she said. Her hand slipped beneath his knee, and she applied surgical tape over the dressing. There was the sucking, snapping sound of surgical gloves being stripped off; then a warm palm was laid on his buttocks. "Nice buns. Wish I was seeing them under different circumstances."

"Angela!" Thanks to her wandering hand, memories of

the last time they'd been in a bedroom together came forcing their way into Richard's thoughts. It was not a good place to go.

She gently began to work his leg back into his pajamas. "I'm sorry, I always go for the cheap quip. I know how much pressure you're under, so let's try to lighten the burden at least a little. Whether we ever become sexual partners doesn't matter to me. I'm your friend. I always will be, and I'll always stand by you as you work through … well, you know."

Her kindness and understanding when he felt like he had been so unappreciative of her loyalty and friendship had Richard feeling like he was drowning. Angela pulled back, looking alarmed as he gasped for breath.

"Panic attack?" Richard managed a nod. He didn't have enough air to speak. "I'll write a prescription and send Estevan."

The hammering of his heart filled Richard's ears. He couldn't wait for Estevan to drive to a drugstore and come back. *He couldn't breathe.* Richard caught her wrist and managed to whisper, "Xanax. In a pillbox. In the drawer." He indicated the bedside table with a jerk of his chin.

As she pulled out the silver-and-enamel box, the vivid memory of the day his mother had bought it washed over him. The family was spending Christmas in Germany, skiing and enjoying the Old World celebrations. They had gone to Rothenburg to shop because the weather was so bad, they couldn't ski. Snow was swirling down the narrow, crooked cobblestone streets. Overhead, the upper stories of the medieval houses almost touched.

Many of the buildings had been converted into shops. It

was in an antique store that they had seen the eighteenth-century snuffbox. The picture on the lid was of a man's face. He wore a tricorn hat, a powdered wig, and a domino mask. The eyes behind the mask were made from two tiny sapphire chips. There was something in the smile that curved his lips, and the way the gem chips flashed, that Richard found fascinating. He had wondered who he had been? If this had been his snuffbox? Had he commissioned it, or had it been a gift from a lover? When Richard had opened presents on Christmas, the box had been wrapped as a birthday present. He had used it as a pill case ever since that fifteenth birthday.

The five-pointed white pills seemed to be rebuking him. Not all that long ago he was priding himself on resisting using the drug.

But that was before Kenntnis was captured and the fate of the world had been dumped on him.

Richard plucked one out and dry swallowed it. He groped for Angela's hand, clutching it tightly. Her skin was slightly slick from the residue of powder from the glove. "I'm sorry. Thank you for hanging in there with me. I know I'm a lot of trouble, but someday things will settle down and we'll have a chance to maybe … figure things out." It was an awkward conclusion and elicited the response it deserved.

"Yeah, like that's going to happen anytime soon," Angela said sourly.

✦   ✦   ✦

"IN ORDER TO understand Richard, you really need to understand his relationship with his father." The speaker was of medium height with graying brown hair and a neatly trimmed Elizabethan-style beard and mustache. He was handsome and very well dressed and had a clipped accent that reminded Rhiana of Richard.

Jack and Rhiana's research before this meeting had fleshed out the bare-bones information that Sandringham owned an investment firm. They now knew that it was a boutique firm with a list of very wealthy, very private clients, both foreign and American. They knew that Sandringham had divorced more than twenty years ago and never remarried. There were whispers that he was gay, but others they had spoken to attributed those rumors to spite and jealousy engendered by his success. Rhiana had wondered why this successful, well-connected man would ever agree to talk to them, but when Jack had said they had some questions regarding Richard Oort, the man had immediately suggested the Beekman Tower Hotel.

Drew Sandringham sat on one side of the small table in the bar of the Beekman hotel. Rhiana and Jack sat across from him. Through the wide windows Rhiana had a view across Manhattan. The UN Building caught the light off the East River. Directly across and some ten floors down from their aerie, a woman wearing a parka over her housecoat wandered out the door of her condo and into the tiny rooftop garden. She was a doll-like figure.

"Oh?" Jack said in that encouraging tone designed to invite more comment.

"Of course, it's terrible pop psychology," Sandringham said with a short laugh. "But in this case, it is spot-on. Richard has spent his life trying to please Robert and win his approval, without, I may add, any notable success." He lifted his martini glass to his lips and took an appreciative sip. "Carl really does make the best lemon drops in Manhattan," he added in an annoying non sequitur that had Rhiana longing to throttle him.

The sun appeared to be impaled on the tops of the more distant skyscrapers. Out over the river the clouds were tinged pink, peach, and blue. The light of the setting sun turned concrete and glass into spikes of gold and crystal. It was all breathtakingly beautiful. Rhiana tried to reconcile her old life with the new. The new one had advantages. Money, luxury, power. It also had stress beyond belief. Maybe life had been better when she just felt deprived and resentful. At least back then she could dream. Now she only seemed to have nightmares. Sandringham's voice recalled her to her surroundings.

"Richard tends to form strong attachments with older men who can fill that father figure void. I know." He gave them a flash of perfect white teeth, and with a forefinger traced the line of his perfect mustache.

"And you know this how?" Rhiana didn't like the proprietary nature of the man's smile.

"Richard worked for me for a few months after his return from the conservatory in Rome. At his father's insistence he had left before completing his master's in voice and piano. He knocked about New York for a while, but his vocal auditions never yielded any roles. I'm sure some of that was his height. Tenors tend to be short, and female singers tend to be very, very large, and Richard is slight as well as short. But I also think some of it was his insecurity. You need one hell of an ego to hold a stage for three-plus hours. Richard has always tried to be overlooked. Hard to do when he's so very handsome." Sandringham paused for another swallow of his martini.

Rhiana wondered why Sandringham was talking so much. It seemed like an excess of information. Her drink arrived. Rhiana took a cautious sip.

"How do you like that one?" Jack asked.

"It's good." The nutmeg and cream damped down the sharp taste of the brandy. Rhiana had another sip of the Brandy Alexander.

They all waited until the waiter left the glass verandah before Sandringham continued.

"Anyway, Robert asked me to hire Richard as a favor to him. Robert and I were at Harvard together, and were very close friends, so I was happy to oblige."

"But he only lasted a few months?" Jack asked.

"Yes. Richard was a dead loss as a stockbroker. But he had other … gifts."

"Who got blamed for Richard's failure? You or Richard?" Jack asked.

"Robert knew who to blame."

Was that the faintest hint of glee? Rhiana couldn't really tell. Sandringham hurried on.

"Not to say that Robert hasn't been unfair at times." Sandringham sighed and took another sip of his whiskey. "Still, it must be difficult being the longed-for son and ending up such a disappointment."

"In what way?" Jack asked.

"Well, Richard's been totally outstripped and eclipsed by

his sisters. Amelia a surgeon, Pamela an attorney, and then there's Richard ... a cop. After all the opportunities Robert gave the boy."

Rhiana was at a loss. The note in Grenier's office had seemed to portend something, but there wasn't anything here.

"Well, he's left the girls in the dust now," Jack said, weighting the words to give them significance. Rhiana shot him a glance, wondering where he was going with this.

Sandringham arranged his features into an expression of polite inquiry. "Oh?"

"Yeah, he's now the head of Lumina Enterprises."

Rhiana shouldn't have been surprised that an investment broker would recognize the name. There was a flash of some indescribable emotion deep in Sandringham's eyes. The businessman took another deep swallow of martini.

"Well, that's quite a lot to take in," Sandringham said slowly.

"Yeah, little bastard," Jack said softly. He leaned in across the small table. "Go on, you can say it."

The man's mouth worked for a few seconds; then he burst out, "This is unbelievable!" And the floodgates opened. "That little cocksucker threatened me ... *me* as if I were some kind of common criminal. And then tattled to daddy, breaking a thirty-year friendship irretrievably. I'll *never* forgive him."

"What happened?" Jack asked. His voice was warm and inviting, exuding comfort, and inviting trust.

Sandringham lowered his voice and took a quick glance around. The only other occupied table was across the verandah. "Richard and I were lovers."

The words struck Rhiana hard. *But he was attracted to me. I know he was.* Rhiana remembered the time she had bandaged Richard's burned hands. She had watched his breaths quicken, brushing across her hair and cheek.

She had lost the thread of the conversation. When she started listening again Sandringham was saying, "… a dinner party for a couple of clients. All I did was suggest that he let Yuri sample what I had been enjoying for months. Like he hadn't been sucking my dick and letting me pound that cute ass, but no, he insulted my potential client, cost me the account. I admit, I … lost my temper. Upshot, he quit, and we haven't spoken in years. Not until he threatened me last month. At his mother's funeral, if you can believe it. Then a few weeks ago Robert called and told me he was taking his business elsewhere. He was so cold. When I pressed him to tell me why, he said what I'd done to Richard was unforgivable, and that we would not speak on this or any other matter ever again. Our friendship was over." The man looked honestly hurt.

"Do you think Robert knows that you and Richard were intimate before this … incident?" Jack asked.

Sandringham considered that. "I don't think so. He made it sound like I was some kind of rapist."

"Mr. Sandringham, what if I told you we, Rhiana and I, have the power to give you virtually anything you want? Life-changing money. Power. Love—well, at least sex." Jack gave his charming smile.

"I would say I'd like some proof. I'd also say if it means doing Richard a bad turn, you don't have to give me anything at all."

"Well, we'd like to have a man like you in our camp, and we want to see you happy."

"What do you want me to do?" Sandringham asked.

"Break Richard." Sandringham smiled and nodded. Jack continued, "One more thing. We're trying to keep the pressure on Richard and the company until we can"—Jack gave a smile that was all teeth—"bring him down. Any suggestions?"

"Oh, you leave that to me. Richard's family offers a plethora of opportunities."

"Fine, we'll leave it to you. All of it."

Jack held out his hand, and Rhiana took it. She was still trying to cope with what she'd learned. They took a few steps, only to be stopped by Sandringham asking, "Who are you people?"

Jack smiled again. "The new world order."

On the elevator Rhiana watched the numbers flare to life and then die again as they dropped through the forty-two floors.

"Do you still want him?" Jack's voice was quiet.

"Yes."

"You can't change him."

"Maybe not." She paused, feeling the pressure against the soles of her boots as the elevator slowed and stopped. "But I can own him."

CHAPTER ELEVEN

JUST ONE OF SUFFERS

A FTER FOOD HAD been supplied for the weary travelers, they adjourned back into the living room. Grenier's belly rested on his thighs and pressed painfully against the waistband of his trousers. Once again, he had overeaten. He felt so empty all the time now that his magic had been stripped away. He wiped his fingertips across his eyes, removing the betraying moisture. Overt emotionalism also seemed to be a symptom of his loss. For a moment he hated Richard, cursed the Old Ones, and thought back over the actions he'd taken in those final hours. Thought how he could have done things differently … better. How one small change would have given him the victory.

He reached up and surreptitiously unbuttoned his pants and gave a gusting sigh of relief as his distended belly bulged free. Grenier felt embarrassed over his lack of self-control, but it really didn't matter any longer. He no longer had to face the tyranny of the television cameras, so he could indulge himself. Sometimes it was hard to look at the image in the mirror. He had been a very handsome man. That was gone now, hidden behind a layer of lard.

On the other hand, he no longer had to mouth platitudes to the believers and launch verbal grenades at political and spiritual opponents on his nightly television show. He felt a surprising surge of relief.

And I'll never again have to kneel with blubbering politicians as they use me as a Band-Aid for their latest financial or sexual indiscretion. I'd call that a silver lining. And that thought enabled him to face Richard's entrance into the living room with a degree of equanimity.

The young man had dressed, gray slacks, a silk turtleneck beneath a beautiful Norwegian sweater. The elaborate colors of the pattern gave a bit of color to his pale face. Sam watched him with frowning concentration. The Kraut pulled a set of Turkish worry beads from her handbag. The beads were amber, and they gave small clicks as she fingered them. Grenier wondered if she was a former smoker who'd found a new hobby for her nervous hands.

Armandariz took the crutches from Richard. The judge supported Richard into the leather-upholstered recliner and carefully raised the leg support. He obviously wasn't gentle enough, for a grimace of pain flashed across that handsome face. Once he was settled, Richard looked at them all and gave a small smile.

"So, are introductions in order, or have you handled all that?" he asked.

There were murmurs of assent, but then the young FBI agent spoke up. Her tone was belligerent. "All except *you*. I haven't met *you*."

"How do you do? I'm Richard Oort," he said, and inclined his head.

"I know your name. I want to know what you did to me," Sam demanded.

"I used a device, a weapon, to remove your ability to ever do magic. One of the side effects is that it also restores sanity, provided the mental illness isn't due to a chemical imbalance."

"Blah, blah, blah. But what does that *mean*? I mean, really? I know that whatever you did hurt like hell, but I'm not scared anymore. Well, I'm scared, but I'm not scared of *everything* anymore, and I understand *why* I'm scared."

"Yes, it's sensible to be scared of monsters," Richard said with another smile.

The judge laid a hand briefly on his son's shoulder. Richard gave his father a startled look, and Grenier got the feeling this was not a family that indulged in gestures of physical affection. "Richard, you have three people who know nothing about the real state of the world. I think giving the full lecture would not be amiss."

Richard pressed a hand briefly to his forehead. "I don't even know where to start. Kenntnis gave you the lecture," he said, looking appealingly up at his father. "Maybe you could—"

"*You* are the head of the Lumina."

Grenier settled himself more comfortably in the deep bucket chair and laced his hands over his belly. "And I'm here to offer a little insight into the other side," he said loudly. "We'll muddle through."

Richard closed his eyes. The silence stretched on and on. Grenier wondered what the young man was thinking, feeling. Finally, with a sigh, Richard opened his eyes and looked at them.

"Our world, our universe, and this dimension, or multiverse as Kenntnis called it, is under attack by creatures from other dimensions."

He laid it out in a bald, uncompromising statement. Not surprisingly, Sam and Dagmar had the look of people humoring a mental patient. Richard, empathetic, sensitive to others, and painfully insecure, read their reaction. He stuttered into hurried speech.

"There are a lot of other dimensions. Multiverses. I don't exactly remember how many Kenntnis told me, somewhere in the twenties, I think. Anyway, there are points where they connect with our universe. There are creatures in those other multiverses, and ever since we first stood upright, they've been pushing through the barriers between the universes and feeding on us."

"Feeding how?" Sam asked. "What the fuck does that mean?"

"They feed on emotional energy," Grenier said, deciding to throw Richard a lifeline. "And those of us who served them also learned to feed. It's a heady sensation. Every human has a little of it. It's why we love to look at car wrecks, why *schadenfreude* is such a *wonderful* emotion."

"Point being that the Old Ones don't like good emotions," Richard said, and Grenier realized the young man was trying to wrest back control. Grenier smiled inwardly. It was going to be fun playing tug-of-war for the conversation.

"Kenntnis once said that we're unique in how we experience love and joy," Richard continued. "But fear and hate, pain, and suffering, those we all share alike, and sadly they are very easy to engender. These creatures stoke the flames of ethnic hatreds. They push us to kill over skin color. Most pernicious of all, they urge us to kill in the name of our gods." Passion had brought color into the sensitive face, a ring into the voice, and his pale blue eyes glittered.

Grenier glanced at the other listeners, wanting to judge their reactions. The sister was looking at her brother as if seeing a stranger. There was both pride and discomfort on Robert Oort's face. *Yes, you hate strong emotion, don't you, you rigid prick?*

The worry beads had fallen, forgotten, into Dagmar's lap. Her gaze was calculating, measuring. Sam stared, a frown between her rather straight brows, resentment etched on her features. Angela, however …. her hands were tightly clasped, her lips parted, quick breaths lifting her breast. Attraction and arousal vying to be read as mere friendship and affection.

Syd glanced at the walls of the penthouse as if expecting them to collapse in on them. "What about natural disasters? Like those tsunamis and earthquakes and stuff?" he asked.

Pamela gave the agent a sardonic look. "I think the operative word in that is *natural*."

"Oh, there are weather spells." Grenier enjoyed watching the Oort girl blanch briefly. "But they're the toughest magical spells to weave, so we don't try them very often. And an earthquake spell …" Grenier shook his head. "It would take an enormous amount of power, and if you guessed wrong you might crack the planet. Remember, we want you to *suffer*, not be annihilated."

Richard gave him a cold-eyed stare. "You might want to remember that *you're* one of the sufferers now." Ice edged each perfectly enunciated word.

Grenier *had* forgotten, and for an instant he hated the young man for making him remember. He gave Richard a smile from the teeth out. "We should all also recall that magic isn't the only way they accomplish their goals. For that we've got politics."

"I always knew the Republicans were the spawn of Satan," Angela quipped.

"And your boys on the left are very good at hand-wringing and shedding crocodile tears without—"

"Let's not have this reduced to political and partisan squabbling," the judge interrupted. "We have bigger problems."

"Let's get back to this eating thing," Syd said. "Why not just feed on cows heading into the slaughterhouse?"

"I think it has to do with cognition," Richard replied. "Cross said that when a species develops a cerebral cortex it attracts the Old Ones. Apparently, part of the pleasure is the prey's awareness of what's happening to them. Blind animal panic isn't good enough."

"So, what do they eat when they can't get us?" Sam asked.

Richard shook his head. "I don't know. Each other, maybe." Grenier found himself on the receiving end of that blue-eyed gaze. "Do you have any insights you'd like to share with the class?" Richard asked.

Grenier stood and took up a position in the center of the room. "I know they're not all the same. I know rivalries exist. I can't guess how deep they go, or if they prey on each other." He was suddenly acutely aware of his unbuttoned pants. "My magic enabled me to use mirrors to thin the barriers between the dimensions. That's where the Old Ones and I would communicate. That's been the extent of my contact. Well, until recently."

"*Through a glass darkly,*" Richard said softly, quoting Corinthians.

"Exactly," Grenier said. The zipper on his fly began a slow, inexorable slide under the pressure from his belly. He folded his hands in front of his crotch.

"So that's why the mirrors in the trailer, and in Colorado Springs, and at your compound were all occluded," Angela said. "None of the tests I ran could ever tell me what had done that."

"It was the touch of the Old Ones. They're not natural to our universe, and so they have a destructive effect on our reality," Grenier said hurriedly. He hustled back to the chair, and surreptitiously zipped his pants while Richard continued.

"Thousands of years ago there were actual gates between the dimensions constructed by the Old Ones, and they passed back and forth with relative ease. Then Kenntnis came—I don't exactly know when—and with the help of people like me, and this...." Richard lifted the hilt. "The gates were closed. There were still incursions, but they were more like rips or tears in the fabric of reality. Some of the Old Ones on this side of the dimensional barriers were killed, but others became so powerful that they couldn't be banished or destroyed with just the sword. I should add that that's purely conjecture on my part, but it's the only thing that makes sense."

"So, do we have a method for killing gods and myths?" Pamela asked, and it was half a question, half ironic statement.

Grenier looked at this Oort daughter with interest. Here, it seemed, was a sharp and satirical nature akin to his own. He spoke up. "It's possible that a rejection of them by humanity, together with the sword, might do the trick. But I don't think it would be easy. Some researchers think there's a god gene."

"I thought your crowd rejected science," Angela said.

"No, we *fear* science," Grenier corrected. "As the bright boys and girls keep answering the questions and dispelling the mysteries, it gets harder and harder for those of us in the pulpit to keep the sheep believing."

"So, every priest, every minister—" Syd began.

"No, I don't think so," Richard said quickly. "Not all of them are cynical manipulators like him," and he nodded toward Grenier. "I've met men and women of faith who served the ideal of a loving, forgiving, generous god that had been fostered by Kenntnis, and they've done a great deal of good in the world."

Cross walked into the living room. "I believe I heard my cue."

He grinned and nodded at Richard. "Is my timing impeccable, or what?"

"It's something," the young man said dryly, but he smiled. Grenier studied the Old One curiously. It was a fractal, a splinter of the greater creature that kept dividing itself, as Judaism spawned Christianity which spawned Islam. A traitor to his own kind, Cross had thrown in his lot with Kenntnis.

Cross looked at Syd. "Consider how you've progressed as

a species. You've gone from human sacrifice to animal sacrifice to ritualistic sacrifice, and if Kenntnis had succeeded you would have learned to be merciful and generous to each other just because it would be the right thing to do."

"And not out of the fear of Hell or the promise of Heaven," Richard added softly.

"Of course, I don't think you humans have it in you. But Kenntnis was the eternal optimist," Cross concluded.

Angela jumped in and asked Cross, "Aren't you surprised to find Grenier here?"

"Nah. He's a rat and we're the only high ground in a rising flood," Cross said.

Angela clearly wasn't giving up on enlisting allies to change Richard's mind and have Grenier booted from the building. "Do *you* think it's a good idea to let him in?"

The homeless god shrugged. "Sure, why not. He might be helpful." The little coroner looked disgusted, but she subsided.

Richard turned to Dagmar. "As I said to you earlier, Lumina isn't just a business. The company is a front for an ancient and secret society that has fought against these creatures for millennia. Kenntnis threw all of his wealth and power behind the quest for knowledge because he believed that science and rationality would ultimately trump magic, religion, and superstition. But now Kenntnis has been effectively neutralized as a force in our world, and the gates are opening again."

Grenier cleared his throat. "And in this brave new world the Old Ones will probably meet people's fondest expectations. Angels will fly and saucers will land, and magic will actually work."

Cross cleared his throat. "Not everyone who says they've been abducted by aliens is a nut. We've been taking humans for millennia."

"Why?" the judge asked.

"To breed more magic into your genetic code," Cross answered as if the conclusion were obvious. "The more magic you have, the deeper into you we can reach. That's how we got stuck with that bitch Rhiana. She's the result of a long breeding operation—half human, half us."

"The genetic angle is why Kenntnis so heavily funded stem cell research," Richard said, directing the statement at Dagmar. "He was trying to find a way to erase those genes."

"Would that make everyone like you?" Pamela asked her brother.

"Possibly ... maybe ... I don't know."

"What do you mean, like you?" Sam asked belligerently. Grenier wondered if she was reacting against her attraction to Richard and was hiding it under her abrasive challenges. "How are *you* any different from the rest of us?"

No, not rejected passion, Grenier decided; the young FBI agent just hated not being the most gifted, most talented, toughest person in the room. And she was still smarting under the knowledge that the gate had driven her mad thus revealing her deepest fear—that she was actually *weak*.

The flush washed up into Richard's pale cheeks as he reacted to the hostility, but embarrassment was also a component of his discomfort. *Yes, little man, you are different, and you hate it. You also invited it; the East Coast blue blood walking a cop's beat.* Grenier longed to say the words out loud, but Cross broke in.

"He's an *empty one*, a Paladin, born without a scrap of magic."

Richard nodded. "A magic spell per se has no effect on me. I can be hurt by the results of the spell—if you pull electricity from a wall socket, for example, the electricity can hurt me." His eyes slid toward Mark who gave him a smile as they both recalled their first meeting. "But you can't put a glamour on me or use a spell to convince me I'm in love with somebody."

"We also can't feed on him," Cross said. "He's a cipher to us."

"The real importance of my genetic makeup is that I can use this." Richard again lifted the hilt of the sword. "I can draw it, and it kills Old Ones."

"Yeah, but you removed my magic, so I ought to be able to use it now, too," Sam said. The challenge hung in the air.

Angela jumped in. "It doesn't work that way. You've had your magic negated, but you still carry the genetic code. You can't use the sword."

It was clear from the young agent's expression that she neither liked the answer nor believed it. Richard proved again he could read nuance. "If you don't believe us, you're welcome to try."

Richard tossed the hilt to Sam, who caught it with the grace and quickness of a cat seizing a bird out of the air. She studied the hilt, then laced her fingers through the curves and looked inquiringly at Richard.

"Place your free hand against the base of the hilt. Pull the hilt away as if you're drawing a sword from a scabbard," he instructed.

"I'll cut my hand."

"You won't get that far," Richard said. "Even if you could draw it, you wouldn't get cut. It doesn't cut me. And don't ask me why because I have no earthly idea."

"So, it is because of this … this thing … that Kenntnis has left you his entire business?" Dagmar asked while Sam swept the hilt over and over away from her hand to no result.

"Yes." There was a pause and Richard added, "I guess." The tag diluted the effect of him being a man in charge.

"*Mein Gott,*" the German repeated again.

It took Sam another few minutes of trying before she accepted the truth of Richard's statement. *So,* thought Grenier, *she's quick, coordinated, and very stubborn.* Finally, she admitted defeat and returned the hilt to Richard.

"Well, this kind of sucks," Sam said.

"On the plus side, you're not finger-licking good anymore," Cross said to the young woman.

"What?" Sam said. It emerged as an incredulous squeak.

"We can't feed on you after you've been touched. Well, when you die you can feed us. Death sort of trumps all the other emotions," Cross said. "Speaking of … is there anything to eat in this joint?"

Richard pointed toward the kitchen, and Cross left.

"So now you have a general idea of the state of things," Richard said. "My biggest fear is what happens to the world with Kenntnis out of it. Cross said something once that made me think that Kenntnis might be like a platonic ideal, or the very idea of rationality. And it does seem that since his capture people are having a harder and harder time keeping a grip on reality."

"Not that they were doing all that well before," Angela muttered.

"So, what you're saying is that people are going to start living in their own private David Lynch movies?" Sam asked.

Grenier entered the conversation again. "They won't be just private delusions. Before Richard sheared away my power ..." He held up his stump and was pleased when Richard flushed. "I could feel the power rushing past me like flowing water. It wasn't hard to dip in and have the potency to do almost any kind of spell. That's a big change. Before Kenntnis was bound I had to engineer the appropriate fear, pain, grief, or hate; I would feed, and then cast the spell. You're going to see a lot of strange and inexplicable things happening, and each time they happen it will weaken the fabric of our reality."

"Yes, but don't you have to learn how to do these spells?" Pamela asked. "I can't believe I just said that," she added. She pressed a hand against her forehead (it seemed to be a learned and shared gesture of the Oorts) and shook her head.

"Before the loss of Kenntnis, yes," Grenier answered. "But now I rather suspect that a supreme act of personal will, will suffice."

"Monsters from the id," Angela muttered.

"So, our most pressing issue is freeing Kenntnis," Richard said. The judge entered the conversation.

"I believe we had this conversation before. On Christmas Eve you said we needed a physicist to advise us since Kenntnis is trapped by this slow glass. Do we have a physicist?" The words were pointed.

The blood rushed into the young man's face, and he hung his head.

"No, sir. I'm sorry, I should have done that."

Well, damn, thought Grenier. *I wish I had known about this little family dynamic before. I could have brought Richard to his knees in no time. I applied pressure at all the wrong points.*

Of course, now that Grenier was in New Mexico and had thrown in his lot with the Lumina, he badly needed Richard to be strong and tough and decisive. Which meant he was going to have to find a way to buffer the young man from the Right Honorable Robert Oort.

Dagmar suddenly stood and walked over to Richard. "That's for another day. Right now, it is more important that you have the loyalty and support of *all* your people." Grenier couldn't be sure, but he thought she glanced briefly at the judge.

The German continued, "Allow me to be the first of your employees to accept your condition of employment, sir," and she leaned down so Richard, from his seated position, could more easily touch her with the sword.

CHAPTER TWELVE

WHEN LOGIC FAILS

"THINK OF IT as a drug test," Dagmar said.

The man—Richard risked a surreptitious glance down at the employee list—Fred Mickelson, blinked rapidly as if processing the words. Mickelson was tall, with a sunken chest and an incongruous little kettle belly. He had been sitting in the high-backed leather chair that faced the desk, but then rose jerkily to his feet and stood, shaking his head.

"No, this is too weird."

For an instant Richard thought about saying this had been in the instructions Kenntnis left for him, but he knew he was a terrible liar, and it would only make a bad situation worse. Thus far they hadn't lost that many employees with his strange request. Richard decided he could afford to lose Fred. But Dagmar wasn't giving up without a fight.

"Look, I'll go first," Dagmar offered. "Just to show you it's fine."

Richard shifted his grip on the hilt of the sword, picked up his cane with his right hand, and pushed to his feet. After some discussion they had all agreed that the appearance of a blade out of nowhere and the musical overtones that filled a room would rattle even the most loyal and unflappable of employees. So, the sword had been drawn before Fred entered the office, on the theory that coping with only one weird thing—a boss asking to touch them with a sword—would be less upsetting than dealing with the whole strange package.

Now they just have to cope with the fact that I seem to be a total nut job, Richard thought as he limped up to Dagmar and laid the blade of the sword on her shoulder.

Since Dagmar had already experienced the sword, she was able to bear the touch with equanimity. That had been another debate, about whether Dagmar should react as if she were in pain when we put on the little show. The consensus had been that she shouldn't.

"Better to cut the puppy's tail off all at once instead of by inches," had been Weber's opinion, while Pamela's attitude had been, *"Better to receive forgiveness than ask permission."*

However, it was phrased, Richard hated he was starting his tenure as head of Lumina Enterprises by lying to his people. Somehow, he bet that was *not* in a Tony Robbins video.

He pivoted on his cane and cocked an inquiring eyebrow at Mickelson. The only thing that had made this even remotely bearable was that the pain experienced by the employees who had allowed themselves to be touched by the sword had been much less than Angela's and Weber's. Which suggested that Kenntnis had used Cross's ability to "see" magic, and deliberately hired people who had a low quotient of magical aptitude. Richard reminded himself to ask the homeless god if that was true the next time he wandered through.

I wish Cross had found a different Paladin, too. Why did I ever go down that alley that night? If I'd just called for backup.

You couldn't, the radio didn't work.

I could have driven away.

Couldn't, the car had died.

And honestly, once he had heard Rhiana's scream of terror there was no question about whether he was going down that access alley between the buildings. But why couldn't it have been an ordinary mugger? But no, it had to be monsters. *Monsters that killed your partner* came the hateful little reminder. Richard realized with a flare of guilt that he hadn't reached out to Sterling's fiancée since his passing. *But so much had happened: his mother's suicide, the decision to confront Grenier, his capture and torture, Kenntnis being lost to them, becoming the head of Lumina …*

Mickelson's voice drew Richard back. "I have to do this if I'm going to keep my job?"

"Yes, I'm afraid so. But if you wish to leave, you'll receive a generous severance package," Richard said.

"Okay. I'll do that. I've enjoyed working here, and Mr. Kenntnis had his odd quirks, but this is just too strange."

Richard propped his cane against the side of the desk and held out his hand. "I quite understand." They shook, and Mickelson's palm was slick with sweat. He really had been put to a Hobson's choice—do something nuts or lose your job. Richard respected Mickelson. Telling him to piss up a rope had taken some guts.

"Jeannette will arrange all the financial details," Dagmar said. Mickelson headed for the door.

In addition to money, Richard did feel he owed the man some warning. "Fred." He looked back while his fingers nervously explored his shirt buttons. "Look, be careful. Outside these walls things are ..." Richard mentally picked up, considered, and discarded a number of words. *Crazy, dangerous, perilous, threatening.* He finally settled on one. "Unsettled."

The accountant nodded and left.

Dagmar pulled her phone out of a pocket and checked the screen, then her watch. "Shall I set up the call with Kenzo?"

It took Richard a moment to place "Kenzo" in the bewildering array of people who now seemed to work for him. Kenzo Fujasaki, Lumina's CFO. Right. Check. Oh, no, he so didn't want to talk to him. Richard shook his head, set the hilt on the desk, and watched the blade vanish. He still found it unnerving, and he wondered where it went.

"Put him off for another day."

Dagmar had a mouth like a strawberry, full and soft, but now those lips compressed into a tight line. Richard felt like people got that expression *a lot* when dealing with him, and it just added to his fear and doubts.

"Sir, events are streaming past us. We've got bank closures in the Far East, price controls being set by the EU, borders being sealed. Every market is fluctuating wildly. We need to transfer and stabilize assets."

Uncertainty became a fluttering deep in Richard's gut. If Lumina Enterprises collapsed financially, he wouldn't have the resources to combat the Old Ones. But what he *really* needed for this fight was Kenntnis, not money.

Richard said as much, and then added, "I've got to get him out of this slow glass stuff if we're going to have a snowball's chance."

Dagmar's disapproval became contrition. She grabbed a handful of her hair and shoved it back. "Oh, shit, the physicist. I haven't done that. I'm sorry, sir, I keep getting distracted by some new …" She paused, searching for a word.

"Crisis? Catastrophe? Disaster? Cluster fuck?" Richard suggested.

The COO sighed. "All of the above, sir. I'll get on it now. We have a huge research facility in Rochester. I just need to make the call.," she said, and left.

The high-backed leather chair beckoned to him. It was a lot more comfortable than the executive chair behind the desk, and the reasons weren't all physical. Richard sat down, sighed, and closed his eyes, but it didn't keep his mind from whirling like a pinwheel. *Breathe, relax. Breathe, relax.*

Jeannette's voice came over the intercom. "Sir, your brother-in-law is on line two."

"Did he say what he wants?"

"He says he has an investment opportunity for you."

Richard sighed, drummed his fingers on his knee, and considered his eldest sister's husband. Ever since Amelia had brought him home, Brent van Gelder had some get-rich-quick-scheme. None of them had ever panned out, and it had made him resentful. Richard resented him because it was Amelia's work as a surgeon at Mass General that kept her family afloat, and Richard thought Brent was more a burden then a help to his sister.

"Tell him I'm in a meeting and I'll call him back."

"Yes, sir."

Since the discreet announcement that Richard was now

the new CEO of Lumina Enterprises had appeared in the *Wall Street Journal*, he'd been getting calls from old college chums and high school buddies. Funny thing was Richard never remembered *any* of these people being particularly friendly to him. Then he had become Jeff Bezos and suddenly they all had great memories of all the good times back in the day.

Richard's gaze fell on the morning's *New York Times*. It had been inexpertly refolded and left on the edge of the granite desk. He pulled it over, and then rubbed the tips of his fingers together, trying to remove the sticky aftermath of a jelly smear. Coffee stains had set the words to weeping. Someone had started the crossword and given up with a scrawl of red ink across the puzzle. Probably Sam. Patience wasn't her strong suit, and she didn't look like the type who could do the *Times* crossword.

He started scanning the *Times*. Papers had always been filled with news of tragedy, but now there were so many stories there was no longer room for lighter news about actors' relationships, movie reviews, and heartwarming features about *dog saves owner*. It was a deluge of death, and the numbers were staggering. *Bombs and mortars in Varanasi, Hinduism's holiest city, kill two thousand.*

His eyes skipped away to another story, and he read—

The NTSB easily determined the cause of the crash. The small commuter plane ran out of fuel. When questioned, members of the ground crew stated the plane didn't need fuel, and that it crashed because the pilots and passengers didn't believe. What they had failed to believe varied widely from person to person, but what remained a constant was the complete lack of guilt over the accident …

The hairs on the nape of Richard's neck rose, and a cold line traced its way down his spine. *This* was what Grenier had been talking about. People believing crazy stuff. And not just believing; some of them might actually be able to *do* crazy stuff. As logic and rationality leached out of the world, planes might fly powered by belief alone. Unfortunately, there had been no magic for the crew and passengers on *this* flight. Richard groped in his pocket for the snuffbox, fished out a tablet, and dry swallowed the Xanax. He threw the paper into the waste can next to the desk.

The big copper-paneled doors swung open, and Angela entered. "No tea, painkillers, and sympathy for that one?" she asked.

Richard shook his head. She looked at him with concern and started toward him, hand outstretched. He dodged the impending touch by rising and limping over to the window. It wasn't that he dreaded her touch or didn't like it, but it felt dishonest to allow the contact. Despite her assurances that she could be satisfied with friendship alone, he wasn't sure about his own feelings and desires, and he did not want to give off mixed signals. That always hurt worse than honesty. He yanked his thoughts away from the memory of Weber's fingers twining through his, the warmth of his hand on his shoulder. *Yeah, being just* good friends *sucks when you wanted so much more.*

Down in the parking lot a woman struggled against a brisk west wind. The tail of her long coat twisted behind her. She clutched a cardboard box to her chest. Farther along the line of parked vehicles a man slammed the trunk of his

Nissan Leaf closed. Richard couldn't help but notice that there wasn't a single SUV among the employee cars. In fact, they were all fully electric vehicles.

"So, what's the tally?" Angela asked.

"Out of eighty-four employees, five left," Richard answered.

"That's not too bad." Richard could feel her breath soft on the back of his neck.

The lonely isolation he had been feeling seemed suddenly too much to bear. It might not be fair, but he was going to take comfort in another's touch. He turned and rested his chin on the top of her head, his arms slipped around her waist. Her curls tickled, and a faint citrus scent from her conditioner wafted up.

God I'm a shit. Not two minutes after vowing not to do this ... I'm doing this.

Angela suddenly stepped back. Reaching up, she brushed back the lock of hair that continually resisted being combed into place, allowing her fingertips to brush softly across his forehead. Richard closed his eyes and leaned into the cool touch.

"You look tired," Angela said softly. "Do you want to lie down?"

Richard opened his eyes and looked down into her brown eyes. It was still surprising and more than a little pleasant to get to look *down* into a woman's face. "It's brain tired. What I really need is to give my mind a rest. Do you think I could try a swim today?"

"Sure. Just limit the time, and if it hurts in a bad way instead of a good way, quit."

✦ ✦ ✦

THE ELEVATOR DOOR slid open. Damon was so lost in his thoughts that he didn't initially register Richard standing in the foyer of the penthouse, and he nearly bowled him over as he stepped out. The tip of the cane skittered on the parquet marble floor as Richard started to fall, bathrobe flying open as his arms windmilled. Weber dropped his briefcase and caught the smaller man around the waist, registering the bare skin against his hands. Color washed into Richard's face, and he gave a hiss. Weber put it down to his cold palms against the younger man's warm skin.

"Sorry, shit, sorry. Didn't see you there."

"I'm not *that* small," Richard replied with a smile, though he wasn't meeting Damon's eyes.

Weber registered the swim trunk and the towel draped around Richard's neck. "There's a swimming pool in this joint?"

"I'm afraid so. Also, an armory and a shooting range, and generators and wall batteries, and a seed vault, and … well, you get the picture."

"Jesus. I can't decide if this is the Avengers' headquarters or if you're a supervillain."

"Like everything I suppose it depends on your perspective." The blue eyes drifted to the briefcase.

"Just stopped by to check on you." Weber raised his voice when he heard the rustle of a newspaper from the living room. "I see you're recovering so I can be on my way." Their eyes met in an intense look, and Weber shifted his gaze to the briefcase.

"Great, I'll drop you off in the lobby," Richard said brightly, and he limped onto the elevator.

Justice Oort appeared in the archway. Weber gave him a wave. "Good morning, your honor, how you doin'?"

"Very well, thank you." Weber felt like those blue eyes were cutting through his skin and seeing right through the subterfuge. He gathered up his briefcase and backed onto the elevator. The doors closed and he leaned against the wall across from Richard.

"Shit, do people just confess in the courtroom when your dad stares at them?"

Richard chuckled. "Not quite, but famous lawyers have been known to cry." His expression darkened and he stared down at his slippered feet.

"Well, while we've got some privacy." Damon snapped open the case and handed Richard his badge and the Heckler & Koch.

"Oh, thank God," he breathed. The pistol went into his left pocket, the badge in his right.

"I brought a box of cartridges, but it's gonna get pretty obvious if we put those in your pockets, too."

"Leave them with Joseph in the security office."

"You trust him?"

Richard gave him that blazing smile. Damon focused on snapping shut his briefcase. "My employees all seem to have undertaken a quiet war against my father and my sister."

"Good on 'em. Where do I enlist?"

"Oh, I think you've been leading the charge, General Weber." Richard reached out as if to place his hand on Damon's arm, then the hand fell back to his side.

The elevator arrived in the lobby with a soft bounce and *ding*. Richard held the door open and gave Damon an almost desperate look. "Come to dinner tonight? I'm surrounded by people who either don't like me or don't trust me or *need* things from me. I could really use someone who is just a friend."

Damon gripped his shoulder. "I'll be there. Franz's grub will definitely be better than the Swanson's turkey dinner I was planning on. What time?"

"7:30 PM."

"See you then." Richard allowed the door to close.

Weber stared at the blank metal for a few more moments then made his way into the security office tucked away behind the receptionist's desk.

Joseph was in there, eyes flicking between the screens showing the various camera feeds both inside and outside the building. Weber noted the elevator that went to the penthouse was noticeably absent. He breathed out a sigh of relief. He didn't need Richard's terrifying sire to see him handing back the tools of Richard's trade in direct contravention of the judge's orders.

Once again Damon opened the briefcase and stacked three boxes of cartridges on the African American man's desk. Joseph gave him a small smile and an approving nod. "I'll see to it he gets them, and none will be the wiser."

"Great." Weber started to leave, then paused in the door and looked back. "You keep him safe, ya hear."

"You can count on it."

✧ ✧ ✧

THE MOMENT THE elevator doors opened, Richard could hear splashing and sharp breaths. There was already a swimmer in the basement pool. A flash of resentment shook him, but he limped on through the blue-tiled archway. Maybe it was somebody he could stand to have around as long as they didn't *talk*. He longed for privacy.

The room that housed the pool was designed to evoke a Roman bath. Off to the side steam waved languidly over the top of the hot tub. On the other side were the doors to a steam room and a cedar sauna.

The ripples in the water distorted the figure, and it wasn't until the swimmer approached the shallow end and Richard had reached the edge of the pool that he realized it was indeed somebody he couldn't stand. It was Sam. In the days since she had arrived, she had been in his face, mocking every remark he made, wondering loudly when they were ever going to fucking *do something*, playing the kind of macho boy games that brought back horrible memories of high school gym class and Richard's worst days on the police force.

Sam executed a neat somersault, braced her feet against the side of the pool, and pushed off again. The young agent must have caught his shadow in the water because she stopped mid-stroke and began treading water in a slow circle.

It gave him ample opportunity to watch the play of muscles beneath the skin of her arms, the sharp bones in her clavicle, the brown hair slicked against her skull. Through the slowing ripples he could see the top edge of the high French-cut one-piece swimsuit defining the slender length of her legs. She made him think of the Scottish legends of *selkies*.

"Come on in. The water's fine," she said.

"I don't wish to intrude," Richard muttered, hoping that would suffice to explain his sudden retreat. The tiling around the pool felt like it had been oiled, and the metal-shod foot of the damn cane kept slipping as he carefully turned away.

He heard the water churn from a couple of hard kicks, then jerked to a halt when Sam grabbed the trailing hem of his robe. "Fuck, it's your pool."

Rage set his temples throbbing. *I could have fallen!* But then he realized he was acting like a spoiled child. With his temper once again under control he turned back to face her. She had rested her arms on the edge and was staring up at him.

"Are you always this ..." She made a complex gesture with one hand.

"What?"

"Polite?"

"Is that a bad thing?" Richard asked.

"Yeah, it is when you're so fucking self-effacing that you're practically *invisible*. You're supposed to be in charge of this joint."

Sam suddenly grasped Richard's bare ankle and gave a sharp yank. The metal tip of the cane chattered and squeaked as it slipped across the glass tile. Richard struggled to catch his balance, stepped instinctively onto his right leg, and yelped in pain. Which turned into a glissando wail as he toppled sidewise into the pool.

A house slipper floated briefly in front of him, then started to sink. And he was likely to follow it toward the bottom because the weight of the pistol in his pocket and the now leaden terry cloth bathrobe. Holding his breath, he first removed the Heckler & Koch and got it onto the side of the pool. He then began struggling with the belt of the bathrobe. Sam was suddenly at his side. Their hands bumped together and tangled. He thought she was trying to help him, but then her slim hand darted into his swim trunks and grabbed his cock. Richard was appalled, but it couldn't stop a line of fire running up into his belly. He had been celibate for so long that outrage couldn't trump his body's reaction. Unable to prevent the gasp, he ended up sucking water.

Coughing and spluttering he finally shed the robe and surfaced to hear Sam say, "Whoops."

She gave him a predatory grin. But the smile never reached her eyes. Instead, resentment glared out at him.

Richard flopped the sopping robe onto the side of the pool, pushed his hair out of his eyes, and managed to croak, "Are you insane?" He could feel the chlorine stinging the wound in his leg.

"Nope, I just find insecure people really boring, and I'm *never* reassuring. So, do you want to fuck?"

Richard had carried a dual major in college—psychology and music. He knew this for what it was, a boy's trick. Use the crudest term possible, remove any possibility of personal or emotional contact, and reduce the person being propositioned to an object.

"I'm sorry, but I can't help the fact that I've seen you vulnerable, scared, and crazy." He paused, and then added significantly, "And that *I'm* the person who made you well."

They were face-to-face both treading water. Richard watched the self-satisfied smirk melt, replaced with blazing anger. Richard tried to control his own anger.

Sam went splashing away to the ladder, hooked her arm through the rungs, glared at him.

"Jesus, take a pill. I was just fucking with you," Sam said.

"Hmm, somehow it doesn't appear that our definitions of that word align."

She grabbed the ladder and pulled herself out of the water muttering, "You are such a pompous prick." Snatching up her towel, she stalked for the elevator, bare feet slapping wetly on the elaborate tiled floor.

"Sam." Richard tried to give his voice that snap of command that came so easily for Weber, and he must have come close, because the young FBI agent stopped and turned back slowly. Richard stroked over to the side of the pool and folded his arms on the edge.

"What?"

"Look, we can play macho games with each other, and keep score in blushes and outrage, or we can work together. Your choice."

She walked back and squatted down in front of me. "I want to understand you."

"I'm not that complex."

"I resent you."

"I know."

"I think I really do want to fuck you."

Well, he hadn't expected *that*. "We'll … uh, discuss it," was the best Richard could manage.

CHAPTER THIRTEEN

THE WORLD IS COLLAPSING

A N INTENSE WET dream yanked Richard awake. He wouldn't have minded the damp and the sticky touch of semen if he'd actually had the comfort of an intimate moment, the touch of someone he loved and who loved him in return, but to awaken with that acrid and musty smell, belly coated, and yet still feel so deeply alone. He gave a shudder, eased himself out of bed, grabbed the crutches, and hobbled into the bathroom.

The travertine tile in the bathroom was cold underfoot as he stripped off his pajamas. He ran hot water and swept the washcloth across his groin, feeling goose bumps bloom on his skin. As he cleaned himself, he remembered his first gymnastics coach who said Richard was like a cat because he hated to be sweaty or smell. It wasn't meant as a compliment. The man hated cats. He hadn't much liked Richard either.

He limped into the closet, dumped the pajamas in the hamper, and pulled out a new pair. He tried to balance on his crutches without putting any weight on his injured leg. He failed and yelped, then decided to be a smart wimp and instead leaned on the built-in chest of drawers to pull them on.

That done, he stood in the closet door, staring at the bed

and trying to imagine sleep. It wasn't going to happen. Moonlight poured through the windows, making it easy to navigate around the living room. He had to be quiet. If any of them woke up they'd come and cluck at him and force him back to bed.

He leaned the crutches against the piano, settled on the bench, opened the lid, and brushed his fingers softly across the keys. It was just a feather's touch, but it drew a whisper of sound. Richard froze, but there was no reaction from the bedrooms. He relaxed again and tried to think about the day, but only two memories stuck.

Weber's hands closing around his waist. Holding him up with surprising strength.

And the swimming pool and Sam.

Almost five years. Fifty-five months. Two hundred and thirty-nine weeks. His mind balked at working out the number of days.

As a teenager Richard had been scared to death to take recreational drugs, and he'd never been able to hold liquor worth a damn. Give him a few drinks and he'd inevitably end up in somebody's bed. Which brought him face-to-face with what had been his greatest vice—sex. If he did a burst of pop psychology on himself, he'd say it was because he felt lonely and unloved, was touch starved (the Oorts were not a physically affectionate family) so he sought intimacy, and constantly mistook sex for love.

Or maybe I just really liked sex.

At least until sex became inextricably bound up with pain and guilt about his sexuality.

I just want someone to hold me. Love me.

So maybe he ought to take Sam up on her offer. The thought conjured Sam's sardonic half-smile, the image seeming to hang in the air in front of him, and he knew that even if he did get into bed with Sam, it wouldn't be lovemaking. It would be fucking and a competition, which would only add to his anxiety. And anxiety meant impotence.

Angela would be more supportive. She'd already proven that.

And he'd be using her.

And if he were honest he was forcing himself to consider the two women to try and avoid thinking about the person he really desired.

Richard closed the lid on the Steinway. The crutches dug into his armpits as he made his way to the window. His breath fogged the glass, blossoming and retreating with each exhalation. Richard rested his forehead against the glass and relished the ache from the cold.

I shouldn't be thinking about this. We've got bigger problems than my dick—

There was the slap of bare feet on the polished floor. Richard jerked upright and whirled, eliciting a groan of pain, to see Grenier waddling out of the dining room.

He was carrying a large mug and a plate piled high with slices of cinnamon toast. Steam formed a waving pennant over the top of the mug and carried the rich smell of Mexican chocolate and cinnamon throughout the room.

"Can't sleep?" the former minister said.

"No, I'm sleepwalking. What do you think?" Richard immediately regretted the tone. It made him sound petulant. He folded his lips together trying to keep any other ugly little croakers from emerging.

Seemingly unruffled, Grenier held out the plate, an implicit invitation. Richard was going to refuse, but his stomach gave a sharp rumble. He hadn't been able to choke down much dinner, and the butter, powdered sugar, and cinnamon drenching the bread proved irresistible. The bread was still warm in his hand as he took a slice. The first bite sent powdered sugar puffing upward to dust his upper lip. Hot and sweet burst across his tongue. It tasted wonderful.

"What's wrong?" Grenier asked.

Richard couldn't hold back the sharp, short bark of sardonic laughter.

"What isn't?"

The man settled his bulk into an armchair. "So, putting aside for the moment the existential threat of alien creatures invading the Earth from alternate dimensions, tell me what's really bothering you."

Opposing instincts and emotions buffeted him, each struggling for primacy. Intellectually Richard could neither forget nor forgive what the man had done to his mother. And to himself. But Grenier was the first person who had expressed an interest in just talking with him instead of harping at him.

That made Richard feel disloyal, and he started to run frantically through everyone in his support circle as he tried to prove to himself that there was someone else, anyone else, he could turn to other than the man who'd run an electric current through his balls.

Grenier began to talk, and it was like he'd been reading Richard's mind.

"Really, Richard, who else have you got? Angela? She's in love with you, and you're not in love with her. If you turn to her, she'll read way more into it than you want. Then there's your terrifying sire." Grenier rolled his eyes. "Dear God, is the man never satisfied?"

No, Richard answered internally.

"Ms. Reitlingen hasn't totally grasped that the P&L statements aren't your most pressing problem. And your sister ..." He just raised his eyebrows.

He and Pamela exchanged an average of twenty snipes a day.

"Sam resents you because she's beholden to you. Syd worships you, which must be wearing. And you don't get to work with your best friend and mentor or have him at your side." Was there a knowing gleam in the hazel eyes? It was gone before Richard could pin it down. "Because crime is on the rise, and he has little time for you." Grenier paused to consume a slice of toast. "Which leaves you with ... well ... me."

Richard looked hard into Grenier's plump face. "I can't trust you," he said rather weakly.

"I'm not asking you to, Richard. But you can talk to me. Because you can absolutely trust me on this—there is no way I am leaving the protection of this place and you. Which is why I want you to succeed in all your endeavors."

Richard finished off the cinnamon toast and returned to the piano bench. Running nervous hands through is hair he tried to order his chaotic thoughts.

"I don't know where to start, and I don't just mean about this conversation. I mean about everything. I don't know where to put my energies. Dagmar wants me to learn about the company and run it. Angela bugs me constantly about Kenntnis. Papa reminds me that if we don't have the company, we won't have the funds to do whatever it is we're going to do about Kenntnis. But I have no idea what to do about Kenntnis." He loosened he fingers that had clutched in his hair.

"It sounds like you're *doing* a lot but accomplishing very little."

"Yeah, that sounds about right," Richard sighed. "Everybody's got an opinion. But everybody wants me to do something different." He pressed the palm of his hand against his forehead as if that could somehow force order on the churning mess inside his head.

"You listen. Then you go away, and you make the decisions. Maybe with the help of a single advisor," Grenier said.

Richard raised an eyebrow at him. "And would that be a role you're envisioning for yourself?" he asked dryly. "Because if it is ... don't."

Grenier smiled and consumed another piece of toast in three big bites. "I'm many things," he said thickly around the wad in his mouth.

"Selfish, self-centered, cruel, power hungry, greedy?" Richard suggested.

"But not stupid," Grenier concluded blandly. "Also very, very scared, so I wouldn't guide you false."

The eighteenth-century French clock struck the quarter hour. Richard didn't look because he dreaded knowing the actual time. He knew he was going to pay a heavy price for this bout of insomnia. All the tasks that would fill the coming day crashed into his head and a thundering headache began to throb in his temples. He pressed the heels of his hands hard against them.

"What is it that's bothering you? Really?" Grenier asked.

The words slipped out. "I'm scared." And the harsh truth of that admission left Richard limp.

Grenier gave a snort. "You sure as hell weren't scared when I captured you. Oh, sure, you were frightened at the prospect of more pain, but you weren't frozen like you are now. I saw the man you're destined to become—if you get out of your own way."

"That was different. I had a plan. I knew what I was doing. I didn't know if it would work, but there was at least the chance." Richard limped over so he could look down at Grenier. "And I'm not frozen. Just the opposite. I feel like I don't even have time to breathe."

"Or think. Which means you can't plan. It's a feedback loop, and a bad one."

"*I know* that." His voice seemed to boom in the room. He quickly moderated my tone. "Thank you so much for stating the obvious."

"You need to take some time to relax. Your mind will work better."

"I can't. The world is collapsing."

"But very, very slowly." Grenier frowned, rolling the mug between his palms. Richard could tell the former minister was puzzled and disgruntled, so he decided to push.

"And why is that?" Richard asked.

"I don't know. I thought the gates would open, nations would collapse, and I'd be a satrap in the new world order.

But it isn't happening that way."

Richard was struck by that, and it helped answer a question that had been nagging at him. "Maybe that's why our government, and all the rest of the world's governments, aren't reacting," he mused. "You can ignore or explain away a little weirdness, and nobody wants to believe this is really happening."

"And by the time the weirdness becomes too big to ignore, or people realize it is happening, it might be too late to stop the Old Ones." Grenier drained the last of his cocoa. "I don't know what's happening at the gate at my compound, but my guess is that the Old Ones will moderate the craziness. The word will go out from thousands of pulpits that the demons appeared because Hell was trying to prevent the Lord's return. That's what I would be saying if I still had a pulpit to preach from."

"The Second Coming isn't supposed to happen in Virginia," Richard countered.

"Pffft." Grenier waved away the objection. "I could explain that away in a second." His voice took on a deeper, more musical resonance. "America is the only true bastion of freedom and opportunity in the world. America is the nation most loved and favored by God."

In that moment Richard could totally see how Grenier had become one of the most famous and successful evangelists in America. Richard knew it was bullshit, but he still felt a flutter of pride at the words, because he was moved by the certainty and sincerity in Grenier's voice. *Words can be such dangerous things*, he thought.

Richard shook his head to break the spell and asked, "So,

what will happen when … *if* the government does decide to act?"

"The gate will be defended by thousands of the faithful."

Richard shivered even though the room wasn't cold.

✧   ✧   ✧

PAMELA WAS LISTENING to four distinct conversations that were occurring at the dining room table.

Dagmar and her father—

"… Rochester lab is locked down, both of the New Mexico scientific labs are also under lockdown. I've called, but the scientists at Sandia and Los Alamos say that what I'm describing is impossible, and our Lumina scientist say they can't do anything without inspecting the slow glass construct."

Dagmar was making excuses. Pamela wanted to tell her not to bother. The judge wouldn't buy it.

"I don't think you're devoting enough time or energy to it," the judge said, proving Pamela's point if only to herself.

"Okay, yes, you're right. It isn't my top priority. This company is my top priority. It must be managed."

Because Richard sure as hell isn't doing it, Pamela thought. She glanced at her brother, seated at the head of the table, and watched him flinch and the color rise into his pale cheeks. He'd obviously overheard the exchange. Good, maybe it would get him to focus.

Syd and Sam were arguing with each other.

Syd said, "I think we ought to formally resign. Hell, we may be fired anyway."

Sam countered, "Hell, no, we want to keep a toehold in the agency. And we can't abandon everyone."

The cop and Grenier—

Weber's rough voice was saying, "We're the only first world country that still has the death penalty." The incongruity of that statement emerging from a policeman's mouth had her turning her attention to him.

Grenier's rounded sonorous vowels were edged with amusement. "I personally like that old-time justice along with my old-time religion. Give me an eye for an eye."

Weber gave Grenier's stump a pointed look. "You best not be planning any of that old-time payback justice on Richard ... or any of us. And we make mistakes. We try not to, but it happens, and I don't want to deal out death unless I'm damn sure we've got it right."

Grenier leaned over to say to both Pamela and Angela, "Did you hear that? Lieutenant Weber says you are both incompetents." His bulging belly brushed against her arm. Pamela pulled it close into her side.

"No, he didn't," Pamela snapped. "He was pointing out there can be prosecutorial overreach and mistakes do happen."

Angela stared at the former minister, hatred blazing in her dark eyes. "And since there is no God to sort it out, we'd damn sure better not do anything irrevocable. Oh, that reminds me." She looked at Weber. "That body ... not a Taser. Those were sucker marks."

"Suckers don't leave burns. And I haven't heard of any cephalopods escaping from the aquarium." It was a ponderous attempt at humor from the cop, but his eyes kept darting around as if he were looking for a way out.

"That's because it was caused by magic," Angela said. It was clear this was the continuation of an ongoing argument between the two of them.

Weber's lips and eyes squeezed shut. Repudiation by silence. The skin around the cop's jaw sagged, and pouches hung beneath his eyes. Weariness created the effect that his face was melting.

Pamela took a few more bites of salmon loaf with cream dill sauce and had to praise the genius who cooked every meal for both the residents of the penthouse and the employees in their dining room. She'd never seen a company where meals were provided, but she decided she approved.

She caught movement out of the corner of her eye. Richard had stood up and was limping into the kitchen. He had his finger pressed against his temple. Angela made a move as if to follow but sank back down in her chair when Weber shook his head. Pamela had no such compunction. She followed.

Her brother was inspecting a tray of pastries. Napoleons, eclairs, Sacher torte, cannoli. Pamela stared at the diabetes-inducing array and shook her head. Large silver carafes steamed and burbled, filling the air with the smell of fresh-brewed coffee. A basket held fifteen varieties of tea. Richard turned at the sound of her footsteps and forced a smile.

"The last rehearsal I hosted; I opened up a Sara Lee frozen cheesecake. I did tart it up a bit with some frozen raspberries." He selected a caffeine-free peppermint tea out of the basket.

"Stomach bothering you?" Pamela asked. He nodded and

filled the cup with boiling water from one of the carafes. "It should give you a hint. You shouldn't be doing this."

"Pamela, I can't work all the time. I've got to take a break, or my head's going to explode. So just leave me alone, okay? You can go downstairs and work all you want."

"Putting aside that I think this is frivolous, your own security chief thought it was a risk."

"That was before Joseph investigated." He pulled the tea bag out of his cup and tossed it into the trash compactor. The smell of peppermint tickled at her nose. "Bob, Lee, and Susanna are going about their lives without any overt signs of craziness. When they enter the lobby, they'll be scanned for weapons, and Cross has promised to see if any of the three are armed with spells. I think we've got it covered. Oh, and thank you for your concern," her brother said, and he didn't make any effort to disguise the sarcasm.

Sam walked into the kitchen carrying her dirty plate. "Your band is here," she said.

Pamela watched Richard struggle with himself and decide to let it go.

"Thank you," he said.

Angela came wandering in with an air so casual that it made it clear there was nothing at all casual about her arrival. She set her plate on the counter. "May we listen? I've never heard you play."

An expression of acute discomfort swept across her brother's face. "I'd really rather you didn't. When you have an audience, it isn't a rehearsal any longer. It becomes a performance."

Dagmar entered the kitchen. "My husband is the same

way," she said to the room at large. "He practices six hours a day locked away in a converted greenhouse out behind the main house."

"So, your children never see either of you?" Angela said in tones of sweet inquiry.

"I don't think professional women should have kids. You end up doing a shitty job on both fronts," Sam said in that tone she had that brooked no argument.

It was clear Dagmar was going to argue.

Pamela looked at Richard with his back against the center island, and the three women surrounding him. Richard squeezed his eyes shut for a moment, then slipped between Angela and Dagmar, heading for the door. It looked more like flight than an exit.

Pamela followed.

As they crossed the dining room Pamela heard a thunk followed by the soft cry of vibrating strings as a cello case bumped into a wall, shaking the instrument inside.

There were three strangers in the living room. A tall, dark-haired man with a half-smile and a crooked bow tie was inspecting the art. A young woman with waist-length blonde hair had her violin case hugged to her chest and kept turning in circles, surveying the room with a look of childlike wonder. An older man with crew cut gray hair and pants that rode too high on his waist was drawn to the collection of canopic jars on an inlaid table. He looked up at their entrance and said, "Could you bring some of these by the school sometime? My world history class has only seen my slides from the Cairo Museum."

"Sure," Richard said. "I'll give you my assistant's number

and we'll get it arranged."

"Oh, Richard, there are so many beautiful things," the blonde said in a breathy little-girl voice.

Maybe the woman couldn't help it. Maybe her voice really sounded like that, but Pamela had always suspected the baby dolls of putting on an act. Pamela also watched the interaction between her brother and the blonde, trying to judge if she was another one of his victims. Pamela had watched so many women, many of them her friends, make fools of themselves over Richard. This time it didn't seem to be the case.

The tall man with the bow tie turned to Richard. "There's art in here worthy of anything in the Uffizi."

Richard nodded his head in acknowledgment, and stammered into far too detailed an explanation. "It's not really mine. I mean, I live here, and it might ultimately be mine ... well, at least for my lifetime, but I'm ... we're hoping the real owner comes back ... I'm just sort of a caretaker ..." He stuttered to a halt.

Grenier, wandering through with his splayfooted fat man's waddle, reached out and patted Richard on the cheek as he passed. "Too much information, little man." Pamela watched as Richard yanked his head away.

Weber, Syd, and her father joined them, and the three women, their argument apparently tabled for the moment, also entered. Introductions were made. The tall art lover turned out to be Lee Titelbaum, a law professor at UNM. He fell into easy conversation with her father. Syd and the high school history teacher and cello player, Bob Figge, found a common interest in fishing. Susanna Monroe chattered brightly with Dagmar and Angela. While Sam sulked by the bookcases, Weber was drifting from conversation to conversation, his eyes flicking back to Richard periodically.

Richard threaded his way between chairs and music stands, retreating to the piano. He began sorting through music.

CHAPTER FOURTEEN

GUESS THIS IS MY PROBLEM

THE SOCIAL CHITCHAT wasn't all that comforting. Nuggets of disturbing information were being dropped in casual, dismissive ways, indicating just how much people wanted to pretend that things were normal. Damon sympathized; he was doing the same damn thing. Figge reported that truancy at the high school was running at forty percent. At the law school it was, oddly, the professors who were missing. The mall where Susanna worked was an echoing cavern filled with Muzak and no customers.

Richard remained at the piano going through books of music. His shoulders were tense, jaw tight. Because he didn't want an audience? Because he didn't want to hear these conversations any more than Damon did? Because the kid was living in a fishbowl with so many damn people watching him, guarding him, lecturing, critiquing, demanding, in short just kibitzing at him all the damn time?

And was he any different?

No, brain, fuck you! I just want to keep Rhode Island safe. I don't want anything from him.

There was a thin thread in the back of his mind whispering *that's not true.* Damon pushed it aside, he just wanted the world to feel normal again.

And the only person who could apparently do that was a slight twenty-eight-year-old who had already endured too much.

The conversations began to hiccup to an end. The three string players picked up their cases and moved to the chairs that had been arranged in a semicircle near the piano. The others began to settle on sofas and in armchairs. Outside the wide windows, the wind whistled and moaned through the boulders and tossed fine grit against the glass.

There were sharp snaps as clasps were opened, and the hollow thrum as the violin, viola, and cello were pulled from dark velvet-lined interiors. Richard struck a note on the piano. There came a mewing as bows were drawn across strings, and tuning pegs adjusted. The scrape of bows on strings set a counterpoint to the wind's melancholy cry and Weber suppressed a shiver.

Richard slid onto the leather padded piano bench, opened the sheet music, and then worked his hands, flexing and stretching the long, slim fingers. He closed his eyes and nodded slowly for a few seconds. Damon wondered if he was mentally playing the first few opening bars. The mewing stopped.

Damon suddenly felt completely out of place and ill at ease among these people. The German woman who helped run this multibillion-dollar company and whose husband was a concert violinist. The Federal court judge, his lawyer daughter, Angela with her medical degree. Even Syd and Sam, they were FBI agents, which meant they had either degrees in accounting or in law. And here he was with his associates degree in police science. He'd used his GI bill to get that much college after leaving the army, but he didn't fit in with these people. He didn't fit in at all. He wasn't sure why Richard kept him around.

"I'm heading home," Damon blurted. He reached up and touched his ear self-consciously. "It would be wasted on me."

Richard's head turned so fast it must have stressed his neck. The blue eyes were pleading, almost desperate. Damon could read them and the young man's expression as clearly as if he'd spoken—*Please, don't leave!*

Why do you want me here? Weber mentally queried.

Richard wet his lips, seemed about to speak, then turned away—a physical rejection, hurt etched in the tense line of his neck, the hunch of his shoulders. Damon took two steps, a jumble of complex emotions churning in his gut, then abruptly changed direction.

"Okay, I'll stay," he muttered awkwardly. Richard looked up at the sound of his voice and gave him one of those blazing smiles. Weber gave a one-sided shrug and answered with a rueful smile of his own. He took up a position next to Sam, his shoulders resting against the bookcase.

She leaned over and whispered, "Somehow I don't think they're going to be playing the Foo Fighters or even BTS."

Damon choked back a laugh. "Pretty sure you're right about that."

"Gonna be Old Dead White Guy music," she grumbled.

"Hey, I'm an old white guy."

She gave a one shoulder shrug. "At least you're not dead."

"Not yet, but the way—"

Angela glared and shushed them. The Kraut was giving them the evil eye, too. Weber subsided.

"Okay," he whispered into the young agent's ear. "We need to get cultured now."

Everybody settled onto available furniture except the judge, who started walking toward the bedrooms. "I want to finish the reports I was reading last night before bed."

Richard's expression as he watched his father's retreating back was like a punch to the gut for Weber. He had thought he had it bad with his pop, a bitter man who struggled to find work after the mines closed and drank too much on the weekends but had supported his son's desire to get the hell out and had encouraged him to join the military when he turned eighteen. Robert Oort seemed to know every soft and vulnerable spot in his son's psyche and Damon suspected he played on them with as much ease as Richard played those ivory keys.

The long lashes were lowered to cover the hurt. Richard finally looked up, cleared his throat. "Do you mind?" Richard asked the members of his quartet with a nod toward the ad hoc audience.

His tone made it clear what he wanted them to say. Which was strange, Damon thought, because Richard had pretty clearly wanted *him* to stay, so why not the others? The musicians exchanged glances, but no one wanted to seem rude. They all nodded and said it was fine if folks listened. Richard sighed, nodding his head in acquiescence.

✧   ✧   ✧

SIX MEASURES WAS all it took. Six measures and the tension in Richard's chest uncoiled. They were playing Mendelssohn's

Piano Quartet, opus 3 in B minor. The sound shimmered in the vaulted roof above their heads. Richard loved the stretch and play of the muscles across the backs of his hands. Even though the rise and fall of his right foot on the pedal caused the wound in his thigh to twinge, he didn't care. Playing had always made him feel incredibly strong. Especially when they got to an allegro or scherzo movement. Feeling the muscles in his forearms bunch and jump as he attacked the keys with speed and power made him feel like he was a superhero controlling sound, creating a vortex of music. There was nothing but the music, the notes on the page, and matching breaths with his fellow musicians. It was utterly different from when he sang, then he felt horribly exposed and *seen*.

As he played the presence of the listeners was forgotten as he lost himself in the fall of notes.

Until his father walked back through the living room carrying a stack of reports. They were at a particularly wonderful section in the final movement. Richard desperately wanted Robert to hear it, embrace it, realize that Richard hadn't just wasted the time, money, and education. *Music has value,* he thought desperately. *Professional or not it adds to the general joy in the world.*

He threw himself into the run, trying to coax perfect sound from the piano. Richard glanced over at the judge, but he didn't look up from the report he was reading, just walked into the foyer and called for the elevator. The elevator *dinged* as it arrived; it was in a discordant key from the quartet. Richard's fingers tangled, and suddenly he was three beats behind. Feeling like he wanted to cry for having ruined something so perfect, he lifted his hands, counted, and jumped back in with the others.

Once more he allowed the music to do its magic and take away the pain, the loneliness, the worry, and the fear. The music swept away all thought. He was possessed by it, swept along, lost to the world. They were approaching the resolution. It felt as if the passion of the music had entered his chest and gone shivering throughout his entire body.

It was exactly what it felt like when he drew the sword.

Then the phone shrilled, harsh and metallic, cutting across the floating music, breaking Richard's trance, and bringing back the world. He was not a man prone to displays of emotion, especially not pique, but this time he couldn't disguise his fury. He brought his hands crashing down on the keyboard in a jangling, dissonant chord. The strings faltered into silence. Angela darted to pick up the receiver.

"Hello? Hello?" she said, but the phone kept ringing.

"There," Sam said and pointed at a phone on the bookcase.

It was the first time Richard had really noticed it, and apparently it was a different line because no other phone in the penthouse was ringing. A faint sound reached him from the bedroom side of the penthouse. Richard mentally corrected, a phone was ringing, and it sounded like it was in Kenntnis's ... now Richard's bedroom.

The phone was at Weber's elbow. He lifted the receiver and carried it over to Richard.

"Oort," he snapped, irritation throwing him back into old habits, answering as if he were once again at APD headquarters.

"Will you accept a collect call from Dr. Edward—"

Richard was startled to hear an actual operator, but he'd been trained well by my parents. "No," he said quickly.

And then he heard a young man's voice in the background. *"No, wait!"*

Another voice, deeper, gruffer, with an Aussie accent, said, "That's it then, lad. That's your phone call—"

"Back off, flatfoot!" the younger voice shrilled.

The operator's voice, losing some of its soothing phone sex quality, asked, "Sir, do you wish me to terminate the call?"

The fact there were cops, Australian cops, involved had Richard intrigued, so he said, "No, it's all right; I'll accept the charges."

There were a few clicks on the line; then the boyish voice said, "Thanks. Is this Lumina Enterprises?"

"Yes. Who is this, please?"

"Eddie Tanaka, Dr. Tanaka," came the hurried addition. "I'm in Australia. I haven't got a passport, or any money, and that bastard on the freighter took my ID—"

For some reason Richard's pique was gone and he was finding this oddly amusing. "And now you've been arrested," he interrupted.

"Yeah, this is my one phone call, and I really need help, and—"

"Okay, I can see where *you* have a problem, but why is it *my* ... or rather Lumina's problem?"

"Because dickhead!" Richard yanked the phone away from his ear at the bellow. "I work for fucking Lumina!" The shout became a roar. "I was given this number to memorize before I left for Indonesia. I was told to call it if I was ever in real trouble! Well, I'm in real big fucking trouble! Everybody at my lab was killed except me, and I had to jump ship, and it took me four days to get to Australia in a goddamn Zodiac, and I'd run out of food, and then these dumbasses arrested me—like how many Japanese-American terrorists have *you* ever heard of?" The fury and desperation were rising again. "And then I picked *you* for my *one* call instead of a lawyer, and so far, you've been a real fucking disappointment, so get off your dead ass and get me some help!" Tanaka was once again shouting.

There was silence, and Richard listened to desperate panting from the other end of the line, while his mind tried to process all that he'd just heard. Only one thing was really sticking. *Everybody at my lab was killed.* Then, in an almost conversational tone, Tanaka added, "And by the way, who the hell are *you*?"

"I'm the head of the Lumina," Richard answered before he could think about it and carefully parse and pick his words.

Richard was suddenly distracted by someone clapping. He looked over his shoulder. It was Grenier.

Far away in Australia he heard his employee say, "Oh, shit. Um ... sorry?"

✧   ✧   ✧

"WHY IN THE hell didn't we know about this?" Richard demanded of Dagmar as they swept through the office doors.

Pamela, trailing after them, watched her father's head snap up at the profanity and the harsh rasp of her brother's voice.

"If everyone was killed there wouldn't be anyone to report the events," Dagmar said quietly.

"And no one is fucking monitoring these outlying interests?" Richard countered, and he glared at Dagmar.

"Richard!" The name cracked like a whip, and the judge came out of the big chair behind the desk. His face was stiff with disapproval. A momentary and errant thought disturbed Pamela's focus. She wondered why her father had always been so uptight about cursing.

Amazingly Richard rolled over the rebuke. "We've had thirty-six scientists and technicians murdered in Indonesia." The judge's disapproval dissolved as he processed this information.

"Obviously this is something we need to look at and make adjustments." Dagmar's head was erect, back stiff.

"Do ya think?" Richard growled. As her father emerged from behind the desk, Richard swung in the other side and sat down. Pamela realized it was the first time Richard had approached the desk and chair without forcibly reminding her of a terrified dog circling a trap.

"I want the dead recovered," Richard continued.

"That might not be easy," Pamela said.

"Tough," Richard snapped. "We have relatives who've lost loved ones to violence. They'll need the comfort of having the dead returned."

Dagmar nodded. "Yes, sir."

"Next question, was this wide-scale rioting and violence, some sort of spasm with their national politics and we had the bad luck to have it roll over us? Or were *we* the target?"

Dagmar looked baffled and shook her head. "Well, find out, and while we're making that determination, let's get warnings out to every other Lumina holding. Next, we need to get Dr. Tanaka papers, and get him back to the States. I want to hear his report personally."

Pamela stared at this stranger behind the desk. When had her brother become effective? Maybe his stint in the police hadn't been all bad. It seemed to have given him a spine transplant. Or he found dead people more compelling than corporate reports... Pamela couldn't say she disagreed with him on that score.

Their father joined the conversation. "It's hard to quickly obtain a passport."

"We're a big company. They expedite for corporations all the time," Pamela offered. "And you've got contacts, Papa ... Congressman Waters."

Richard was flipping a fountain pen between his fingers and frowning. "Tanaka's in the hands of the police, and that's never an easy situation to resolve. I'd like to have someone with legal training handle this. Pamela, I'd like you to go to Australia."

It was couched as a request, but it was really an order. To her.

Pamela damped down the coiling resentment and tried to keep her tone level as she asked, "Why me? Why not Papa?"

"Because you're right, with Papa's contacts we can get the papers arranged. We'll send you on the Lumina jet. By the time you get him back to the States we can meet you at the airport with a passport."

"There's just one small problem with this plan," Dagmar

said. "Our pilot is in jail in Virginia," she said in response to the various querying looks she got.

Pamela looked back over at her brother, and saw that the sharp, commanding certainty had vanished, replaced by that lost vulnerability that always irritated her. Her mother used to get that look, too.

"He is? What happened? I didn't know. If I'd known, I would have—"

"Oh, for pity's sake, you can't feel guilty over something you didn't know about," Pamela snapped. Richard shot her a withering look, but it did succeed in banishing the fragile, haunted expression.

"This must be the fellow who was flying the helicopter when we came to—" Their father broke off abruptly, and his mouth worked as if trying to expel a bite of something rotten.

"Came to rescue me," Richard said, his tone flat. "Why can't you just say it, sir?"

Well, the family melodramatics seem to be working overtime tonight, Pamela thought.

"Why was he arrested?" Dagmar asked, breaking the pattern, and bringing them back to the topic.

"Violating federal airspace. We were in the no-fly zone around DC," the judge answered.

"Is this going to be a hard rap to beat?" Richard asked.

Pamela shook her head. "I don't think so. Once again, we've got Papa. He's a member of the federal bench."

"And *you* have the power that comes from being a very rich man," Dagmar reminded Richard.

Pamela watched the weight of that statement fall onto her brother. For a moment Richard's expression became distant and faraway. Pamela wondered what he was thinking. Whatever it was, he shook it off.

"I know this isn't exactly pertinent, but why do we only have one pilot?" Pamela asked.

Richard shrugged and shook his head. He looked over to Dagmar, who said, "The plane was primarily for Mr. Kenntnis's convenience. We could request to use it, but he preferred his employees flew commercial." Dagmar shrugged. "It was one of his many quirks."

"All right. Papa, you'll handle getting this gentleman ..." Richard gave Dagmar an inquiring look.

She supplied the name. "Brook Kanadjian."

"Brook out of jail. Meantime, we'll wire money to Dr. Tanaka, and try to at least get him out of jail until Pamela can get there. And let's buy another plane and hire another pilot. We're going to need them."

Dagmar nodded. "I'll get on it, and I want to find out why we had a breakdown of communications."

The judge cleared his throat, a dry, precise sound. "I think I can accomplish this more easily if I'm in Washington instead of the wilds of New Mexico. As Pamela pointed out, I do have contacts."

Richard suddenly lifted his head, and Pamela watched a number of emotions go washing across his face. It all happened too fast for her to get a read of what he was thinking.

"I think I ought to go with you." It was the absolute last thing she had expected out of her brother. At their father's expression Richard rushed on. "I mean, it doesn't seem like the government is responding to this ... this invasion at all. I know what's going on, and I've got this." The hilt came out of his coat pocket and was laid in the center of the desk. "I think I need to try to work with them."

Dagmar hustled forward, rested her hands on the granite surface of the desk, and leaned in on Richard. "With all due respect, sir, that is crazy. If they learn of the sword, they might take it. Why would you take such a risk?"

But Richard didn't look at her. He watched their father with an intensity that bordered on desperate.

Pamela thought Dagmar was right and said so, then added, "And they won't just take the sword. Since you're the only person who can use it, they'll take you, too."

"I believe I made just these points in Washington in December," the judge said.

"Yes, sir, you did, and they made sense—then. But things are just getting worse and worse. Pretty soon we're not going to recognize our world, and I'm afraid if we don't mobilize now, it will be too late. Nothing we do will have any effect." His gaze went around the room, resting briefly on each of them. "We need allies, and we need help. We're going."

CHAPTER FIFTEEN

CRACK TEAM OR CLOWN CAR?

A PHONE RINGING late at night always elicits gut-clenching terror. Rhiana jerked awake in her nest of Egyptian cotton sheets and fluffy down comforter. The bed was a giant Georgian with massive posts rising toward the hammered copper tile ceiling. She had them remove the high rails and the heavy, blue velvet curtains. She had slept in a gossamer tent in Kenntnis's penthouse, and even though the material was vastly different, it brought back memories. *Memories of betrayal.*

Fighting her way out of the covers, Rhiana scooted to the side of the bed and snatched her cell phone off the bedside table. As she answered she saw the time—3:40 AM.

Shit, maybe it was her mom or dad.

She wasn't sure why she'd called her adopted parents and given them her number. That was a different life that she was so totally done with, but she had, and she didn't really want to think too much about it.

"Hello? Hello?"

But it wasn't one of her reputed siblings. It was Doug Andresson.

"Hey," he said. "I'm in a little jam. I need you to come—"

"What do you mean you're in a jam?" Rhiana combed

her hair out of her face and tried to focus. "How can you be in a jam at the compound?"

"Well, actually, I'm in town. DC." He tried to infuse the words with an insouciant little bounce.

"What? What the fuck have you done? Didn't I tell you to stay there?"

"Yeah, well, I was bored. You promised me anything I wanted, but you didn't get back to me when I called. I'm important, and you treat me like shit." He sounded angry and sulky now.

The desire to strike at him clawed at the back of her throat, but she forced herself to moderate her tone. "So, what's the problem?"

"You need to come here."

Here proved to be a hotel that straddled the boundary between official Washington, where power walked, and the decaying neighborhoods where crime preyed on the poor. Jack pushed open the pitted-glass doors. Rhiana had enlisted his help because she didn't want to meet Andresson alone again. It was starting to feel natural, even comfortable, to call the tall spiritualist when she needed help. She knew it made her vulnerable and he might take advantage, but right now she didn't care.

In the east there was a hint of gray as dawn slouched toward its arrival. Rhiana reluctantly turned her back on the sky and followed Jack into the lobby. A night manager dozed behind the desk. There wasn't a cage protecting the plump and pallid middle-aged man, but there was a prominent sign on the counter that stated NO CASH KEPT ON PREMISES.

A few stained sofas and an armchair huddled around a

scarred coffee table that was littered with People and Time magazines, several years out of date. There was the smell of cheap coffee brewing and of microwave eggs being prepared for the breakfast buffet.

"Keep him asleep," Rhiana said softly to Jack.

The clerk yawned, stirred, and started to open his eyes. Jack looked down at the big square-cut diamond ring on his own right hand, murmured, and the gem blazed with light. A tendril of white fire left the ring and touched the man's forehead. The clerk collapsed back into the chair, mouth open, snoring sonorously.

They moved down a hallway toward the back of the hotel. There was a faint wet-dog smell from the recently cleaned carpet. It hadn't had a notable effect. There were still stains ground into the blue Berber.

Rhiana tapped on the door, and Doug opened it a bare crack.

That alone told her it was bad. "Oh, good, it's you, come in. Hey, who's he?" Suspicion sharpened the words.

Jack slammed a shoulder into the door, forcing the smaller man backward. "I'd suggest you not question the lady," Jack said. "She's your—" The words cut off abruptly, then Jack said in a suffocated tone, "Oh, shit. Oh, Jesus. Oh, Lord God."

Rhiana rushed into the room. The cloying and yet almost metallic scent of blood filled the room. There was a man sprawled on the floor, back up against the dresser. His hands were cupped around the knife protruding from his belly. Blood stained the skin and drops actually hung in the hairs on the backs of his fingers. Quivers ran through his body, and his eyelids were fluttering. He was alive, but only just.

Not so the naked girl in the bed. Black hair hung in thin corkscrew ringlets. Some of them were draped across her face and helped hide the protruding, bloodshot eyes. Her tongue was like a piece of purple liver thrusting from between her lips. A man's belt was wound around her throat and pulled tight. Livid bruises mottled her face and shoulders, and her breasts showed bloody bite marks.

Jack was gagging. Rhiana fell back against the door. It gave beneath her weight and latched shut. Her thoughts seemed to be spinning, colliding, and shattering. Nothing made any sense.

"What ... what ... what ..." was all she managed to say.

"I was softening her up. A little play before we got down to action. I went to get a glove, who knows what a cunt like that might be carrying in her cooch, and while my back was turned, she got her cell phone and called her pimp. She kept crying, and telling me to stop, that this wasn't what she did, and then this asshole ..." Doug glared at the bleeding man on the floor. "Let himself in. I think that fag at the front gives him a passkey so they can do a shakedown on their patrons. I'm settling with him next. Anyway, he tries to start something, but I got my knife. Then she starts to scream, and I had to shut her up." Doug shrugged as if what had occurred in this room were the most natural things imaginable. "She shouldn't have fucked with me."

Jack had pulled out a handkerchief and was wiping his mouth.

He backed up to stand next to Rhiana. "Okay, what now?"

She looked into Andresson's flat black eyes and wanted to call the police. Wanted to call Richard to come and take this man away and lock him up, so Rhiana never had to see him or deal with him again. But he was an essential part of their plans. Their answer to getting Richard. But Andresson was awful, and he terrified her. Jack was looking at her, sensing her indecision. He took her by the upper arm and gave Doug a stiff smile.

"Excuse us just one minute." He pulled Rhiana into the hall and made sure the door was shut. "How is this guy our problem?"

"Because he is. I've been put in charge of him. He's an empty one, a person with no magic. If we … when we get the sword, he'll use it. And I was supposed to keep track of him. Keep him safe. Keep him happy. Oh, God, if they find out …" She spun in a frantic circle, fingers clutching at her hair.

Jack caught her by the wrists and forced her to stand still. "Okay, we get rid of the evidence. We take him back to the compound, and you keep him supplied in hot and cold running girls, booze, anything he wants."

"What if he kills another one?"

Jack stared at her; his expression quizzical. "What do you care? If you time it right, you can have a snack."

"Yes. Yes. You're right, of course. I'm not sure what I was thinking …"

"That you were human?" he suggested.

Rhiana suddenly wanted to cry. Crossing her arms, she clutched at her elbows and thought. "We need to make this go away."

Jack nodded. "Yes, but unless you've got Harvey Keitel playing the fixer from *Pulp Fiction* I'm not sure just how we do that."

"We'll send the room away." With her forefinger she reached out and lightly touched the diamond in his ring. "Want to learn how to create a tear in reality?"

✦   ✦   ✦

A FEROCIOUS WINDSTORM had the hem of Richard's overcoat beating at his knees, and some of the gusts threatened to knock him off his precarious three-point balance. Angela watched him try to dig the tip of the cane more firmly into the concrete of the tarmac without success. It also threatened his perfectly coiffed hair. His forelock kept falling into his eyes to be impatiently brushed back.

The western horizon was obscured by a wall of approaching dust, and dirt was pinging against the metal skin of the newly purchased Lear with enough force to be heard over the screaming wind. Angela, Weber, and Richard stood in a tight circle trying to shield each other.

Weber put a long arm around each of the much smaller people and pulled them close so they could hear each other over the howl and moan of the wind. "You know if you need me, you just have to call. I'd come with you now, but somebody's got to try to keep the force intact, and the city safe."

Weber's eyes, irritated by the flying sand, were running water, but Angela suspected it was not the wind alone that had brought moisture to his brown eyes. Richard started to reach up and wipe away the trailing moisture from the older man's cheek, but he quickly turned it into an awkward swooping gesture that landed his hand safely in a pocket. He looked down, bright color rising in his cheeks.

I've lost him, Angela thought.

You never had him, the more rational, hard-nosed part of her replied.

"Same goes for me," Angela said. "But hopefully you won't have any need for a pathologist or a coroner. Weber and I will keep the home fires burning 'til you get back."

They stood in silence, and Angela watched Richard struggle with his emotions. The haunted expression on that handsome face deepened as he watched his father climb the stairs and vanish through the hatch into the jet. The judge was trailed by Dagmar, Syd, and Sam. The Lumina security detail—Joseph, Estevan, and Rudi—were arrayed around the perimeter of the plane. At the foot of the stairs Pamela stood checking a list. The paper fluttered wildly in her hand from the force of the wind. Grenier, his hand on the railing, looked up at the stairs with the disgruntled expression of a man faced with an irksome and daunting task.

"Looks like you're loading the clown car at the circus," Angela remarked.

"Thanks, that just fills me with confidence," Richard muttered.

Weber cocked his head and gave his lopsided grin. "And just how did the Bozo Brigade convince you to take them all along?"

Richard sighed. "Well, let's see, Sam and Syd think they can help by contacting friends at the FBI, and Sam has offered to shoot people as necessary."

"That girl is just plain scary."

Richard nodded in agreement. "Papa needs to go so he can get Brook out of jail and arrange a passport for Tanaka. Pamela has to fly to Australia with said passport to collect Tanaka and bring him to me, and the other Lumina plane is in Virginia." Richard paused to catch his breath.

"Your sister must hate being your girl Friday," Angela said, and she didn't regret the pleasure it gave her.

"Oh, probably. Where was I? Oh yeah, Dagmar. Dagmar is still trying to teach me the business and she won't let me play hooky, and Grenier refuses to be separated from me and the sword because he's convinced, he'll be killed if he's not attached to me at the hip."

"Well, he ain't wrong," Weber grunted. "Of course, there's more than a few people *right here* who'd like to kill the son of a bitch."

Angela had a very strong sense that Weber was one of those people, and it was weird. Angela herself had nearly been killed by one of Grenier's magic spells, while Weber had been well away from most of the uncanny stuff, yet the muscles in his jaw were tightening and his breath had gone short.

Richard gave the older man a grateful smile then shook his head. "Thank you for being fierce on my behalf, but Grenier might actually be the most useful card I can play. He's been a Washington fixture for almost twenty years. He knows the President and a good number of legislators. He can back me up."

"While admitting he's an evil sorcerer who wanted to

bring the monsters into the world. Yeah, that's a real winning hand," Angela said.

They all looked over at Grenier again just in time to see the preacher shake his head, like a bull bedeviled by flies, seize the rail of the plane's stairs, and begin trudging ponderously upward toward the hatch.

"We'll just gloss over that."

"You better be tap dancing naked *and* hand-waving to go along with that gloss," Weber huffed.

Angela watched as Pamela suddenly darted up the stairs and tried to squeeze past the former minister, but she caught her heel on a riser and almost fell. Grenier's arms shot out, and he gathered her into an involuntary embrace. There was a moment when they looked into each other's faces. Pamela pulled back, and Angela watched her say something.

The pilot appeared in the door. He was short, wide, and pugnacious. He pointed ostentatiously at his watch and yelled over the wind, *"Hey, Oort, you may own this fucking plane, but I'm flying the goddamn thing. Let's go!"* The man disappeared back into the plane.

"He does know he works for *you*, right?" Weber asked. Richard held out his hand, palm down, and waggled it back and forth. Weber shook his head. "You've got, like, this superpower for attracting bossy assholes."

"It's a gift," Richard said.

"Kind of a self-own there, Lieutenant," Angela said, giving him a limpid look. "Since technically Richard still works for you, so I guess that makes you one of the bossy assholes, huh?" The older man was staring down at her with his mouth open. Angela grinned and added a Homer Simpson

"Doh!"

His bewilderment turned into a scowl as Richard and Angela both laughed.

Harumphing a bit Weber demanded, "You use the sword on him?"

Richard gave him a withering look. "No, why ever would I do that?" Sarcasm dripped off the words. "He's just going to hold my life in his hands. Of course, I used the sword on him."

"Hey, watch the lip, as the Jawa here pointed out ..." Weber jerked a thumb at Angela. "You do still work for me. So, here are my orders. Make the politicos listen and get Kenntnis free."

"Yes, sir!"

Weber stared at him for a long moment, then smoothed the windblown hair off Richard's forehead. "You take care, okay?"

She watched Richard's breath go short, and he gave a sharp shake of his head. "Well, Jerry's right," he muttered. "We should probably get this flying circus in the air. Bye, Angela, Damon. Please ... both of you stay safe. I couldn't bear it if anything—" He broke off abruptly.

"Same goes for you, Rhode Island," the big cop replied, and clapped Richard hard on the shoulder.

Angela stepped in close and gave him a chaste kiss on the cheek. "You're going to do fine. You've got this," she said softly.

His jaw tight, Richard gave a sharp nod then limped up the stairs followed by his security.

Angela glanced up at Weber's rigid face. "He'll do better

if you're there," she said.

"I can't … I've got … things are …"

"Bad all over," Angela snapped. She jerked her head toward the plane where the stairs were starting to fold up. "And he's the only one who has a chance to make things better, but to do that he needs someone at his back who doesn't want anything from him apart from wanting to help him."

Weber stared down at her with a strained expression. He suddenly gulped in a large breath and then sprinted for the plane waving his arms over his head.

"Wait! Hey, wait!"

The stairs unfurled and Angela watched Weber race up them two at a time. The hatch closed and she stepped back as the plane began to taxi away. She held up her hand in farewell.

"You all take care," she whispered. "Be safe. Be brave."

Squaring her shoulders, she walked back toward the gate and her waiting car. It was time to wrestle some demons.

✧ ✧ ✧

RICHARD HAD FELT a cold emptiness as he had limped up the stairs, but then Weber had decided to join them and the constriction in his chest eased. Pamela looked like she'd bit into something unpleasant as Weber had rushed past her. Jerry was in the cockpit flipping switches. A soft whine rose in intensity until it was a rumbling growl. The vibration ran up through the soles of Richard's shoes and into his bones.

Dagmar hung over the pilot's shoulder. "The radar

works? It's to your satisfaction?"

"Yeah, yeah. Lady, the day I can't avoid a missile, even in a piece of shit plane like a Lear, is the day I hang it up. Now go put your attractive little ass in a seat." Jerry looked up and saw Richard watching. "You, too."

Richard gave him a mock salute and moved into the body of the plane.

"I don't think much of the gentleman's attitude," Dagmar said stiffly. "Brook is far more *ángenehm*." Richard's mind provided the translation—*agreeable*.

"I didn't hire him for his personality," Richard said quietly. "I hired him because he's a former navy pilot who has spent the past few years flying food and medicine into the world's hellholes. I figured he could probably fly us out of any fix in which we might find ourselves."

"I now believe I *love* this gentleman," Dagmar said with a smile.

Richard gazed down the fuselage of the Lear. It seemed cramped after the Gulfstream. *How quickly you get accustomed to living the life of the very rich,* Richard thought.

"What are you smiling about?" Dagmar asked.

A bit shamefaced, Richard told her, and her bright smile bloomed again. It intensified the laugh lines around her eyes and Richard had the sudden realization that she was probably a person who, in normal times, smiled a lot. He felt a momentary flare of guilt that he was adding to her burdens. Then he looked at it logically—*monsters/me, monsters/me.* It was probably the monsters that were causing more heartburn than he was.

"Yes, soon you'll be deciding which yacht you want to

buy based on the draw of the keel, and which harbors you can actually enter versus having to take the helicopter into Monaco," Dagmar teased.

"If I *ever* become that person, you have my permission, in fact, I *order* you, to shoot me," Richard said trying to match her light tone.

"I don't like guns. I have never shot a gun," Dagmar said.

"Okay, then have Sam do it." Richard glanced over at the young agent. He leaned in and whispered to Dagmar, "She'd probably welcome the chance." Dagmar laughed, nodded, and took a seat. Richard pushed farther back toward the tail of the plane.

His phone began buzzing and vibrating in his pants pocket. Richard dug it out and looked at the screen. BRENT VAN GELDER. He put it away. He didn't need to be bothered by his brother-in-law right then. Pamela was leaning across the aisle arguing with Grenier.

"I just don't understand why you are coming. You violated your parole. You jumped bail. They will put you in jail."

"Your brother will protect me. And you can defend me. I'm sure you are formidable."

Pamela harrumphed and flung herself back against the seat. "This is so stupid."

Richard knew she was referring to him. Taking a deep breath, he tried to explain. "Look, I think it will help having him with us. The very fact I would tolerate having him around, or that he would work with me, helps make our argument." Richard glanced over at the former minister. "God knows, we've done a lot of damage to each other." At his words Grenier lifted his right arm and inspected his stump closely; he then gave Richard a thin smile. "The fact we'd work together rather proves how serious things are."

Pamela just folded her arms and looked pointedly out the window. Grenier and Richard exchanged a glance. They had discussed this. What Richard didn't mention was the other part of the conversation.

"I'm coming because you, dear boy, are going to need some respite from your terrifying sire. You'll be grateful to have me along."

Richard stole a glance at his father's profile. The judge's eyes were closed, and his Bose headphones were already firmly in place. Richard knew he hated to fly. He wasn't sure if it was the actual flying, or the disruption of being out of his familiar, comfortable space. And he had sure as hell been swept out of his familiar comfortable life by his only son. Wife dead by her own hand but driven to it by Grenier's people. The family home burned to the ground, again by Grenier's lackeys.

And you're bringing him along … why?

Richard shook off the thought. He knew Dagmar didn't like his father, he knew both Angela and Weber didn't like his father, and now he could add Grenier to that lengthening list.

He's my father. He came for me at the worst moment of my life. He's here now helping me.

They're wrong.

CHAPTER SIXTEEN

WHERE ANGELS WALK FEAR FOLLOWS

RHIANA HUDDLED AGAINST the swooping, graceful back of the Victorian fainting couch. Her bare feet were tucked up under the floor-length bathrobe, and she had an intricately crocheted afghan pulled up to her chin. It was both scratchy and greasy as wool and lanolin vied for primacy.

The heater kicked on, and the rush of air through the vent set the crystal drops on the chandelier to shivering and ringing. She was beginning to think the chandelier had been a mistake. The ceiling wasn't really high enough to support its four-foot length. Maybe she'd repaint. The rose and green wasn't working for her anymore.

Thoughts about interior decorating worked for a few brief moments to take her mind away from the hellish scene in that hotel room. Andresson was safely back at the Virginia compound, and no one seemed to know—or at least no one remarked—about his absence.

Rhiana knew that women were being delivered to the dark Paladin. She didn't want to know any more than that.

The darkened glass in the large oval mirror with its floral-patterned gilt frame swirled with purples and black ribbons of color. She waited for her father to speak, but the mirror returned to its non-reflective state. Suddenly viscous drops of black and purple oozed from the crystal pendants on the chandelier. Hundreds of drops pattered like a blighted rain onto the polished marble floor. Madoc's body appeared like pulled taffy. The human form stabilized, and he gave his collar a twitch.

"I haven't seen you in a while," Rhiana said, trying to keep her voice level and the tone casual.

He offered no excuse or explanation, just said abruptly, "How are you coming on securing the Paladin and the sword?"

"It's coming," she replied.

"Well, it just got easier because Oort is in Washington." Rhiana sat up. "It seems this has taken you by surprise, implying you weren't *coming along* with this very necessary task."

She ignored him and asked, "Any idea why he's come?"

"We presume it's to sound the alarm to your kind. We'll be monitoring who he meets, and try to limit his contacts, but you should act quickly. *Now that you know.*"

His exit was more conventional than his entrance. He walked out the door of her Georgetown mansion. Rhiana wondered if he'd noticed that he'd lumped her in with humanity. Three months ago, it had all been how special she was, how superior she was to humans, how much they valued and treasured her. Now ...

Your kind.

❖   ❖   ❖

THERE HADN'T EVEN been time to unpack before Richard had

shooed her out of the homogenized space that had been rented for this incongruous gaggle of people. The condo had good-quality leather furniture, a flat-screen TV hung on one white wall, and pale gray carpet underfoot. The only unusual feature was a baby grand piano in the living room. The big armchair near the gas fireplace was beckoning, and Pamela pointed out that there were only two hours left in the business day. He had overruled her, and in a particularly snotty way.

"I've got two people in jail. I know it's a huge effort, but maybe you could at least try to care," he had said.

"And what are you planning to do? Sit around and play the piano?" she'd shot back in her nastiest tone of voice.

She didn't know why finding that damn piano in the rental had irritated her so much. Maybe it was the way Dagmar petted and cosseted her brother, and how Weber had just thrown over his job and responsibilities to join them.

But Richard wouldn't fight. He just turned and walked away from her, back toward his bedroom. Which was another sore point for Pamela. Richard had a bedroom to himself while everyone else had to share.

Weber had remained at the condo with Richard, as had Grenier, who had said he would make calls to some of the organizations that orbited the Republican Party.

The rest of them and one of the guards as driver had piled into the big SUV to start their various tasks. Without Dagmar's gift for artless patter, and Sam and Syd's affectionate squabbling, it would have been a tense and silent ride to the government buildings. They had dropped Dagmar at

Treasury where she had an acquaintance who was now an Under Secretary.

Sam and Syd went on to FBI headquarters to beg forgiveness for Syd's sudden departure and do a little reconnaissance.

Since it was so late in the day her father began at State, where he could at least start the paperwork for Tanaka's passport while Pamela headed off to deal with the jailed pilot. A bail bondsman was obtained, and she soon had Brook freed and accompanying her back to the condo. She had expected another grizzled vet like Jerry, but Brook Kanadjian was a good-looking, dark-haired man in his mid-thirties. She found herself hoping he wouldn't be one of the employees who quit when faced with the sword.

Everyone, except Sam and Syd, who both lived in the area, had rendezvoused back at the condo for dinner, which had consisted of a stack of pizzas. Grenier had managed to eat one of the extra-large pies by himself. Then, after bestowing a garlic-and-pepperoni-laden belch on them, he had demanded money from Richard. When Richard balked, Grenier pointed out that the town ran on rumors. Rumors abound in bars, and alcohol always helped to prime the pump. The former preacher was still absent.

Pamela was snuggled under the down comforter reading a travel book about Tuscany and still tasting the too greasy pizza. There was a light tap on the door. Pamela recognized the pattern. It was Richard.

Holding her place with a forefinger, she closed the book and said, "What?" She didn't make it sound welcoming.

The door opened, and Richard walked in. He was dressed

casually in blue jeans, boots, a cashmere sweater, and a ski parka.

"You're going out?"

He nodded. "I'd like you to come with me. It's time you see what we're up against."

The feather comforter felt suddenly even cozier. She held up Under the Tuscan Sun. "I'm reading. And I'd have to get dressed again," she said.

"Yes."

"This is really important?"

"Yes."

"You're not going to let this go, are you?"

"No."

Richard when he was laconic irritated her more than all the other times, but she got up and dressed. Weber was waiting in the living room along with Rudi and Estevan.

When did we become people who traveled with body-guards? When did my brother become that person? she wondered.

Weber cocked an ironic eyebrow at her, seeming to have read her thoughts because he leaned down and whispered, "Just because you're paranoid doesn't mean there aren't people who are actually after you."

"What are we doing?" Pamela demanded.

"Gathering intelligence. And in your case ... convincing you this is all actually real."

"I know it's real," she huffed, turning on her heel to walk away.

"You know it. But you don't believe it. Richard's hoping tonight will convince you."

As they stepped out into the hall, their only neighbor on the floor was also leaving. His dog, a tiny white ball of fluff, began yapping shrilly. Her owner was a tubby little man who wore three-thousand-dollar suits and pink-tinted glasses. He gave them a look, sniffed, thrust his button nose in the air, and tried to march past them, but Rudi cut him off and chivvied him up against the wall. The man's complaints were as shrill as his dog's.

"Hey, you should have sold out, man," Estevan said with a grin. And Pamela remembered Dagmar saying something on the plane about how she had tried to buy his condo for Joseph, Estevan, and Rudi to share, but the owner had refused, hence the crowding in their condo.

Bet he's sorry now. We really are a menagerie. I wouldn't want to live next door to us. She was also a bit breathless over the amount of money that had been spent in the past three days—Lumina had bought another jet, hired a full-time employee to fly it, purchased a large, luxury condominium in central DC. The whole thing was mad.

The doorman held the door, and Joseph held open the back door of the limo. Richard, Pamela, and Weber, along with Joseph, sat in back while Rudi slid behind the wheel, and Estevan took the passenger side in the front seat. They pulled out into Washington's insane traffic. Even at this hour of the night the city pulsed with energy. They seemed to just be driving aimlessly, moving into suburban hell. Up ahead was a multiscreen movieplex with its surrounding growth of chain restaurants like mushrooms sprouting at the foot of a dying tree. They were soon tangled in three lanes of heavy traffic trying to leave the theater, and finally they were stopped among the cars.

Joseph suddenly ordered tersely, "Go!" as he threw open the back door.

✧　✧　✧

RICHARD GRABBED HIS sister's wrist, and Damon gave her a boost from behind as they all three ducked out the back door of the limo. White streamers of exhaust filled the air as if this were a herd of steel buffalo exhaling all around them. Mingled with the reek of exhaust was the hint of brine from the Atlantic, and Weber had a memory of breathing the moist air off Lake Superior. It was strange his memories went back to his childhood. He had spent much of his adult life in deserts—Afghanistan and Iraq and then New Mexico.

Richard dragged Pamela into the backseat of a beat-up Neon while Weber jumped in the front seat next to Sam who was gripping the steering wheel. The light changed, and the rumbling herd rolled forward. Brake lights flashed and flared as drivers jockeyed for position. A small opening appeared in the lane to their left, and Sam sent them rocketing through it.

The young agent drove with a mad flair that Damon could only admire. His defensive driving course was years in the past. Maybe it was time for a refresher, he thought, as he glanced into the rearview mirror to look at Richard and Pamela. The woman had a death grip on the panic strap above the door, and a particularly fast turn sent her careening into Richard. Weber winced in sympathy as Richard hissed in pain as she fell against his injured thigh.

"Could you slow down!" Pamela snapped at Sam.

"Nope."

Weber tried to pass off his chuckle as a cough. From the glare Pamela aimed at him he hadn't succeeded.

They drove in silence for close to an hour, ending up in a Baltimore neighborhood that wasn't quite residential or quite urban. There were a number of three- and four-story buildings and lots of shotgun houses in between. Dumpsters, overflowing with hunks of drywall, lumber, and old appliances, lined the street. Renovation and gentrification were clearly under way.

They pulled into the driveway of a two-story house. Sam flashed the headlights, and the garage door opened. She rolled in. The door closed, plunging them into total darkness. Then the overhead fluorescent lights came on.

A tall, powerfully built African American man stood holding open the door into the house. Weber recognized him as Syd's partner, Bob Franklin. He had been with Richard and Damon as the gate had opened, and he had come to Richard for help when Syd had become catatonic. He waved and beckoned. Sam hopped out and opened the back passenger door. On Richard's side. The young agent offered her hand to help him out which he accepted. Weber quickly did the same for Pamela. She refused his hand.

Despite the cold, Sam wore only a bolero-style leather jacket over a silk shirt, a short jean skirt, and sharp-toed, high-heeled boots. She bounced up to Franklin, and he enfolded her in a bear hug.

The big agent released Sam, then turned to the Oort siblings. Richard inclined his head. "Agent Franklin."

"Good to see you again, Mr. Oort, Lieutenant Weber,"

the black man said.

"Thank you for offering us this help," Richard replied as they shook hands.

"Oh, there's a price," Franklin said, and Weber tensed a bit at that. Franklin didn't miss it and he and Weber measured gazes. Weber could see the heavy bags hanging beneath Franklin's eyes. They were so pronounced it looked like he'd been punched. Franklin then glanced over at Pamela. "You brought an extra."

"My sister, Pamela Oort," Richard said.

"Bob Franklin." They shook hands. "Pleased to meet you, ma'am," the agent said.

"And you," Pamela responded though it sounded rather begrudging.

"Please come in," Franklin said.

Despite the late hour there were a lot of people in the house. Syd was among them. Many had that hyperaware quality that marks cops of every stripe, but to Damon's surprise there were also a number of spouses and children.

Franklin's wife was a good deal younger than the agent, and their three children ranged in age from two to seven. Weber guessed it was a second marriage and a second family. On the overstuffed sofa four little kids slept among the flowered throw pillows. The little round faces were red from the heat of the fire and the effort of sleeping so deeply. Nestled among the floral pattern they looked like elfin children asleep in a garden.

And I'm 0 for 3, he thought. *Thank God only he and Marjorie had had a kid, and Denny was grown and off living his own life now.*

Logs crackled in the fireplace, and a few older kids were shaking an old-fashioned popcorn popper over the flames. The opening kernels sounded like small explosions, and the scent set Damon's mouth to watering. He briefly laid a hand on his gut and reflected that he didn't need any more junk after stuffing pizza and guzzling beer earlier in the evening. Unfortunately, the air was rich and tempting with the smell of Cajun spices and the yeasty scent of beer.

It would have seemed like a party but for the grim expressions that formed lines around the agents' mouths and lurked like shadows in the backs of their eyes. Bowls of gumbo were shoved into their hands. Damon noted that Pamela accepted a beer while Richard declined. Weber glanced down at the gumbo and the beer in his own hands and shrugged; the diet could start tomorrow.

He drifted through the crowd, picking up fragments of conversation. Much of it centered around the power vacuum that was forming at the heart of the federal government. Rumor had it that the White House was divided, with some staff urging the President to address the nation, set up an international conference, take action. Another faction argued that what was occurring could not be handled by ordinary human agencies, and so a stream of religious leaders was parading through the West Wing. There was a nod at inclusiveness, but most were of the president's traditional Protestant denomination.

Wilder rumors circulated around the Pentagon, that the military was planning to take control. No, the President would be imposing martial law, it wouldn't be a military coup. Congress dithered, passed resolutions, debated, tried to pass additional spending bills, hire more police, reinstate the draft, demand the president work with our European and Asian allies. In short nobody seemed to have a clue about what to do.

Weber went in search of Richard and found him in a knot of agents.

"... talk to local law enforcement," Richard was saying.

"And tell them *what*?" a woman agent asked, and her tone was sharp and brittle.

Richard's tone stayed patient and even. "To keep visible. Maintain a presence in their towns and cities. If we're AWOL it will only add to the sense of fear and chaos. We're the guardians, the bulwark against chaos," Richard concluded.

Weber gave a small headshake because amazingly it didn't sound pompous or overly dramatic because Richard believed it so totally.

"Well, maybe he didn't become a policeman *just* to outrage the family," Pamela said quietly, and Weber jumped. He hadn't heard her come up behind him. "But why are they all here? Honestly, why am *I* here? Do they actually think *my brother* is going to fix this or has *any* idea what to do?"

"Well, clearly they've got more faith in him than *you* do," Weber answered. "And I told you why you're here. So, you'll maybe, finally, start to understand that this shit is real," Weber whispered back.

"We got a report out of South Dakota that angels have been appearing in some little town, and the people have been *giving them their children*," said a burly young man wearing a SWAT gimme cap. "By the time a team arrived from Pierre they found the town deserted. Everybody was gone, two thousand people, *just gone. Poof.* Their sheriff and deputy didn't help *them.*"

"Crime is up everywhere," another man offered. "Way past what any of us can cope with."

Weber felt a stab of guilt. He had run out on his department. On his duties. *But maybe helping Richard was the best way to do his job?*

"The President needs to mobilize the National Guard," Syd said.

"And I ask again," the woman broke in. "To do *what?*"

"Yeah," came a mutter from the back of the crowd. "The National Guard worked so well down in Virginia."

Richard dragged a spoon back and forth through his untouched gumbo. He had lost that certainty and fervent zeal, and had what Damon thought of as his stricken fawn look.

"I'm going to be meeting with senators and representatives," Richard said. "We'll find someone who'll ... who'll ..."

"What?" a voice demanded.

"Listen," Richard said.

"I don't want 'em to listen. I want 'em to fucking *do* something."

"Okay, folks, let's go into the study," Franklin called.

All the agents shuffled into a room at the back of the house. Weber made certain Pamela was carried along with them. French doors offered a view across a small backyard crowded with a swing and slide set, a sandbox, and a big gas grill. There were a surprising number of books on the shelves, and the desk was dominated by a twenty-three-inch computer monitor. Cables snaked from the computer to the sixty-inch flat-screen television hanging on the far wall. A skinny man whose hair was rumpled like a pale brown haystack slouched in the desk chair, keyboard on his lap, fingers flying across the keys. He appeared to be playing an online game.

Franklin laid a hand on the bony shoulder of the man at the computer. "Ready, Danny?"

"Yeah, like, ages ago."

"You're sure they won't suspect?" Syd asked.

Danny made a face and pressed the palm of his hand against his chest. "Am I not the best? Seriously, I built in a trapdoor, and set up an automatic routine to imitate a hacker. They'll be chasing my little myth while we take a look at the satellite feed."

"Okay," Syd said vaguely. "I guess that makes sense."

There was the quick clatter of keys, and an image stabilized on the computer screen and the television. From his vantage Damon couldn't see the monitor, but he had a great fucking view of the television. The cliff face was veiled in mist, and Weber remembered the choking, burning quality of the air. Figures that defied description moved through the coiling mist. Damon heard Pamela give a small gasp.

"I've seen what Hollywood can do with special effects," she muttered through stiff lips, and she started to turn away.

Damon grabbed her by the shoulder, forced her around to face the television again. "Then why won't you look at it?" he demanded. "Because you know it's real. You can *feel* it, even through the fucking TV."

"We're down to orbital cameras now." Franklin's voice carried through the room. "People come apart mentally in there. Then we tried sending in predator drones, but they all crashed."

"Technology doesn't work where there's an Old One, or that much magic," Richard said quietly.

Around them there was a soundless reaction like the shifting of muscles on some large animal from the thirty people crammed into the room.

The image clicked away from the cliff face, and there was a flare of golden light. "There!" Richard said. He pointed. "Can you magnify that?"

More clicks, each one making the image larger, brought into focus a curving wave of glass resting in the center of a small meadow. Inside the glass there was a pale glitter like gold and diamond dust. On one side of the glass structure loomed a great gate. It had grown a lot from when Weber had last seen it. The image on the television flickered and rolled as Danny sent commands to the satellite cameras and tried to get an angle through the opening.

"That's the best I can do," the computer tech said.

There was another shift from the crowd, and this time a murmur of distressed comments, for what they seemed to be seeing was a distant sun against a backdrop of stars.

"What the hell is that?" someone called.

"A galaxy far, far away," Damon replied grimly. There was a smattering of hollow laughter. "Not joking," he added, as he remembered going into that world of snow, freezing cold, and mountains that walked to help Richard rescue a lost child.

Richard's eyes met Damon's. "They don't seem to have altered the terrain around Kenntnis. And he doesn't seem to be guarded."

"Do the acres and acres of crazy-making crap count?" Sam asked blandly, and Richard blushed in embarrassment.

Franklin looked over at Richard. "Syd says if we free this Kenntnis guy these gate things will vanish. Is that true?"

"Well, I don't think it's quite that easy," Richard said. "But their effects will certainly be diminished. And we'll have the help of somebody who knows how to close the gates and fight the Old Ones. He's done it before. A long time ago."

"But nobody can go in there and keep functioning," another person called from near the back of the room.

"Speaking of, could we turn that off?" Pamela said as she pointed at the television. "It's making me ..." She couldn't seem to bring herself to say it.

Weber said it for her. "Afraid. It makes us afraid."

Danny looked to Franklin, who looked to Richard. Her brother nodded. A few keystrokes and the screen went dark.

"Richard, do you suppose people like me and Sam, people who've been touched with the sword—do you think *we* could go in?" Syd asked.

"The sword doesn't make you brave. It just makes you sane," Richard said gently.

"And if you're sane you'll probably want to *run away from the monsters*," Sam quipped. This time there wasn't even a titter of gallows laughter from the people in the room.

Richard looked seriously up at Franklin and Syd, then swept the assembled agents with an intense blue-eyed gaze. "And while they can't feed on you after you've been touched, or use you to power their magic, they can still kill you."

Franklin laid a hand on Richard's shoulder and addressed

the people filling the room. "Look, the director's AWOL. We're getting orders out of Justice that are just plain nuts. I saw what this sword did for Syd."

Syd grabbed his daughter and pulled her forward. "And my Sam."

For an instant the young agent hesitated, then grudgingly admitted, "Yeah, he ... it fixed me."

"Well, I'm going to do it," Franklin resumed. "Anybody else want to join me?" He looked around challengingly. There were confirming nods from everyone.

Richard had the hilt of the sword in his hand. The room went very quiet. People watched him with varying degrees of skepticism, fear, and dread. He drew the sword, and skepticism vanished. Weber leaned back against the wall. Each time the sword was drawn now the musical overtones became deeper, stronger, and more resonant.

Just before Richard began using the sword, Weber spoke up. He hated to do it, but it had to be said.

"Richard," he called sharply. "What about the children?"

CHAPTER SEVENTEEN

WE'RE SURROUNDED

THE WATER IN the swimming pool was bathtub warm, and it didn't take long before Richard's strokes had slowed, and he was taking a breath every two strokes instead of every four. Only the pain as his wound pulled and tugged kept him from just giving up and sinking to the bottom of the pool.

The hilt hung on a lanyard around his neck, and it felt like it was also trying to drag him to the bottom. *Ironic that the sword would be the thing that tipped the balance.* Richard tried not to read significance into the thought.

Back home he would have left it rolled up in a towel. But not here.

Here it was never leaving him.

Pamela had fallen asleep in the car on the drive back from Franklin's. Even her terror over Sam's breakneck driving style hadn't been able to keep her awake. One particularly fast turn sent her falling against him. Richard had clasped an arm around her shoulders to steady her and had the disorienting sense of protectiveness.

Weber had whispered, "Should I take a picture? Might come in handy as blackmail."

Richard had huffed out a quiet laugh, looked down at her

soft brown hair spilling over his shoulder. "Who knows, maybe someday we'll actually manage to like each other," he had whispered back.

Richard kicked harder trying to force his body to obey. The sound of the churning water was both muffled and hollow in the echoing, tile-lined room. They'd gotten back to the condo at 1:00 AM, but his sleep had been fractured by the memory of crying children. The adults had experienced the sword, so they knew how much it would hurt, but most had still wanted their children protected. Only one woman had refused, saying she didn't want to deny her child his dreams and imagination. She had taken her son and left.

Her argument had actually shaken Richard. Maybe kids did need pretend games and imaginary friends to develop normally. What if the sword took those away? He didn't understand this weapon, and the man ... creature who could have enlightened him was well out of reach. Which left him relying on his own judgment, and honestly, he didn't have much faith in his judgment. Fortunately, Franklin was made of sterner stuff. He shrugged off the woman's objections as dumb as hell. *"What a load of crap. I can still imagine. In fact, I can imagine a whole hell of a lot more than I'd like."*

Richard had warned that he might not feel that way when his children were crying in pain. But again, Franklin had brushed if off. *"It can't be any worse than a vaccination for school, and this is a hell of a lot more important than a damn shot for whooping cough."*

So, in addition to reassuring Richard, the conversation had also provided him with a way to describe what happened when he used the sword. *Being inoculated.* It beat every other phrase people had come up with. When Cross called it *the touch* it sounded creepy. When Pamela called it *submitting to the sword* it sounded like an S&M sex act. Dagmar had suggested *the dubbing*, but that was even worse. *Inoculated* worked.

Richard tucked, somersaulted, caught the side of the pool with his feet, and pushed off again. Estevan's shadow fell across the water. A surge of resentment surged through him. Here he was, rich as hell, and he had to be guarded around the clock. Never to again know privacy. The deep end seemed a long, long way away. The muscles across his shoulders and down his triceps shivered with effort. It was time to admit defeat. Richard sidestroked over to the ladder, pulled off his goggles, and climbed out.

Estevan held out a towel. Richard dried off. Next Estevan held out his robe. It felt so odd to have people waiting on him. Richard muttered an awkward thank you, and they left the pool and gym area and headed for the elevators. It was inevitable. It was karma. It was kismet. They met Shih Tzu Man and his dog on the elevator. He was clutching a long pooper-scooper, and he treated them to his usual glare. The little dog, however, seemed to be calming down about them. She just sniffed their ankles. Richard felt it was safe to lean down and give her a pet though Estevan looked like he wanted to drop-kick the little thing. The dog looked up at him. He looked down at her, and she reverted to form. She backed up against her owner's legs and started yapping. Naturally that was when the cell phone in the pocket of Richard's robe started to buzz and vibrate.

"Oort."

"This is Senator Aldo's office."

"What?" he said trying to hear over the frenzied barking.

"ALDO, Senator Aldo."

Thankfully they reached their floor before Richard also felt like he also wanted to see if a Shih Tzu could fly. The senator from Nebraska held no official leadership position, but his influence went wide and deep. He was one of those figures the American people, whether Democrat, Republican, Independent, or Apathetic, seemed to embrace. Members of his own party deferred to him, the loyal opposition feared him, and the president heeded him. He sat on the Intelligence Committee and Foreign Relations, and he chaired the Armed Services Committee. It meant he'd most likely been briefed about conditions at the gate. The fact that he was calling was significant.

"The senator would like to see you tomorrow at 11:00 AM in his office. Can you be there?"

"Yes. I'll be there."

✧　✧　✧

TRAVELING FROM THE bitter cold of Washington, DC, in late January to the sultry heat of an Australian January, had Pamela kicking herself. How had she not thought of this and packed appropriately for a trip to the southern hemisphere? On her way to the Air Raid City Lodge, the taxi passed a mall in downtown Darwin, and she had the driver stop. A quick stop in a department store where she bought jeans, a T-shirt, and sandals. "I'll wear them," she told the salesgirl, and had them put her wool slacks, cashmere sweater, and pumps into the bag.

During the seemingly endless flight, she'd spent time on what passed for research in the modern age—she'd Googled Darwin, Australia, and read all the tourist information sites. They had all agreed that Darwin had the youngest population of any city in Australia. Her brief foray into the mall had provided anecdotal proof of that, it was filled with lots and lots of young people. *Of course, most malls were filled with young people.* In a perverse way she had found it comforting to watch teenagers indulging in mating behavior while they ate junk food in the food court, and girls adorned themselves in the plumage of jewelry and hair combs in various shops. *At least the young were unaffected by the world falling apart,* she thought.

Once in the lobby of the lodge she called up to Dr. Tanaka's room.

"Hello?" It was a surprisingly young voice, and he sounded hesitant and suspicious.

"This is Pamela Oort. Lumina sent me. Are you ready to go?"

"Oh, shit, yeah." And the connection was broken even as she was opening her mouth to tell the scientist what she looked like.

She took up a position where she could watch for a Japanese American entering the lobby. The room was buzzing with activity: people booking tours, and a party of young Germans, all wearing backpacks, checking in at the front desk.

Moments later an incredibly tall, incredibly thin Asian man dressed in jeans, a white T-shirt, and tennis shoes hurried into the lobby. Pamela stood up, but he looked right past her. Instead, he zeroed in on an older, heavyset woman. He said something, and she shook her head. Frowning, he moved on to the next closest woman. For some kind of physics genius, he seemed pretty damn clueless, Pamela thought. After the fourth such encounter Pamela took pity on the other guests and walked up to him.

"Dr. Tanaka?" she asked.

"Yeah."

"I'm Pamela Oort."

"Wow, uh, okay. Huh, I didn't think you'd look like ... well, like you ... do."

"And just how do I look?" The moment the unwary words emerged Pamela wished she hadn't uttered them.

"You're really pretty." She drew herself up and gave him the patented Oort disdainful glare right down the nose. He seemed unfazed and, in fact, continued to dig deeper. "You don't expect that from a corporate drone."

"Are you trying to be rude?"

"Oh." His mouth worked as if he were chewing on something. "So, that came across as rude rather than as a compliment?"

Pamela looked him directly in the eye, but he wasn't being sarcastic. It still didn't incline her to be charitable. "Obviously," she said, and was pleased when he blushed. "Do you have anything in your room?" He shook his head. "Do we owe anything on the room?" He again shook his head. "So, we're ready then." Turning on her heel, she headed for the door. Tanaka took two long strides like a wading stork and fell into step with her.

"Actually, I'd like to get something to eat before we leave. I was using the computer in the business center and I kinda forgot to eat."

The reminder set her stomach to growling. There was a small galley on the Gulfstream, but there hadn't been time to stock it fully, so the choices were currently limited to cold cuts and bread for sandwiches and a variety of beverages. A hot meal and a martini sounded lovely. She called Brook to see if he wanted to join them, but he told her he was stocking the galley in preparation for the return flight—twenty-three hours in the air plus a stop to refuel in Los Angeles. As expected, her father had done a good job; not only had Brook been freed, but all charges against him had also been dismissed.

As they walked toward the door Tanaka said, "Actually I used up a lot of the money you sent me buying computer time." He glowered at the front desk and added, "It's just bullshit. It's so cheap, but these hotels just stick it to you."

"Your work must have been very important," Pamela said.

"Oh, shit, this wasn't work. I can't do my work without an accelerator. No, my raid group was entering a dragon's lair, and it took a lot longer than I thought it would." This time she didn't have to explain her expression to him. He looked momentarily guilty, then sulky, and finally devastated. "I just wanted to feel like things were normal again," he muttered in a tone barely above a whisper.

Feeling suddenly contrite for her earlier behavior, Pamela laid a hand briefly on his upper arm. "I know. I understand. I wish things were normal, too."

As they stepped into the tropical heat and Pamela waved for a taxi, she reflected on how terrifying that statement actually was; that an online computer game where one fought dragons felt more normal than the world they presently inhabited.

✧   ✧   ✧

BOTH GRENIER AND Richard's father had told him that Senator Aldo had the same office that John Kennedy had occupied back in the 1950s. It was appropriate. Both Kennedy and Aldo had been military men. Both were Liberals. Both entered Congress in their early thirties. Where they differed was in ambition and background. Aldo had chosen to remain in Congress rather than run for president, and he had not come from wealth. He had grown up on a farm and watched a way of life vanish under pressure from corporate farming. In his autobiography he'd written that the experience had killed his father and shattered the family. All of it combined to make him a fierce defender of the common man.

Grenier had also told Richard that Aldo valued courage and independence, so he arrived solo. *Well,* he thought, *solo was a relative term.* Joseph, Rudi, and Estevan waited with the limo in one of the underground parking garages. Over the years Richard had met a lot of politicians, dated their daughters, seduced a few of them, and even slept with a couple of their sons. Politicians, simply by virtue of being politicians, held no mystery or awe for him, but he still wished the judge had come with him. Robert Oort's calm gravitas would have been so much more effective than he could ever be.

Reflecting on all of this as he walked down the hall, Richard tried to slow his heartbeat and take deeper breaths. The three-beat rhythm of his footfalls and the awkward swing of the cane added to his nervousness. The hilt had been mounted on top of the cane so it wouldn't cause any problem when he went through security. It registered as inert, but it would have seemed too strange to have had it in his pocket or, worse, in its holster. It did overbalance the cane, however, and made it hard to control. The fact that Richard's palm was sweat-slick with nerves didn't help either.

At the far end of the hall a group of tourists clustered around a portrait. If there was one thing the police academy taught it was situational awareness. Richard never entered a room without checking out every person in it, and he always got seated where he could watch people entering and leaving—even if he had to use a mirror to do it. Which meant he noticed the swing of long black hair, and the light glittering off a line of earrings running from the tips of her ears to the lobes. She had also been much on Richard's mind during the intervening weeks since their last meeting in that dell in Virginia. *Rhiana.* He wasn't hallucinating; she was here.

Preparing for a spell to be thrown, Richard stopped and tightened his grip on the hilt, ready to yank it free and draw the sword. But Rhiana didn't do anything. The tour was moving again. As they disappeared around a corner, she glanced back at Richard from beneath the brim of her fur hat. Richard made a hobbling run down the hall and spun around the corner. The tourists were still moving, the sound of shuffling feet and winter coughs loud in the enclosed space. They were all large, pallid, and older. The beautiful girl in a sable coat was no longer among them. Richard had a vivid memory of Grenier vanishing into a crack in a wall in a church in Colorado Springs.

Rhiana had her own way of evading him.

As Richard retraced his steps, he tried to comfort himself that there was more than one senator on this floor. They wouldn't know it was Aldo he was visiting ... Richard stopped lying to himself. *Of course, they would know.* There were appointment calendars and sign-in sheets. He glanced down at the white tag pasted to his label. Security informed and badges issued.

Secrecy was never going to work. If anything, they needed *more* transparency, more light shined on what was actually happening to the world. Richard pushed open the door into the senator's outer office.

The staff didn't make him wait. Moments later Richard was in Aldo's personal office. Richard was surprised when Aldo left the power position behind the desk and indicated a pair of deeply upholstered chairs clustered around a low coffee table. They sat down, and for a long moment just regarded each other. Richard sensed the older man was taking his measure.

Fortunately, quiet had never bothered Richard. He'd never felt the need to rush into conversation, and it gave him the time to study the man as carefully as he was being studied. Even in repose Aldo was an imposing figure. Six foot four, with broad, thick shoulders, and a neck as wide as his ears. Despite his age he hadn't run much to fat. Richard glanced over at the Heisman Trophy on the bookcase, and the framed Silver Star that hung above it. Suddenly he felt very intimidated by this man. Why on earth would he listen to anything he had to say?

Aldo leaned back in his chair, fingers steepled before his face. "So, the message made this sound like the fate of the nation was hanging in the balance, and you were our only hope."

The talking heads on the news channels described him as blunt rather than charming. Richard concluded that they weren't kidding. He felt his face flame with embarrassment, and his knee began jiggling nervously. Richard laid a hand on it, trying to hold it still. "Well, I wouldn't … I don't know who phrased it quite … well, it's half true," he stammered.

"Which half?"

It should have come across as harsh, but Richard caught the twinkle in the man's eyes. He smiled. "Oh, come on, sir. You didn't actually think I'd say the second half, did you?"

A smile split the craggy angles of his face. "You'd be surprised. Politics is an egomaniac's game. A lot of my compatriots would totally have taken a bow."

"First, I'm not a politician. Second … you are."

A rumbling chuckle shook the barrel chest. "Touché. Fortunately for you I know your father. Six years ago, Judge Oort and I joined forces to oppose presidential signing statements. I respect your father, despite our political differences, and somehow, I don't think his son would be a liar."

"I'm not, sir."

"So, what is it you want to tell me?" Aldo asked.

Richard caught the piercing gleam in his brown eyes, and suddenly he knew what to say. "I don't need to tell you anything, sir. You're on the Intelligence and Homeland Security committees. You've no doubt seen the satellite images. You know this goes *way* beyond a foiled plot to detonate a nuke. That it's much, much worse."

He leaned slowly back in his chair. "Those are classified. One call and I could put you in a world of hurt."

"And I can say I never saw those images. Remember, I was *there* when the gate first opened."

"A gate. Why do you call it that?"

"Because it's an opening through which an invading army is entering our world, and the government isn't doing squat. What's happening in Virginia and Jerusalem and India requires a unified and international response." Richard found he couldn't sit still. He jumped up and started limping back and forth. "It may be there's a military solution to what's happening, but whatever action we take, it needs to be coordinated and guided from the highest levels. This isn't something the governor, the state police, or the National Guard can handle. America is the last superpower. The President must act. I need to get in to see him. And you're the man who can make that happen."

Aldo lowered his hands and began beating out a rhythm on the arms of the chair, while his big, square-jawed head swiveled slowly, assessing the pictures on the wall. Richard followed his gaze. Most of them were photos of the senator with five different presidents.

After a long moment he looked back at Richard. "Initially

the FBI supported your position, but they've backed off that, and now they're in agreement with the NSA and Langley."

"And what might the NSA and Langley be saying?" Richard asked.

Aldo's lips never parted when he smiled. The corners of his mouth just stretched, making his cheeks more prominent. "That's classified."

Richard discovered that frustration could have an actual taste. He clenched his hand on the cane and gritted his teeth, as he struggled to hold back the profanity.

"Yeah, it makes you crazy, doesn't it?" the senator said softly. "I'll tell you this much. Lobbing a bomb into an area where guns, radios, cameras, and so forth don't work wouldn't be all that effective."

"Meaning they tried it," Richard said heavily. He sank back into the chair.

Aldo just smiled again. "But of course, a place where weapons don't operate would also have some really interesting applications for a government that understood and controlled that technology."

This time Richard couldn't keep control. The words burst out, hot and intemperate. "It's not technology! It can't be controlled. And any moron who tries is going to end up dead or worse."

"There's a worse?"

"Oh, yes. And these things that are pouring through the gates are going to prove that to us."

Suddenly Aldo leaned forward. He was so tall that he came almost completely across the coffee table, leaving his face only inches from Richard's. He could smell the breath mint he'd chewed. "And why should I believe *you* over all these security experts and alphabet soup agencies?"

It was not in Richard's nature to get in people's faces; it was something he'd had to learn. But learn it he had. He leaned forward and was surprised when Aldo retreated. Richard pursued the advantage, saying, "Because I've come here at no small personal risk to offer my help. I could have stayed in New Mexico and been safe for a little while longer. But sooner or later it will be *everywhere*. It will cover the world. *Unless we do something.*"

Aldo leaned back in his chair and regarded Richard for a long, long time. "What do you do, son?"

The question surprised him, and Richard answered instinctively. "I'm a policeman."

"I thought you were the head of Lumina Enterprises."

"I'm that, too, but ..." Richard pulled out his badge case, opened it, and studied the badge. The light from the ceiling fixture gleamed on the gold shield. The hilt, perched precariously atop the cane, leaned heavily against his knee. and for one strange, distorting moment the shield seemed to expand until it filled Richard's sight, blotting out the room.

He was jerked back to the moment when a hand fell heavily onto his shoulder. Aldo was looming over him, holding a glass of water.

"Here."

"Thank you." He took a sip. Clearly lack of sleep was catching up with him if he was having waking hallucinations.

"Well, you're not telling me everything. Not by a long way," the senator said. He paused. The silence was excruciating. Then he suddenly added, "But that can wait until we sit down with the President."

Richard nearly spilled the water in his lap in his haste to set aside the glass and stand. "You'll do it? You'll get me in?"

"Can you tell us why people are losing their minds?"

"Yes, sir, I can."

"Can you tell us what these things are?"

"Yes."

"Can you tell us how to fight them?"

"Yes."

Richard hoped his bravura performance was enough to hide the fact that his final answer was a lie.

"You'll be ready to go at any time?" Aldo asked as he moved back to his desk.

"Day or night, sir."

"I'll be in touch."

It was dismissal. Richard gathered up his cane, then hesitated at the door. He looked back. "Sir." Aldo looked up from the papers he was reading. "By helping me you could be endangering your life. Please, be careful."

"Always am."

Yeah, but you don't know that one of them was in the hall outside your office.

That they can walk through walls.

That they can use magic against you because I wasn't able to inoculate you.

Because that really would *have been a bridge too far.*

Richard grappled with his tumbling thoughts, then let himself out, and went limping through the outer office. It was humming with activity. He noted that the senator's staff tended to be young and passionate. At one desk a couple of staffers were reviewing legislation. At a corner table a trio of young women shook actual letters out of a mailbag.

As Richard passed the receptionist's desk, she looked up and gave him a white-toothed smile. Her perfectly coiffed and sprayed hair didn't move.

"Have a blessed day," she chirped.

Richard got into the hall, leaned against the wall, and fought back nausea.

They were surrounded.

CHAPTER EIGHTEEN

PLEASING FATHERS

THEY FOUND A restaurant right on the beach. Pamela watched the waves rush forward and then retreat with a hiss and a chuckle, like mischievous children begging the grown-ups to chase them. Running in pursuit of the white foam were tiny, long-legged birds pecking at the wet sand.

Pamela leaned back in the fan-backed wicker chair and took another sip of her green appletini. Her lobster thermidor had been wonderful and very rich. Eddie Tanaka was still masticating his way through a giant plate of fried seafood and French fries. He had downed five refills of Coke thus far. She could only conclude that he burned off the calories with the caffeine high. She had finished first because Eddie had been punctuating bites with tales of his escape from Indonesia.

"I was really careful not to speak English. I mean, I'd watched them burn down the American and the British embassies, and I speak some Japanese so I could fake people out, but man, it was scary. I got down to the docks and managed to get on this old freighter. I got lucky—one of Talafani's crew had landed in jail, and he didn't want to brave the city when things were going nuts. I was there. I'm tall, and I didn't seem nuts. So, he hired me."

He stuffed a breaded jumbo shrimp into his mouth, and Pamela watched his throat work as he swallowed the massive bite. A Coke chaser and he was back talking.

"You know how people are always talking about the romance of working a tramp steamer, exotic ports of call, sloe-eyed women in the exotic ports—well, I can tell you it's a total crock. They ought to ban kids' reading Hemingway. Anyway, Captain Talafani worked us like slaves, and I was awful seasick, but he expected me to keep working anyway." The outrage rang in his voice. "I'm *never* eating curry again. We had a lot of curry, and it just turns your vomit yellow and it's like eating it again only worse."

"TMI, Dr. Tanaka," Pamela said.

"Oh, yeah, sorry. Even though this was a really big ship …" He spread his arms out like a fisherman displaying a prize catch. "There were only fourteen of us on board—automation's really changed things—and none of them would talk to me." He considered and then added, "They didn't talk to each other either, but I didn't totally get how much they were channeling Greta Garbo until one guy punched me in the stomach. That made me sick all over again, and I was blowing chunks—"

Pamela interrupted a new rendition of exactly what he'd eaten and how it looked when it came back up. "The police said you came ashore in a lifeboat. Why did you leave the ship?"

"'Cause Talafani was steaming right back to Libya, and I wasn't sure I could get home from there." For an instant his gaze seemed lost, and distant, and frightened. He quickly ate an oyster.

"I really sucked up to the captain. He liked this gross, really sweet tea with condensed milk in it, and I kept bringing it up to the bridge for him. I finally got a look at the charts, and realized this chunk of coral represented the Sylph. That was the ship's name. Anyway, I saw we were close to Australia, so I stole food out of the galley, filled some empty bourbon bottles with water, and hid them in the lifeboat. I waited for the first moonless night, and then lowered the lifeboat, and dove into the water after it. I had to swim like hell to catch up with it. It got caught in the ship's wake."

"You dove off the side of a commercial freighter?"

Eddie shrugged. "I grew up in San Diego, practically in the water. And I was a competitive diver in high school and college. It was no worse than a platform dive." He mopped up more ketchup with several French fries and gobbled them down. A few more massive bites and the last of the breaded fish was also gone. He drained his glass, burped, and sighed.

"All set?" Pamela asked.

He nodded. "You're taking me back to California, right?"

"Actually, no, my brother needs to talk to you first."

"He can come to California." He sounded pugnacious, and Pamela decided it wasn't the right moment to argue with him. Then he added in a little boy's voice, "I want to go home. I want to see my folks."

For the first time she realized how terribly young he was, and she saw the fear that he'd been holding at bay.

✧   ✧   ✧

THE VISIT TO Britches, Washington's premier old-line men's clothier, had been necessitated because Grenier could barely zip his slacks closed over his burgeoning paunch. As he had told Richard, he needed a new wardrobe before he was arrested for indecent exposure. The young man had taken a look at the pale skin and graying chest hair revealed by the gaping buttons and quickly agreed.

Grenier had really stressed that they make this outing together because there were things he needed to report, and he didn't want that gray presence of the judge interfering with Richard's natural cunning. Aside from the ever-present guards they were alone, which suited Grenier just fine. He hated the judge's constant hovering over Richard. It had stopped seeming protective and had started to feel more like a doctor making sure a mental patient didn't do something dangerous or foolish. Grenier had only been with Lumina for a short time, but he couldn't find the young man who had defied him, challenged him, and played him for a fool. Instead, Richard had retreated to hesitant childhood.

While these thoughts ran through his head, Grenier was issuing orders to a young salesman. "I want a gray suit with a small pinstripe of lavender. I want a blue suit with a pinstripe of yellow and brown. And I want the buttonholes enlarged. I have to work one-handed. Also, a selection of slacks and shirts, and a black sports coat. Go." He waved the young man away. "Oh, and shoes, wing tips in black and brown, size ten—"

"And who's going to tie them?" Richard asked. He had his back to Grenier and was sifting through a stack of cashmere sweaters displayed on a polished cherrywood table.

Grenier flushed and couldn't control the glance down at his stump.

The rush of fury, regret, and grief left him breathless. He regained control and said smoothly, "An excellent point. Thank you, Richard." He turned back to the clerk. "Loafers, then, and let's try a C width." He joined Richard and said in an undertone, "Even my feet are getting fat. I didn't know that could happen."

"You could try eating less."

"Leave me a few of my pleasures. You've taken so much from me." Their gazes locked, and Richard looked away out the front window. Grenier watched Richard stiffen. "What?"

Richard indicated a car driving slowly past with a jerk of his chin.

It was a BMW convertible. The driver's long black hair floated around her, and though her eyes and much of her face were hidden behind large dark glasses and a muffler, it was clear she was gazing at the store.

"My, my," Grenier said.

The car passed the store and suddenly accelerated away.

"So, you said your barhopping had yielded results?" Richard asked.

"You're not going to deal with that?" Grenier asked and pointed at the rapidly dwindling car.

"What would you suggest? Run down the street with the sword drawn? Shoot her in the head? And she's careful never to give me a chance to get close to her."

"So, this isn't the first time you've seen her." Richard shook his head. "Why haven't you mentioned it?"

"Because everyone would start clucking."

Grenier chuckled. "Good point." He hurried into speech after seeing Richard's impatience. "Ah, yes, what I've learned. The Cardinal of Washington, DC, has sent for a team of experts from the Vatican. No details on what kind of experts, but I think it can only mean one thing. They're going to try an exorcism."

Richard gave a short bark of laughter. "Whoa, wow, I bet the Old Ones are scared now."

"I think the Old Ones will let it … work." Grenier bracketed the words with quote marks in the air with his one hand. "Miracles will occur, stigmata will bleed, the Madonna will cry, maybe even the face of Jesus will appear in some interesting foodstuff. The Catholic faithful will be ecstatic. But in the evangelical churches the preachers will be thundering from their pulpits that this is the Antichrist, and that the Catholics, by worshiping a false god, are preventing the real Jesus from returning."

"Oh, the Catholics hate the Protestants, and the Protestants hate the Catholics, and the Hindus hate the Moslems, and everybody hates the Jews." Richard softly sang the old Tom Lehrer song.

"Exactly. Also, word about the sword is leaking out. People are talking, at least in the bureaucracy. If we verify its existence, I think you'll have takers just like you did with those FBI agents."

"Career bureaucrats may not set policy, but they actually run the government," Richard mused. "We need a mechanism for meeting with them. I can't just go walking in and out of agencies whacking people with a sword."

"If Aldo succeeds and you manage to see the President,

he may mandate it," Grenier said.

The young salesman returned. "Sir," he said diffidently to Grenier, "I have a selection of clothing for you to try."

"Thank you, I'll be right there," Grenier said. He waved the man away. "There's one more thing we need to consider—media." Grenier watched as Richard's nostrils narrowed with disdain. He threw back his head and laughed. "God, you old blue-blood families and your elitist attitudes. It's the twenty-first century, baby." He reached out and patted Richard on the cheek. He was surprised when Richard didn't jerk away as he had every other time Grenier tried for physical contact.

Richard sighed. "I know you're right. You've got the experience. Are you willing to take it on?"

Grenier struggled to hide his surprise. "You're actually going to give me some responsibility?"

"Yes."

"Power?"

"Limited."

"Okay. Money is no object, so let's have some very slick and very scary commercials made, and air them nationally. Interviews, articles, blogs, Web sites, podcasts, chat rooms ..."

Richard's phone rang. "Oort."

Grenier watched as all the color drained from the young man's face, and his eyes seemed suddenly dark and sunken. Richard hung up the phone and looked up at Grenier.

"Aldo's been killed."

✧ ✧ ✧

THE VIBRATION FROM the engines seemed to have permanently embedded itself in her bones. Pamela sighed and leaned her head against the plane's window. At least the seats in the company jet were wide and very comfortable. They even went flat so you could sleep. But that constant thrum! She shook her head and picked back up the Bose headphones. They helped with the engine noise and the Eddie noise. The young scientist snored like a log stripper.

There had been a bit of a kerfuffle when they stopped to refuel in Los Angeles. Eddie had tried to get off, saying he needed to stretch his legs, but Pamela had caught the furtive look toward the small building and the cars in the parking lot, and said no. It hadn't escalated because Pamela had the very good idea to have Brook stand in the door of the plane and openly wear a pistol. Apparently, Tanaka's high IQ allowed him to add two and two.

Pamela looked out the window again. They were flying over the great flat empty of the Midwest. Much of it was snow covered, and Pamela wondered what the people in those small towns and farms thought, or even knew, about what was happening. It was a part of the country that grew wheat, made cheese, and sent kids into the army and Republicans into Congress.

Eddie awoke with a snort and a mumble. He gave her a bleary-eyed look across the aisle. "Hungry. Gonna make a sandwich. Want one?"

She shook her head and turned back on the music she'd been listening to, and watched the clouds they were now flying over. Occasionally wisps of cloud swirled up, smoke like, to caress the wings of the plane.

Eddie returned from the galley with a true Dagwood sandwich, piled high with turkey, pastrami, and liverwurst. He settled back into his seat; his jaw seemed to crack in half as he took a bite. He glanced out the window, let out a whimper, and lettuce and lunch meat rained into his lap.

Pamela unsnapped her seat belt and rushed over to him. "What? Are you all right?"

He pointed wordlessly. His hand was shaking. Pamela looked out the window at another plane that was rising through the clouds like a breaching silver whale.

There were winged *creatures* beneath the wings and belly of the plane. Holding it up. Slowly one of the massive heads turned and *looked* at them.

Pamela jerked down the shade over the window, as if that could somehow protect them. The door to the cockpit was open, and Brook turned a face gone white with fear toward them, and yelled, "Hang on!"

Then a sudden banking of the Gulfstream sent her falling against Eddie. He caught her, and they both clung to whatever they could grab until the plane came out of its dive. Even after they leveled out Pamela didn't try to pull free. Instead, she wrapped her arms around him, too, taking comfort in his human touch.

✧   ✧   ✧

"WOULD THE TWO of you care to explain why I had to arrange the murder of a United States senator?" Madoc said as he continued to stare in rapt contemplation of the delicate Japanese painting of cranes in a snowy landscape.

They were in the Freer and Sackler Galleries at the Smithsonian Institution. Despite Madoc's mild, almost plaintive tone, Rhiana took a step back and to the side, so she was standing partly behind Jack. Neither of them dared to answer.

"I thought you were getting the sword and neutralizing the Paladin. Not letting the Paladin nearly reach the President. So, when do we get the sword?" Madoc asked.

"Why does it matter so much?" Jack asked. "You've told us the sword alone can't close a gate. So what if Oort gets to the President, or the Joint Chiefs, or the Chamber of Commerce for that matter. They throw more troopies at you, you kill them or make them nuts, and hey, it's all-you-can-eat night, right?"

"Because you fool, *we* have a Paladin. If we also have the sword, we can kill competitors." Jack flinched. "Now go and get this done." Madoc sat down on a bench and stared at the paintings again.

Neither of them spoke until they were walking down the Mall toward the gleaming white spire of the Washington Monument.

"So, what's with the art connoisseur? The past three times I've met with him, it's been in art galleries or museums," Jack said. The sound of his voice sent a trio of crows flapping up into the sky like animated apostrophes. "Or is he just planning which ones he's going to steal after the great monster conquest?"

"They don't get creativity. Music's alien to them, too. They don't even like to hear it," Rhiana answered. The dried winter grass crunched beneath the soles of her boots. There was a brisk wind whipping the hem of her sable coat around her ankles. It smelled of impending snow.

"Huh. I wonder what that means."

"That they're aliens," Rhiana said shortly.

Once again silence stretched between them, then Jack said, "So, it sounds like it's not all Universal Monster Brotherhood." He tried to keep it light, but the worry crept in. "I thought I was safe because I was on your team, so to speak, only now I find out there's an NFL and an AFL. Did I pick the wrong team?"

"I don't know, Jack; you want to try getting traded?"

Her long hair, caught by the wind, snaked across her mouth and eyes. She clawed it back and held it in a mock ponytail as she said, "You need to call Sandringham. He's got to get this done."

"He will," Jack said. "He's a smart, methodical guy. He's not going to rush this and blow it. He knows these people. For years. He'll play it right."

"But we need to rush. If the others learn we have a Paladin and we're after the sword, they're going to gang up on us. We need the sword to protect us," Rhiana said, and it gave her a perverse pleasure to watch Jack's expression go from worried to outright sick.

"Great, I'm in a fucking shark cage."

"Yeah, well, I'm in it, too! I'm the one who said I could get him."

Jack stopped walking, stepped in front of her, and put his hands on her shoulders; they were warm and heavy. "Rhiana."

But she didn't see Jack or hear his voice. Instead, she

heard and saw Richard. He had said her name. And then he held out his hand to her and said, *And I choose you.*

If only that had been true.

Emboldened by her silence, Jack slipped an arm around her shoulders. "Hey, at least it won't be so lonely with two in the cage," and she felt his lips against her forehead. She yanked away from him.

"Don't! Just don't. I don't want *you.*"

✧ ✧ ✧

JOSEPH PICKED THEM up at the private airstrip in Maryland, and Pamela was surprised to find Richard had ridden out with him. She wasn't surprised that Weber had come along, too. Once she realized her brother was there it was inevitable that Weber would be as well, they seemed to be joined at the hip.

As Richard entered the body of the Gulfstream he held out his hand to Eddie. "Doctor Tanaka, I'm Ri—"

Before he could finish the young scientist was on him, gripping Richard tightly by the shoulders, and Weber was tensing, his hand reaching for his pistol. "Oh, God, it was awful. There were these things, and there were things in the sky ... with a plane ... and they killed everybody." The words fell from his lips like spilled marbles, he was utterly incoherent and obviously terrified.

Richard laid a hand on Eddie's shoulder and given it a gentle squeeze. "You've been incredibly brave and very smart to have managed to escape." Then Richard surprised Pamela by adding, "But maybe we should let my sister explain." He leaned in to say softly into Eddie's ear, "She's very good with words." He gave Eddie that smile that had always irritated the hell out of Pamela, but this time she was grateful for it because Eddie relaxed and nodded.

Pamela quickly recounted what she had learned from Eddie about the events at the lab, but when she got to a description of what they'd seen beneath the wings of the other airplane, she was having trouble keeping her voice level and her hands from shaking.

"It saw me, Richard. It looked right at me." She looked away, staring down at the floor.

Richard put his arm around her shoulders and gave her a tight hug. "I won't let it," he'd said softly, and she was surprised when she felt gratitude welling up like a warm bubble into her chest, and even more surprised when she realized she believed him, and she somehow felt safer.

Richard had started to turn for the door when Weber had said quietly, "Richard, before we bring home another stray you need to do the thing."

The two men's eyes met for a long moment, then Richard nodded, reached behind his back and removed the hilt from its holster.

"This is the hilt of a sword ..."

Pamela didn't need to hear it again, and honestly Richard had said it so many times now that it was beginning to sound rote. She sank back into a seat, arms hugging her chest. Depending on how the scientist reacted they could be here awhile.

Weber surprised her by taking the seat opposite her. "How you doin'?"

"I'm fine—" He raised an eyebrow at her. She bit her lip and shook her head. "I'm not okay. That thing ... it'll know me if it sees me again." She wet her lips with the tip of her tongue. "And it wants to hurt me."

Weber laid a hand on her knee, gave it a comforting squeeze.

Richard had reached the point where he drew the blade. The overtones filled the cockpit while Eddie breathed out, "Cool beans! Gotta be a pocket universe," he was jabbering. "Non-Euclidian or some—" The blade touched his shoulder, he gave a grunt of surprise and pain and collapsed.

It didn't seem to have hurt him as much as it had others, and Eddie had soon recovered. As they trooped to the car, Pamela said to Weber, "Dr. Tanaka's reaction does rather support Richard's theories that a grounding in math, science, and music seemed to reduce a person's quotient of magic."

"Which is kind of weird when you think about it; most people would probably say that creativity is magical."

"Maybe that's what *they* wanted us to think," Pamela replied.

During the ride to the condo Richard gave Eddie a crash course on the world according to Lumina, and Pamela turned on her phone and checked her messages. She had three from Amelia. Only the final one told Pamela what was on her older sister's mind.

"Hey, Pammie, I know you're with Richard and I know he's really busy, but could you please get him to call Brent back? My husband's about ready to kill our brother, and I'm in the middle, which is not a fun place to be. Thanks. Love ya."

Pamela looked over at her brother, but Richard was deep

into the explanation, and she hesitated to interrupt. Then when they reached the condo Grenier took one look at their wan faces and ordered everyone into the kitchen, saying, "My mother always said that when people are stressed, scared, and tired you feed them."

"Whether your mom ever said that or not is probably irrelevant," Weber grunted. "I expect you'd love any excuse for a second lunch or tea or whatever." Grenier gave him a withering look as they headed into the kitchen.

They started to follow, but their father held Richard back. The judge had his glasses perched on his nose, and he was frowning down at a piece of paper. "I have a list of legislators we need to visit. Not one of them is as powerful as Aldo, but perhaps a coalition can be formed."

Richard had stepped away. "Not now."

"This needs to be—"

"I said, *not now.*" And Richard walked away.

Pamela's stomach became a small aching ball when she watched her father's face twist with pure rage. The judge stalked away, and Pamela dithered between running after him or joining the others in the kitchen. *Richard shouldn't have been rude,* she thought as she tried to catch her breath. *But Papa keeps bemoaning the fact that Richard is so biddable.* There had been plenty of times when he snapped at Richard for not taking control of his life, making decisions, and living with his choices.

But the one time Richard did, the big choice when he became a policeman, Papa was furious. Maybe Richard never can please him.

She was horrified by the traitorous thought. She shook it off and rushed into the kitchen.

CHAPTER NINETEEN

WHAT WE'VE GOT IS YOU

DAGMAR HAD WEBER sautéing the Italian sausage for the lasagna. Rudi stood at another burner toasting fresh garlic to go on the bread. The blade of a knife clacked against the wood cutting board like a rhythm-impaired flamenco dancer as Sam chopped the ingredients for an enormous salad. *Figures she'd be good with a knife,* Damon thought.

Syd was dropping lasagna noodles into a pot of boiling water, and Joseph was grating cheese while Estevan pulled down plates and grabbed silverware out of the drawer. Richard came into the kitchen, followed soon after by his sister.

"How can I—" Richard began.

"You can sit down," Damon ordered. Richard gave a half-nod, moved to the table, and dropped heavily into a chair. Pamela gave Damon a look he couldn't fully interpret then moved to Dagmar to ask how she could help. She was handed a box of brownie mix and a package of pecans and told to start on that.

Weber looked back to Richard to see that the young scientist, Eddie Tanaka, had landed on his left, and Grenier on Richard's right. The preacher was idly spinning a wineglass by its stem while Eddie had his chair so close that his thigh was almost touching Richard's. Weber had noticed that as they moved from plane to car, and car to condo, and around the condo, Tanaka had walked directly next to Richard, his arm often brushing against Richard's shoulder. Damon snorted softly, wondering how Richard liked having a duckling.

Estevan began setting the table. Richard motioned him close and said something that Weber couldn't hear. A jab in Damon's ribs reminded him to keep an eye on the sausage. When he eventually got to look back to the table, a laptop had appeared, and Tanaka was hyperfocused on the screen. He had his elbows on the table and his chin cupped in his hands, watching satellite images from the gate. Damon suppressed a shudder. He had to respect, but also faintly resented, the scientist's ability to look at the pictures with fascination rather than the gut-churning terror it engendered in himself.

Since the lasagna was now being assembled, and he was no longer needed, Damon drifted closer so he could listen in.

"Rhiana called it slow glass," Richard offered as Eddie continued to watch and didn't respond.

"She must not be very bright. That term was used in a really great science fiction story, 'Light of Other Days' by Bob Shaw, but the *technical* term"—Eddie leaned back in his chair and gestured at the computer—"is a Bose-Einstein condensate. But this doesn't look like a condensate." Eddie suddenly jerked his head around to look at where Joseph spun the handle on the Mouli, grating Parmesan cheese over the garlic-and-butter-drenched bread. "Oh, gross," Eddie said. "Cheese on garlic bread is gross."

There was an almost audible sound as everyone tried to shift gears mentally. Joseph looked down at the skinny young scientist.

"So, don't eat any. *We* all like it with cheese."

Eddie got a funny look on his face, and his lips moved as if he were repeating something to himself. "I'm sorry," he said formally to Joseph. "That was rude of me."

Richard took back control. "So, if it's not a condensate, what is it?"

"I think it's a spin glass," Eddie said.

"And what's that when it's at home?" Weber asked.

"It's a way to slow or even freeze light so you can study its properties," Eddie answered.

"Why the fuck would you want to do that?" Sam asked as she washed her hands.

"Because it's really cool, but here's an explanation even *you* might get," Eddie said. "It's got economic applications. It's a way to build a quantum computer that would be screamingly fast. Whoever succeeds gets really, really rich."

"But how does this trap Kenntnis?" Dagmar asked before Sam could blow a gasket.

"And these things are real?" Syd's question tripped over the COO's.

Eddie started with Syd's question. "Yeah. They've been created in the laboratory. Cornell, Wieman, and Ketterle won the Nobel back in 2001. But they don't withstand contact with the real world, so this thing"—he gestured at the computer screen—"shouldn't exist. Of course, who the hell knows what's real anymore. And it certainly can't trap a person." He laid a pencil against the screen. "It looks to be only a few centimeters wide."

Richard cleared his throat, a nervous little sound, and he looked from person to person, ending with Dagmar. He cast his eyes upward. "Well, actually I don't think ... in fact, I'm pretty sure ... that Kenntnis isn't human."

Dagmar sank into a chair. "Oh, dear, I was coping so well, and now you add this."

"We're talking about my employer. The man I've worked for for seven years?" Joseph asked.

"'Fraid so," Richard said.

"Rhiana said ..." Richard closed his eyes trying to recall. "Slow glass traps light, and she said that's all Kenntnis was—just light."

Eddie hunched into the computer screen again, narrowing his eyes.

A few clicks of the mouse enlarged the image.

Eddie leaned back in his chair. "Okay, let's assume for a minute that I'm not crazy and something that you thought was a person was actually just a stream of photons. And you wanted to trap it. The experiments have shown that you can store light's information in the form of an atomic spin wave. Atoms spin like tops, so they sort of act like little bar magnets. So, what you do is introduce the light signal—a probe laser, but in our case it's this guy, Kenntnis—into the glass. At the same time, you use another laser, a pump or control laser, to create electromagnetically induced transparency. Then the light interacts with the atoms, which changes the atoms' spin states coherently, and that creates a joint atom-photon system, and that's called a polariton."

"Help," Syd said, and the word was a plaintive squeak.

"I guess another part of being such a big brain genius is you can't put anything in simple English," Sam remarked to the room, indulging in a little payback.

Eddie looked up at the young agent. "Yeah, I guess you'd need it simple."

Sam leaned down and held up two fingers. "That's *two*. One more and I'm gonna punch you real hard in the stomach." Eddie looked alarmed, Sam looked satisfied, and Richard looked pissed.

"Stop it. I don't have time for this kind of childish bull-shit."

"Hey," Sam squawked. "That's one to *you*."

"I mean it."

Damon had never heard that tone in the young man's voice before, and he felt a flare of pride.

"Go on," Richard ordered Eddie.

"Okay, well, what that means is that it weighs down the massless photons and continues to slow down the pulse's speed. You keep adding mass and eventually the light pulse stops moving, and the information that the pulse carried is stored in the atomic spin wave. It can be released again as a light pulse, and it's virtually identical to the frozen pulse." Then the young scientist realized that everyone was staring at him in varying degrees of desperate concentration. "You're taking this seriously?" he asked, disbelief tinging the words.

Richard turned until he faced the young scientist full on. "Yes. We really are."

"But this isn't real," Eddie protested feebly.

Grenier spoke up for the first time. "You said yourself, son, you don't know what's real anymore. Your scientific principles still apply, but they're being affected, warped, by the magic."

"Magic isn't real," Eddie said. The frown and tightly compressed lips showed the level of his denial.

"It is. And getting more real by the minute," Grenier countered. His voice was thick with amused enjoyment.

"That's enough for him right now." Richard stood up. "Dr. Tanaka, you're tired, you need to process what I told you about the Lumina and the multiverses, and you need to come up with a plan to break Kenntnis free. How did you put it? Release the pulse. But right now, I've got other things, mundane but pressing, that I have to do."

Eddie looked up at Dagmar. "You won't let me sleep through dinner?"

She laughed. "We'll ring the dinner bell very loudly."

"I'd like to study that sword thing," Eddie mumbled as he headed out of the kitchen. "But if it won't stay in phase unless he's holding it, how do ..."

Distance reduced the words to a baritone hum, and then they were gone with the shutting of a bedroom door.

Weber stepped to Richard's side. "You should rest, too."

"Can't. Papa had some things to discuss, and Dagmar wants me to ..." His voice trailed away, and he made a vague gesture with his hand.

Damon watched him walk away with an ache in his chest.

❖   ❖   ❖

IT WAS LIKE feeling eyes or tasting a change in the air. *Someone was in the bedroom with him.* Richard opened his eyes to the barest slit. Fortunately, there was enough city glare leaking around the folds of the drapes to make out shapes. A shadow within the shadows hovered at the side of the bed. His stomach gave a lurch, and suddenly his determination to keep his guards outside the condo seemed beyond stupid. These were people who could travel across the continent using a tear in a wall.

Richard dropped a hand off the side of the mattress, and his fingers touched the textured edge of the pistol's grip hidden beneath the bed. Once he had the gun firmly in hand, he shot his right hand up and grabbed the material at the person's throat, dragging him down. At the same time, Richard brought up the pistol and jammed the barrel deep in under the intruder's short ribs.

There was came a *woof* as the air was driven out of his lungs and a strangled squeak of fear. Richard's eyes had adjusted to the gloom, and he found himself face-to-face with Eddie Tanaka. The young scientist's breath, blowing across Richard's face, was unpleasantly sour. The small amount of lasagna Richard had managed to choke down was threatening to make a return.

"What do you want? What are you doing in here?" he demanded, and Eddie recoiled. Richard realized the words had emerged in a harsh, tense whisper.

"I ... I had a question." The words emerged as a croak because Richard had the material twisted tight against his larynx.

Richard glanced at his wristwatch and tried to process that. "You came into my bedroom at *3:12 AM* to *ask me a question?*"

"Yeah."

"It couldn't wait until morning?"

"I couldn't sleep," came the disingenuous answer.

"Well, *I* could. Was."

Not that it had been easy. Watching the red sauce bubbling had taken Richard back to the house on Quincy, and Aldo's death had left him feeling like this entire excursion had been a waste of time and fucking dangerous as well. Richard truly didn't have a clue about what to do next. And added to all this there was Rhiana. He had spotted her BMW ineptly following the limo as they had returned from the airport. Since it was no secret where they were going Richard had said nothing, just let her follow, but it was scary and confusing. If he could ever have three seconds to himself, he needed to analyze her behavior and try to figure out what was behind it.

Tanaka frowned. "Oh, yeah. Didn't think about that. Do ... do you think you could take the gun out of my side? And then answer my question?"

Richard sighed and released him and set the Heckler & Koch back under the bed. "Okay."

"You always keep a gun with you?" Tanaka asked.

"That was the question?"

"Uh. No. But do you always keep a gun with you?"

Richard was suddenly wavering between screaming annoyance and laughter. He thought back on his psychology classes in college. *Asperger's. It had to be Asperger's syndrome.*

"Yes."

"Why?"

"Because people keep trying to kill me."

Tanaka's eyes widened. "Wow. Really?"

"Yes, really. Can we get to the question?" Richard prodded.

The scientist sat down on the mattress. His hip was pressed against Richard's thigh. Fortunately, it wasn't his right leg. "I've never seen anybody die before ... before ... Indonesia," the young man said. "When my grandma was dying, I wouldn't go in the hospital room until it was all over. And I get the shakes just thinking about ... what happened."

"Dr. Tanaka, forgive me, but it's late and I'm tired. Is that question at least on approach? Will it be arriving soon?"

"Oh, yeah, sorry. And could you call me Eddie? I get real uncomfortable when people call me doctor." Richard nodded. "Anyway, they said you used to be a policeman. So, have you ever killed anybody?"

"Yes." It was such a small word to encompass so much, but Richard didn't amplify.

"Is it hard to do?" Eddie asked. "I mean, would the way I feel about seeing people die affect ... I mean, keep me from—"

"Killing someone?" Richard broke in.

"Yeah. Did it bother you? When you killed them?" Eddie asked.

Richard stood on the edge of a sea of complex emotions—horror, grief, guilt, pride, excitement. He was afraid he'd drown if he went in. "Yes. Look, Eddie, if you don't have to kill people, I don't think you should."

"But I want them to pay! For what they did ... to everybody!"

Richard laid a hand over the young scientist's and felt

Eddie's fingers close convulsively over his. "You figure out how to free Kenntnis. That's a far better thing to do for the memory of your friends," Richard said gently.

Eddie stood, and his hand slipped free. Richard's hand felt suddenly very cold. "Thanks." He got almost to the door before he slewed around like a gawky foal and added, "Oh, yeah, I'm sorry I woke you up." Eddie slipped out of the room.

Richard pummeled a pillow, trying to get some lift in the feathers. He was now wide-awake, and he was faced with another trek back up the hill to Congress today. He tried to think about what he had to do, had to say, who to convince, but disjointed thoughts and memories kept flashing like brief bursts of lightning through his mind. He saw the blood pumping from a head wound when he'd shot the perp who nearly killed his partner. The bone chips flying when he'd killed Snyder. There was another thought buried deep. Richard dug it up and looked at it. He wanted to confront the man who'd brutalized him and let a bullet peel back skin and muscle and listen to him scream. It wouldn't be hard; Drew Sandringham was a quick flight up the coast in New York City.

The brutal fantasy shattered when faced with the tangible reality of killing a man he'd known for most of his life. Maybe he wasn't really a killer. Which should have made Richard feel better, but instead he felt only depression, as if he didn't have the grit to do what needed to be done.

All these thoughts of death had him thinking about morgues, which triggered a memory of a conversation with Angela just before they had left. She had told him about the dead scientists from the Santa Fe Institute. Like a puzzle piece, it snapped into place with the killings in Indonesia.

Richard lunged out of bed and made a limping run into the living room.

Laptops, their lids gleaming silver, lay on various surfaces like tiles in a giant's Mahjongg set. He found one open and still running. Logging onto VICAP, Richard typed in *scientists* and *murders*.

The list of incidents scrolled by for a long, long time. And that was just crimes in the United States.

✧   ✧   ✧

EARLY THE NEXT morning, Grenier looked up from his book at the sound of Richard's voice approaching down the hallway of the condo.

What emerged into the living room looked like an Aaron Sorkin walk and talk scene in a television show. Richard, walking quickly, the limp now barely evident, was pulling on gloves. Dagmar was on one side, Weber on the other. Tanaka, towering over everyone, looked like a wading stork. Behind him were the judge and Pamela, and bringing up the rear were Joseph and Rudi.

"I've blanketed all of our scientific facilities with security," Dagmar was saying.

"And alerted local law enforcement?" Weber asked.

"Alerted and paid off as necessary depending on the part of the world where they are located," Dagmar replied.

"Is it enough?" Richard ran an agitated hand through his hair. "Depending on how badly they've been affected by the gates, the guards might turn on our people. And they're functionally mercenaries. We bought them. Someone else could buy them." His breath was growing short, panic lacing the words. "Do we need to get our people out?"

"We could charter planes and hire pilots, but where do we take them?" the judge asked.

"And if we remove them from the companies and facilities, we're going to see a profound drop in productivity and income," Dagmar added.

"Dagmar, scientists, engineers, health care workers are being targeted and killed. I've *got* to protect my people. I can't worry about money right now. And we've need to get the warning out to universities and laboratories everywhere."

"We're working on that," Pamela said sharply. She was holding a man's fedora.

"Work faster." Richard threw out his hand, and Pamela gave him the hat. But he just held it by the brim and kept turning it over and over in his hands.

The physicist saw his moment and pushed Angela aside. "Richard, I think I have a plausible answer to your question," Tanaka said.

"Which question was that?" Richard looked up from checking his inside breast pocket. "I ask so many people so many questions every day that I end up not remembering anything I said to anybody." He lifted out a checkbook, looked satisfied, and put it back in the pocket.

"About why the craziness and … magic …" Tanaka stuttered over the word, and Grenier smiled to himself. "Hasn't spread faster and gone deeper."

"Which is?"

"Okay, so our universe is a universe of laws and probability. Take an action, you get a reaction and an expected result. And we can reproduce those results time after time after time," Tanaka said.

"The basic scientific method," Richard said. They were moving again, the people breaking into discrete streams as they flowed around the furniture. "And by laws you mean like gravity?"

"And relativity, and the first and second laws of thermodynamics, and conservation of energy, yeah, that kind of thing. Of course, down at the quantum level there is an element of chaos in our universe."

Richard's expression was both dismayed and frustrated. "I don't have time for this."

"Yeah, right, okay, so let's ignore that for now."

"Yes, let's."

"Anyway, I put together what you told me about how magic violates natural law, and how every magical act tears a hole in the fabric of our reality. Then I talked to Mr. Grenier." Tanaka nodded to him, and Grenier nodded back. "About how he did magic, and it became pretty clear that the same spell won't get the same result every time. It might use electricity, but how it manifests can be totally different. So, it seems that magic is random and essentially chaotic. Magic is the result of a supreme act of personal will, which makes it antithetical to our multiverse of probability and order."

"But isn't magic normal and natural in the other universes?" Richard asked.

"Yes, they have their own laws, however weird they might be, but they're alien to ours, so *our* multiverse is pushing back, *resisting* and to some degree neutralizing the effect of the invaders."

"So, you're saying it's a stalemate."

"No, I don't think we're going to be that lucky. I mean, I'm flying blind here, but I ran some calculations, and it seems that the continued pressure from these other multiverses bulging into our multiverse will begin to break down our reality. The more magic, the more erosion to our physical laws. The more erosion, the more magic. Eventually … well, I don't know. Do we just get torn apart and subsumed into these other multiverses? Or do we become a place of functional chaos that's indigestible to the other multiverses, and we mess them up, too?"

"That strikes me as the very definition of a Pyrrhic victory."

"So, we have to close the gates," Pamela spoke up, and for an instant the cool facade pulled back and Grenier saw her fear, but Richard reacted to the sharp, hectoring tone.

"Yes, thank you. I am abundantly aware of that."

"What happens to the creatures who've come through these gates after we close them?" Dagmar asked.

Richard didn't sugarcoat it. "They're here." The German blanched, and Richard gave a short laugh. "What? You were hoping they would shrivel up and die if they got stranded?"

"I could hope."

"Nice thought, but wrong. Remember, some of the ones who came through thousands of years ago are *still* here."

"And we build churches and temples and mosques to them," Weber muttered.

"So, what do we do about them?" Tanaka asked.

"Same thing our distant ancestors did. Hunt them down and kill them," Richard answered. There was something coldly implacable in the young man's eyes.

The scientist was shaking his head. "We haven't got any ancient ancestors. What we've got is *you*. *You're* gonna have to hunt them down and kill them." For an instant Richard seemed to shrink as if the words had weight, but then the shoulders stiffened and squared.

"And that is *precisely* why he needs allies," said the judge. He turned his gaze to his son. "You're due on the Hill in fifteen minutes. I do hope you've prepared what you're going to say. This is not a situation where you can simply skate through relying upon charm and a smile." Robert Oort paused, then added rather petulantly, "I would have gone over your statement if you'd finished it last night."

The long veiling lashes were quickly lowered, but not before Grenier saw the flash of pure rage in Richard's eyes.

Yes, yes! Do it. Say it!

But the moment passed, and Richard seemed to become smaller again as he said, "I should have, sir, but I was making notes at 5:00 AM. I didn't want to wake you."

Grenier sighed and threw aside the book, stood, and gripped Robert Oort's shoulder.

"What?"

"You are such an ass." Pamela's inhalation was almost a moan. "My safely and my life depends on your son. So, I'd appreciate it if you'd *cut it the fuck out*."

"What are you talking about? It? What does that mean?" Robert demanded.

"Cutting him down, demeaning him, undermining him

constantly—"

"How dare you, sir!" the judge bellowed, and shrugged off Grenier's hand.

"Stop it! Both of you!" Richard yelled. "Stop talking about me as if I'm not here. That's pretty damn demeaning, too." He turned to Joseph. "Is the car at the door?"

"Yes, sir."

"Then let's go."

They left, and Robert Oort stepped in close to Grenier. He was tense with fury. "I know the game you're playing. He is *my* son."

"Then fucking act like his father," Grenier shot back.

The judge spun and walked away. Pamela glared at Grenier. "He's trying to help Richard."

"Really? From where I'm standing it looks like he's working for the other side."

"Oh, fuck you," Pamela said, and she also walked away.

"You know, right now I almost like you," Weber said, and he buffeted him on the arm.

"*You* could be more help, too," Grenier said pointedly.

For an instant the other man's face went slack; he gave a hum partway between confusion and agreement and walked away.

Yeah, you keep on hiding from it, you big dumb fuck.

CHAPTER TWENTY

LET ME BRING YOU HOME

"W E'VE GOT TO stop meeting this way." The rolling baritone turned the words into a pronouncement.

Richard looked up from the report he was reading. Grenier, his bulk swathed in a red-and-black-striped bathrobe, stood in the kitchen door.

Richard raked him with a look, sighed, and shook his head. "You look like a circus tent." He pushed away the cup of cold tea. The light reflected colors off the oily slick on the surface reminding him forcibly of the swirling sickening colors near the interdimensional gate.

"My, my, feeling a tad bit pissy tonight, are we?" Grenier waddled in and began pulling out the ingredients for cinnamon toast and hot chocolate. "So, how did it go? Promises of support? Are you off to the White House in the morning?"

"The only sound other than my voice was the rip of paper as I tore out the checks I'd written," Richard said. He had hoped to make it sound sarcastic. He sensed it had only sounded pathetic.

"You should have used the stick, not the carrot," the former minister grunted. "*I'll throw my not inconsiderable millions behind your opponent in the next race if you don't come through for me, you ball-less wonder.'* Something like that."

"Somehow I don't think we've got two years." Richard watched his knuckles whiten as he closed his hands into fists. "They are such weasels and cowards."

"What did you expect? They're politicians."

"Aldo was a statesman." The bittersweet scent of chocolate began to fill the room.

"One of the last," Grenier grunted. "And now he's dead, and I'm sure many others have received discreetly worded warnings. It's exactly—"

"What you would have done," Richard gritted before Grenier could get it out.

"Absolutely." Grenier pulled the pan of steaming cocoa off the stove and filled two cups.

Richard cupped his hands around the warm ceramic sides of the mug and realized the condo had gotten very cold. He found himself looking at the reflective surfaces of the stainless-steel appliances.

"What?" Grenier asked, picking up on Richard's alarm.

Richard set aside the cup, stood, and drew the sword. "Maybe this is overkill and paranoia but ..." He quickly touched every reflective surface in the room.

"Ah, yes, that was probably wise," Grenier said. Richard sat back down, and they drank in silence. The toaster gave a loud, annoyed-sounding *ding*. Grenier moved to the counter and began scraping butter across the bread. "You know your father is going to blame you for the failure to garner any support."

"Thank you, really what I needed to hear in the dark

hours of the night."

"Yeah, your father is definitely the stuff of which night-mares are made."

"Don't." Richard held up a warding hand. "I really, really don't want to go there. I don't have the emotional surplus for it right now."

"Actually, you do. You got mad at him today. I'd go so far as to say furious. You should have followed through. Told him to go to hell."

Richard squirmed under the penetrating hazel gaze and hated himself for the wash of heat through his body, and feeling like a vise was closing around his chest as the anger came sweeping back. "He knows my pattern," Richard said levelly, once more burying the hurt and the longing.

"Thus, ensuring you will repeat it. You're so cowed from his constant criticism that you can barely function when you're around him. My advice is get your father the hell out of here, and start using your not inconsiderable gifts—charm, charisma, and that wry little sense of humor that breaks out at unexpected times. You're also cunning and conniving—as I learned to my detriment and far too late—and I bet you could play dirty if you needed to. So, stop censoring yourself, watching every word, and weighing every action. Oh, and among your gifts … your handsome face. *Use it.*"

Beneath Richard's usual writhing desire to elude and reject praise, the germ of an idea began to coalesce. He grabbed for it, then pulled back mentally, trying to coax it into focus.

"Papa says—"

"I don't care what Papa says." Grenier abandoned the toast and moved in on Richard. "He distrusts beauty. I'm betting he blamed your mother's beauty for drawing him to her. Then he discovered they didn't suit at all, adding to his distrust of beauty so he rejects the thing that attracted him and also led to what he no doubt views as his greatest mistake. And *you* embody it."

Richard surged out of his chair. "You *really* don't want to go there after what you did to my mother."

Something in his eyes sent Grenier skittering in retreat back to the counter. The older man cleared his throat. "Yes, well, then let's focus on Daddy Dearest instead. Stop being so damn scared that he won't approve. He's *never* going to approve. He doesn't like you. He never will. So, give it up."

It struck with blinding clarity, the way hearing a true statement often did, and in that moment, it hurt more than any physical blow or wound Richard had ever received. He pushed away the devastating conclusion and clung like a drowning man to the memory of what had happened in Grenier's office when his father had come to rescue him. The judge hadn't said he loved him, but he said the answer to the agonized question—*I hope someday you'll love me, too*—Richard had written in a letter was *yes*.

So, saying yes was the same thing.

Wasn't it?

No. It really wasn't.

Grenier hadn't been a pastor for almost thirty years for nothing. He saw the hit, and he surprised Richard by adding softly, "I'm sorry."

Richard drew in an unsteady breath, then said airily,

"Doesn't everybody feel misunderstood by their parents?"

Grenier studied him for a long moment, then nodded and finished thickly powdering the toast with confectioner's sugar and cinnamon. He returned to the table with the plate, and Richard took a piece. Butter oozed onto his fingers. "If the monsters don't get me, heart disease will," he said lightly.

They ate in silence for a few minutes, and it felt oddly companionable sitting at the table with Grenier even after what he had said. Richard didn't want to think too deeply about that. Instead, he said casually, "Rhiana was loitering outside the Capitol today," after finishing off a second slice.

Grenier set down his fifth piece of toast. "And she did ... what?"

"Nothing. Just watched me." Richard took a sip of cocoa. A skin had formed over the top and tried to affix itself to his upper lip. He wiped it away and gave it a frown before continuing. "You know, she phoned me. To warn me that someone was going to try to kill me."

"Hmm. And from this you glean ... what?"

"Bear with me for a minute. There was this girl in high school who really liked me. Somehow everywhere I went, she'd turn up. She took up fencing. She started swimming."

"Did you go out with her?"

"Eventually."

"Did you nail her?"

Richard gave an exasperated sigh. "Not that that has anything to do with anything, but yes. Anyway, I think Rhiana's doing the same thing, because when you get right down to it, she really is just a kid. I also think she's finding that life in Monsterville isn't as wonderful as she expected, and ..." Richard coughed as he breathed in powdered sugar. "Bottom line, the crush endures."

Grenier immediately saw where Richard was going. "And you're going to try and use that to lure her back from the dark side of the Force."

"I'm seriously considering it."

"You'd be stuck with her," Grenier warned. "It'd be like bedding a cobra. And it's going to annoy a lot of other women." His full lips quirked in a smile. "Probably a few men, too."

Richard shot him a withering look. "She comes back. She frees Kenntnis. I don't see a downside."

"Just to *you*."

"So, you're not in favor of this?"

"I didn't say that. I just want you to go into this with your eyes open."

"Believe me, they're *wide* open."

"How are you going to ditch the watchdogs?"

"Enlist one of the watchdogs in my desperate need to get laid." Richard pushed back his chair, picked up the report, and headed for the door.

"That probably won't require a lot of acting," Grenier called, and Richard felt his ears turning red.

✦   ✦   ✦

"AMERICANS NEVER TAKE anything on faith. We question. We challenge. We think."

The music was stirring and patriotic. The images were of American triumphs—Henry Ford and his assembly line, the

Wright Brothers at Kitty Hawk, American GIs being embraced in France in 1944, the flag going up at Iwo Jima, and finally a montage of space shots culminating with the first step onto the surface of the moon. The narration was supplied by Grenier. His voice was rich and comforting, and it echoed with pride. The final image was the notation THIS MESSAGE WAS PAID FOR BY LUMINA ENTERPRISES. The whole thing made Weber squirm.

"Little manipulative, isn't it?" the cop asked.

Grenier dropped a hand onto his shoulder. "That's the entire point of advertising."

"I'd call it more like propaganda," Weber responded.

Grenier gave a dismissive shrug. "Call it whatever you like, but this is merely our setup, our mood piece. We'll start getting a lot more pointed and specific in subsequent ads. Danny has done an incredible job with the website and has literally hundreds of links to scientific and rational sites."

"You mean like debunkers?" Damon asked. Grenier nodded. "Then I see a problem." Grenier cocked an inquiring eyebrow at him. "According to you the magic is going to start being real. That means the debunkers are going to start having a hard time debunking shit that is *actually happening*," he said.

Grenier stroked a palm across his beard. "An interesting point," the former evangelist said. "We may need to—"

At that moment Sam came striding into the living room. Pamela was with her, and the lawyer's face was tight with tension.

Damon jumped up from the sofa. Dread was settling into his stomach. "What's wrong?"

Pamela opened her mouth, but Sam grabbed her hard by the wrist.

"Emergency girl shopping," the FBI agent said. Her expression was flat and hard, giving away nothing.

Weber cocked his head and gave her a sardonic look. "Sam, if you're ever playing poker, you probably don't want to bring Pamela along. Judging from the strength of her reaction this probably has to do with Richard. So, I ask again, what's going on?"

Sam shrugged, then said, "Richard's gone rogue."

"What the fuck does that mean?"

Pamela broke in. "That he's slipped away from his security. He's somewhere in Maryland, and he doesn't have any protection."

"And you know this how?" Grenier asked, but Weber saw a strange expression flash like summer lightning deep in the other man's eyes.

"Because I put a tracer in the foot of his cane, and one in his money clip. The schedule said he was having drinks with Congressman Wilson at the Mayflower, but GPS puts him on the coast in Maryland," Sam answered. "Estevan was supposed to be with him, and I was trying to handle this without Joseph finding out, but now it's going to be this big deal and Estevan will probably get canned. I was just planning on killing Richard," Sam concluded.

"Perhaps Richard has his reasons, and since he is the head of Lumina you should perhaps stay out of his plans," Grenier said in a low warning voice.

Damon rounded on him. "You know about this. What's he up to?"

Grenier's lips worked for a moment, then he shook his head. Damon moved before Sam could. He grabbed the disgraced preacher by the collar twisting it tight into the abundant flesh of his neck. Grenier's fat cheeks began to redden as he struggled to breathe.

Sam's hand was laid over his. "Ease off, dude. He can't talk if he can't breathe."

Weber released him so abruptly that Grenier staggered and had to throw out a hand to steady himself on a nearby chair. "Meeting Rhiana," he croaked out.

Pamela's hand went to her throat, Sam let out an expletive, and Weber found himself saying, "You son of a bitch, you bastard, you're behind this. You sold us out." Weber grabbed Sam's arm. "You've got the tracker. Let's go."

"I'm coming too," Pamela said.

Damon gave her an exasperated look. "Look, no offense, but we don't really need any learned argument from legal counsel. I need a badass." Weber jerked his head at Sam. "And she's as badass as they come."

"Damn right," Sam said.

"Too bad. I'm coming. I may be able to talk some sense into Richard," Pamela said.

Weber cast his eyes toward heaven but nodded. The trio headed for the front door.

"Wait! Don't!" Grenier called, but they ignored him. Damon glanced over his shoulder and saw the preacher reaching into his pocket as the door began to swing shut behind them.

Damon lunged, grabbed the edge of the door before it could close, and rushed back into the condo as Grenier was punching buttons on his phone. The cop crossed the room in two strides, yanked the cell phone out of his hand, threw it on the floor and slammed his heel into the glass.

"Oh, no, you don't. You don't get to warn your buddies," he growled.

"I'm warning Richard because you're going to fuck this up. He's trying to turn her!" Grenier yelled.

"Yeah, right," Damon snorted, and taking the former minster in an armlock he handcuffed him to the leg of a heavy table.

HE MADE IT a point to apologize for the venue. The Riverside Inn wasn't elegant, but Richard explained that they could lose themselves in the crowds who flocked to the restaurant in search of the famous Chesapeake blue crabs. Rhiana had sounded breathless when she said that was fine. She also assured him she would come alone. Richard made appropriately trusting and grateful noises, but he still had both his guns and the sword, and another reason for the Riverside— he could get lost in the crowds if he had to run for it. He just had to hope his leg wouldn't object too much. He eyed the Hendriks gin martini in front of him. *Or too drunk.* This was the first alcohol he'd had in over five years.

Despite Richard's warning that the restaurant had all the ambiance of a bus station, Rhiana still turned up in a clinging, floor-length silk dress that left one shoulder bare. The color was a peacock's tail; blues, greens, and lavenders shimmered through the folds.

Yes, Richard thought, *this is prom night, and I'm the dream date.*

Richard looked around at the graying wood plank walls, the photographs of crusty old sea captains, lighthouses, and fishing boats, and the scarred wooden tables covered by long sheets of newspaper stock. The smell of drawn butter and citrus hung in the air. He was definitely going to have to do something to recover his status as dreamboat. Napkins and crab mallets were thrust into small buckets, and plastic bibs were available. Conversations and the pounding of wooden mallets attacking the shells of the crabs roared through the room though the sound abated somewhat at Rhiana's entrance as men gawked and women glared.

Richard had peeled off enough twenties that he had managed to secure a corner table where he could watch both the front door and the kitchen entrance, and there was a window just to his left. He had parked his car directly under that avenue of escape.

He brought his attention back to Rhiana as she reached up and pushed her long black hair behind her ears. Richard watched the play of muscles beneath her smooth skin, and how the movement set her silver earrings sweeping across the tops of her shoulders. The metal had been pulled and twisted like spiderwebs, and trapped within them were scattered jewels: amethysts, emeralds, pearls, and sapphires. Richard suppressed a shiver, hoping he wasn't going to join them, caught in her net.

No, I'm the one angling. I've gotten her this far. I just have to set the hook.

He felt a brief pang of guilt. He was taking such advantage of her of her youth, her inexperience, and her lonely need. But she was one girl and when weighed against the fate of the world and all the people currently living in it, he really didn't have a choice. Richard pushed aside the remorse.

Richard continued staring at her, struck again by her incredible beauty as she walked to join him. As she slid onto the bench next to him, the scent of her floral perfume washed over him, and he felt a flush rising in his chest. She suddenly gave a smile that was both shy and young, and wise and mysterious. Apparently, *fortunately*, his hesitation and calculation had been read as him being mesmerized, but he needed to say something. Never had so much been riding on a seduction, and never had he felt more inadequate.

You're good at this, an inner voice berated. *You've talked how many people into bed over the years?*

But he couldn't come across like a third-rate Lothario. Rhiana was young, but she wasn't stupid. Sincere. He had to be—*feel*—sincere. Did he feel sincere? Richard sincerely thought she was beautiful. He sincerely thought she was dangerous. And he sincerely thought she was the key to freeing Kenntnis and stopping the madness. He had a brief memory of Damon grinning at him, the feel of his hand on his shoulder, and he sincerely regretted a path that was about to close forever. *It was never open,* he reminded himself. No, he had to make this work.

He sucked in a deep breath but before he could speak a waiter bustled over and took Rhiana's drink order. Once he was gone Richard leaned over and said quietly, "Thank you for your call, for trying to warn me. It came a little late, but I appreciate the impulse that generated it. It was kind of you, and it meant a lot to me." He reached out and very lightly brushed the back of her hand where it rested on the table.

A slow blush rose into her cheeks. "I ... I shouldn't have done it." She got control over her voice. "I got in a lot of trouble."

"Your ... father," Richard said. She nodded, and he saw the shadow of fear and pain in her eyes. Pity gripped him, and he took her hand. "Did he hurt you?" She gave a tense little nod. Richard felt anger surging through his chest. They were *all* of them just using her.

The waiter swept by and deposited a pina colada in front of Rhiana. Richard wanted to strangle him. He gathered his scattered thoughts.

"You gave up ... so much—" he began, only to be interrupted.

"What? *What* did I give up?" She tried to sound bellicose, but there was sadness beneath the anger.

Richard shrugged. "A different life. Relationships you might have had." This was dangerous territory, so he said it very cautiously.

"There was only *one* I wanted."

Richard hung his head but made sure he could still watch her from beneath his lashes. "I know. It was entirely my problem. I was worried about your age, and other things ..."

"And now?" she demanded.

"We're in a different world."

She took a sip of her pina colada. He gulped down another mouthful of his martini. If this worked, they'd end up in bed together. Alcohol had always been part of his many seductions. Maybe it would work again, and overcome his fears, guilt, and regrets.

"I'm eighteen now," Rhiana said suddenly.

"I'm glad, but it really doesn't matter any longer."

"Why not?"

He leaned back and gestured at her. "Well, look at you. You're …" He deliberately hesitated.

She leaned toward him, expression intent. "What?"

"Beautiful. Sophisticated. Powerful."

Her cheeks were bright with color and the green eyes shone with excitement and affection.

She really is so young, and I'm being such a cad. Richard pushed away the thought and concentrated on the long list of murders he'd uncovered. Some of them people who worked for him. Though he might not have known it, he had still nonetheless failed them. He knew what he had to do. Whatever the cost, he had to turn this girl.

"Fathers are … difficult. I'd be in trouble, too, if mine knew I was here … with you now. He would say I was a fool." An ember of anger began to burn beneath Richard's breastbone. His entire life he'd done what the judge wanted, except for one time. Couldn't he trust Richard to take what he'd taught him and do the right thing? His breath caught, and he returned to the moment. "That you couldn't be trusted. That you'll hurt me," he finished.

"I won't hurt you." She reached out and gently touched his cheek, allowing her fingers to linger against his skin. She smelled of jasmine and girl.

And then artifice became reality, at least so far as Richard's body was concerned. He had been denying the physical for such a long, long time and desire sent heat flaring through him. Richard suddenly felt light-headed, and he was grateful for the napkin in his lap.

Her face was very close. It was the next logical move. Richard kissed her.

Her lips were warm, soft, and pliant, but she was so inexperienced, and doubt once again shook him. Then he remembered what he'd seen in Virginia, and it hardened his resolve. He caught her full lower lip gently between his teeth, then allowed his tongue to explore her mouth. She tasted of pineapple and coconut and ice cream, but there was also an underlying harsh oily taste. *She's not human. She's not human*, came a nervous little voice. *Not* totally *human*, Richard corrected, and he also noted that it began to fade, and she tasted more like a girl the longer they embraced.

They broke the kiss when a waitress came over. The beads in her beautiful, cornrowed hair clashed like tiny cymbals. She gave them an indulgent, knowing smile.

"Y'all ready to order?"

Rhiana leaned against Richard's shoulder. "I don't know how to eat these things."

"I'll show you. They're actually kind of fun, in addition to being delicious. And they're a great way to work out your aggressions." Richard ordered for them and got refills on their cocktails.

After another fortifying sip of liquid courage, he said, "Rhiana, forgive me if this is out of line, but you seem … sad."

Richard knew he was pushing things fast, but it was going to be damn hard to keep arranging to play hooky so he could go on dates with the enemy. He needed to seal the deal tonight.

She rolled her glass between her palms and hid behind the curtain of her hair. "Sometimes I'm lonely." She set aside the glass and began to shred a roll. "I grew up in this world. I'm comfortable here. The only people I see are Jack and An—" She broke off abruptly and took a big drink of her pina colada.

"Jack?" Richard inquired as casually as he could manage.

"Rendell. I'm teaching him magic." Richard filed the name away. "They've been trying for years, centuries, to get someone like me, but once I did what they wanted—" She broke off and stared unseeing into space.

Richard rifled through what she had said and left unsaid and took the risk. "Because you're comfortable here, they relegated you back here, in the human world. Does that make you human again, at least in *their* minds?" Rhiana was listening intently, and he saw that thought strike home. She slowly nodded. Richard took another sip of martini and said slowly and carefully, "But Rhiana, if they think of you as human you may not be safe." She turned stricken fawn eyes on him. "I'm sorry, I don't mean to frighten or hurt you."

"It's okay. I put myself here."

What had been artifice and performance became reality. Pity seized him and Richard put an arm around her shoulders and rocked her gently, murmuring into her hair, "Then let me bring you home." She sagged against him; all resistance gone.

Movement at the front door caught his attention. Three people were entering. Pamela, Damon, and Sam.

"*Fuck!*" The expletive burst from Richard lips. Rhiana lifted her head, stiffened, and drew away.

CHAPTER TWENTY-ONE

BROKEN DREAMS

U NTIL THIS MOMENT Pamela had never seen the much-talked-about Rhiana. She knew that Cross hated her (she suddenly found herself wondering at the absence of the strange creature) and said she couldn't be trusted. Angela and Weber both hated her, but Weber conceded that she was beautiful first, and then decried her betrayal second. Now that she was actually looking at the woman ... girl, Pamela concluded that beautiful didn't begin to describe it. Here was a worthy match for Richard, and Pamela briefly thought she could hate Rhiana, too.

Richard had come out of his chair and was wending his way through the tables toward them. Pamela had never seen such an expression on her brother's face, and she suddenly didn't feel so confident in the rightness of their rescue. Rhiana also stood up, giving them the full effect of her dress.

"Crap, if you wanted a *hooker*, why didn't you say so?" Sam said in her crude, piercing way. "We could have brought one to the condo and saved all of us a fuck of a lot of trouble."

Richard grabbed the FBI agent's wrist so hard that Sam's hand went white. *"Shut up!"* And it was also a tone Pamela had never heard out of her brother.

"Richard, we were worried—" Pamela began.

He flung away Sam's hand and leaned in on her. "I am so *sick* of all of you handling me and fussing over me. *Leave me the fuck alone!*" His voice was a low harsh whisper.

Weber grabbed the smaller man by the shoulders and jerked him around to face him. "That is *not* okay. You should have discussed this with *me*. You don't pull a stunt like this without planning it with your team. And your team is not that fat fuck who used to *work for the goddamn monsters*." His jabbed a finger at Rhiana. "Like *her!*"

Pamela saw the girl flinch, then rage suffused her face. A woman screamed, and Pamela let out a moan of fear. Richard's head whipped around.

Rhiana had begun to dissolve, her body pulling apart like strings of red and purple taffy, but before her face vanished Pamela saw where tears had run down her face, ruining her makeup.

The windows in the restaurant all blew in. Shards of glass stung Pamela's cheeks, and she felt one large splinter lodge itself in her back. She screamed at the sudden, stabbing pain. Weber pulled Richard to his chest, and turned toward the back wall, shielding him with his body. Sam had vanished and Pamela finally spotted her sheltering under a table. Pamela joined her just as other screaming people were doing the same.

There was a cry of terror from the kitchen, and the sound of an explosion. Cooks and servers came running through the swinging doors leading to the kitchen. Flames came boiling after them. Panic was spreading through the room. Richard pulled the hilt off the end of the cane and drew the sword.

"Listen!" The basso overtones together with his shout brought everyone's attention to him. "The windows are out. Those closest to a window, go out that way. Those of you near the front, line up and use the front doors. There is *plenty* of time. Stay calm. Help them," he ordered Sam and Weber.

Pamela took an elderly woman's arm and helped her out the door. She could feel blood trickling down her back and soaking into the material of her sweater.

Within minutes the restaurant was cleared; the flames were taking hold, dancing like red and orange fans in the empty window frames. In the distance Pamela heard approaching sirens. The briny scent of the sea was overlaid with the wet heavy smell of impending snow, and the stench of burning plastic and wood.

"I'm sorry," Pamela whispered to Richard as they all stood in the parking lot.

"How did you—" Richard began.

"I put a tracer in your cane, and I'm *not* sorry. So go fuck yourself," Sam said. Her tone was pushing for a fight.

Richard almost joined the battle, but then Weber said, "We're all here because we're trying to *protect you.*"

Richard abandoned Sam and turned, raging, on Weber. "I am not weak. I am not helpless. I know you think I'm just a useless fa—" He bit off whatever he was going to say. "But I didn't do this on a whim or out of caprice. I had a plan, but thanks to all of you it's been fucked beyond repair, and the situation is now a whole hell of a lot worse. She'll never believe I didn't betray her and arrange this so she could be humiliated. She's a fucking kid, but a kid with terrifying powers, and you've, you've ..." He gave a strangled, inarticulate sound and pushed Weber hard, causing the older man to stagger back.

Richard began backing away from them. "Go away. Go back where you belong. Get out of my ... life. It's what you want."

Pamela thought it was meant for all of them, but her brother's eyes were fixed on the cop. Richard spun on his bad leg and almost fell. Weber's hand jerked out as if to catch him even though at least ten feet separated them. Richard flung himself into a nondescript parked car. All three stood silent as the taillights dwindled and vanished.

Pamela risked a look up at Weber. The gutted and devastated look on the cop's face had unexpected tears rushing to fill her eyes.

"What a fucking prick," Sam said, but it sounded defensive.

Pamela cleared her throat and wiped her eyes. "He didn't mean it. He's angry. He'll cool down, and realize he was out of line."

Weber stepped back. "Nah, he was right. I walked away from my duty, my job. I'll get myself home. You guys go on. Get back to the condo. Stay safe." He dug his hands into his pockets and walked away.

❖   ❖   ❖

RHIANA WALKED THE darkness until she felt the pull of the gate and then allowed herself to re-form. Not too close to the gate. Truth be told, it disturbed her, too.

Rhiana scrubbed at her cheeks, feeling the sticky wetness of her tears. The naked boles of the trees marched away from her and stretched bare limbs toward the white sky. The smell of snow was stronger here. Growing up in California she had never seen snow. Once her adopted parents had taken the family to Knott's Berry Farm just before Christmas, drawn by the lure of man-made snow. It had felt like ice, as if someone had dumped a truckload of sno-cones on the ground. Kids had tried to inner tube and sled on the hill, but it had felt like a fake and a cheat, like so much of her life.

Had he planned this? Had Richard really done this to hurt and humiliate her? That woman had said that awful thing about her. Rhiana looked down at the dress she had picked with such care, and she suddenly reached down and tore away most of the trailing skirt. It *was* trashy, not elegant. She'd made a fool of herself.

She remembered the one-time Drew Sandringham had come to her house for a meeting. The way his upper lip had lifted, and his nostrils narrowed, and she realized the house was tasteless and gaudy and *she* had made those choices.

Her thoughts shied away from that painful memory. She tried to focus on her hurt and her anger. Richard was going to pay. She would find a way.

But his lips had been warm and soft, the kiss deep and passionate.

He couldn't have faked that.

Another memory stabbed and impaled her. *"Richard and I were lovers."* Drew Sandringham's voice in that bar in New York City.

Richard had gone to Weber. The old cop had called her a monster. He had shielded Richard with his body. *What if they were together?* Richard must have told the policeman where he would be. How else could they have found them?

She coughed out a sob and walked on through the Virginia forest.

A lump of darkness caught her eyes. Something lay on the fallen leaves and pine needles.

"Hey," Rhiana called, and her voice sounded dull and flat in the darkness. There was no movement or reaction.

She approached cautiously. It was a young woman dressed in student-chic blue jeans, oversized pea coat, boots. Once, in another lifetime, Rhiana had dressed that way. A small section of the girl's scalp was bare and bloody. The hank of long hair lay tangled around a branch as if the tree were playing cat's cradle. Rhiana's head twinged in sympathy. The girl had been caught and slowed by the grip on her hair. It was a measure of her desperation that she had pulled so hard she'd let her hair be ripped out. Or maybe Doug had done it just for the fun of it. And then the knife had been applied to her gasping throat. In the cold the blood had coagulated into a viscous pool. Rhiana remembered when this one had been snatched off the campus of UNLY.

Another of Doug's toys. Only now he'd taken to breaking them.

She covered her mouth with a hand and began to sob. For the dead girl. For herself. For her broken dreams.

✧　✧　✧

IT WAS 3:00 AM before Pamela managed to get to sleep. She shared the room with Sam and Dagmar and their steady breathing as they slept seemed to mock her. She had texted Weber at 2:00 AM. He wasn't sleeping either, because he texted back he had checked into a hotel at the airport and would be flying out at 6:00 AM.

When Pamela finally emerged from her room, she found the psychodrama continued. Joseph had tried to fire Estevan. Richard had intervened and overridden the security chief's decision, which left Joseph fuming. Estevan was sulking. Dagmar tried to keep up an artless patter of conversation, and Grenier had the air of a man enjoying a drama in which he had no stake or investment.

And the judge capped the morning by lecturing Richard about how lack of planning was always a recipe for disaster. Richard had listened in silence, then stood and said, "It was planned, and it would have worked if they hadn't interfered."

"But in fact, it *did not* work, and you endangered yourself in this foolish act of bravado. I don't know if this is a function of being a policeman, but acting like some kind of movie hero is not the way to succeed," the judge concluded.

"Thank you, sir. Dagmar, don't we have reports to review?" Richard said, and they left.

Shortly after, Pamela and her father left for their scheduled appointments at the Justice Department. Which proved to be utterly fruitless. Three of the four people they were supposed to see weren't in, and it seemed to take an inordinate amount of time to ascertain that they weren't in. The person who did keep the appointment was distracted to the point of incoherence. She kept checking her watch, answering the phone even though it hadn't rung, getting up to look out the window.

It was now past 1:00 PM and Pamela was hungry, the cut on her back stung, and her frustration was at the boiling point because they had wasted the entire morning. Finally, Robert admitted defeat, and they went in search of lunch.

They selected the Tabard Inn, one of Washington's more elegant eateries. As they approached the front doors, a man stepped out of a parked taxicab and approached them. It was Drew Sandringham, and Pamela greeted him with pleasure. She hadn't seen him since her mother's funeral.

"Drew." She gave him a hug. "What are you doing in DC?" she asked. "Where are you staying? We should have dinner."

But the glance, smile, and hug he spared for her were fleeting. All his focus was on her father. She looked over at the judge, and dread settled like an icy shawl across her shoulders. She had never seen her father look so forbidding and so *furious*.

"How dare you approach me," Robert said. His tone was low and intense.

Pamela stared at him in confusion. "Papa?" She was ignored.

"Hear me out, Robert. After thirty years of friendship, you owe me that at least," Drew said.

What the hell? Pamela thought as she watched her father struggle with himself.

"You have two minutes."

"I won't need that long." Drew took a long steadying breath. "Look, I won't deny that what happened, happened.

It was undoubtedly a bad call, showing poor judgment on my part. But Richard isn't the innocent in all this. Whatever he might have told you."

"He's told me nothing. Ever. And I have not asked. I learned about ... the incident ... from another source."

"Then you probably don't know that Richard and I were lovers long before that night. He came to my bed within three weeks of starting to work for me." Drew rushed on. "And trust me, I wasn't his first. There had been a young man, an actor, but he'd left for California. I was the replacement."

Oh my God, now so much makes sense. But I know he was sleeping with my friend Gail. And there was Margo, but he did spend so much time with Paul that summer. Pamela's whirling thoughts bumped against each other in a chaotic game of point/counterpoint.

"So, he was the aggressor. Seduced you, did he? Or did he force himself upon you?" The judge's words were as cold and sharp as glass.

Drew looked wryly amused. "Oh, Robert, you've always been oblivious. I'm surprised you managed to father three children. People like me, we recognize each other. I've known from the time he was ten that Richard liked boys. When you asked me to give him a job I was delighted. I knew I'd end up fucking that tight little ass."

Pamela was shocked by the crudity. It was completely unlike Drew. A dull brick red blotched her father's pale cheeks, and Pamela realized that it had been calculated. A shot aimed with perfect accuracy to cause the maximum amount of hurt and shame. This was not a man attempting to make peace with an old friend. Something far darker was at work here.

"I don't believe you," the judge said, but the words sounded weak.

"Alannis knew. I assumed that was why she ..." Sandringham executed a knowing gesture with no more than a turn of the wrist.

My God, he's implying that Richard caused Mama's suicide. Papa will never buy that. He knows how Richard adored her.

But all the color had drained from Robert's thin cheeks. Her father whirled and rushed away. His strides were long and so fast that he was almost running. Pamela dithered, unable to decide whether to follow or confront Drew. Sandringham's satisfied smile made the decision.

"Why?" she demanded.

Sandringham didn't pretend not to understand. "Payback."

"You'd shatter their relationship for spite?"

"And what relationship is that Pamela? There's never been love there. Just fear and the desperate need to be loved on one side, and disapproval on the other." He tapped his chin with a forefinger. "Hmmm, I wonder if Robert always sensed that Richard was a fag?"

And Pamela realized that the man she'd thought of as an uncle, and a far more acceptable one than her real uncle, hadn't given a tinker's damn for her, or Amelia, or their mother. It had always been about Robert and later Richard. Sickened, she turned away, but her father had vanished. She knew where he would go, and feared what he would do.

Which meant she had to reach the condo first. She pushed Drew aside and jumped into the taxi he had just vacated.

✧   ✧   ✧

DAGMAR SPREAD ANOTHER set of reports across the coffee table in front of Richard. The numbers seemed to get tinier and tinier the longer he stared at them. Meaningless ant tracks across a white desert. Richard hadn't really wanted to work; he'd just wanted to get away from his father.

His mind kept straying back to the events of last night. What could he have done differently? Maybe told Weber his plan and involved him in the decision. Damon wasn't an idiot. He would have seen the logic in what Richard was doing. Yes, if he had succeeded, he would have had to be with Rhiana permanently, but why would Weber care? When he'd discovered Richard was gay ... bi ... he had requested a transfer to get *away* from him. He'd only come back to help because ... well, fate of the world, and whatever else he might be Damon was a brave, decent man, former military, and he knew when he had a greater duty.

Richard should have suspected Sam, checked for bugs and tracers, but damn it, he was in charge; she shouldn't have been spying on him.

He kept seeing Damon's hurt expression.

And Rhiana's devastating hurt. *She's a fucking kid, but a kid with terrifying powers ...*

And hurt kids lash out.

He held up a restraining hand to Dagmar while with the other he dug out his phone. Hit Angela's number in Favorites. She answered on the second ring.

"Glad to know your alive—"

"I'm sorry, I'm in the middle of a thing so I need to make this fast ..."

"What happened?"

"I tried a ... a thing with Rhiana and it sort of went pear-shaped."

Dagmar mouthed to him. *You think?* He waved her off.

"Anyway, I'm concerned she might try to get back at me through my friends, so I wanted to give you a heads-up. Please be on your guard."

"Damn the girl. And I can hear you beating yourself up. Stop it. It's not your job to save everybody."

His felt his lips quirk in a wry and bitter smile. "Actually, it kind of is." He sucked in a deep breath. "Sorry, but I really need to go."

He clicked off the phone and looked around the room, seeking a respite from the roiling mix of guilt, fury, and worry. Eddie was sprawled on a love seat set at right angles to the long sofa. The faint rumble of a bass line leaked around the edges of the young scientist's headphones, and his head bobbed in time to the beat. A laptop rested on his chest, and he was typing furiously. Richard craned and got a glimpse of the screen. More numbers. He could hear Grenier moving about in the kitchen. *Time for afternoon tea, it seemed.*

"We're spending eighty-seven thousand dollars a day," Dagmar said.

That got his attention. "Did you just say *a day?*"

But before she could answer, the front door flew open, crashing against the wall, and Pamela hobbled rapidly through it. Her face was blotched red and white, partly from the cold, but Richard knew from the set of her mouth that she was in distress. The anger he had been nursing faded into alarm, and he hurried to her side.

"What's wrong?" Richard took her arm and helped her into a chair.

The commotion drew Grenier, who emerged from the kitchen, a dishtowel hanging in his plump hand.

"Slipped on the ice," she said tightly. She grimaced and leaned down to rub at a rapidly swelling ankle.

Richard gave a small hiss of pain as he dropped onto one knee, slipped off her shoe, and gently palpated the ankle. After years in gymnastics, he had a good feel for injuries. This one wasn't bad. He looked up and said as much and was dismayed when her gray eyes filled with tears. In all the years of their childhood he had never seen Pamela cry. The only time he'd ever heard her weep was when she called to tell him about their mother's death.

"Richard, Papa is coming. He's ... he's ..." She stammered to a halt and looked around the room. "Drew talked to him." The words came out in a whisper.

Nerves fluttered deep in Richard's gut. *He'll know. He'll find out, but Kenntnis had fixed all this.*

"He knows," Richard said soothingly, though he suspected it was as much to convince himself as it was for her.

The incredulous look he got in response told him that somehow the situation had changed, and dread settled like a cold fist deep in his gut. The front door opened. Richard could see Rudi's broad back where he stood guard in the hall. Then every other bit of his surroundings disappeared, and all

Richard could see was the expression on his father's face. He stood up so he could face what was coming on his feet instead of on his knees. Pamela clutched his hand, and Richard could feel himself choking on fear.

"Out! All of you. Everyone who is in the condominium, out!" the judge commanded.

Dagmar stood and moved very deliberately to Richard's side. "Would you like to continue with our meeting, sir?" she asked.

"No. Go." Richard's lips felt numb, and he could barely force out the words.

Dagmar went to the love seat and gave Eddie a shake. He lifted one earpiece of the headphones. She gave a terse gesture. He swung his legs off the love seat and sat up. They headed toward the bedrooms.

"No," came the snapped command from the judge. "Outside. You, too, Pamela."

"No. I'm staying." Her response left Richard gaping. Eddie clutched his computer like a child hugging a favorite toy and scuttled for the front door with Dagmar close on his heels. Grenier paced ponderously past him, gave his shoulder a squeeze. Richard felt dampness from the towel.

"You know what you need to do," Grenier said quietly. The seconds seemed to stretch endlessly. Richard couldn't stand it.

"Sir, what—"

"Be quiet! I will deal with you presently and privately!"

The front door closed behind the trio. Richard scanned the chiseled planes of his father's face, and saw no softness, no love, nothing but anger and disgust.

CHAPTER TWENTY-TWO

NOW IT'S WAR

WITHOUT PREAMBLE ROBERT asked, "Are you a homosexual?"

For one wild moment Richard considered lying. After all, he'd been lying to his father for his entire life. Why stop now?

"Papa, he's always had girlfriends," Pamela said, trying to break through the heart-stopping tension. Richard was touched by the unexpected defense.

"He'll answer for himself," Robert grated, and spun back on him. "Do you sleep with men?" The words were enunciated so sharply they seemed to cut. They also dripped with disgust.

"I ... I ..." Richard coughed to clear the obstruction in his throat and found himself mentally making excuses, none of which would cut ice with his *father*. The judge was devout, their particular brand of Christianity viewed homosexuality as a grievous sin. He was a Republican. He had helped write an amicus brief to the Supreme Court arguing against the rights of gays and lesbians to marry. The argument had been based on his strict constructionist views of the Constitution, but in this moment, Richard realized that beneath all the legal language there was only bigotry.

He was just so sick of it. Of all of it.

Of him.

"Yes. Yes, I do."

A sound of disgust emerged as if words weren't sufficient. Then Robert found them again, and they cut like glass. "This is what your mother was alluding to in her note. She tried to bargain with God for *your* worthless soul! *You* caused her death!" Pamela gasped, and Richard took a step back because of what he saw in his father's face.

Richard knew he was codependent to the point of absurdity, but if there was one thing being a cop had taught him it was how to assign blame. Anger began to lick at the edges of the shame and fear.

"No, sir. You don't get to lay that off on me. Grenier's people played on Mama's love for me, and her weakness and neuroses, with fears of me being condemned to hellfire and eternal damnation. If you want to bust somebody's chops, go bust Mark's!"

His father's deep blue eyes raked him up and down. Bitterness, disappointment, and anger were all there. "To get *you*." The word dripped disgust. "Alannis risked her health and emotional stability. Because she wanted a son."

Richard wasn't prepared for the explosion of rage that seemed to scorch behind his eyes. Where was the gut-shivering fear and guilt? Caution was also missing. It seemed like some other person was talking when he heard himself say,

"Not the way I heard it. Uncle Ridley said *you* were the one who forced the third pregnancy. Over her doctor's objections. And when her postpartum depression led her to start drinking and using the pills, instead of *helping* her, you hid her away in institutions. You were more worried about what it would do to *your* reputation than you ever were about Mama. She was always terrified you'd send her back. So, when you're looking for reasons for her suicide, *maybe you should try looking in a fucking mirror!*" Pamela made an inarticulate sound.

The blow came so quickly and was so unexpected that Richard didn't register it until pain exploded across his cheek. The force of the backhand slap drove his cheek against his teeth and Richard tasted blood. Pamela gave a cry that turned into a sob.

And his courage crumbled. His father had never before struck him, and Richard realized he was about to lose another parent. He raised his hand, a pleading gesture. There had to be a way to fix this. Apologize enough. Twist himself into a new shape. *Become* what his father wanted.

"Papa, I'm sorry. I shouldn't have said that. Please, I'll—"

But Robert turned away. "Come, Pamela, we're leaving. We shall go to your sister's."

And the world started spinning backward when Pamela said, "No, Papa. I'm staying with Richard." She got out of the chair, took hold of Richard's arm, and clutched it tightly to her side.

"I see. Well, when you come to your senses, you may join us in Boston."

As Richard watched his father's retreating back, he explored the vast hollow that seemed to have opened in his heart.

"Papa," Richard called.

"You will not address me, sir. We are finished." The bedroom door closed behind him.

Blood from his torn cheek was slithering down the back of his throat, filling his stomach with nausea. A shiver ran down his arms and into his legs. Richard turned and headed blindly for his bedroom. Pamela hung at his side, gripping his arm tightly with both hands.

"It'll be all right. He'll think about this and calm down and be back. If he can trust that you'll never do ... it ... that ... again."

Richard paused, his hand on the bedroom door. "I can't make that promise, Pamela. And why should I have to? I've spent my life twisting myself to fit his image of what I should be. Well, I'm done." He drew in a shuddering breath. "Just tell me when he's gone."

Richard closed the door on her worry and desperation, pressed the heels of his hands hard against his eyes. His back found the wood of the door and he slid down until he hit the floor, the pain in his leg negligible when compared to the emotional agony. Suddenly the adrenaline was gone from his system, leaving behind only nausea and a shaking he couldn't control.

He didn't quite reach the toilet before he vomited.

✧   ✧   ✧

THE FAIR HEAD was bent over papers as he sat at the desk. Richard looked up, irritated by the intrusion, and Grenier realized in his agitation he hadn't knocked.

"Pardon me, that was rude. I'm sorry, but, Richard, I

308

must speak with you."

He paused, and Richard growled, "Fine. Speak."

"They're manipulating you. This didn't happen by accident. They're trying to force you into an emotional reaction that will play right into their hands. Think; you minored in psychology. Don't be a fool. They're isolating you, and—"

Richard leaned back in the chair far enough to cause the springs to squeak and laced his fingers behind his head. "You think I don't know that?" His voice was filled with amusement.

"Well, I ..."

The smile flickered briefly, like a glimpse of sun through clouds, and the young man said in an almost singsong, "Richard's been abandoned by his daddy, so he's going to rush off and find a replacement. Kenntnis is the logical choice, so of course Richard is going to go in and get captured by the bad guys. Does that pretty much sum it up?" All Grenier could manage was a slow nod. "Actually, we're going home."

"What about alerting the government?"

"I did my best. I prodded the dinosaur as best I could. No, I think Eddie and his kind are the better bet for us. Lumina has scientists all over the world. We're gathering them up, and they'll figure out a way to free Kenntnis. *Then* we'll be back."

Grenier was suddenly aware of how badly his back hurt and how weak his knees had gone. He dropped into a chair. "I'm so relieved. And ..." His mind searched for a less pejorative word than he'd been going to use. "And impressed."

Again, the smile appeared. "You could have said it."

"What?"

"What you were really going to say—surprised, amazed. Now get out of here and start packing."

✦   ✦   ✦

PAMELA PRESSED HER cell phone tighter to her ear, tossed the sweater into her suitcase, and sank down on the bed as her sister said, "He took everything. Paul's college fund, my retirement, his retirement. He took out a second mortgage on the house." Panic had turned Amelia's voice into a shrill flute.

"What did Brent do with the money?" Pamela asked.

"There was this business deal, the United Emirates Fund. We ran it by Drew." Pamela's stomach gave a roll at the sound of the name. "And he said it looked good, so I agreed to the first payment, but there were more, so many more, and Brent didn't tell me about them. He just took all our money!" The words became an anguished cry. "Oh, Pam, we're going to lose our house!"

"How did Brent even find out about this deal?" Pamela asked.

"He met this man at the racquet club. They had lunch together, and the man invited him in. You know how Brent is, he likes to feel important."

"What about Papa? Is he there?" Pamela asked.

"Yes, but what can he do? He doesn't have the money to pay off the loan, and we can't even go home with him because his house is gone, too. Burned down because of all this Richard mess." Tears thickened Amelia's words. "Papa forbid me to call Richard, but I have to. We've got no place else to turn."

"Well, call him."

"I was hoping you'd talk to him first. Brent's been calling and calling him, and Richard's never called him back. I didn't know if Richard was mad at me, or …" Amelia's voice trailed away.

"No, no, he's not angry," Pamela said quickly. "He's just had so much … he's been so busy … don't worry, we're going to fix this."

Pamela ended the call and went in search of her brother. She found him in his bedroom. He was also packing one-handed while he talked on his iPhone.

"Yes, Kenzo, I understand. If you think that's more secure, then let's do it—"

"I've got to talk to you," Pamela said. He waved her down, and she added in a much sharper tone, *"Now!"*

"Let me call you back," Richard said. "No, no, go ahead and get started, we'll just talk in more depth later." He turned to Pamela. "What?"

"Amelia just called me. Brent's managed to lose everything—house, savings, everything—in some business deal gone bad."

Now it was Richard's turn to sink down on the bed. He ran a hand through his hair. "Oh, crap, that must be what Brent kept calling about."

"Yeah, it would have been helpful if you'd *taken the damn call.* So now you can call Kenzo back and arrange to have him payoff what they owe and *fix* this." Richard was frowning at the far wall. "Are you listening? Did you hear *anything* I just said?"

"Yeah, okay, we'll take care of the money, but I'm wondering if it goes deeper than that. Do you have any details?"

"Just that it was called the United Emirates Fund." She hesitated, then added, "And Drew signed off on it."

His jaw tightened at the mention of the man's name. Richard moved to the door of the bedroom and called down the hall, "Dagmar, check out something for me."

She stuck her head out of her room. "What?"

"The United Emirates Fund. And find out how they got a line on my brother-in-law, Brent van Gelder."

"Right-ho."

"And make it fast," Richard added. He took out his phone and punched in a number. "Jerry, I need you and Brook to file new flight plans. I want you to head back to New Mexico with some of the staff. Tell Brook we need to add a stop in Boston." He ended the call and reacted to her look. "What?"

"Papa's there," Pamela reminded him.

"I know."

She took a deep breath. "If you have to go to the house, I'll come with you."

"I'd like that."

✧   ✧   ✧

IT HAD ONLY taken four years as a cop to make Richard suspicious and paranoid. He couldn't imagine what he would have been like if he'd put in his twenty. Dagmar had gotten back to him, and it was just what he'd feared but also expected. Drew had been behind it all. He'd covered his tracks pretty well, but Richard had the resources of Lumina behind him. Between Dagmar and Kenzo they had the corporate threads untangled in four hours.

War had been declared on anyone with the last name of Oort or in any way associated with him, and Drew had been one of the soldiers for the other side. Richard decided grimly that he would deal with Drew soon enough, but right now he needed to protect his family.

As the big limo rolled quietly down the suburban Boston streets, Richard had the sword drawn just in case. Pamela sat next to him. Joseph drove while Rudi rode shotgun. The blade of the sword was deep matte black with just the hint of lights deep in the darkness. There wasn't a net of swirling light in the air around the blade. That reassured him; when magic or Old Ones were present the lights came out. Richard sheathed the sword and put the hilt in the holster at the small of his back. What he was going to say to his eldest sister and brother-in-law was crazy enough—without waving a sword about as he did it.

Trees overhung the street, and every available curb was taken up with parked cars. The long line of redbrick row houses were all dark except for a few porch lights spilling their light down the steps leading up to high stoops.

"I just don't understand why they didn't buy a house with a yard after Paul was born. Get out of the center of the city," Pamela said in that exasperated tone siblings reserve for the perceived foolishness of one other.

"Because this one's close to the hospital," Richard answered reasonably.

He'd phoned the hospital to make sure Amelia hadn't been called in for an emergency surgery. She hadn't. Dr. van Gelder was at home this evening.

"That's it," Pamela said pointing.

Joseph braked, and the brother and sister climbed out. The cold, damp air carried the scent of brine off the bay, rotting leaves, car exhaust, and wood smoke. Richard had grown up with these East Coast smells, and now he found himself longing for the bite of winter-dry air, turquoise skies, and the smell of burning piñon.

Just a few more hours. The Gulfstream was parked at Logan International. Since Syd and Sam had opted to stay in Washington, he had plenty of room for his family.

"Just shark around," Pamela added. "We shouldn't be long."

"No, ma'am, I'll double-park. I don't want to be around the block if you need me," Joseph said.

"Joseph's right," Richard said. "Come on. It's 11:00 PM at night. There's not going to be a lot of traffic."

Side by side they climbed the steps up to the front door. The brass knocker held an elaborate swirl of initials, *V* and *G* overlaid on an *O*. Pamela hesitated with her hand on the knocker.

"How do you think Papa is going to react?"

"Badly."

"Are you ... scared?"

Richard analyzed that. What he felt was the churn of bile in the pit of his stomach, but he was having a hard time figuring out what emotion was fueling the burn. "Nooo," he said slowly drawing out the word. "I feel anxious because I don't like fighting. But I'll fight if I have to. So, knock."

CHAPTER TWENTY-THREE

THE LAST THING I FEAR

THE HAMMERING OF the knocker against the brass plate seemed to echo down the street. He heard footsteps approaching.

"Who is it?" His sister Amelia's voice, soft and gentle. She had always been the turtledove trying to broker peace between Pamela and Richard.

"Richard."

"And Pamela."

The door was flung open, and Amelia grabbed him in a tight hug. If she'd looked tired and old in December at their mother's funeral, Richard reflected that she looked like a grey ghost now. She was still dressed in her Professional-Woman-Uniform of knee-length skirt, sensible pumps, sweater, and a gold chain at her throat.

"You could have just called. You didn't have to come. But, oh, I'm so glad to see you both. Come in, come in."

They stepped into the entry hall that ran straight through to the back of the house. To the right a set of stairs hugged the wall, with an Oriental runner splashing color down the middle of the steps. The left wall was punctuated with doorways—living room, dining room, kitchen—and overhead the crystal teardrops in the small chandelier flickered with rainbow colors. From the living room there was the flicker of light from a television, and he heard the *Tonight Show* music. Richard swallowed hard. It had always seemed like Amelia had telepathy.

"Papa's gone to bed," she said quickly.

"Who was it?" Richard heard Brent call.

And then he emerged from the living room, tying the belt of his bathrobe, one foot scuffing for a fleece-lined leather slipper. He was sporting several days of beard growth, and dark pouches hung beneath his eyes. Richard had been a cop for enough years that he'd seen every variety of despair, depression, and drunkenness. Brent was sporting all three. His face hardened when he saw Richard.

"So, you couldn't return my calls when it would have made a goddamn difference, but you turn up now? Why? Just to gloat?"

"First, I'm sorry I didn't call. Second, you were deliberately targeted and led on so you'd lose your money, but third, it wouldn't have happened, Brent, if you weren't such a goddamn moron."

"I don't have to listen—"

"Shut up." Both sisters jumped and Brent took a step backward. Richard felt perversely pleased since Brent was six inches taller than himself. "And actually, you do have to listen if I'm going to bail you out. You've been living off my sister for eleven years, always looking for the big score. Well, it's time for you to butch up, get a job, and start acting like a man—but you're going to have to do it in New Mexico."

Brent just kept opening and closing his mouth. Amelia was frowning. "What do you mean we were targeted?"

"I'll explain it all on the flight," Richard said.

"Flight? We're not going anywhere—" Amelia began.

At the same time, Brent said, "New Mexico? Why the hell would we go to New Mexico? It's the middle of fucking nowhere. We might as well be on the moon."

"You may end up being glad that it's remote. This mess you got into made me realize that you're in danger, and next time it might not be as benign as just bankrupting you. I need you where I can keep an eye on you and keep you safe." Brent was looking sulky again. Probably because Richard had used the word *mess*.

"Richard, this is ridiculous," Amelia said. "I have a job here. Paul's in school; we have a house—"

"Actually, you don't, unless I pay off the mortgages. This is not a negotiation. This is me rescuing you, or at least doing a preemptive rescue. They'll use you against me, and it might work. I don't know if I could let them hurt or kill my family, so I just can't risk it."

"Kill us? What are you talking about?" The fear in Amelia's voice had the words emerging in a strangled croak. "And who are *they*?"

"I really don't have time to explain all of this—"

Pamela laid a hand on his arm. "I'll do it." She put an arm around Amelia's waist. "Meli, the world has changed. You really aren't safe, and only Richard can keep you safe. Why don't you go in the kitchen and start some water for tea. I'll be there in just a minute." She gave her older sister a push toward the kitchen door. Brent followed her, but, of course, he always had.

Pamela turned to her brother. "We need to enlist Papa if

we're going to have any hope of convincing them."

Richard knew she was right, but he felt that clutch of fear that, if he was honest, had always seemed to be the primary emotion associated with his father. Just as suddenly it was gone, and Richard found himself *wanting* to talk to him.

The narrow staircase seemed claustrophobic. Richard trailed his hand along the wall beneath the ascending framed family photo gallery and began marshaling his thoughts. He didn't exactly know what he was going to say, but he had the shape of it. Perhaps he wasn't as confident as he thought, because his knock was the merest breath of a sound.

"Yes?"

It didn't sound like his father been asleep. Maybe he'd been up here all the time listening to the conversation downstairs, but then Richard remembered that Robert had always had the ability to come instantly awake. You could roll the man out of bed at 4:00 AM and he'd give you a perfect sound bite or a dissertation on the Constitution. It was the one trait Richard shared with him.

Richard didn't answer, just walked into the guest bedroom. Robert sat up and switched on the bedside lamp. Richard noted that the ceramic base was painted with flowers, and the carved Chinese rug on the floor had a floral pattern. Amelia's two china patterns were also floral, as were the bedspreads and even the sheets. *But she lives in a row house with no yard.* Richard shook off the errant thought, musing that it was crazy how one's mind would flit away when faced with something you really didn't want to do.

"What is this, sir?" His father's voice was icy.

Richard wanted to match his cool, but he once again

found anger blazing through his body. It was so intense it made him light-headed.

"You're going to go downstairs and tell Amelia that she has to move her family to New Mexico," Richard ordered. "Because she'll do exactly what you tell her to."

"I will not have you influencing my grandson."

"And I won't let *you* get him killed." That shocked the judge, and for an instant his features sagged. "Don't act like an ignorant rube. You know Paul is in no danger from me, despite what you might rule from the bench as you argue *religious liberty* bullshit. We're being torn apart, and Drew and the Old Ones are behind it. He lured Brent into this disastrous business deal, and ... well, you know what he did to *us*. He's working for the Old Ones. But since subtlety failed, they may try more direct measures. Our family isn't safe. They'll use them against me, and like I told Amelia, I don't think ... no, I *know* I don't have the strength to resist them if they threaten my family. So, they're coming back with me so I can keep that from happening."

The covers were thrown back so violently that they looked like a tsunami wave breaking across the footboard. The judge swung his legs out of bed and headed for the closet. "Very well, you've made your case." He pulled his suitcase out of the closet. "But I'll be watching—"

"Actually, sir, you might notice that I rather pointedly did *not* include *you*."

Robert froze, and his back stiffened. Slowly, slowly he turned to face Richard. "I don't understand."

"I'm done with you." The words seemed to be coming from a vast distance. It wasn't what he'd expected to say, but it felt right. Richard could have left it at that, but all the years of pent-up anxiety and anger clamored to be expressed. "For years I've tried to figure out what you wanted from me. I did everything to please you, including giving up everything I wanted. But then I got hurt, and I realized I couldn't live afraid anymore. You're the last thing I'm afraid of, so it's got to end. You never have loved me, I see that now, so I guess I'm not giving up all that much."

"That's not true. I'm not … demonstrative; I show my love in other ways, by trying to teach you your duty—"

"No, you tried to make me into *you*. You're a complete narcissist. What you wanted was to look into my face and be looking in a mirror. All this crap about service and duty. Yeah, you meant it, but it was *my* duty to serve *you* by being a reflection of you."

Richard couldn't read anything in the spare planes of that face. He turned, started for the door, put his hand on the knob, hesitated. Richard turned back to face his father one last time. "Oh, by the way, I didn't quit the police force when you ordered me to. I told Weber to shit-can my letter of resignation." Richard pulled out the badge case and flashed the gold shield. "See, I'm still me. Not you."

Paul's room was at the far end of the hall. A night-light cast a soft glow, and on the ceiling stick-on stars glowed in the faint light. *Star Wars* posters hung on the walls, and the floor was littered with toys. Richard caught his heel on a toy truck and struggled to keep his balance. The little boy, sprawled in the bed, didn't stir. One bare foot thrust from beneath the covers, and Paul was muttering. He was in the throes of a dream, and it looked to be fun because he was smiling.

Richard gently touched his nephew's shoulder. "Paul, Paul, wake up." The gummed lashes pulled slowly apart. Sleep was congealed in the corners of his eyes.

"Uncle Richard …" It was both a question and a statement.

"Paul, you have to get dressed now."

The boy looked to the window and frowned. "Is it snowing? Is that why it's so dark?"

"No, it's still night, but we have to go." Richard threw back the down comforter and helped the child to his feet.

"Where are we going?" Paul mumbled around a yawn. He pulled open a drawer and pulled out underwear.

"You're coming with me to New Mexico."

"There are cowboys and Indians there, aren't there?" Richard helped him tug a sweater over his head, flattening the tousled hair.

"Yes."

"Will I get to see them?"

"Uh-huh."

"Oh, good."

"Do you have a suitcase?" Richard asked.

"Uh-huh. On the shelf in the closet."

Richard grabbed the chair from the desk, stood on it, and unearthed the case. "Let's pack some of your toys. Just your favorites, 'cause we can't take all of them right now." The lower lip protruded and trembled. "Everything's going to be sent to you, and if anything gets lost, I'll buy you new ones," Richard said.

"Really?"

"Promise," and he crossed his heart.

"Okay." Paul dumped the armful of toys into the open suitcase. A few switches were tripped by the rough handling, and lights blinked and there were halfhearted hiccups of sound from the abused toys. "Okay, I'm ready. Let's go," Paul said.

Richard zipped shut the case, hefted it, and followed Paul into the hall.

There were sounds of drawers closing from the master bedroom. Obviously, his father had done his job, but Brent's mutters of complaint were like a piece of heavy equipment growling nearby. Paul and Richard went downstairs and found Pamela in the dining room, loading an antique silver tea set into a suitcase.

"I don't want movers packing or handling Great-grandmother's tea service," she said. Richard nodded.

"Can I have some milk?" Paul asked.

Pamela gave him a hug. "Sure, kiddo, you need help?" He gave her an offended look. "I'm eight."

"Right, go ahead." She waved him off, then looked at Richard. "Everything ... okay?"

"Yes, yes," he said, and then with greater force and more certainty added, "I think it might be now. There's just one more thing I need to do."

✧   ✧   ✧

IT WAS 3:00 AM, and exhaustion and the steady drone of the engines had sent almost everyone to sleep. Richard was too tense to sleep. Pamela and Eddie's story about the creatures supporting the plane had him on edge, so he had the sword drawn and he kept pacing the length of the fuselage—over and over again.

The bed that the Gulfstream contained had been opened, and Paul, a blanket tucked around him, was deeply asleep. Amelia and Brent sat nearby. Her head was on his shoulder, and his head was thrown back against the window. Richard had no idea how she (or anyone else for that matter) could manage to sleep, because Brent was snoring like a chainsaw. When you added in Eddie's snores it was a nasal symphony.

Dagmar, a seasoned traveler, had inserted earplugs. Rudi and Joseph had been soldiers and could sleep anywhere. Grenier was in the galley making a sandwich.

Estevan and Pamela were playing cards, but her face looked drawn, the muscles in her neck looked like corded steel, and she kept staring out the window at the blackness beyond. Richard reached out and yanked down the shade.

"You've been looking out that window for three solid hours. Stop it."

"But what if they're out there?"

"And you watching obsessively is going to help … exactly … how?" Her lips tightened into a thin line. "We've got a former Air Force fighter pilot on the controls. I'm keeping the sword drawn. We're going to be okay."

Grenier came waddling back down the aisle, dropped into one of the commodious leather seats with a grunt, took a bite of his sandwich, and then brushed breadcrumbs off the mound of his belly. "The sword does seem to confuse them," he offered.

Richard's iPhone rang. He checked the number and felt a

smile curving his lips. From his sister's reaction it was clear it had been a really ugly one. "I think you deserve to hear this," said softly to his sister, and he hit the speaker icon.

"What the hell have you done?" It was Drew, and he sounded furious and frightened.

"Hi, Drew, so good of you to call."

"I've got a—"

"A call on your note. Yes, I know. I bought your building, and all the outstanding paper. All you have to do is payoff your loan ... Oh, but wait, your company is experiencing some cash flow problems, isn't it? Hmmm, I wonder why?"

"Why?" came Sandringham's question.

Richard knew what Drew meant, but he decided to draw out the torture. Richard was beginning to understand why cats played with mice.

"Why the financial problems, or why as a more general question to the universe? You blew it, Drew." Richard could no longer maintain the light, bantering tone, his voice deepened, gravel in the low tones. "You threw in with my enemies, and you overpromised on what you could deliver. They're not going to be happy with *you*, and I'm *really* not happy with you. You should have considered that I control one of the great fortunes of the world before you decided to screw with me and mine. And just so you know, right now my *only* interest is in using that money to fuck you. I've wrecked your company, and I'm throwing you out in the street. Sort of a nice symmetry, don't you think? It's what you did to me. At least I won't put you in the hospital. Your new friends might take care of that, however. Bye, Drew, have fun being broke and hunted."

"Wait, Rich—"

Richard cut the connection and put the phone back in his pocket.

Pamela was staring at him in shock. *"Who are you?"* she asked.

"The man he was destined to be," Grenier said.

Hateful? Richard thought. *Vengeful? Merciless?*

He excused himself and retreated to the aft of the plane, where Kenntnis had a private office. Closing the door behind him, Richard sank down behind the desk and tried to analyze what he was feeling. What worried him most was that among all the other emotions coursing through him there was another like a thin dark thread weaving through his mind and heart. *Pride. He felt proud.*

Richard stared at the empty chair across the desk. In November, Kenntnis had sat where Richard was now sitting, and Richard had occupied that other chair. Kenntnis had discovered that Rhiana was not completely human, and Richard been called in to discuss what should be done about her. It had become a debate between Kenntnis and himself about their respective roles. Richard had told him he had to be in charge. Little did he know how prophetic that would turn out to be. Richard had decreed that Rhiana was not to be harmed. Because of that single decision on his part, Kenntnis was gone, and he was well and truly in charge.

And proud of having destroyed a man's life.

It was not a good place to be.

CHAPTER TWENTY-FOUR

ALL READY FOR THE APOCALYPSE

VERTEBRAE POPPED AS Richard stretched his arms over his head, and he realized that for the first time in weeks it didn't feel like his muscles were twisted tight with tension. He felt at peace. *I came home.* The thought surprised him. His first year in New Mexico he had found it brown, dusty, windy, and ugly. The mañana attitude drove him crazy with his uptight, rush, rush, rush East Coast style. His intention had been to work a few years with APD and then look for a job someplace civilized. But years had gone by, and Richard hadn't sent out the resumes, and that afternoon in Washington, as he had tried to figure out where to go and what to do, Richard had imagined he smelled the sharp pungent bite of roasting Hatch green chiles, and the spice and evergreen aroma of burning piñon crackling in kiva fireplaces.

He just hoped that Amelia and her family would fall in love with New Mexico as he had. He had them settled into a gated community only a few miles to the south of the Lumina building, and Joseph had seen to the installation of an expansive security system in their new home. Given Amelia's credentials, he had no doubt she would soon be hired at one of the local hospitals.

He turned his back to the window and perched on the

windowsill while he critically surveyed the office. There was room in the far corner for his piano. He'd have Jeannette arrange for movers. Actually, he'd have her clear everything out of his apartment; he was never going back there.

Richard was just settling into the chair behind the desk when Cross slouched in. He was stuffing the final enormous bite of a cheese Danish into his mouth. "Well, you finally look like you belong here. You should have dumped Daddy a long time ago," he mumbled around the wad of dough.

"First, I was the dumpee, not the dumper, and second, we don't talk about this. Ever. Got it?"

Cross gave a mock salute. Richard leaned over and depressed the intercom. "Jeannette, a couple of things. Figure out what time and day it is in Tokyo. I need to talk to Fujasaki. And please close up my apartment. Bring the books, music, and piano here, and you can store everything else."

"Yes, sir. Ms. Reitlingen is here. Should I send her in?"

"Yes, please."

Richard jerked his chin pointedly toward the door. "See how Dagmar asks if she can be admitted. Why don't you do that? Why do you just walk in?"

Cross shrugged. "I'm a god. And Kenntnis let me."

"You can use the second reason to keep doing it," Richard said.

"*Was ist loss?*" Dagmar said. Then shook her head. "Sorry, I've been talking with Peter. What's—"

"I've got a question."

"Let's see if I've got an answer," the COO said. "I'm bright, my dear, but amazing as it might be, I don't know everything. *Nearly—*"

"Cut the burble." She gave Richard an impish smile and subsided.

"Why did a building this size only house eighty-four people?"

"Give the boy a gold star," Cross said. "I've been wondering when you'd notice. Kenntnis left it up to me to decide if and when you were ready for the real tour. When you didn't fall for the daddy trick, I figured you just might be bright enough to see past the obvious, and tough, smart, and brave enough to survive, at least for a little while longer. So now you get all the secret *schnaba.*"

"Does that include a decoder ring and a secret handshake?" Richard asked in a tone that was almost sickeningly sweet.

Cross glared at him. "You got a fucking magic sword, what more do you want?"

"It's not magic," Richard said piously. "It's an ancient weapon of alien design—"

"Yeah, you can try giving 'em the explanation, but anybody who sees you draw it is gonna go, *'yep, that's a fuckin' magic sword.'* Shall we?" Cross indicated the office door with an elaborate sweep of his hand.

With Cross in the lead, they began a tour of the Lumina building. On the fifth floor someone was typing on a computer keyboard, a sound like rain pattering on plastic. The heater kicked on, the rush of air overrunning the sound of the typing.

"This building is a fortress," Cross said. "A place for us to ride out bad times should they come. It wouldn't be comfortable, and you can forget about privacy, but we can house three thousand people in this building." The heater shut off, and the sound of the lone typist returned.

"Where do they sleep?" Dagmar asked. "Air mattresses," Cross answered.

Richard shook his head. "No, bunk beds. We might be able to house more people that way. If it comes to that. I'm still hopeful that Eddie and the other scientists are going to find a way to free Kenntnis," Richard said while Dagmar scribbled on her iPad Pro.

"The rest of the floors are pretty much the same, so we can skip them," Cross said and led them back to the elevators. When they reached the lobby, Joseph was waiting. He nodded a greeting.

"Show Richard the real security setup," Cross ordered.

The chief of security crossed to the circular reception desk, murmured an apology to Paulette, and reached down by her right leg. "Sorry, not getting fresh," Joseph said.

"Oh, please, get fresh," Paulette replied. She had a lilting French accent. The long lashes brushed the tops of her high cheekbones, and the tip of her tongue lightly touched her lower lip.

Joseph grinned at Richard. "Does that count as sexual harassment?"

"Do you want me to stop her?" he asked.

"Hell, no," Joseph said, and they all shared a laugh.

There was a loud click followed by the quiet hum of motors, and heavy steel panels came rolling up out of the floors and sealed the windows. Within seconds the lobby was plunged into darkness. Halogen spots in the ceiling switched on.

"These can be keyed from a number of locations in the building," Joseph said. "Your office, my office, the penthouse, and on the third floor."

Cross piped up. "You know how we're tucked in among the boulders. Well, anyplace we don't have big rocks to protect us, steel and concrete barricades have come up to keep any mad bombers away."

"Every window is sealed?" Richard asked.

"Yes," Joseph said. "But there are pumps and scrubbers to pull in outside air."

"And what happens if someone cuts the power? It's going to get pretty dark and hot or cold, depending," Richard objected. The thought of being sealed in here, away from the touch and sight of the sun, had his claustrophobia jumping to grab his throat and shorten his breaths.

"The roof, the south wall, and the west wall are covered with solar panels. We also have battery storage for night and during cloudy weather as well as diesel generators," Joseph concluded.

"So, we should go down there now," Cross said.

Back in the elevator Cross touched the button for the swimming pool which was one level below the garage. The elevator doors opened, and the light from the halogen spots danced on the gently swaying surface of the pool.

"Not just a swimming pool ... water storage. There used to be big cisterns down here," Cross said. "But Kenntnis knew you liked to swim, so he had this built. He figured we could store the water this way."

Richard was stunned and oddly warmed by the thought

that Kenntnis had put such effort into his comfort. "When did this get built? I've only known you people for a few months."

"Right after Thanksgiving. It only took a couple of weeks. Enough money and you can get anything done."

Dagmar walked to the edge of the pool, leaned down, and trailed her fingers in the water. She stood up and shook the droplets of water off her fingers. "I have to ask, if this is meant to be a water source, aren't the chemicals going to be a problem?"

"The water purification system is in the next room."

"How do we replenish the water if the city's water system goes down?" Richard asked.

"We'll get to that. Let's finish the building first," Cross said.

He led them through the room holding the purification system. The next room housed the backup generators. Cross pointed at another door. "That room has stockpiles of diesel, gasoline, and replacement solar panels. Do you want to see it?"

"I better. Let's make sure they're actually there."

"Taking that definition of assumption, a little too much to heart, aren't you?" Cross asked.

"No," Richard said.

The room did indeed contain the promised fuel and panels. They traipsed back past the pool, and through a door at the opposite end. The rooms held vast stockpiles of food.

"Okay, now the cafeteria and industrial kitchen make sense," Richard mused.

"Okay, next level."

Cross fished a key out of the front of his sweatshirt, inserted it in the lock in the elevator, and sent them down another floor. "Kenntnis didn't want any kids wandering in here." He looped the chain and key over Richard's head. "Here, it's yours now."

They stepped out into an armory. The collection of weapons ranged from TOW missiles and M-16s and grenades to spears and bows and arrows and swords. The accompanying ammunition, both low- and high-tech, was also present.

"*Mein Gott,*" Dagmar whispered.

The room to the left was a training gym stocked with weights, aerobic machines, and the accouterments necessary for gymnastics. Fencing masks and padded vests hung on one wall. On the other side of the armory there was an indoor laser shooting range.

"So we don't waste ammo," Richard murmured as he picked up the laser pistol and sighted down the barrel. "Damn, he thought of everything. Is that it?"

"Nope. Now we go outside."

They returned to the lobby, and Cross led them out the back door. They walked past his packing-box shelter, squatting like a wart against the clean steel and glass lines of the building. Boulders and concrete retaining walls were only a few feet away. Cross turned and looked like he was walking directly toward the rocks, and then he disappeared. When Richard got close enough, he spotted the narrow opening between boulders. The passageway extended about six hundred feet, and the rocks towered ten feet above his head.

Suddenly the terrain opened up into a tiny, narrow box

canyon. Tufts of buffalo grass, brown now from winter's grip, crackled under the soles of his shoes. There were a couple of cottonwood saplings which signaled the presence of water. There was a small shed and a frost-free hydrant in among the trees.

"We dug an illegal well so we have our own source of water," Cross explained.

Richard pulled up the handle on the frost free and jumped back at the gush of water. Cupping his hand, he braved a sip and felt a sharp pain behind his eyes from the chill. It tasted sharp and wonderful.

"We run a pipe and refill the swimming pool," Cross said. "As for the planes, we own a big hunk of mesa to the north. The runways are dirt 'cause we didn't want to raise too many flags by starting a big permitting fight. And there are cisterns of jet fuel buried on the property. And there's a reason we have a bunch of electric cars that can be recharged off our solar panels and batteries in addition to the penis cars."

"So we are all ready for the zombie apocalypse," Dagmar said grimly.

"How about we stop it instead?" Richard suggested. He glanced down at his elegant Zegna suit. "People always dress so badly in a zombie apocalypse." Cross gave a snort, and Richard was pleased to see a small smile curve Dagmar's lips and her brow clear.

They returned to the office and watched while New Mexico treated them to one of its spectacular sunsets. The rounded cones of the Three Sisters, extinct volcanoes, looked like the backs of broaching blue whales silhouetted against a riot of gold, crimson, purple, and blue. Well, at least the two humans were enjoying nature's fireworks, Richard thought. Cross was eating his way through a jar of mixed nuts that he found in the bar.

Pamela walked in.

"Hey, she didn't get announced," Cross said in a tone that was both triumphant and accusing.

Pamela gave the homeless god a puzzled, irritated look. "What?"

Richard waved it away. "Never mind. Hey, guess what, I'm Bruce Wayne." This time he was on the receiving end of the puzzled, irritated look. "You know ... Batman?"

"Nah," Cross said. "You're that wimpy Peter Parker."

"Who?" Pamela asked.

"Spider-Man," Cross and Richard said in chorus.

She rolled her eyes. "Dinner is almost ready." Cross jumped up and tossed the empty jar into the trash with a long throw like a basketball player, giving a "score" pump with his arm.

"Angela's coming." And then she added in a too casual tone, "And I left a message for Weber inviting him to join us, too."

Richard stopped midstep and looked at her erect back. Tried to analyze his feelings. Tried to picture them as a couple. Tried not to be depressed. Told himself he was just trying to protect her ... him ... both of them.

Instead, he found himself blurting out, "He's married. Separated, but they haven't gotten a divorce."

"Good God, Richard, must you try to make everything into a romance?" she huffed. "You two parted on bad terms. I wanted to see if we could heal that breach."

Feeling oddly relieved, Richard asked, in what he hoped was a casual tone, "So, is he coming?"

"I don't know. I haven't heard back from him."

Maybe he doesn't want to come. Doesn't want to see me after the way I treated him, Richard thought as he leaned against the back of the elevator ignoring the conversation going on between Pamela and Dagmar.

They stepped into the penthouse living room to find Eddie slumped on the sofa with his laptop and headphones.

They walked past him and into the kitchen, where Grenier was inspecting a bottle of wine. "I think a Malbec with pork loin," he was saying to Franz. "Ah, good, someone else to open this. I can't really do that with only one hand." He gave Richard a pointed look.

"I would have helped you, Monsieur Grenier," Franz said.

"I didn't want to disturb you while you were putting the final touches on that Sacher torte," the former minister said. Dagmar went to help him.

Amazing aromas were issuing from the ovens while Franz bustled about putting the final touches on dessert. Richard hadn't realized he was starving until that moment.

Eddie wandered in. "Is it dinner yet?"

Grenier was handing out glasses of wine. Richard was feeling relaxed, actually rather self-satisfied, and pushing aside his reservations, he took one.

Angela arrived and was introduced to Eddie. The coroner took a sip of her wine, then looked around with a questioning expression.

"Where's Damon?"

"I did invite him," Pamela said.

Richard dropped his eyes, watching the swirl of red in his glass. "We ..." He coughed and continued. "We had a little ... disagreement."

Pamela answered, "He came home before we did."

"Well, he hasn't been at work," Angela said. The buzz of conversation died.

Dread hit his stomach. Richard set down the wineglass and was startled when the stem snapped. Wine flowed across the granite countertop and began to drip onto the floor. Richard once again had a flash of the blood pooling on the floors of that small house, and he gagged. Pulling out his phone, Richard dialed Weber's home number. It rang and voicemail picked up.

"You know how this works."

"Damon ... Lieutenant, it's Richard. Are you there?" Silence. Next, he tried Weber's mobile. It went to voicemail on the first ring. He looked around at the circle of concerned faces. "His ... his cell's been turned off."

And deep inside Richard a murmur of fear and guilt became a shout.

I sent him away. I sent him away, I sent him away. And I didn't arrange to protect him.

❖   ❖   ❖

IT TOOK A while for Jack to respond to her knock on the hotel room door. When he finally opened the door, he was rubbing his eyes, his hair was tousled, and he wore only pajama bottoms, and his feet were bare. Rhiana looked at the face of her diamond-encrusted watch and realized it was 2:00 AM. Sleep, like hunger for traditionally human food, pricked her only after days spent on this side of the gate. Even in human form she sipped and supped from the chaotic, roiling emotions of the crowds she passed on the street, and the person trapped in the smashed car at the scene of an auto accident, or a married couple fighting in a restaurant. There was a reason her father called Earth a buffet.

"Jesus, Rhiana, what's wrong?" Jack asked.

"Nothing. I forget about time and night and rest."

"Nice for you. You want to come in? What's up?" His words were still thickened by sleep.

Rhiana followed him into the room. It was a nice room. Georgian inspired with a king-sized four-poster bed. The sheet and comforter were twisted and rumpled. A sofa and a couple of chairs clustered around a gas fireplace. There was a desk in an alcove. An open laptop sat on top, sending slow flashes of color across the wall as the screen saver roiled. It had seemed strange to her that Jack lived in the Hay-Adams Hotel across the street from the White House. Now it made sense. He was a man and a bachelor. Why not have maid service, room service, health club, pool? Especially when you didn't have to pay for it.

"What do you need?" Jack asked as he pulled on a bath-robe.

"If I did something that got Richard to come back it would be a good thing, right?"

He scratched absently at his chest, his finger probing at the mat of brown hair. "Well, yeah. What did you have in mind?"

"Oh, I already did it."

"Okay." He waited.

Rhiana clasped and unclasped her hands. She walked to the window and looked out at the White House. "I got Doug to help me."

"Okay," Jack said again, only more slowly, and she heard the distaste frosting the edges of the word.

"I gave him that cop, Weber," Rhiana finished in a rush. She didn't have to explain who Weber was. They had all obsessively studied the people around Richard, looking for any opening that could be exploited.

"Jesus!" Jack ran his hand through his hair. "You're for sure going to have to kill him now. He'll never forgive you."

"He won't necessarily know I did it. It might just—"

"He'd be an idiot if he didn't. Jesus, Rhiana." Once again, his hands went to his hair, frantically combing and tugging. He paced a small circle. "We're trying to take over a world, and you're acting like it's high school." Guilt and embarrassment fueled her fury, and she felt the bonds encompassing her human body threatening to shred. "We had a plan—" Jack continued, and she cut him off.

"And your big plan didn't work! You and Sandringham with all your psychological crap about daddy transference. Richard *didn't* go after Kenntnis. He went home. *I'm* the one who'll get him back."

"Okay, fine. You're a genius. I just hope you're right and he actually comes back. But why come bother me at two in the morning?" He moved to the minibar, turned the key, and pulled out a miniature of bourbon. Screwing off the cap, he drained it in two swallows.

"I thought you should be kept informed. You are my assistant," and the words sounded ludicrous even to her.

"Bullshit." He turned back to face her. "It's because you're scared and feeling guilty, and you want me to tell you it's all going to be okay, and your fantasy crush won't care that you gave his best friend to a fucking *psychopath*."

Rhiana groped in her pocket and pulled out a penny. "He's not just his *best friend*. There's something between them. I saw it in their faces. So, he will absolutely come back." She set the coin to spinning and sparking in her hand. "And you will never, ever speak to me like that again." The flare of copper fire danced across the wallpaper as Rhiana murmured the spell. Jack's back stiffened in surprise and fear. Rhiana reached out a hand, fingers curled like talons. The spiritualist gasped, and a hand flew to his throat. She pulled him toward her. His cheeks were a dull brick red. She released him, and he fell heavily onto his knees. His fingers clutched convulsively at the nap of the carpet as he sucked air into his oxygen starved lungs.

Rhiana walked toward the door. She didn't quite reach it before Jack said, "There's one thing you need to remember, princess." His voice was hoarse, and he could barely speak above a whisper. "You really should be nice to the people you meet on the way up, because you're sure as fuck going to meet them on the way down."

CHAPTER TWENTY-FIVE
COST-BENEFIT ANALYSIS

"**Y**OU BETTER HOPE he's *not* in there," Syd said as they all gazed down at the topographical map of Virginia.

They were once again back at Bob Franklin's house in Baltimore. This time the warm smell of roasting turkey and garlic mashed potatoes had replaced the smoky bite of gumbo. Another difference was the lack of spouses and children. It was just agents and Richard's entourage. Joseph, Estevan, Rudi, Pamela, Cross, and Grenier.

Richard had tried and failed to convince his sister to remain behind. Cross had been philosophical about it all. As for Grenier, he hadn't wanted to come, but Richard knew they needed the man's knowledge of the Old Ones as well as the knowledge he could provide about his private Virginia compound. Richard was convinced they had taken Weber to the compound, so he wanted the former preacher with him. Unfortunately, it had required Richard to deliver an overt threat, that Grenier would be thrown into the street, to obtain his grudging agreement.

I wonder if he still *likes the man I've become,* Richard thought.

Danny had been running through satellite images to try to turn Richard's hunch about Weber's whereabouts into a certainty.

"They've set up a perimeter of marines called in from Quantico. *Nobody* gets in," Franklin said, amplifying on Syd's statement.

Richard shook his head. "Not true. There's one group they've agreed to allow inside the perimeter. There's a team arriving from the Vatican to perform an exorcism."

Grenier paused with his fork halfway to his mouth. "Are you seriously suggesting that you put on a dog collar and traipse out in fancy dress to confront monsters and rescue the damsel?" He dropped his fork and made quote marks around the final word. His tone held a sneer. It looked like Richard hadn't been forgiven after all.

"Hey, those dress thingies priests wear can hide a boat-load of guns," Sam broke in with delight.

Pamela wrinkled her nose as if a bad smell had wafted past. "Cassocks! They are called cassocks, not dress thingies." Sam threw her a finger.

Apart from Pamela, Sam was the only woman present, and they both stood out like lilies in the midst of a redwood forest. All the agents were *big*. The only other woman in the house was Franklin's wife, Michelle, who had set out the food and promptly disappeared. She didn't seem real happy to have them back. Richard couldn't blame her.

"Uh, Sam, I think this one is going to have to be a stag party," her dad said.

Sam's mouth opened and closed a few times before she finally said, "Well, crap." Syd grinned and ruffled his daughter's short, bobbed hair.

"And remember, guns won't work in there," Franklin

reminded her.

Cross mopped up gravy and cranberry sauce with a crescent roll, and then stuffed the entire dripping mess into his mouth. He mumbled around the doughy glob, "Well, that might not be *strictly* true. They might work if the sword was nearby and drawn."

"Now we're talking," Sam said. "Hey, I could dress up like a nun."

One of the younger agents, Richard couldn't remember his name, leered and said, "Ooooh, Sammy as a naughty nun. Will you spank me with your ruler, Sister?"

"No, Jay, but I'll kick your nuts up through—"

Pamela spoke up. "Sam and I could go. For all the marines will know, the nuns might be there to hand you holy water and wipe your sweating brows while you contend with demons."

Richard looked back to Cross. "Okay, that's promising, but I'd have to draw the sword well before we reach the compound to keep the guncotton from being affected." Richard sighed. "I suppose it's unavoidable. I hate looking like a *Highlander* reject—"

"Yeah, little on the short side," Sam broke in. Richard gave her an exasperated look. She held up her hands. "Jeez, sorry, just trying to relieve the tension, but go ahead."

"Are you normally this manic before an operation?" Richard asked, honestly curious.

She shrugged. "I want to kick some monster butt. You know, a little payback."

"Are you good now?" he asked. She pressed her lips into a tight line and made the zipping motion. "As I was saying, I think I need to keep the sword drawn all the time now. So how do I do it if the hilt isn't actually in my hand?"

"You can't," Cross said. He craned his head and looked down his nose at the untouched plate of food resting on Richard's knee. He'd never seen a starving vulture, but he had the very real sense it would have looked just like Cross in this moment.

Richard knew he wasn't going to be able to eat. He was projecting businesslike competence, but his gut felt like he'd eaten ground glass washed down by battery acid. He handed over his plate to the homeless god and said, "You can't tell me that Charlemagne or Arthur or other paladins in ancient times didn't wear the sword openly."

"Yeah, the hilt was sticking out of the scabbard, but the blade wasn't there." Cross encompassed them all in a wide grin. "It's actually kind of funny. All those incredibly gaudy scabbards you see in museums, they were just for show. Something to draw the eye so people would be less likely to notice there was nothing actually *in* them."

"So, there is no way to keep the blade present without me holding it?"

"Yep."

"Well, that's a terrible design." Richard pulled the pill case out of his pocket and dry swallowed a Xanax and a Pepcid.

"Take it up with the designer—if we ever manage to bust him loose." Cross cleared his throat and added, "*Uh*... a question, if it turns out Fuzz Boy is in there, and you go in after him, do you want me along for this little party?"

Richard pressed a hand against his forehead and prepared to say out loud what, up until now, he had kept to himself. Pamela was not going to like it.

Finally, he said, "Yes, I want you along because if anything happens to me—if I get killed—you need to grab the sword and run for it. With your powers you can find someone to replace me. Find another Paladin."

Cross said, "I don't want to be trying to do magic in there. First, if I'm close enough to you to take the handoff, that means I'm close enough for the sword to affect *me*, and it's going to fuck up my powers. And second, my brethren *way* outclass me. I get into a full-blown magical pissing contest with them I'm gonna get squashed."

"I'm not advocating that you do that. I fall, you grab the sword and high tail it out of there."

"Got it," Danny, the computer geek, sang out, interrupting them.

There was a general shuffling as everyone gathered where they could see the screen of his laptop computer.

"This is surveillance from the Hyatt Regency at Reagan National. There's Weber."

He pointed, and a fist seemed to clench in the center of Richard's chest. Weber looked so tired … and so sad as he emerged from the hotel. The time stamp on the recording read *3:40 AM.* The shuttle to the airport was waiting in front of the doors. It looked like Weber was going to be the only passenger. He began to climb the steps into the van.

"And there." Danny froze the tape and pointed again. "That's where it happened."

A figure Richard recognized rushed up behind Weber. *Doug Andresson, his evil counterpart.* Andresson grabbed

Damon in a tight choke hold while at the same time punching him hard in the temple. Richard could almost feel Andresson's fists connecting with *his* face and belly again. Weber collapsed onto the steps of the van. The driver stared, mouth agape. Andresson then casually drew his pistol and shot first the driver of the van and then the doorman who was pulling a cell phone out of his pocket. Andresson dragged the driver's body out of the driver's seat, across Damon's prone form, and tossed him out onto the pavement. He then dragged Damon farther into the shuttle, settled into the driver's seat, and the van drove away.

"The dark Paladin, Doug Andresson." Grenier gave Richard a significant look. "You still want to take the sword anywhere near the gate? Knowing they've got him?"

"We can't go in without the sword, and they've taken Weber to the compound—"

Pamela was shaking her head. "There is nothing on this video"—she thrust a forefinger at the computer screen—"to support that. Have you got anything beyond a *feeling*?"

"Where else would they keep Andresson?" Richard asked tightly.

"Oh, I don't know—a hotel? Someone's house? We know there are humans who are working for these … things." Pamela's eyes slid pointedly toward Grenier.

Grenier was unaffected by the accusing look. "No, Andresson's at the compound. They'll want him close to hand. I know I did."

Syd shivered. "That place ain't good for humans. It's gotta be a hell of a lot worse now. I don't see how the dude can take it."

"Because he's our very own version of a monster wrapped up in human skin," Grenier said. "He's the coldest psychopath I've ever met."

"Hey," Danny said. "I've been checking traffic cams to track the van, and there's a tag to this shitty movie."

They all rushed back to the computer to watch as the shuttle van was abandoned in an industrial area of DC. A BMW convertible with the top up pulled up next to it. The trunk popped open and Andresson bundled Damon's unconscious body into the trunk. It was hard to distinguish the features of the driver, but it was clear it was a woman, and Richard had seen that particularly BMW any number of times while he had been in DC before. There was little doubt it was Rhiana.

So, this was where his act of mercy had taken him.

Everyone was looking to him. It was his call. The question was whether anyone else would agree. "They have Damon. We're going in. We don't have a choice," Richard said.

Grenier snorted. "Of *course*, we have a choice. We could *not* go in. There are going to be casualties in this war. Weber just had the bad luck to be the first, but he's a military man. He'd understand. You feel guilty because of your attraction to him, and because you sent him away, so you're acting—"

Richard was emotionally raw; the whipsawing by the man from support one minute to what felt like betrayal the next, and saying *out loud* in front of these hyper-macho men how he was sexually attracted to Damon, was more than Richard could handle.

It felt like something exploded behind his eyes. Almost

before he realized it Richard found himself spinning around, and his hand closing around Grenier's throat. The rolls of flesh gave under his fingers, and the hazel eyes widened in alarm. The man outweighed Richard by a hundred pounds at least, but Richard drove Grenier back across the room and slammed him up against the wall. Anger had Richard's breath coming so short and shallow that he couldn't manage to say a word, and Grenier couldn't speak because Richard was choking him.

"I take it that's not an option," Sam drawled. She tapped Richard on the shoulder. "Maybe ease off, dude? You can kill him another time."

Richard abruptly released Grenier and sprang back, horrified at his own rage.

Would I have killed him?

Who am I?

✧   ✧   ✧

DESPITE THE BLACKOUT curtains having been pulled against the ever-present light haze of Washington, DC, and a comfortable bed, Richard still couldn't sleep. That was partly due to the fact that the suite at the Mayflower hotel was filled with the guttural snores of men sleeping heavily. Joseph was taking this third watch, and he nodded to Richard but didn't speak when he padded into the sitting room carrying his laptop. Settling onto a sofa, Richard logged on to the APD computer to review Andresson's rap sheet. The list of assaults on both men and women soon had his gut burning.

People had accepted Richard's decision that they had to

go in, but he could sense the support was soft. While it was a high certainty that Weber was in the compound, there was still some doubt among his allies, so he needed another reason. The reason was obvious. Kenntnis was there. Lumina needed him. The team could try to free him. Or if that was a bridge too far, they could at least do some reconnaissance. But for that to make sense Richard needed someone who understood how Kenntnis had been trapped.

Rather than wake up people in New Mexico, Richard logged on to the secure and encrypted Lumina server to see who might be awake. He wasn't surprised to find Eddie online, and he just so happened to be the person Richard needed.

<Hi. What are you doing?> Richard sent.

<Playing WoW. I'm fighting a balrog.>

<Want to face some real monsters?>

<No! Actually—HELL NO!>

<Want to take a close look at spin glass?> Seconds ticked by.

<Are you there?>

<I'm here. You're going in?>

<Have to.>

<They have him?>

<Yes.>

<I liked him.>

<Don't make it past tense.>

<Sorry. Is it okay I'm scared?>

<Yes, I'm scared too.>

There was another long moment with the cursor just blinking at Richard; then a single word appeared.

<Okay.>

✧　✧　✧

ANDRESSON WASN'T A moron, Damon had to give him that. Rather than handcuff him to the wooden bedpost where he might have gotten enough leverage to break the wood, or any other convenient closet rod or shower rod, the psycho had broken into the wall of the bathroom and cuffed him to one of the pipes in the wall. They were depressingly sturdy. The other thing depressingly horrible—actually horrific—were the rusty red stains in the bathtub. Damon had been a soldier and then a cop for over twenty years; he knew blood stains when he saw them. Somebody, or more like *somebodies* given the amount of blood, had been butchered in that tub. Weber figured his blood would eventually join the rest once the Monster Bitch figured out Richard wasn't stupid enough to come to his rescue, and Andresson got bored with his newest toy.

Weber was pretty sure he had a couple of cracked ribs, and his wrists were rubbed raw from the cuffs. Both eyes were blackened, his lips were cut, and his jaw cracked whenever he tried to work up some saliva in his dry mouth. He was hungry and he'd been forced to piss down his leg. He was pretty sure he was going to die in this filthy bathroom (Andresson clearly wasn't much into cleaning). He just hoped it would happen soon and be relatively quick but given the pleasure the man had taken in delivering the beatings, Damon feared it would not be quick. And was certainly not going to be painless.

Fear made his stomach wobble. He tried to push it back. Think about anything else. He wished he could apologize to Carol. She hadn't deserved the marriage he'd once again fucked up. He wished he could drink margaritas and eat *chile con queso* at *El Pinto* with Angela. He wished he could tell Richard he was sorry ...

The door to the bathroom swung open and Andresson sauntered in. A bottle of beer hung negligently between his fingers. Damon was desperately thirsty. He could survive without food for a good long while, but he needed water ... or a sip of beer if that was all that was available.

"Hey." His voice was a harsh rasp. "If you don't get me something to drink, we're not going to get to continue our fun. So, what do you say?"

For a few seconds the man just blinked at him, then throwing back his head, he let out a braying laugh. "Good point, pig, I want to keep you breathing until that faggot shows up to rescue you."

Damon almost said *he's not a moron, he won't come,* but he bit back the words. If he kept up his strength, there might come a time when luck would favor him and he could ... might be able to escape. If he just got back some strength and could swing up and get Andresson in a leg lock around his head ...

The man stepped in close and held the bottle to Weber's lips. He greedily drank down the beer. Some of it dribbled over his lips, stinging in the cuts left from Andresson's fists.

"I wish I hadn't gotten stuck with you. Wish it had been that stuck-up bitch of a sister, but princess and her cuck seem to think you were the better choice to get Oort out here.

How does it feel having that fag all hot for you? Bet it makes your asshole pucker right up."

"My God, you really are an ignorant cracker, aren't you?" Damon sighed. That earned him a hard punch in the stomach. Weber had to fight to keep from vomiting up the precious beer.

Andresson stormed out of the bathroom, slamming the door behind him. Damon found himself chewing over what the psychopath had said. *They think he's hot for you. Why would they think that?*

Because he is. And you've known it for months.

Weber closed his eyes tightly, sucked in a breath.

For God's sake, Rhode Island, stay the fuck away.

✧   ✧   ✧

IT TOOK SEVEN hours before Eddie walked through the door of the Mayflower suite. Richard was grateful the Lear jet had still been in New Mexico to bring the scientist to him. Pamela had been arranging for their disguises, Joseph had worked with Syd and Franklin obtaining vehicles, while the computer geek, Danny, displayed a real flair for finding forgers to prepare the documents they would need.

Eddie moved immediately to the desk in the sitting room and began perusing the room service menu. "You didn't eat on the plane?" Richard asked.

"Yeah, but this'll be better."

Richard suddenly realized that he was hungry, too. They called in an order and settled onto the couch so Richard could receive another crash course in physics. Most of which he feared, *no, knew*, he wouldn't understand.

"Okay, so, you know we're going into the compound. Kenntnis is trapped there, and I figured as long as we're there we may as well try to bust him out. So how do we break this spin glass?" Richard asked.

The gawky young scientist leaned down, untied his tennis shoes, and pulled them off. He rubbed his stockinged feet on the carpet, hissed as he sucked in a breath through his teeth, removed his glasses and pinched the bridge of his nose, plucked at his collar, cracked his knuckles. Richard wanted to throttle him.

"In a lab we'd turn back on the pump laser, and that would start the probe laser ... uh, that'd be Kenntnis ... moving again. But it looks like they used light from that star that we saw through the gate as the pump laser, and I don't have a clue how to turn back on a laser that's powered by a fucking *star*."

That left a hollow pit in Richard's stomach. He grasped for anything that might be promising. "That glass looks to be only five or six inches wide," he said. "What if we just pushed it over and broke it?"

Grenier waddled in and checked abruptly at the sight of Eddie. Richard ignored him.

Eddie shook his head. "You don't want to do that because you run the risk of disrupting the light pulse. Remember, whatever this guy was, his knowledge, mind, everything is stored on an atomic spin wave. If you just break the glass, the information that is Kenntnis might end up scrambled. Also, the longer it's ... uh, he's stored, the more he degrades. He's functionally frozen, but the atoms still move slightly, and that alters the stored information."

"So, we need to get this done and get it done soon."

"And right. Getting it done right would be also good," Eddie added.

"So, when you turn on this pump laser, what is it about that laser that will make Kenntnis move?" Richard asked.

"The light from the laser."

"And how much light does it take?"

"Normally, not much. But nothing about this is normal."

Richard removed the sword hilt from the holster at the small of his back. "There's always a swirl of light around the blade whenever I've drawn it where magic or a tear in reality is present. The more the magic or the bigger the tear, the brighter the light."

"I'm guessing with that gate the sword will turn into a torch," Grenier interrupted.

"Exactly." Richard turned back to Eddie. "So, could we focus the light from the sword onto the spin glass?"

"The pump laser is tuned to the frequency of the probe laser. It's not like frying an ant with a magnifying glass," Eddie said.

"Kenntnis made the sword," Richard said. "I think it might actually be a part of him. Tuned to him, so to speak."

Taking his lower lip between thumb and forefinger, Eddie pulled at it. "Maybe we could use mirrors and lenses to focus and intensify the sword's light," he mumbled. The torment of his lip was interfering with his diction. "It might work. And even if it doesn't it will also tell us a lot. It'll help me figure this thing out."

Richard nodded. "That was my thinking. We'll try for a

double rescue, but we'll be happy if we end up with intel and *one* rescue."

Grenier cleared his throat and took a step toward the two men on the couch. "What?" Richard asked, and he knew his tone wasn't all that friendly. He still hadn't forgotten or forgiven how Grenier wanted to just abandon Damon.

"*Now* this plan actually has some merit. So let me offer my help."

"You're a fat man with one hand," Richard snapped. "What possible help could you be?"

Alarm pulsed across his face. "Oh, God, you think I'm … Heavens no, I'm not going *with* you. I'm not going anywhere *near* them. And there's nothing you could do that would make me go with you, but there's an alternative to going in the front door."

"What?"

"There's a tunnel. It runs from my basement wine cellar to a quarter mile past the fence. The exit is screened by trees."

For a moment the rest of the sentence didn't register. Richard was remembering that basement. Remembering the toe of Andresson's cowboy boot connecting with his balls, and his fist crunching against Richard's face. The look of absolute joy on Andresson's face at the pain he was inflicting. *He took Damon. He has Damon.*

Eddie asking a question brought Richard out of his frantic memories and worries. "Why would you have something like that?"

"For a very smart man, you're singularly stupid sometimes," Grenier drawled.

"Hey!" The word emerged as a strangled squawk.

Richard waved down Eddie's outrage as Grenier placed a finger at the side of his mouth and cast his gaze up toward the ceiling.

"Let me think—I was a traitor to humanity, in league with monsters from other dimensions. *Of course,* I had a bolt hole."

Now it was Richard's turn to feel a growing outrage. "And you didn't tell us this earlier. *Why?*"

He shrugged. "I was hoping you would look at the situation, see it was hopeless, and give it up. But if you have a chance to free Kenntnis ... *now* it makes sense to go in."

"Lieutenant Weber wasn't worth it, but this Kenntnis guy is?" Eddie said.

"Yes."

And Grenier's eyes were on Richard because he knew, on some small level, Richard had made the same calculation.

CHAPTER TWENTY-SIX
NEEDS MUST WHEN THE DEVIL DRIVES

THE LIMO, TOWING a small U-Haul trailer, rolled down the two-lane blacktop, headed deeper into the Virginia countryside. On either side leafless trees seemed to claw at the flat gray sky. Pamela, wedged against the left side of the car, could just see one of the Vatican flags fluttering on the hood. She and Sam were pressed thigh to thigh, and Pamela realized that what she felt digging into her leg was one of Sam's guns that had been strapped beneath her nun's habit.

Despite the February cold, sweat was prickling on her scalp beneath the heavy cloth of the wimple. Pamela tried to put it down to ten people in a car designed to comfortably carry eight, but she knew it was a lie. This was nerves, and nothing else.

Rudi was driving; Joseph was up front with him along with another FBI volunteer, the wiry, skinny man who had teased Sam about being a naughty nun. His full name was Jay Haskell.

The men all wore the Catholic dress. Her brother's face above the black of the cassock and the white collar looked like the chiseled features of a Della Robbia angel. Rudi and Estevan both looked at ease. Pamela suspected years spent as altar boys. Franklin and Joseph seemed clothed in dignity.

Syd, Jay, and Eddie seemed the most uncomfortable. She glanced over at Sam. The agent was stunningly beautiful, as the wimple formed a frame for the oval face, setting off her dark eyes and the slashing line of her eyebrows.

A large, heavy cream parchment folder embossed with the presidential seal and adorned with gold seals and fluttering ribbons rested on Richard's lap. Dagmar had explained that Kenntnis had received a Presidential Medal of Freedom back in the Reagan administration, and the portfolio looked impressive. Eddie had brought it with him when he returned from New Mexico, and the indefatigable Danny with his flair for criminal activity had fancied it up with more seals and ribbons. They also had forged letters from the pope and the Cardinal of DC.

Richard had his hands folded on top, and the family gold signet ring glinted on his right hand. Pamela wondered what her father would think of this mad endeavor. But hadn't he himself invaded the Virginia compound to rescue his son? *We've got to stop making a habit of this,* she thought.

Joseph had voiced strong opposition to using the forged documents. He had been a marine and felt any soldier would want orders from his immediate superior officer, not a bunch of shit from civilians, especially foreign civilians. Richard had overruled him.

"It's going to be one more ring in the circus I'm going to be ringmastering."

Pamela wondered what he had in mind.

A few miles farther on, a soldier, dressed in mountain camouflage, stepped out from between the trees and held up a hand, palm out. They rolled to a stop. The soldier approached cautiously. He was a baby-faced private with a heavy machine gun slung across the front of his body. The weapon looked outsized against the bony and knobby wrists of a boy just flirting with manhood. Joseph had the window rolled down by the time the young marine had reached the side of the car. The soldier reacted to the sight of the collar. Tension flowed out of his shoulders, and he shifted the gun to the side and behind him.

"Where's the officer in charge, son?" Joseph asked.

The boy pointed southwest. "A mile further on, Father."

"Radio him and tell him the contingent from Rome has arrived."

It could have been a hundred miles. It seemed like hours passed before they reached the final line of defense against the dimensional gate. Here, a barricade had been constructed across the road. Humvees were pulled onto the shoulder on either side of the road. The silhouettes of the trees seemed subtly wrong. Pamela peered closely and wondered what she was seeing.

Syd leaned across his daughter to say, "Camouflaged artillery piece, and there's a couple of tanks in there, too."

Rudi pulled forward until the limousine had its grille nudged against the red-and-white-painted board that formed the levered gate. Richard rolled down the window and handed the pile of documents to the lieutenant in command, a handsome black man whose high, chiseled cheekbones hinted at Native American in the mix. He looked through the papers, and Pamela felt her stomach clench as he began to frown. This was taking too long. The lieutenant would call someone higher in the chain of command, and they'd all be arrested.

Richard suddenly threw open the door, jumped out of the car, and assaulted the marine with a barrage of rapid-fire Italian complete with expansive, swooping gestures and much pointing at his watch. Joseph also got out of the car, leaving the door open, and pulled the young officer aside. He said in a low voice, "Kind of crazy they'd send us a guy with no English, but also kind of typical. Can't you help us out here?"

There was a low, unidentifiable sound, growing in intensity.

Pamela glanced around looking for the source but couldn't locate it.

Richard let fly another rippling batch of Italian. A thunderous frown lay across his brow. Joseph pretended to listen, nodded, made a placating, patting-the-air gesture, muttering, "*Si, si.*" The chief of security turned back to the officer. "Look, son, the sooner we get in there, the sooner this thing ends."

The drone and whirr grew louder, and suddenly a new factor literally flew into the equation. The sunlight was blotted out, throwing them all into deep shadow, and they were deafened by the whir and clatter of wings. Everyone, soldiers and fake priests alike, ducked and looked up. The sky was choked with thousands of birds of every variety. Geese, sparrows, ducks, crows, all fleeing northward as if carried on a hurricane wind. Feathers drifted down, and then dead birds began dropping all around them. One smacked onto Richard's shoulder and slid down his chest, leaving a red smear against the black material of his cassock. He gave a cry of disgust.

Rudi's hands clutched convulsively on the steering wheel. It was hard to see through the front windshield, but what Pamela could see was alarming. She jumped out and joined Richard. He was looking beyond the clouds of birds at a sky gone purple and black. Shapes writhed within the sullen clouds. The lieutenant produced a small sound between a gasp and a whimper. Pamela wanted to scream, but her throat and mouth had gone too dry.

Richard gripped the marine by the shoulder and broke character, saying in English, "Get your men out of here, Lieutenant! Get them out *now!*"

The marine was terrified, but managed to stammer out, "Our orders are to hold here."

"If you do, you'll either die or go mad. You can't do anything more. *We*, however, might be able to."

"You can't go into that," the lieutenant cried as dead and dying birds continued to rain down around them.

Richard's face had gone bone white down to the lips. "Can and must. Please, Lieutenant. Will you let us pass?"

"You're fucking crazy! Okay! Fine. Do whatever you want." The marine ran away up the road, bawling into his radio, "Fall back! Fall back!"

The soldiers were shaking, flinging down their guns, dropping to the ground crying. Discipline eroded into blind panic.

Richard drew the sword.

The overtones were *massive*, and the swirling light around the blade illuminated the ground all around him. The panic abated, even among the birds, who stopped pecking and bashing into each other and just flew. On the ground the troops began to listen, and an orderly retreat began.

Diesel engines growled and rumbled to life, and trucks and Humvees began to pull away.

"What are we waiting for?" Pamela asked.

"For them to get clear," came the tense response from her brother.

"Well, the bad guys sure as fuck know we're here now," said Sam as the overtones from the sword continued to press against their eardrums.

✦　　✦　　✦

IT SOUNDED LIKE distant thunder or pounding rain against the glass. Rhiana ran into the living room to see hundreds of birds flinging themselves against the windows. They smashed against the glass, shattering fragile wings, and breaking their necks. She shrieked, disturbed by the wanton destruction, and then screamed again when the glass broke, and the birds poured in. She flung her arms over her head, trying to ward off the assault. Feathers drifted down around her. When she finally raised her head there were birds perched on the mantel, on the backs of the chairs and sofas, on lamps, and clinging to the chandelier.

She held out her hand, and a large crow hopped onto it. The skin of its feet felt almost scaly, and the claws pricked her skin. Its head cocked back and forth, a movement both sinuous and mechanical. The hard black eyes glittered as she got the message. Humans were on the edge of the compound. The weapon was with them. The *Paladin* was with them.

There was an edge of fear and alarm in the query that was more felt than understood—is *Prometheus secure?*

It was followed by an imperative. *You will come. Now!*

A flick of the wrist sent the crow exploding into the air. She had been rough, and its claws left bloody scratches on the back of her hand. Rhiana circled the room, clasping and unclasping her hands.

He knew. Was Weber still alive? Dead would be worse. She should never … She needed to make sure he never found Damon. Never saw what Doug would have done to him by now. The man had served his purpose.

Her attention was caught by the couch. It was smeared with white and gray bird dung. Rhiana had a sudden vision of herself as a wrinkled old hag, surrounded by familiars in a house that reeked of animal droppings, and alone, utterly alone. Her human body shredded as she ran for a mirror.

He mustn't find him. He mustn't ever know what I did. What I allowed to happen.

✦   ✦   ✦

EDDIE WAS BLATHERING. "… they didn't attack us. For it to be *The Birds* the birds would have had to attack us. This is like the anti-*Birds* because they were all dying instead of attacking us—"

"Eddie," came the soft admonishment from Richard. He laid a hand on Eddie's knee. "Calm down. Focus."

"Shit. Sorry."

"Where's Cross?" Syd asked.

"I don't know," Richard answered. "He'll be there when

we need him." Richard drew the tips of his fingers slowly up the side of the blade. The net of light caressed his hand. When he pulled his hand back, the light flowed after it like pulled taffy. Pamela found it disturbing. Eddie was staring at it hungrily.

Sam shifted, glared at Richard. "You *know* that or are you just hoping?"

A faint smile touched her brother's lips. "I don't know, Sam. I only know I can't do this alone." Pamela noticed how thin Richard's face had become. "So, I have to have a little … faith."

Joseph lifted the topo map and peered through the windshield. "Turn off here."

Rudi spun the wheel. They left the road and went jouncing across the shoulder and into the cover of the woods. Branches snapped as the car rolled through the trees and scraped across the top of the trailer with a rending shriek.

"That's a great sound. Chalk on a blackboard," Franklin said.

"Wow, if that's how chalk on a blackboard sounds, then I'm really glad blackboards were something that belonged to the Dark Ages," Eddie said.

Syd laid a hand over his heart and pretended to wilt. "Ow, that hurt."

"We're not old, Syd," Joseph said. "We're seasoned."

"Actually, I think you're old," Eddie said, and Sam wrapped her arms around her waist and started laughing.

It spread like a yawn, and suddenly everyone in the car was whooping with laughter born of panic. Pamela wiped her streaming eyes, looked around at the red faces, and realized that for the first time in her life she *belonged*. A lump formed in her throat, and suddenly the tears were from emotion. She sniffed and hoped no one would notice. But Richard was looking at her. He stretched out his right hand, reaching across both Sam and Syd. She reached out and clasped it.

Suddenly they broke through into a small clearing. Joseph glanced over at the topo map and gestured to Rudi. The younger guard took his foot off the gas, and they rolled to a stop. The engine sound died away, pinging as it cooled. The tops of the pines whipped back and forth as the wind roared through them. For a long moment no one moved; then Richard opened the door, and they all exploded into action.

Once out of the car, they stripped off their cassocks and habits. Sam and Pamela helped each other with the pins that held on the wimples. "Man, it would suck to be a nun," Sam said, and she ripped away the material and ran frenzied fingers through her short hair.

Rudi and Estevan walked in circles, kicking at the fallen leaves and needles as they searched for the hatch. Eddie opened the top of his shoulder pouch, reached in, and pulled out a velvet-wrapped package. He untied it and threw back the material to reveal mirrors and lenses.

Joseph helped Richard shrug into a tight-fitting leather jacket so Richard wouldn't have to release his grip on the sword. Next, the older man buckled the belt of a pair of cycling chaps around Richard's narrow waist, and then knelt in front of him to thread the zippers on the legs. Pamela watched and had a sudden memory of the color plate in their grandfather's copy of *Men of Iron* showing the young knight Miles being dressed for battle. She shivered.

Rudi and Estevan pulled up a metal hatch. Dirt, needles, and leaves cascaded off the gray metal. Estevan came down the ramp of the trailer trundling a large red-and-silver motorcycle.

Pamela circled the bike. "I've never really known you, have I?" she said to her brother. The smile she got back was rueful, and Richard shook his head. "Well, we'll fix that once this is all over," she said briskly, and blinked hard again. It had to be nerves that had her so emotional. Fortunately, Eddie drew attention away from her.

"I thought it took two hands to ride a motorcycle," Eddie said.

"Not this one," Richard answered. "Gilera Ferro 850 automatic. One hand to steer. The other hand to use the sword."

Bob Franklin had a quiver full of arrows slung over his back and was stringing a large bow. Jay lit cigarettes, puffed, and handed them out to everybody.

"Don't puff, just keep them lightly between your lips. We don't want them to burn away before we reach the house. I've got extras, but let's play it safe."

"And we're lighting them here because ...?" Franklin asked.

"Because fire won't burn near the gate," Richard said. "At some point they will seem to go out."

"And we're gonna be climbing ladders, and maybe fighting bad guys. These cigarettes are gonna be a handful of tobacco," Rudi said.

Jay looked disgusted. "Doesn't anybody fucking smoke anymore? When they stop burning, you're going to tuck them behind your ear." Jay demonstrated with an unlit cigarette.

Joseph handed out nightsticks. Jay and Syd transferred metal canteens from a box into backpacks. There was a greasy residue around some of the caps, and Pamela coughed as the throat-biting smell of gasoline hit the back of her nose.

Richard thrust a helmet at Eddie and swung onto the bike.

"Where's *your* helmet?" Pamela yelled as Richard gunned the engine.

"I need my peripheral vision," Richard yelled back. "Eddie, if I give you a gun, can you manage not to shoot me? I don't need you to actually hit anything, just keep people's heads down."

"I'd only have one arm to hang on with." Eddie's voice quavered like a fifteen-year-old's.

"Never mind."

Pamela watched the resolve harden the young scientist's chin. The look he gave her brother was pure hero worship. "No, that's cool. I can do it."

Joseph handed him a pistol, grip first. "When you're on the bike, keep your arm straight out to the side and pull the trigger. Don't try for anything fancy, just aim toward any people or ... other things you might see. Here, try it once so you see how much pressure you actually need."

Eddie strained, the trigger snapped back, the gun roared, his arm jerked up, and the pistol flew out of his hand and landed in the winter-withered grass. The smell of gunpowder brought back memories of Fourth of July parties and fireworks on the beach near their house in Newport, and suddenly Pamela wanted to cry; for her lost mother and absent father, and a world that made sense.

"This isn't a good idea," Joseph said to Richard. "You should have gotten the sidecar so I could have ridden shotgun."

"I'm going to be weaving through trees to get to Kenntnis. That's why it had to be a bike, not a car, and the passenger has to be Eddie. He's the only one who can inspect the glass," Richard said.

"No, no, I can do it. It just took me by surprise," Eddie said.

Richard nodded. "Let him try again."

Estevan ran over and retrieved the pistol. Eddie took it, closed one eye, and aimed at a tree across the clearing. This time he didn't lose his grip on the gun. Wood splinters exploded out of the tree trunk.

"*I aimed* for that tree," Eddie said loudly and looked around at everyone.

Rudi patted him on the shoulder. "You're a natural."

"We need to start humping," Syd called from where he stood at the tunnel entrance.

Joseph checked the face on an old-fashioned spring-wound watch. "It's about two miles, and then we need to clear any bad guys out of the house and set up. That's going to take at least forty minutes."

"I'll start moving in twenty," Richard said. "See you at the compound."

"Don't worry, boss, we'll be there."

Pamela joined the group gathered around the hatch. She looked back at her brother, and suddenly it hit her—this might be the last time she ever saw him. She ran back and gave him a fierce hug.

"Come *on!*" Sam yelled.

CHAPTER TWENTY-SEVEN

MONSTER MAGNETS

E DDIE CLIMBED AWKWARDLY onto the backseat of the bike and wrapped his arms around Richard's waist. It felt like being hugged by a Kodiak bear.

"Not … quite so … tight," Richard managed to squeeze out.

"Sorry, sorry. I've only been on a bike once before. My dad hated these things and forbid any of us to ever ride one. But my half-uncle Chet came through San Diego when I was thirteen. He was on his way to Mexico, and my dad was at a conference at JPL, so Chet got to stay, 'cause my dad really hated Chet. Anyway, he took me for a ride. He had this big old Harley."

Richard was having to concentrate on the uneven ground as he guided the bike back toward the road, so he was barely listening. Eddie kept going.

"The problem was that Chet didn't mention that the exhaust pipes run the length of the bike, and man, they get really, really hot. That's why I was so careful when I got on this bike, because after the ride I just slid off Chet's bike 'cause I was, like, scared and tired and feeling really guilty 'cause my dad had told me to never, ever get on a motorcy-cle, and I was wearing shorts, and I rested my calf against the exhaust pipe and got a third-degree burn on my leg. It was so gross, it smelled like roasting pork at a luau. Anyway, my mom was so scared that Dad would find out that Uncle Chet had been at the house, and that I'd ridden on a motorcycle, that she didn't take me to a doctor. That's why I've got this scar. Solarcaine and Neosporin don't do much on a third-degree burn."

The artless, never-ending blather had Richard's neck tensing. He was almost wishing he had worn a helmet. It would have kept out the verbal diarrhea. They reached the road, and Richard opened it up. Eddie let out a glissando wail. The trees flashed by like a gray film unwinding. Richard's ears began to burn from the cold.

They went into a curve, but Eddie stayed stiff as a board and bolt upright. Richard had to fight to keep the bike from falling. Eddie started yelling in his ear. Richard got them through the curve, and half-turned his head to shout, "When we take the turns you've got to lean into them. Go with the bike so you don't throw us off balance. Remember, I only have one hand to steer."

Richard looked down at his left hand balanced on the handlebars with the blade of the sword pointed straight forward. The swirling lights around the blade were bright enough to throw a spear of white light into the sullen red gloom here beneath the clouds. Richard wondered how much darker it was going to get, and if the sword could keep pace.

Another curve was coming. Eddie tightened his grip on Richard's waist and placed his head on Richard's shoulder. This time he stayed in sync with Richard's body, and it worked perfectly. The bike leaned over. Eddie gobbled a little as the pavement rose up toward them, but Richard couldn't control the whoop of delight. They came back up smoothly.

"That's the way to do it. Good job." Richard threw back his head and laughed.

"Who are you, and when did you steal my uptight boss?" Eddie yelled into his ear.

Richard didn't answer because he saw the stone gatehouse up ahead.

THE CHEMILUMINESCENT LIGHT sticks worked surprising well. They were bright enough that Pamela could see the shadows of the men in front and behind her bobbing and swaying on the tunnel walls. Sam was disgusted at the march order, which had her and Pamela sandwiched between Joseph and Franklin and Rudi in the front and Syd, Jay, and Estevan bringing up the rear. When Sam squawked, Joseph had pointed out that Franklin had a compound bow, he had a hunting knife, they had a longer reach, and they were stronger than Sam. Pamela for damn sure didn't mind being in the middle.

When they'd first entered the tunnel, there had been the buzz of whispered conversation, but that had died away. Now only an occasional cough or the scrape of shoe leather on grit marked their passage.

Pamela tried to identify the men by the sounds of their breathing. Syd had a habit of pulling air through his teeth, a sort of tuneless hum. Estevan was a quick, sharp panting.

MELINDA M. SNODGRASS

Pamela wondered how much air was actually reaching the young man's lungs. Joseph's breaths were slow and calm, as were Franklin's.

She had been told to expect it, but as they moved toward the compound the thin wisps of smoke stopped rising from the lit cigarettes. She tightened her ponytail and tucked the cigarette behind her ear. Pamela normally hated the smell of cigarette smoke, but now she missed it because nerves had somebody's bowels in an uproar.

Another fart erupted somewhere back in the line. It was a series of squeaking pops like someone walking on bubble wrap. Her reason to come along now seemed thin, and her determination dropped with each passing minute. She wondered how Richard was doing and envied him the open air. She wished she could have ridden the bike with him but knew intellectually that it had to be Eddie. She prayed they would find Weber. That he wouldn't be dead. She prayed that none of them would die.

✧ ✧ ✧

TWISTED METAL GATES lay to either side of the road, torn down by the FBI when they raided the compound. Richard gunned the engine, and the bike leaped forward. He had a brief glimpse of a man's face poking out the door of the gatehouse before they flashed past, but there didn't seem to be any organized security. A crowd of people were streaming down the road toward the gates as if they'd been summoned, but they seemed confused, just a milling mob.

"Eddie! Be ready to use that gun."

He should have spoken sooner, because a man darted out of the crowd and flung himself at the bike, as if hoping to bring it down with the momentum of his body. Richard swung the sword and took the attacker in the solar plexus with the flat of the blade. Even over the rumble and roar of the engine Richard could hear the man's screams as the magic was stripped from him.

"I'm going to lean way forward. Use my back to steady your arm, and start shooting," Richard instructed Eddie.

Richard dropped until his chin was almost on the handlebars. One bump in the road took him by surprise, and they hit his chin, and he bit his tongue. The warm coppery taste of blood filled his mouth. Richard felt Eddie's elbow gouging into his right shoulder blade, and then the roar of the pistol so near to his ear deafened him. They were getting so close, and *no one was reacting*. Eddie fired another shot. Again, there was nothing. Then on the third shot finally a reaction. A woman in the crowd threw up her arms and fell backward.

The crowd lost cohesion like a ball of yarn unspooling. Only two people remained in the road, a man and a woman. The man reached out as if preparing to grab the handlebars. Richard abruptly straightened and swung the sword. This time he didn't have a chance to turn it and use the flat of the blade. The dark metal peeled back the dirty sweater and the flesh beneath. The man looked down, reacted in surprise, then slapped his palms down on the cut as if trying to hold in the blood. Richard reversed his swing and brought the blade down on the top of the woman's head. She collapsed.

"Are they still following?" Richard yelled back over his

shoulder.

Richard felt Eddie half-turn. "Yeah, they're trying, but we're leaving them in the dust." To Richard's gunfire-deafened ears his words sounded distant and muffled.

"Are you all right?" Richard asked next, because Eddie had just shot someone, and that was never easy to handle. Richard glanced at the blood on the blade. It was rippling under the wind created by their speed.

Eddie was quiet for a few moments and then yelled, "They cut up my friends. They had it coming. So yeah. Yeah, I'm fine." The logic didn't exactly track, but if it kept him calm and functioning Richard was all for it.

Then the strange red orange light was blotted out by something huge overhead. They both looked up, and Eddie screamed.

Richard had the impression of darkness and thousands of tiny eyes. But he wasn't sure *what* he'd actually seen because there was a wavering all around the creature that made it hard to focus. It seemed to be flat and large and black, as if a stingray the size of a basketball court had taken to the air. Richard thrust the sword point up toward the sky, hoping maybe that would hold it at bay. It felt pathetic, and he felt stupid for even trying it.

A high-pitched keening began. It seemed to resonate in Richard's bones. Richard yanked the handlebars and took them off the road, but the creature stayed with them, and the keening became even more piercing.

It's tracking us. Marking where we are. Summoning others.

It was a guess, but it felt right, and Richard hated that it felt right. He was thinking frantically. He had to touch the thing, kill it before any more monsters arrived. His mind seemed to be chattering as it flipped from thought to thought, and then he remembered sitting on the window seat of his bedroom in Newport reading *The Lord of the Rings*.

Richard released the handlebars, but his balance was good enough that they stayed upright as he sheathed the sword. The engine coughed, the bike shook as the smooth flow of gas stopped, and then the engine died. They rolled a few more feet, and then Richard threw down the kickstand.

"What are you doing?" Eddie was almost sobbing.

"Run!" And Richard gave him a hard shove.

Eddie practically fell off the bike. Richard grabbed his arm and started running toward an opening in the trees. Every jarring step sent agony through his partially healed thigh. There was a small meadow just beyond it. The seared grass hissed against the leather of his chaps. The shadow hung over them. Eddie was in bunny mode, and he didn't respond to Richard tugging at his arm, trying to get him to stop. He didn't have a choice; Richard kicked the scientist's feet out from under him. The young man face-planted in the dirt and dead grass, and Richard threw himself down on top of him.

"Come on, come on down, you bastard. Squat on us!"

"No! No! I don't want it to come down! Are you fucking nuts!"

Eddie was crying.

Richard really wished he had time to explain, but the creature was spiraling closer. Richard waited and tried to appear shattered and terrified and hopeless. *Doesn't take much acting,* he thought. He had his right hand resting against the base of the hilt. The air was filled with a hot metallic scent. He risked a glance. It was close.

He used his heartbeat to count the seconds, then leaped to his feet while at the same time drawing the sword. Richard took three running steps and launched himself into the air, arm and blade extended. He pushed it so hard that he felt his shoulder catch and twinge.

The blade was frothing light like the biggest Roman candle ever made. The foible connected. There was a jar that shook his arm and slammed into Richard's still imperfectly healed side, and then the resistance was gone, and the blade sank deep into the shadow. There was the thunder of sound like a sonic boom directly overhead, and the thing was gone.

Richard failed to stick the landing. His right leg collapsed from beneath him, he staggered and fell onto his back. He gripped the hilt so tightly that his fingers cramped, but he was proud of himself, he didn't drop the sword. The light from the blade shot into the air. The clouds burned away, and normal sunlight poured through the hole in the clouds. For a few moments Richard just lay there trying to catch his breath and taking joy in the touch of sun.

Then he hobbled back onto his feet, grabbed Eddie by the collar, and hauled him up. They got back to the bike and climbed on.

"Start. Please start," Richard crooned. The engine roared back to life. They were still in the game.

✦   ✦   ✦

ANDRESSON SPRAWLED ON a glider on the front porch of the big stone house. His hand rummaged in a box of Honey Nut Cheerios while he frowned off toward the gate. He looked up at the sound of Rhiana's footfalls, stuffed a big handful of cereal into his mouth, and gave her a black frown while he masticated. His nose looked mashed and a bit off to the side and there was a smear of blood beneath one nostril.

"Where's my food? I can't fuckin' cook anything. I told them I wanted a surf and turf. I thought somebody would be back by now."

Rhiana forgot he was crazy, forgot he was dangerous, forgot her magic couldn't affect him. She grabbed him by the front of his stained T-shirt and hauled him up out of the glider. The sour smell of an unwashed male body washed over her.

"Where is the policeman? Where is Weber? We've got to get him out of here."

The smile was chilling. "Well, he's going to be a little heavy to carry."

Panic closed off Rhiana's lungs. She wheezed, and then gagged on the harsh taint that filled the air. "What did you do?"

He was starting to look like a sulky two-year-old. "You told me I could do anything I wanted."

"Oh, God, how badly did you hurt him? Is he still alive?"

He offered up his bruised face and broken nose for inspection. "Fucker headbutted me. *And* nailed me in the nuts. I don't mind a little fight, makes it more fun, but *nobody* gets to hurt me. I made him sorry."

The moan bubbled out as if propelled by the spasm that

clenched at her stomach. Rhiana released him and folded her arms over her aching belly. "We've got to get him out of here before *he* gets here. Before he sees. He can't know. He can't find out *I* planned this. Oh, God, what am I going to do? He's at the front gate." The hysteria rang in her ears.

"He? The fag. He's coming here?" Andresson stepped forward eagerly.

"No, no, you have to help me."

"Fuck that. I want that sword."

"You listen to *me*," Rhiana shouted shrilly.

"No. They told me I don't have too anymore. You've done your thing, got the cop to come back. Now it's *my* turn. I'm more important than you." He started back into the house.

Rhiana ran after him and closed her hand on his shoulder. He winced as her nails dug through the material of his shirt and into his skin. "Who told you that? Who said that?"

The smile was pure poison. "Your dad."

He broke free and continued into the house. Rhiana ran after him. "He didn't. You're lying."

The narrow shoulder rose and fell in a dismissive shrug. "Think whatever you want."

They were down the hall and into the master bedroom. Grenier's taste had run to the Baroque. There was a huge four-poster bed with heavily carved dark wood, and thick chocolate brown velvet curtains. A matching armoire and mirrored dresser stood on opposite walls. The dresser mirror was occluded from the touch of the Old Ones. As soon as they were through the door, a girl began whimpering, small animal sounds of pure terror.

Andresson went to the dresser and got a large .357 Magnum. He checked the ammo and headed back for the door. "Oh, and don't worry about your little boyfriend seeing anything, or knowing that you gave the fucker to me. I'll stop him *way* before he gets to the house."

"No!" Rhiana yelled. "You've got to help me."

"You're the one who wanted him here. *You* deal with it. He's in the bathroom," he said indifferently, and left.

"Please, lady. Help me."

Rhiana glanced over at the bed. The girl was naked and tied spread-eagle to the posts. Sweat-matted and tangled red hair lay across the pillow like a flame. Her small breasts were bruised, and in places teeth marks were edged in blood. Her thighs were smeared with blood and sperm. The room smelled of pee, and there was a dark stain on the sheets beneath her.

Rhiana ignored her and moved hesitantly to the door that led into the opulent bathroom. The smells in the room, sperm, blood, sweat, booze, and sewage, caught in the back of her throat like claws.

Weber slumped, unconscious, the handcuffs cutting into his wrists, so the cuffs of his shirt were red with blood. His face was a mass of bruises, his lips cut and bleeding, both eyes blackened; a knife had been used on his chest and blood painted his skin and hair, soaked into the waistband of his trousers. It set her stomach to heaving. That and sheer panic over what Richard would do. The physical confines of her body seemed to blow apart as she fled wildly from the world.

Her last conscious thought was, *I'll tell him I didn't know.*

✦ ✦ ✦

THE TUNNEL ENDED at a cinder block wall. Moisture had wept across the concrete, leaving Rorschach patterns in the gray matrix. A metal ladder was bolted into the blocks. They formed a milling herd at the base of the ladder. Joseph put a hand and a foot on the ladder, only to be stopped by Jay saying, "No offense, Pops, but how about sending someone younger and more agile?"

"How about I bust your face?" Sam suggested sweetly.

"Sam," Syd said. "Save the 'tude for the bad guys."

Pamela watched the waffled soles of Jay's hiking boots disappearing into the darkness. The ladder shook under the man's weight. She didn't like climbing, ever since that fall out of the apple tree in the backyard that broke her arm, and this ladder looked rickety.

Sam shrugged. "Okay, I'm cool with letting Jay be a monster magnet."

Pamela noticed that the rattle of the iron ladder against the concrete lost its rhythm for an instant at Sam's words.

Pamela glanced around the circle of faces. Estevan's eyes had a ring of white all around the iris, and his pupils were wide. She stepped over to him and gave his hand a squeeze. The skin of his palm was clammy with sweat.

There was the sound of grunting from over their heads. Jay's voice drifted down. "It's not opening. Hope it's not locked."

"Shouldn't be," Joseph called up. "Grenier said it wasn't, but that it hasn't been opened in a long time."

"You need some more muscle?" Rudi called up.

"Not enough room," Jay's voice floated down.

"Probably enough room for me," said Sam, and she went eeling up the ladder.

There were more sounds of effort, then a loud *clang* as the trapdoor flew up. Light poured through the opening, and Jay scrabbled for purchase. The unexpected lack of resistance had taken him by surprise, and he lost his footing. Sam clutched at him, caught him by the shirt, but she couldn't hold him. He came half sliding, half falling down the ladder. His ankle buckled as he landed wrong. A string of profanity erupted. Franklin jumped past him and climbed rapidly up the ladder.

One by one they made their way out of the tunnel. As Pamela climbed, her mind kept stupidly repeating *once out of the well, our heroes... once out of the well, our heroes....* But she could never figure out what the heroes *did*, and then she was through the trapdoor and standing in the basement.

Franklin leaned against a tall wine rack. He had an arrow nocked, the bowstring pulled, but not quite to the ready, but they heard nothing and saw no one. There were six rows of eight-foot-tall wine racks, but most of the racks were empty.

The stairs from the basement brought them into a walk-in pantry.

There was very little left on the shelves. A bag of sugar had toppled and torn, making the tile floor both gritty and sticky. Pamela suddenly realized that sweat was beading beneath her bangs, and it wasn't just from nerves. Now that they were no longer below ground, it was incredibly warm for February in Virginia.

Pamela hung back while the law enforcement types used

their training to check the kitchen. After a few seconds they waved her in. The stink from rotting food left lying on dirty plates was stomach churning. A few fat flies buzzed lazily over the moldy scraps. Overlaying the cloying sweet stench of decay was a throat-burning chemical odor. Mold, like soft green velvet, draped itself over the food scraps on the plates.

"Weird," Estevan whispered. "Who's ever heard of flies in the winter?"

They moved on, using doorframes for cover and leap-frogging each other. Pamela could see their discomfort at holding nightsticks and knives instead of guns. The dining room was empty. There were faded places on the walls where art had once hung. The seeded glass doors of the buffet hung open, and one creaked as the hot, biting wind found its twisting way into this interior room. There was no sound beyond the monotonous *creak, creak, creak,* and the sigh of the wind.

"I gotta pee," Estevan said, and his whisper seemed horribly loud.

"Tie a knot in it," Rudi advised.

Apparently, they had been louder than they realized, because suddenly a girl began screaming. *"Help! Help! Please, somebody, help me!"* Sobs punctuated the words.

Sam took off running down the hall, away from the public rooms, back toward what Grenier had said was his private living quarters. The FBI agent was only a half second faster than the rest of them.

"Cops! Always playing the hero," Pamela muttered as she ran after them.

CHAPTER TWENTY-EIGHT
THERE WILL BE CASUALTIES

THERE WAS A ragged sound to the bike's engine that Richard didn't like, but he could certainly understand. The air was horribly dry, and tainted with stinks that bit at the back of his throat and had his eyes watering.

They were moving so fast that at one point both tires left the ground as they crested a small hill. Eddie gasped and giggled, but for Richard the euphoria was gone. Only the skeletons of dead trees and one final hill separated them from the gate. *What in the hell are we doing? We're two guys on a motorbike and arrayed against us are monsters—*

Richard caught movement out of the corner of his eye. *And people,* he added as he spotted the two men hiding in the trees.

One jumped out directly in front of the bike. Richard had a split second to decide what to do. It was too close quarters to use the sword, he didn't have time to dodge him, and if he hit him straight on the bike would go down, and then his buddy would be on them.

Richard wrenched the handlebars hard to the left and hit the brake. The front tire locked, and he felt the muscles in his shoulders and neck spasm as he braced against the hard jerk. He then let the back tire fishtail, spinning them 180 degrees.

Eddie's scream was a high-pitched whistle of terror directly into Richard's ear. The back of the bike slammed into the first man and knocked him flat. The second man started running toward them as Richard fought for control of the bike. They were wobbling, but Richard gunned the engine anyway, and drove straight at him.

At the last-minute Richard pulled to the right and stabbed hard and fast, catching the man in the chest. There was a moment of breath-stopping terror when their momentum sent them hurtling past while the blade was caught in the man's ribs. Richard almost lost his grip, but the sword wrenched loose before the hilt slipped out of his sweat-slicked hand. It still pulled the hell out of his fingers where they twined through the hilt.

As they clawed their way up the final hill, Richard realized that other than that one sentry creature, they hadn't met anything but humans. He glanced down the length of the blade. *The Old Ones fear it. The barest touch and they die,* Kenntnis's voice rumbled in memory.

They were afraid to come too close. They were letting humans face him and the sword and get hurt. *No, die.* Richard's innate honesty forced him to acknowledge that truth. There was a sharp pain at the hinge of his jaw as he gritted his teeth. He wanted something to die other than his own kind. He wouldn't mind killing the creatures that had brought humanity to this, but not these pathetic dregs trapped by a belief in fairy tales and now trapped in madness.

They crested the final hill, and suddenly Richard's thoughts about killing monsters seemed like a bully's bravado. A hot, life-sucking wind swirled in the dell, kicking up errant dust devils that filled the air with a choking grit. It stung the exposed skin on his face and hands. The gate filled the entire cliff face. Mist, like steam from quiescent geysers, trailed from the various glass sculptures that dotted the ground in front of it. Kenntnis's glass tomb was centered among the other sculptures.

"Holy crap," Eddie said, and he was looking off to the side of the gate where another, much smaller opening in the gray stones showed space and that burning star. "Why isn't our atmosphere getting sucked away?"

And now Richard had another gut-burning problem. If Rhiana's magic failed, it was most definitely game over. Somehow Richard had to close at least *that* opening between the multiverses.

But between him and that tear in reality were humans.

And others.

They were just disturbing shapes that his mind failed to grasp, but they were utterly terrifying. Richard felt the rim of Eddie's helmet digging into his shoulder as the young scientist pressed closer to him. Richard desperately wished he had somebody to hide behind, and his thoughts flew unerringly to Weber.

Please let him be alive. Please let him be alive. Please ...

The desire to turn the bike and flee back the way they had come was so strong that Richard's arms were shivering. There had to be somebody else who could deal with this nightmare. But Pamela was here. And Joseph, Estevan, and Rudi. Syd and Sam. Franklin and Jay.

And Weber.

There was no other option. Richard had to be here, too.

❖ ❖ ❖

THE SCREAMS EMANATED from behind the heavily carved door. By the time Pamela got there, Jay and Rudi were pulling security in the hall, and the other men and Sam were inside the room. Pamela stepped over the threshold. There was a girl tied spread-eagle to the heavily carved wood pillars of his four-poster bed. The room was awash with the sour smell of unwashed bodies, the cloying scent of sperm, and the sharp reek of spilled liquor.

Pamela noted the blood smearing the girl's thighs, and the fact she was a true redhead. She would have been pretty had her face not been splotched with bruises and puffy from crying. Mucus smeared her upper lip. Her face and body carried a layer of baby fat. Pamela guessed her to be no more than mid-teens.

Joseph cut at the ropes securing her wrists. Judging from the swollen red skin around the cords, and her puffy purple fingers, she had been there for a long time. Sam was muttering a running string of curses. Pamela pulled off her jacket and laid it over the girl, shielding her from the view of the men.

"Hush. Hush. You're going to be all right now. What's your name, honey?" Pamela kept her voice low and soft, the tone you used to soothe a frightened horse. The girl's sobs died to whimpers as Sam put her arms around her.

"Jessie."

"Jessie, is there someone else here? A man?"

"Uh-huh," the girl said, and her voice shook. "I think he fought back, and then *he* hurt him. Bad. He screamed and screamed, but I haven't heard anything for a while." Sam tightened her grip as the shivering became massive shudders that threatened to pull the girl out of her arms.

"Do you know where he is?" Joseph asked.

"In … in the bathroom."

"Lieutenant Weber," Pamela called, and ran through the bathroom door.

The others followed except for Sam, who kept holding Jessie.

Pamela stood, helpless before the unconscious man. His shirt was open, and there were long shallow cuts down his chest and one nipple had been carved away. Blood coated his chest and had soaked into the waistband of his trousers.

"How do we get him down?" she quavered. "We don't have the key."

Syd stepped forward. "Not a problem, Pam, almost all cuffs use the same key."

Joseph turned to the other men. "Hold him around the waist, we don't want him just falling to the floor. We don't know the full damage yet."

They soon had him down, and Pamela wet a washcloth and began to gently clean the blood from Weber's face, chest, and wrists. Joseph began running his hands across Weber's body. At Pamela's look, he shrugged and said, "Worked with some of the medics when I was in Afghanistan. Looks like a couple of cracked, maybe broken, ribs, and looks like he got kicked hard in the knee, and, uh … other more … uh, private places."

Franklin took charge. "We need to get Jessie and Lieutenant Weber out of here."

"The girl can't go alone, and the cop's down for the count, and we can't spare anyone to take 'em," Jay argued.

"Yes, we can. We probably *shouldn't*, but we can," came the agent's response.

Joseph stepped into the huddle. "Send Estevan. He's just a kid, and he's terrified. He's also strong enough to carry Damon."

Weber gave a gasp and jerked up, fist flying. He caught Pamela on the cheek. She grabbed his hand. "Lieutenant Weber! Damon! It's Pamela. You're all right."

There was confusion in the brown eyes, and he croaked out, "Richard?"

Joseph dropped to one knee and laid a hand on Weber's shoulder, pushing him gently back onto the marble floor. "He's coming." Pamela watched as a look of relief followed by fury crossed Weber's bruised face.

"He should know better," Weber rasped out, and began to cough.

"Jay, try to find a clean glass in this pigsty," Joseph ordered. "The man's parched." The agent whirled and left the bathroom.

As Weber sipped at the water Jay provided, Pamela tore apart the duvet cover, the only material even remotely clean, and gently wound it around the cop's chest. By the time she finished his color was better and his eyes were clear.

"Okay, time to move, we are behind schedule," Franklin said.

They helped Weber to his feet, and he hobbled into the bedroom where Sam was continuing to sit with Jessie, holding her, murmuring quietly to her. Pamela noticed he quickly looked away from the girl as if he was ashamed. It was exasperating; what could he have done since he was a prisoner as well?

At the kitchen they prepared to separate. Sam quickly intervened before Estevan could get his arm around Jessie's waist.

"Don't touch her. She knows you're not the one who hurt her, but right now she can't handle a man's touch," the young agent said quietly. Pamela was again stunned at Sam's sensitivity; she hadn't thought the woman had it in her.

Joseph was giving Estevan final instructions as they all stood in the filthy kitchen. "Get back to the car. Give us one hour. If we're not back by then, get the fuck out of here."

The trio vanished, headed down the stairs into the basement. The rest of the team went from the private living quarters into the public rooms. In the living room there were more dirty dishes piled on end tables and the coffee table. Stuffing exploded like dandelion fluff through the ripped and stained blue velvet upholstery on the couches and chairs. The white carpet looked like an experimental painting. Pamela had a feeling that some of the stains were blood, but she didn't want to ask.

The backpacks were unlimbered, and they pulled out the gasoline-filled canteens and began dousing the furniture, cushions, and the carpet.

"Why haven't we met anyone?" Sam asked the room.

"I think everyone's off planning a reception for us on the main road or at the dell," Syd said. "I think those birds were carrying a message that we were coming."

Jay spun, looking at the walls as if expecting them to

collapse on top of him. "If it's a trap, shouldn't we be getting out of here?"

"And how do we tell Richard we're bookin' out on him?" Sam asked.

"We are *not* abandoning my brother." Pamela's voice sounded about an octave too high. Joseph, Syd, and Sam nodded in solidarity.

Jay looked to Franklin, who shook his head. For a long moment Jay struggled with himself. The syncopated ticks from old-fashioned spring-wound watches seemed deafening in the silence.

"Well then, I guess we better get these cushions against the walls," Jay said. Sam gave him an approving smile and slapped him hard on the shoulder.

They hurried about, propping the split and gasoline-doused cushions against the walls. The no-longer-burning cigarettes were carefully tucked into the rents in the cushions, and Pamela wondered what it was about fire, light, and Old Ones.

"Now what?" Jay asked.

Joseph checked his watch. "We wait, as Richard instructed."

Sam gave a vehement headshake. "Nope. No way. I want to kick some monster butt, and Richard is out there with only a nerd for backup. I say we split our forces. Some hang here and hold the fort, while the rest of us go toward the gate and raise some hell so the nerd can get a look at this glass thingie."

"I'm coming with you," Pamela heard herself saying.

✧ ✧ ✧

It hurt to walk. Hurt to breath. But the worse pain was the knowledge that he'd stupidly allowed himself to become a pawn, and that his capture had allowed the monsters to draw Richard into danger, possibly to his death.

Damon glanced over at the young redhead and again felt shame. He had listened to her cries and screams and sobs interspersed with a man's grunts of passion like a bass line in a symphony of pain and fear and humiliation and been helpless to assist.

The girl sensed his scrutiny and gave him a nervous look. "I'm sorry," Damon muttered.

"It's okay. He was hurting you, too," she whispered. Her face crumpled and she began to cry. "I just don't know if I'll ever be okay ever again."

"I know it doesn't feel like it now, but you will be," Weber said quietly to the girl. He made no attempt to approach her. Being in this tunnel with two men was probably almost more than she could bear. "You're gonna get help. You're gonna talk to somebody and someday it'll be better. I promise you, it will." The girl nodded, tears sliding down her cheeks.

Weber turned to Estevan. "So where exactly is Richard?"

The kid jerked a thumb over his shoulder. "Back there. In that hell place. We all came in through this tunnel. He took a motorcycle, came in through the front."

Weber tried to picture Richard on a bike, failed. "This better not have been just to rescue me."

Estevan shook his head. "That was part of it, but that

scientist dude is with Richard. They're trying to free my boss, my former boss I mean, from glass … or something."

"Okay, you two get out of here."

"What are you doing?" Estevan asked.

"Making sure Richard doesn't get himself killed. You wouldn't happen to have anything that might perk me up?"

Estevan pulled a small miniature of bourbon out of his pocket. "I swiped it from the hotel."

Weber snatched it out of his hands, twisted off the cap, and downed it in two swallows. "Thank you, my brother," he said tossing aside the empty bottle. "Now you two, go."

"Joseph and Mr. Oort are gonna to kill me for letting you go back," Estevan said.

"Nah, they'll know who to blame. Now git." Weber started ed hobbling back up the tunnel but paused after only a few steps. "You got a weapon I can borrow?" Estevan handed over a knife and a billy club.

Weber tipped him a salute and continued on his way.

✦　✦　✦

FRANKLIN HAD BEEN to the compound before and unlike Syd and Sam had not been affected by it, so he led the way. Jay, now armed with Franklin's bow and arrows, and Joseph were going to remain at the house and cover their eventual retreat. Rudi was armed with a nightstick and knives. Sam had a knife in each hand and looked particularly piratical with a cloth band tied around her forehead to soak up sweat. Pamela was awkwardly carrying her nightstick, and as she looked over at Sam she vowed if she lived through this day, she was going to have somebody teach her how to fight.

A hot, harsh wind was blowing against them. Pamela assumed it was flowing through the gate. *I'm breathing the air of an alien universe,* she thought. The powerful gusts made it hard going, and Pamela wondered how Richard was going to stay upright on the bike. A dark red sand glittering with mica flakes pushed across the ground like the final eddy of a wave flinging itself high up the beach. But unlike the wave, the sand never retreated. It insinuated itself between the ground and the soles of their boots, making them slip and stumble, and worked its way around the laces until their socks were thick with sweat and grit.

"Okay, don't go near the sculptures," Franklin said. "That chick, Rhiana, came out of one of them, so they may be doorways or something."

"And don't walk under anything," Syd said, and he shuddered.

"Basically, don't expect the world to remain normal," Franklin concluded.

"What the fuck does that mean?" Pamela asked and felt suddenly both daring and guilty at the profanity.

"Whatever you can imagine probably won't be strange enough," Franklin said.

"Greeaaat," breathed Rudi.

Sam's head jerked up, and then Pamela heard it, too. It was faint and distant like the buzz of a solitary bee. It was the sound of an engine approaching. They picked up the pace, and soon broke free of the dying trees.

There were a number of people in the clearing. They were dirty, skinny, and wandering about in confusion. Pamela studied the faces of the advancing people. They held every possible vile, frightened, mournful, and violent emotion. And Pamela realized she had seen them before in the carved grotesques adorning the columns of European cathedrals and etched in the walls of Mayan temples. What attention the mob could bring to bear seemed focused on the rapidly approaching motorcycle.

Blood sacrifice, crusade, jihad, pogrom. This is where it leads. Why didn't we realize that before it was too late?

And then she lifted her eyes to what lay beyond. The gate, and the *things* that hid in the ... smoke, mist, fog? It defied her ability to describe. Pamela's legs lost all strength, and she collapsed under the sheer weight of terror and wrongness. Syd grabbed her under the arm and yanked her back up. His fingers digging into the soft skin of her armpit sent a flare of pain through her body.

The motorcycle was heading down into the dell. Even from here Pamela could see the flare of the sword. It was so bright it threw light onto the roiling mists, and they seemed to recoil from its light. The filthy, blank-faced attackers began moving toward Richard.

"I'm gonna try to get around these guys so I can help out Richard," Rudi said.

"Good idea let's do it," Sam panted.

And before Franklin could respond they went running off to the left, circling around the mob.

Rudi ran between the curving glass mausoleum that entombed Kenntnis and the opening to an alien sun. Sam was right on his heels. Suddenly Rudi's back arched. The skin on his hands and face reddened and split and oozed blood and fluid. Sam gave a cry of horror and panic and threw herself backward. She lost her balance and fell hard on her tailbone.

The material of Rudi's shirt and pants darkened as they soaked up blood from his rupturing flesh. He writhed like a jerked puppet, and his screams echoed across the dell. Syd started to rush to him only to be tackled by Franklin. Tears were spilling down Pamela's cheeks. They evaporated in the terrible heat.

Rudi collapsed onto the sand. His face was a ruin. Blood and mucus oozed from his sockets where his eyes had exploded. Franklin was cursing, Syd was gagging, and Sam was making a keening cry like a hurt rabbit.

Pamela jerked her gaze away from the horror and saw that the mob was converging on Richard. She clutched her nightstick and yelled, "They're going to try to take down Richard. If that happens, we're *all* dead!" and she went running after the people converging on her brother.

She heard the others' footfalls behind her. She reached the edge of the crowd. For an instant she hesitated, and then she swung the nightstick. It connected with the back of a man's head and dropped him in his tracks. Pamela didn't have time to feel guilty.

They had noticed her. She swung again.

CHAPTER TWENTY-NINE

ROLLING THE DICE

RICHARD WAS VAGUELY aware of himself shouting *no, no, no* as he watched Rudi fall to the ground, and he couldn't understand why they were out here. They were supposed to wait for him at the house, free Damon and *wait at the house.* If they'd followed his orders Rudi wouldn't be … wouldn't be …

He heard Eddie's voice, surprisingly calm, saying, "Get us out of here. I've learned enough, and I don't know how to counter it. The pump laser is still operating. Given this set of parameters I have no clue what to do. I've got to thi—"

The word cut off, Eddie was suddenly making choking sounds, and Richard felt himself being dragged backwards. Or rather Eddie was being dragged, and he was maintaining his death grip on Richard's waist, which meant Richard was coming with him whether he wanted to or not.

There weren't a lot of options, and the only good one meant that he hurt Eddie. Richard offered up a mental apology and slammed the end of the hilt against Eddie's hands. He felt fragile bones shatter, and Eddie's hands fell open.

"You fuck! You bastard!" Eddie screamed a long wail of despair as he was yanked off the back of the bike.

Richard had a brief glimpse of Franklin and Pamela attacking a milling group of people while Syd pulled Sam to her feet, but he couldn't help them yet. He had to get Eddie. Richard planted his left foot and spun the bike in a fast turn, and nearly laid it down as the tires slipped in the slick red sand. His arm shook with strain as he struggled to control the bike. He finally had it upright, and then he narrowed his focus to the core of his body, tightened the muscles in his back and stomach, and found the balance point.

Richard took his right hand off the handlebars and awkwardly pulled the pistol out of the shoulder rig while the heel of his left hand pressed hard onto the handlebars to try and steady the bike against the recoil that was to come. Raising his right hand, he braced his body even more strongly, and pulled the trigger. Richard had figured he'd miss by a mile but was hoping he could spook Eddie's attacker. Instead, the bullet took the man full in the face. Blood, brains, and shattered pieces of skull formed a halo before the body collapsed. For an instant Snyder's ruined face flashed in front of Richard and he fought down nausea.

A woman was running toward Eddie. He lay on his back, chest heaving, mouth opening and closing like a landed fish, bruised hands pressed against his chest. The bike wobbled, threatening to tip. Richard tried to stuff the pistol into a jacket pocket, but the butt overbalanced it and it fell away, leaving Richard feeling suddenly naked, but he pushed aside the dithering thoughts that had him wanting to stop and recover the gun. Instead, he took back control of the bike, roared up between Eddie and the woman, and used the sword to cut her down.

"Get up! Get on! Hurry!" Adrenaline seemed to be popping and fizzing along every nerve in his body.

But Eddie just laid there. Richard put down his foot, leaned way over, grabbed the scientist by the belt buckle, and yanked him up.

"Behind ..." Eddie croaked.

For an instant Richard was befuddled by what seemed to be a non sequitur. Then he glanced into the side mirror.

"Oh, shit!" Richard reversed his grip and stabbed straight backward. The man folded around the blade and grabbed it with both hands. Richard yanked it free and thought he saw fingers dropping toward the ground. Eddie flailed, struggled, and finally got his leg over the bike.

Richard headed for his companions. Out of the corner of his eye he saw a man walking deliberately down into the dell. His right arm was at his side, and a gun hung negligently from his fingers. Richard recognized the narrow, acne-scarred face. Doug Andresson. His counterpart. The man who had taken Weber. Judging from the blackened eye and split lip it looked like Weber had delivered a little payback.

Richard's mind spun like a frightened, maddened top. *He'll get close enough ... into the effect of the sword, and what if the guncotton hasn't been affected? Or the presence of the sword repairs it? Then he can shoot me. And I don't have a gun. I'm dead.*

Richard remembered how the sword had swallowed up the effects of spells that had been thrown at him. *Maybe it would do the same with a bullet?* came the pathetic little thought.

You idiot. This isn't Star Wars. *The sword negates* magic *because magic is alien to our world. There's nothing more natural than a goddamn bullet!*

Andresson was close enough now that Richard could see the smirk of satisfaction. He was so focused on Andresson that he didn't notice the man huddled on the ground. He leaped up and threw himself against the front tire of the bike. It was too sudden, the sand was too deep, and Richard was too tired. The bike, Richard, the man, and Eddie all went down in a welter of flailing arms, legs, and spinning tires. Gymnastics had taught Richard how to fall and how to avoid falling. As the bike was going down, he swung his leg over the handlebars and jumped. Only one thought was beating at him, *don't drop the sword, don't drop the sword.* But trying to hit and roll with a five-foot-long blade was not a lot of fun, and Richard wrenched his shoulder badly as he landed.

He staggered to his feet just in time to see Andresson pull the trigger. Richard recognized the gun now. It was a .357 Magnum, a real penis pistol. A gun for men who liked to prove they were macho. It was stupid to try to outrun a bullet, but Richard threw himself off to the left in the faint hope that he could. The hammer hit the shell, the cylinder spun, but the gun didn't fire.

He remembered someone, Angela, Rhiana, Eddie, Grenier ... someone saying that magic was random, its effect on the physics of this world would not be consistent so there was no predicting the effect the massive amount of reality-twisting energy from these openings into other universes would have on Andresson's weapon. Back in another lifetime Richard and his partner had fired their pistols at the monsters attacking Rhiana, to no effect, but there was *way* more magic flowing here so there was no predicting what might happen with Andresson's gun.

A desperate plan began to coalesce. His timing would have to be perfect, and the results would be fatal if he failed, but it was all Richard had. He began to back away from Andresson, but not too fast, and with not too much agility, channeling the wounded bird leading a predator away from the nest.

As he'd hoped, Andresson squeezed the trigger again. A look of frustration crossed his face when the gun again failed to fire. He charged at Richard, who showed him his heels, running like the proverbial bunny. He felt it pulling at the only partially healed wound on his thigh. He had to make a guess about how much distance he needed to keep between Andresson's gun and his sword. When he'd reached it, Richard abruptly stopped and spun back to face Andresson as the hammer fell for a third time. He was gasping, each breath searing his throat and lungs. He couldn't keep this game up any longer. He just hoped that three unfired bullets would do something more dramatic than just sit there. The fact the cylinder had rotated gave Richard some small measure of hope. If hope failed then he would have to go hand to hand with the man, and Richard had *sucked* at his hand-to-hand training at the academy.

Richard couldn't know with any certainty how close was close enough, but he would have to make his move soon. Richard's eyes flicked between Andresson's face and each footstep that brought him ever closer. He was swaggering now, and he said conversationally, "Didn't think you'd come to rescue an old dude like that cop. Didn't think a little twink like you would go for aged leather." Richard didn't answer. He was staring intently at each step Andresson took, measuring the distance, trying not to react too soon, trying not to react to the slur.

Richard judged it to be the right moment. He took three running steps and threw himself in a long slide toward Andresson's feet.

"What the fuck?" Richard heard him yell, and then came the sound he'd been waiting for, hoping for, maybe even praying for, and on which he'd bet his life.

He heard the roar of three jammed cartridges exploding in the cylinder of the Magnum, and Andresson's shrill screams of agony. Fragments of hot metal seared the exposed skin on the back of Richard's neck, followed by the warm patter of blood. He rolled back onto his feet. Andresson's face was bleeding from a myriad of small cuts, and his right hand looked like something from the butcher's block, with fragments of white bone glinting through the blood.

Andresson cradled his mangled hand. The black eyes that stared out at Richard through a mask of blood were those of a maddened animal. The hate and ferocity were so great that Richard took a step backward. That show of weakness was all it took. Andresson flung himself on Richard.

They went over backward, and Richard hit the ground hard. He clung desperately to the sword, but his hand was slick with sweat and the hilt slipped through his fingers. The basso hum of the weapon was gone, and Richard felt cold and lost. Andresson was pressing his knees into his chest, and Richard felt his ribs creaking under the pressure. His good hand closed around Richard's throat. Fortunately, it was slippery with blood, and he only had the one hand, but red spots were still dancing at the corners of Richard's vision. He punched Andresson hard in the face, but the grip didn't lessen. It felt like he was fighting a berserker.

Richard groped until he managed to grip Andresson's ruined hand and exerted all his strength in a bone-crushing squeeze. The bones really did crush. They shifted and slid and ground against each other. It was grotesque and Richard felt himself gag. Andresson was howling in pain, and the pressure on Richard's throat eased. He rolled sideways and felt a moment of exaltation because Andresson was now beneath him. It didn't last. He bucked like a desperate horse and threw Richard off. They were exchanging wild punches. Some of Richard's connected. More of Andresson's hit. He was hurt, but Richard was exhausted from the strain of keeping the bike upright across that harsh countryside, and his own doubts and insecurities rose up to torment him. *Oort! You hit like a fuckin' girl! Worried about messing up that pretty face?*

Andresson managed to get behind Richard and was bending him backward over his knee. Richard was frantically trying to relax the muscles, bend and flex, but he knew, as panic clawed at his throat, that eventually Andresson would break his back.

And then Eddie came hobbling up, swinging the pouch that held the lenses. He slammed it into the side of Andresson's head, and the man fell to the side. Richard rolled away, and groaned as the muscles and tendons in his back went into a spasm. Richard was facing the gate, and what he saw made his gut clench in terror. The Old Ones were moving. With the power of the sword shuttered, they were moving in on the puny human invaders.

Richard managed to get to his feet and limped toward the hilt. Eddie was sobbing and beating Andresson around the head and shoulders. Richard could hear the lenses shattering.

"You bastards! You fuckers! You monsters! You shits! You killed them!"

Richard registered the knife in Andresson's hand, and though it hurt like blazes, he lunged the last few feet for the hilt, drew the sword, and, whirling, drove the point through Andresson's back just as the blade of his knife cut open Eddie's sweater and shirt and left a long gash in his belly.

"Oh, crap! Oh shit, that *hurt*," Eddie wailed, and clasped his hands against his stomach.

Richard pulled the sword out of Andresson. He wasn't dead, but he soon would be. The red sand was sucking thirstily at the blood that poured down his chest and back. Richard glanced toward the gate. The fogs and mists had drawn close again. The things were retreating, and the comforting thrum of the sword and the nimbus of light were back in place.

He grabbed Eddie's arm. "Let's go!"

CHAPTER THIRTY

TO PULL THE VERY WHISKERS OF DEATH

THEY STARTED HOBBLING across the dell toward their companions, who were rushing to meet them, knocking aside the people with blows from nightsticks and knives. Richard was amazed to see his sister laying about with a nightstick like a Pinkerton beating striking steelworkers.

Suddenly Eddie collapsed and nearly pulled Richard down with him.

"My leg," he moaned, and then Richard saw the long, deep gash that looked like it went to the bone. Adrenaline and rage had kept him going; now both were gone. Richard debated; defend their position and wait for the cavalry? But then there was a sound like thunder and Richard saw an enormous piece of granite breaking free of the cliff face. It bobbed in the air like a child's balloon and floated toward the agents and his sister. If it hit, the cavalry was going to be a smear on the sand.

Richard yanked Eddie onto his shoulder in a fireman's carry and started staggering toward them. He didn't have an actual plan, just the hope that the sword could stop the tons of rock heading toward them even as he knew that would not be the case.

At least I can die with them, he thought.

A cloud of dust, choking and impenetrable, swept over them, carried on a blazing hot wind. The grains of sand burned where they struck bare skin, and it felt like it was trying to force Richard back. With growing despair, he realized he would never reach them in time, and they hadn't seen the death literally looming above them because they were all way too focused on *him*. Richard tried yelling a warning, but his throat and mouth were Sahara dry, and when he parted his lips, he felt the skin tear and he tasted blood. Eddie seemed to be getting heavier by the second.

And then Cross was there. Coalescing out of the flying sand. Or maybe out of the mist, or … or … or … His abrupt arrival gave Richard a chill despite the scorching heat. Oily coils of color swirled around his body; he was well away from the humans, on the gate side of the mob. As Richard watched, Cross threw back his head, his neck swelled, and inhuman screeching cries echoed against the cliffs—it might have been language, but it couldn't be interpreted by a human mind, and it elicited terror. Pamela, Syd, Sam, and Franklin sank down in fear. Richard only managed to stay upright because he had heard these sounds once before—when Cross had challenged his doppelganger in Richard's apartment back in Albuquerque.

Cross's ululating cry was answered by the monsters at the gate, and his body seemed to swell and shrink in time to some alien rhythm, and then the granite slab raced through the air toward the homeless god. He waved it past, and Richard watched in slack-jawed amazement as he let it fall on the crowd—of cultists? Worshipers? Richard wasn't sure what to call them—before they could attack his people.

Richard staggered into the circle of sanity, and Syd and Franklin lifted the scientist off his shoulder. Perversely, instead of relief it started to hurt worse. To Richard's amazement Pamela threw her arms around him and hugged him tight.

"What the hell are you doing out here?" Richard tried to keep the worry and annoyance out of his voice but wasn't sure he'd succeeded.

Sam's pugnacious tone made it clear he hadn't. "Helping you, dickhead!"

Richard couldn't control it; his eyes flicked to where Rudi's body lay on the sand. Sam seemed to fold in on herself.

"It wasn't my fault," she said feebly.

Richard ignored her and said, "I told you to wait at the house. Did you find Damon ... Weber?"

"He's okay. Hurt, but alive. We sent him off with Estevan," Pamela reported.

Richard felt himself slump with relief, but he also was filled with the fervent wish that he could kill Andresson all over again. He wished he could kill him slower. And then he felt ashamed. Richard looked at each of these people who had followed him into a literal hell. He was not going to fail them. He would see them safe.

Suddenly Cross came barreling into the center of the group like a cue ball making the first break. He looked thin, gray, and haggard.

"Okay, kiddies," he said. "Party's over. I've shot my wad, and they've still got many, many wads in reserve. We gotta get out of here." He turned to Richard and gripped his shoulder with a veined and ropy hand. "You've got to fuck 'em up, Paladin, and give us time to retreat."

Richard looked to his people. "Is everything in place?"

Franklin nodded. "Yeah. I still don't understand this plan."

"You need to read more Kipling," Richard said with a smile that felt more like a grimace. "Now get going."

"I'm *not* leaving you out here alone," Pamela huffed.

"I can concentrate better on what I have to do if I don't have to worry about anybody else. Now *go!*"

Pamela surprised him again by giving him another hug. Richard watched as they all started back toward the house. Franklin had Eddie over his shoulder. Richard wasn't sure if the young scientist was still conscious. They disappeared among the bare trees.

"What are you gonna do?" Cross asked. "The sword alone can't cut it."

Richard didn't answer immediately. Instead, he said, "I need you to recover Rudi's body. We're not leaving him in this hellish place."

Cross's head was bobbing like a dashboard toy. "Okay, but how are you—"

"Kenntnis used *music* to shield Rhiana from the Old Ones." And Richard had a sudden vivid memory of how the strings of his piano had vibrated softly whenever Kenntnis entered the room, or the harp in the penthouse.

Cross was nodding again, but this time in agreement. "Yeah, yeah, might work. Music is pure mathematics. Supports your entire universe. Just let me get Rudi and get clear before you start. How you gonna make music out here?" Richard touched his throat. "Oh. Well, okay. Don't get stage fright."

Richard forced another smile and felt his lips tear again. It felt like pulling apart the pages of a rain-soaked book that had been left to dry. "I don't really care if they like it," he said.

Richard gave Cross a push toward Rudi's body. How much time had passed since Pamela and the others had started for the house? How much more time would they need?

Cross opened his mouth, and a roaring like waves through a cavern emerged. There was also the glow of sullen red from the back of the Old One's throat. Every muscle tensed, and then Cross shot away. The sand blew up around him in twisting tendrils. Perhaps it was only a trick of the light and the eddies of grit, or perhaps his body was dissolving into flesh-colored streamers that stretched behind him. The tendrils of light sparkled as he passed through the laser. They enfolded Rudi, and then they were both gone.

It was now all up to him.

And Richard didn't have a clue what to sing. The place in his head where every piece of music he'd ever memorized was stored was an echoing void. Maybe if he picked a composer, he'd remember something. Bach? Perfect mathematics, but mostly religious music. That was a nonstarter. Mozart? Nothing but love songs or religious text. No. Schubert? Too light for such a desperate attempt.

Richard reflected again on how the piano and the harp always seemed to sing to Kenntnis. A crooning whisper of sound as if something had breathed on the strings. It was always the same sequence of notes. Richard was suddenly grateful to have perfect pitch, and an ability to hear a tune once and remember it.

The air burned as it entered his lungs and stretched his rib cage to capacity. He had a terrible feeling that his voice would emerge as a thin thread of sound, but then he realized that the shivering that had always run along his muscles and affected his diaphragm when he sang wasn't happening. This performance was too important to have stage fright. He made it a vocalise, just notes, carried on a column of air.

The power and resonance of the opening note made Richard stumble back as If he could retreat from himself. The sword, which had always hummed with escalating musical overtones, picked up the sound of his voice, amplified it, and carried it into the highest and lowest registers beyond the ability of the human ear to hear. The air shivered with the power of the music. And there was a flare of light from inside the spin glass.

Even from this distance Richard could see the confusion and consternation at the gates. The monsters rolled back like the ragged edges of a thunderstorm scudding away before a powerful wind. All Richard's rage, grief, and hatred got channeled into the singing. The Old Ones withdrew until they were close to the gate, but they didn't retreat past the threshold. Apparently, the sword and the song could hold them at bay, but not repel them completely.

Richard's lungs felt abraded by the air he was forced to breathe. His throat was growing raw, and his tongue seemed stiff and swollen. It was probably too early, but he knew he could no longer stay in this place, facing these things. It would be enough. They would escape, live to fight another day. Richard cast a final look to the glass that held Kenntnis. The diamond and gold motes suspended in the glass were still flaring in time to his singing.

Guilt at abandoning Kenntnis caused Richard's voice to break. Unable to keep singing, he turned and bolted toward the house, running with every bit of strength that remained to him despite the throbbing ache in his leg. He risked a glance back over his shoulder and saw a pack of humans in pursuit. The Old Ones followed, but not too close and not too fast. The power and danger of the sword was still keeping them at bay. Richard stumbled on the rough ground and almost fell. His right hand did touch the ground, but he managed to steady himself and push back up.

A stitch began digging its way up Richard's side. It felt like a knife turning slowly, cutting the ribs and closing down his lungs. Throwing back his head Richard gulped in air. The house drew closer. The front door stood open, and Franklin knelt to one side, waiting. He had an arrow nocked and the string pulled back to his ear.

They were supposed to get to the basement and into the tunnel!

But Richard had to admit he was relieved to see him. He could hear the rasping breaths of his hunters closing in on him. His cunning plan had been to slow down so they would be relatively close when he entered the house. Exhaustion had made it less a choice and more of a necessity. And now they were very close indeed. Richard wasn't sure if it was imagined or reality that he could feel their breaths on the back of his neck. His thighs shivered with effort as he took the stone steps two at a time.

A hand scraped at the back of his jacket. Richard stumbled and went down. There was the hiss of an arrow flying overhead, the sound of impact and an agonized scream. But more were coming. Then strong hands gripped Richard's arms and yanked him to his feet.

It was Weber.

"Come on, Rhode Island," he heard as he was pulled into the living room. Bob Franklin was ahead of them, already running down the hall toward the kitchen and the stairs to the basement.

"Thank God you're alive. They were supposed to get you out!" Richard panted as they ran, though he noticed they were both hobbling.

"I had to make sure *you* got out, too," Damon grunted.

And indeed, it was past time. The cigarettes that had lain dormant under the blanket of magic suddenly flared to life as Richard, the sword, and Damon rushed through the room. The burning ash hit the gasoline-soaked cushions, and they went up with a roar of flame and a blast of heat that singed the back of their necks.

"What the fuck?" Weber yelled.

Behind them people screamed as the flames jumped to their clothes and hair. Richard and Weber were staggering more than running, almost holding each other up. The heat from the conflagration washed across their backs. They reached the kitchen, tumbled down the stairs into the basement, reached the trapdoor and went sliding down the ladder into the tunnel. There was a massive explosion as the fire reached the propane tank at the side of the house, and dirt rained down around them.

"Holy fuck, Richard! *This* was your plan," Weber grated. "Don't you *ever* fucking do anything like this ever again! You hear me."

"Hey, it worked for Mowgli," Richard breathed, as they limped to catch up with the rest of their party.

"Who?"

"Mowgli, from *The Jungle Book*," Richard panted. Damon gave him a look as if Richard were some strange puzzle that could not be understood.

The passage that had suggested the mad plan came back to mind.

"But the buck lived."

"How?"

"Because he came first. Running for his life."

"It is to pull the very whiskers of death."

CHAPTER THIRTY-ONE

SHIT IS GOING DOWN

A COUPLE OF the pursuers who had managed to avoid the worst of the flames followed them into the tunnel, but Jay, Sam, and Syd cheerfully went to dispatch them. Richard called out; his voice urgent.

"Don't kill them, please. Just keep them from following."

"We'll do our best," Sam responded.

They mostly succeeded, but one man tried to take Jay's knife and use it against him. Pamela wondered who he might have been as he bled out his life on the muddy floor of the tunnel. Did he have a family who missed him? Or were they here and among the starving, maddened crowds. The people she herself had beaten without compunction; she had no idea what kind of injury she might have done to them. Perhaps she had even killed some. Nausea clawed at the back of her throat. When did she become that person? Could she go on like this? She snuck a glance at her brother's rigid face and had the feeling his thoughts were spiraling into the same dark place.

The tunnel seemed endless, but ultimately, they reached the hatch. They climbed out to find Estevan hunched over Rudi's burned and bloody body, tears running down his face as he rocked back and forth in grief.

Joseph immediately rushed to the young man's side and gather him into his arms. "Mr. Cross just dropped him like he was *garbage!*" Estevan wailed.

Richard's face was frozen, expressionless. He said stiffly, "Use the abandoned cassocks and habits and make a shroud."

Syd and Franklin had begun unhitching the trailer; they didn't need it anymore, and the car could go faster and was more maneuverable without it. Weber, his strength gone, tottered over to a nearby tree stump and dropped down, exhausted. Jay seemed to be keeping guard. At any rate, his head was jerking left and right as he walked in circles around them. Which left Pamela and Sam to deal with the shroud since Richard had gone over to talk with Jessie.

Then Eddie said faintly, "Hey, guys …" Sam managed to get to the young scientist before he face planted, caught him in her arms, and lowered him gently to the ground.

She pulled back his coat to reveal the torn sweater now soaked with blood as well as the gory leg. "We got another walking wounded here!" she yelled.

Joseph gave Estevan a final pat on the shoulder, ran to the limo, and pulled out a first aid kit. He began bandaging Eddie's wounds.

Sam and Pamela finished constructing a makeshift shroud and managed to get Jay to help them gently roll the body onto the material. Jay rolled an eye at Pamela.

"You're pretty calm about all this."

"I found my mother's body, and we were all present when Grandmother Oort passed. I'm not unfamiliar with death," Pamela replied.

His eyes flicked from Pamela to Richard, who knelt on the ground in front of the open door of the limo where Jessie was huddled in the backseat. "You Oort's are some tough motherfuckers, aren't you?"

Pamela gazed at her brother's back. "Yes. Yes, we are."

✧ ✧ ✧

RICHARD KEPT A good two feet away from the girl. He could see the lingering fear in her eyes, the way they darted in all directions. The way they kept returning to the sword.

"My name is Richard. What's yours?"

"Jessie Vandehei."

"You're safe now, Jessie. But the police are probably going to want to talk to you."

"Why? Why do I have to say anything?" she whispered.

"Because we're coming back to Washington with a body." Richard briefly closed his eyes. "And the police *will* get involved. It's going to be up to you and Lieutenant Weber to make them understand that we did what we had to do."

Jessie looked terrified. "I can't!" she whispered. "He'll find me. Hurt me again. I'll never get him off me. Out of me!" She was spiraling toward hysterics.

Richard wished he could touch her, ground her, but knew he couldn't. He had been where she was, and a man's touch was anathema right now. Instead, he said in the calmest, most matter-of-fact way he could, "I know you're afraid, and you have every right to be, but he's dead, Jessie. He can't ever hurt you ever again."

"How do you know?"

The words seemed to fill his throat, choking him. "Because I killed him."

Her eyes were locked on his. Eventually she seemed to accept that truth. "Okay, but what about the girl? She was part of this, too, and she's still out there. What if she comes after me because I talked?"

"Girl? "Richard asked, but he already knew.

"I don't remember too much. Black hair. Lots of earrings. I asked her to help me, and she just looked straight through me." Jessie's lip began to tremble, and Richard saw the shudders running through her body.

Richard cast Pamela a look. She stepped past him, and briefly gripped Jessie's shoulder. "It's okay. Take your time."

Jessie sucked in a deep breath and continued. "She was telling him about how she wanted ... him." Jessie's eyes shifted to Weber, who was slumped, arms folded on his knees, head resting on his arms.

For a long moment the girl's brown eyes were locked with Richard's. "That girl," Jessie said in a whisper, as if afraid Rhiana would hear her. "She looked in the bathroom and then she sort of ... melted. How can somebody melt?"

"Don't worry about that," Richard said. "And I *promise* you, she will *never* come after you."

✧ ✧ ✧

IT SENT A chill through Pamela. Not because of Rhiana, but because of what she heard in his voice and saw in her brother's face.

Joseph and Estevan gathered up Rudi's body and laid him

gently in the trunk. "It is *way* past time to go," Franklin said.

Richard nodded. Joseph slid behind the wheel. Syd and Sam helped Eddie. Sam insisted that Jessie sit next to the door with Sam beside her.

Pamela grabbed Richard and held him back as he was heading toward the front seat. "You need to wash your hands."

She nodded at his hands. Not only his hand but his wrist and the cuffs of his jacket and shirt were soaked with blood. The blood drained from his face as he gazed down at the stains, and he looked like he was about to vomit.

Pamela pulled out the large bottle of water from the front cup holder, picked up a piece of torn cassock, and, wetting it, she began to scrub at his hand. She could feel his fingers trembling in hers.

"There were so many of them. I've lost count," he said, his voice quavering. "I try to keep count. So I don't forget. So it doesn't start to feel … routine. Acceptable." He raised agonized blue eyes to meet hers. "When did I become a killer, Pammie? I don't want to be a killer," he whispered.

❖   ❖   ❖

ONCE THEY WERE back in DC, the exhausted, silent group had scattered like dandelion fluff in a hurricane. Rudi's body had been taken to the morgue. Damon hadn't known the man well, but they'd compared experiences—Rudi had been a cop in San Antonio before retiring and taking the job with Kenntnis and Lumina. Unlike many cops, and certainly Damon, he'd stayed married until breast cancer had taken his wife. He had a couple of grown kids; one lived in Austin, the other in Denver. A complex mix of grief and rage filled his chest.

Joseph took Jessie, Eddie, and Weber to the hospital for treatment. Weber's injuries were nowhere near as bad as Eddie's nor his trauma and injuries as acute as poor Jessie's, so he checked himself out after being told he had three broken ribs, having some cuts stitched, his dislocated knee restored and braced, and his raw wrists treated and bandaged. He had swallowed a couple pain pills to try and ease the pain from the massive bruising across his entire body, including his nuts which throbbed in time to his heartbeat. At least he'd gotten in one good shot at that bastard Andresson; broken his fucking nose with a headbutt and kneed him in the groin before he'd gotten too injured and exhausted to fight back.

Joseph drove Weber back to the Sofitel Hotel where Richard had rented the presidential suite. Only Grenier was there, and Damon had dealt with him by growling, *"I suggest you get the fuck out of my sight before I rearrange your face."* The former preacher had huffed, declared he'd be in the restaurant, and left. Joseph also soon left as well, saying he wanted to be ready to bring Mr. Oort back once he'd finished talking with the police.

That left Weber with a lot of time to clean up, order room service, finish eating, and return to chewing over the events of the past few days. So by the time Richard, his sister, Joseph, and Estevan entered the suite, Damon had worked up a head of steam and was armed for bear.

As the door closed behind them Richard was saying,

"Nobody is going to go into the compound to look for Andresson's body, and Franklin is a SAC and he made it damn clear that we were running a hostage rescue operation which was wildly successful. We succeeded in saving two people instead of just one."

"Really?" Damon grated, rising with a grunt from the sofa. "Wildly successful? You got one of your people killed. Damn near got Eddie killed."

The long lashes fluttered, and the blue eyes were raised to his. They held an expression that was a combination of shock, hurt, and confusion.

Damon felt the muscles in his jaw bunching and flexing as he gazed down into Richard's face. "And have you bothered to consider that both Eddie and that girl are vulnerable while they're in the hospital?"

"Franklin and the DC police are providing security."

"Richard needs to get out of those clothes and preferably have them burned," Pamela said. Her snotty East Coast accent was at its most snotty.

"No. Not until him and me have this out."

Joseph, having been a military man, quickly evaluated the situation, knew that shit was about to go down, and knew to get the hell out of its path. He dropped an arm over Estevan's shoulder. "We'll leave you all to catch up." The two guards left.

"Say what you need to say, but please do it quickly. I need a shower," Richard said sounding as snotty as his sister.

Damon folded his arms across his chest and glared down at him. "So, props that you killed that motherfucker, and got that girl out, but *you should never have been there in the first place!*" A universe of rage and anger rose up to almost choke him.

"I had to," came the reply.

"Because of me?" Weber demanded.

"Yes," Richard said simply.

It was disorienting, disturbing. Damon didn't pause to parse why exactly that was. "You got Rudi killed!"

"Yes."

"Goddamn it! Fight with me!"

❖   ❖   ❖

THE WORDS WERE a roar, and Pamela retreated to the far wall. The men were only inches apart, and Weber loomed over Richard, but her brother didn't move. Slim, erect, unflinching, he stared up into Damon's face.

"Why are you so angry at me? Because I saved you? I'm sorry, but I can't help how I feel. I'm always going to protect you. I know you can't stand what I am, or that I care for you, but if it will make you feel better, take your best shot. I'll give you one for free." Richard lifted his chin and cocked his head to the side, inviting the punch.

Weber's hand closed into a fist. Pamela stared, fascinated at the way his knuckles looked like pale walnuts, and how the veins stood out like pale blue snakes on the back of his hand. She had thought that would be the extent of it, so she squeaked when Weber actually *took* the swing and hit Richard hard on the jaw. Her brother staggered sideways, caught himself on the back of a sofa, and managed to stay upright.

Richard touched his jaw gingerly, worked it a bit. "Okay. But I think you pulled it. That was far from your best."

He started toward one of the bedrooms, only to be halted when Weber let out a roar and charged. Richard spun around, confusion in his blue eyes. Just as Weber was about to grab Richard in a bear hug, her brother stepped lightly aside and gave the big cop a shove between his shoulder blades. Weber tottered sideways, and the torchiere lamp went over with a crash.

"Stop! Stop! Stop!" Pamela realized she was the one yelling.

At the same time Richard panted, "I am not going to fight you."

The commotion brought Joseph and Estevan. Estevan displayed the barely suppressed glee of the very young enjoying the excitement of catastrophe. Joseph looked disapproving but resigned.

"You're trying to goad me, get me to fight, hurt you to assuage your own guilt," Richard said as he dodged another punch from the older man.

"Do not psycho-fucking-analyze me, Richard!"

"Why not? You're making it so easy," he retorted, evading another bull-like charge from Weber.

Pamela rushed up to Joseph. "Do something!"

"Nah, let 'em have it out," the security chief said. Pamela let out a sound like an outraged cat.

Richard had retreated behind the couch, hands braced on the back. "You feel stupid because Andresson grabbed you. Impotent because you had to listen to him hurt that girl while you could do *nothing*. Well, stop acting like you're so special because I feel stupid, too. *I'm* the reason you were there in the first place because I'm the person who let Rhiana know *how much you matter*."

Richard's eyes went wide as Weber went straight across the sofa using his bulk and momentum to tip it over, knocking Richard to the floor. The big cop dropped his knee onto Richard's diaphragm and closed his hand around Richard's throat.

Panicked, Pamela looked for a weapon. Her gaze fell on the enormous bouquet of flowers that the hotel management had sent up to welcome the CEO of Lumina Enterprises. Running over, she pulled out the flowers. It sloshed most satisfactorily when she picked up the vase.

She ran over to the grunting, gasping males. Though really only one was making any sound. Richard lay completely still beneath Weber's hand, eyes closed, face white except where a bruise was blooming on his jawline. Pamela doused the water over both of them. Weber fell to the side spluttering and cursing.

"Now *stop it*! Both of you. Do something useful. That's what Rudi would probably say."

"That and that we all need something to eat," Joseph added, as he joined them and held out a hand to assist Richard to his feet. Pamela couldn't tell if the water on his face was from the vase or from tears. She decided it didn't matter.

Estevan was helping Weber to his feet. "You fucker," Weber grated, glaring at Richard. "You managed to make me hurt myself more than I hurt you."

"That seems to be a specialty of mine. Hurting the people

I love. Everyone around me, really," Richard said in a low voice.

They watched in worried silence as Richard walked to one of the bedrooms and closed the door ever so quietly behind him.

Frowning, Weber looked over at Pamela. "What the fuck do you think that meant?"

"I have no idea," she said. "But it certainly sounded ominous. And by the way, you are a *gigantic* asshole."

CHAPTER THIRTY-TWO

SACRIFICIAL LAMBS

WHEN RICHARD EMERGED from the bedroom the next morning and told the security chief that he needed to go to the hospital to see Eddie, Joseph had folded his arms across his chest and given him a stern look.

"You should eat some breakfast first. I know you didn't eat dinner last night."

"No appetite." Because after the one-sided fight Weber had announced he'd get himself home, and, guarded and accompanied by Estevan, he'd left for the airport that night. "I'll eat something later. Right now, I really need to see Eddie, and I assume you won't let me go alone."

"You assume correctly. I'll text you when the car is out front. Have Estevan escort you downstairs."

"God, I hate living like this."

"Get used to it," was the comfortless reply.

It took longer than he expected, and Richard found out why when Joseph reached back over the front seat and thrust an Egg McMuffin into his hands. "Eat."

"Yes, dad." There was a bottle of water in the backseat cup holder, and that helped him force down the breakfast sandwich.

When they reached the hospital Richard was pleased to

see Sam canted back in a chair outside Eddie's hospital room. "Yo," she said. Then added, "You look like shit."

"Thank you." She looked disgustedly well-rested.

"Franklin's talking with the Director. Trying to get him to go to the Pres."

"And do what?"

"Declare a national emergency."

"Great," Richard sighed. In his twenty-eight years he had lived through the *"let's all be afraid of Muslims, immigrants, Asians, Black people,"* wing of American politics. He could only imagine what declaring a national emergency would do to an already fractured society. He shook his head and entered Eddie's room.

The scientist was busily wolfing down his breakfast, but he gave Richard a blazing smile when he walked in.

"Hey, boss. We made it. We're still alive."

"Yes." Richard crossed to the bed and took the young scientist's hand in his. "I'm sorry you got hurt."

"It's okay. We were kinda box office though. So, when they make the movie I want that dude from the new Midnight Ninja movies to play me."

It brought a smile. "Okay, we'll work on that."

"I gotta think on who should play you. Gonna be tricky 'cause you're really *short*." He gulped and quickly added, "But really handsome, I mean like amazingly handsome—"

"I accept your interesting version of an apology, Eddie. So, any idea when they're going to release you?" Richard asked.

"Doc's gonna check on me this morning. Could be later today."

"Good. I really want to get home."

"Me, too. I want to see my folks." Eddie sounded suddenly very young and very wistful.

"We'll make sure that happens. But maybe don't tell them what we've been up to. They'd probably make you quit, and I really need you and your brain power."

"Oh, speaking of my brain and its awesome power … I've been thinking a lot about the Bose-Einstein condensate and how to break it. Especially since it's being powered by a fucking *sun*. Anyway, you know how you said this Kenntnis guy was being held with a combination of science and magic. Well, since this sure as fuck isn't natural in any meaning of the word, I wondered that if maybe the magic was removed the entire Rube Goldberg mess would just, I don't know, fall apart."

Richard stared at Eddie, felt a leap of hope followed by a hollow feeling in the gut. There were only two ways that could happen—if Rhiana voluntarily removed the spell, *or if she could no longer cast or power a spell.*

✧　✧　✧

THE NEXT TASK had been to locate her. Richard's badge had enabled him to run the plates on the BMW convertible. To his surprise, the car wasn't stolen or conjured up out of old Volkswagen parts and magicked into a BMW. No, Rhiana had bought and registered it, which gave Richard the address of her Georgetown house.

Lowering dark clouds had rolled in and it felt like snow. Joseph glided the car to the curb. "What if she's in there?"

"Well, that's rather the point, isn't it? I need to speak with her."

"It's dangerous."

Richard gestured with the hilt. "I have this."

"And she might have a gun."

"I'll be careful. And it seems deserted," Richard added, studying the fact the porch light was on, and a pizza delivery flyer was hanging off the knob on the front door flapping a bit in the stiff breeze.

"Then why go in?"

Richard chuckled. "To look for, oh, I don't know... clues?"

Joseph cranked around and grinned at him. "Sass, you're giving me sass. Glad to see it, sir. I think you're finding your footing."

"God, I hope so," Richard muttered as he climbed out of the car.

Though the bad weather had driven everyone inside, Richard didn't really want to be seen trying to pick the lock. He also wasn't very good at it. After ascertaining no one was watching, he ducked down the side of the house, and found the window into the dining room had been broken out.

Tucking the hilt back into its holster, he braced his hands on the sill and boosted himself inside. Drawing the sword, he studied the room. The dining room table held only a bouquet of wilted roses. The smell of stale water and microwave popcorn was an unpleasant mix that had him wrinkling his nose.

Richard moved through to the living room and froze at the sight of dead birds strewn across the floor. A tragedy written in broken wings and shattered necks, the light from the drawn sword had glittered in their staring eyes. Grief pooled in his stomach. They hadn't deserved to be used or to die in this way. Richard wished the sword could restore them, but its power could only protect going forward, it could not undo the casualties of this hidden war in which he now found himself.

As if drawn by his thoughts, sick and diseased colors roiled in the mirrors and even through the teardrop crystals in the chandelier. Richard moved quickly through the house using the sword on every reflective surface he could find.

Others had entered the house before him. Dangling cables showed him where televisions had once stood; there were racks of CDs, but no player; and in the upstairs bedroom, which had been decorated like a scene out of the Arabian Nights, the tall jewelry case stood with its drawers hanging out like tongues. The thieves had missed one earring. The emerald lay sparkling, as green as Rhiana's eyes, in the back of a drawer.

Richard been trained on how to make a thorough search, so he went through the drawers and found expensive cashmere sweaters and fragile lacy underwear. There was nothing hidden in the toilet tank. He went back downstairs to the kitchen to search. There was no food.

Of course not, he thought, *once she had learned her true nature Rhiana had been able to feed on the pain, fear, and hate of ordinary humans.* Then Richard opened the freezer. It seemed there was a small part of her that was still just a teenage girl. Inside were seventeen different flavors of Ben & Jerry's ice cream.

He went back upstairs to the bedroom that seemed to reflect more of the girl than the rest of the house, which felt more like an overly elaborate movie set. Running a hand nervously through his hair he sat down on the edge of the unmade bed. Where would she have gone? His hand fell on the rumpled covers and he felt something firm beneath his palm.

Tossing back the silk sheets and duvet revealed a leather-bound book. He flipped it open. A scrapbook. The chronicle of a young life.

✧　✧　✧

GRENIER GAZED OUT the window at Lafayette Plaza, now renamed Black Lives Matter Plaza. The suite was rife with tension. He and the policeman hadn't spoken again after their exchange the day before, and apparently the cop had left DC. It was a most satisfactory development.

Richard had seemed distracted and preoccupied and had been gone for most of the day. The sister was pretending to work but kept looking toward the door to the suite with ill-disguised worry. Even the normally ebullient Estevan was subdued.

As he watched, fat snowflakes began to spin lazily past the window, and the room became even darker. There was a sharp snap as Pamela switched on the desk lamp. The door to the suite opened and Richard and Joseph entered. The older man assisted Richard out of his topcoat, inclined his head, and said, "I'm going to check in with Brook, make sure we're ready to leave as soon as Doctor Tanaka is released."

Richard looked to his sister. "I take it Eddie didn't get released this afternoon?"

"No, he called around 3:00 PM, said the doctors wanted to keep him one more night. He sounded good," Pamela said.

"He seemed good."

"You were gone a lot longer than I expected."

"I went to look for Rhiana."

"Jesus, Richard! Are you out of your mind?" Pamela exploded. The use of even such a mild expletive was unusual for her, and Grenier raised an interested eyebrow.

"You can relax. I didn't find her. She seems to have left Washington. The question is for where."

"If we're lucky she's left our universe completely," Pamela huffed. "Let her go play her evil-alien-princess games somewhere else."

Richard shook his head. "That would be the worst thing that could happen. There would be no way for us to break Kenntnis free."

"He's one person," Pamela objected.

"I think he's far more than that. First, we know he's not a person, and I just have a feeling that his absence has made things worse. Given the Old Ones more of a foothold in our universe." A faint smile touched his lips. "Of course, if Kenntnis were here he'd be giving me a lecture right now about how I should be thinking and not feeling."

"Which is why you want to find Rhiana, since she cast the spell," Grenier said.

"Exactly. The only thing I found at her house that seemed relevant was this." He handed over a scrapbook.

Grenier began flipping through the pages while Richard

explained he'd found it among the rumpled blankets of her bed. The pages were filled with photos of Rhiana, and press clippings from a small local Van Nuys newspaper as well as the *Los Angeles Times*.

"I expect this is her version of a security blanket or a Teddy Bear," Grenier said. He raised his eyes from the book, and pinned Richard with a look. "But that isn't your actual question, is it? You just want to know if your conclusion that she's gone home to California is correct."

Richard nodded. Grenier almost rolled his eyes. Instead, he gave himself a congratulatory pat on the back for having the amazing forbearance to *not* point out that Richard was once again just looking for corroboration of a conclusion he'd had *already reached* because Richard's insecurities *demanded* that an older male give him that validation.

"Of course, she's going to run home. She's a kid. Think about it, if you'd done something terrible, wouldn't you want to run home to Mommy and have her kiss it and make it all better? Tell you everything will be all right?"

Pamela let out a small sound that carried a weight of grief, and a deadly quiet fell over the room. Richard's eyes had lost any trace of vulnerability and become like blue steel blades cutting into him. That had been too far, much too far, Grenier realized.

"Perhaps not the most felicitous phrasing," Richard said softly. "Since you manipulated *our* mother into committing suicide."

His voice remained dead level, almost conversational, which somehow made it all the more threatening. Grenier reminded himself that if he wanted to take his place as

Richard's major advisor now that the cop had conveniently exited stage left, it was probably best that he *not* get *over his skis,* so to speak, where Richard was concerned.

"I'm sorry. That was thoughtless. Forgive me."

Richard nodded and the ice thawed. Grenier gave an inward smile. There would be time enough for him to manipulate the situation.

It seemed he would end up controlling a Paladin after all. Just not the one he had expected.

✧ ✧ ✧

AFTER THE CONVERSATION with Grenier, Richard had retreated to his bedroom in the suite, sank down on the bed, and dropped his head into his hands. So, now he knew the where. Now only the *what* remained. What to do? What should he do?

He longed to talk with Damon—*no, he mustn't think of him that way. Weber or the lieutenant.* He pushed aside the hurt and small bubble of anger, checked his watch, factored in the time difference, and called Jeannette back at the Lumina offices.

"Oh, Richard. You're safe. I'm so relieved."

"We're fine; well, not all of us." He swallowed past the lump that had formed in his throat.

"Joseph told us about Rudi. We're helping the children with the funeral arrangements, and I took the liberty of contacting the insurance company regarding the death benefits."

"Oh, yes, thank you. I should have thought of that."

"That's why you have me. And Mr. Kenntnis?"

"I'm sorry, but we didn't get him. But we're not giving up. Which is why I called. Is Cross out back?"

"I'll go check."

She put him on hold. Soft Muzak of popular tunes filtered through his phone. Richard decided that had to change and as soon as possible.

Instead of Jeannette it was Cross who came back on the line. "Yeah, what do you need?"

"I have some questions and you're the best person ... thing ... to answer them—"

"Which hotel are you staying at?"

"The Sofitel, why?" But the line had gone dead.

A few seconds later his cell phone rang. It was Jeannette. "Sorry, he just ... *left*. You know, the way he can."

Richard sighed. "We could have done this on the phone."

"I think he's enjoying the ... power boost."

"Yeah, that's probably not a good thing," Richard said.

A few moments later the house phone rang. Expecting it to be the front desk, Richard answered. It was, indeed, the front desk. "Mr. Oort, there's a ... man here who says he works for you, but—"

"He does. Send him up."

"Yes, sir," the clerk said dubiously.

Richard went back into the sitting room and opened the door. Pamela, back at work at the desk, raised an eyebrow. Cross came sauntering down the hotel hall looking more disreputable than normal in stained jeans with a tear in the thigh, dirty tennis shoes, and a T-shirt that was missing one of its short sleeves.

"Where's the fire?" the homeless god asked as he snatched up the room service menu and began to peruse the choices.

"If there *was* a fire those clothes should be in it," Pamela sniffed. "Do you ever do laundry?"

"Hey, I was just fighting ruthless godlike beings to protect your puny human asses, so enough with the judgmental vibes, okay?"

"Pamela, would you mind giving us the room," Richard said before things could escalate. His sister, of course, argued.

"Why?"

"Because technically you still work for the Newport DA's office and what Cross and I are going to discuss might not be technically ... well, anything you should hear."

"If it's illegal you should probably have your counsel present."

"Except you're *not* my counsel. Let me know when you quit. Then we can hire you."

Pamela gave a huff, and rigid-backed she stalked from the room. Her bedroom door closed with something suspiciously close to a slam.

"I like your sister."

"I'm sure she'll be thrilled to hear that. We need to talk about Rhiana." Richard outlined what Eddie had said. "So, what do you—"

"Kill her," the Old One said without a moment's hesitation.

Richard jerked back as if he'd been struck. "No. Nonnegotiable. What if I can convince her to lift the spell?"

"Gonna go all sacrificial lamb on us again?" He tapped a forefinger against his chin. "Yeah, hmmm, let me think ... didn't work out so well last time."

For an instant Damon's ... Weber's face twisted in anger floated before him. "Fuck you," Richard snapped. "And it's different now. She's shaken. I think she's afraid. Grenier and I agree that she's probably run home ... to the *human* home."

"And when she gets her panties in a twist again? Or Old One Daddy either threatens her or bribes her and she turns on us again? What are you gonna do then? You've got no control over her because she can always go where you can't follow."

"You could always take me there. You can move through the dimensions. You demonstrated that today."

"Yeah. No. And remember, your little toy don't work outside of this dimension. It's the embodiment of the natural order and reality of *this* universe."

"So why can it kill any of you?"

"Because you're croaking us *in this reality* where we're as unnatural as all fuck." Cross waved the menu. "Can I please order before we continue this conversation?"

"No. Is there some way we can trap her here? Keep her from walking into another multiverse?"

"Not that I know of. And even if we could how you gonna sell that? *Hey sweetie, do me a favor, free Mr. Kenntnis and in return you get to go to jail forever.* Real compelling argument there, Dickie. Kill her. Simpler and kinder for everybody, really."

Richard gave him a withering look. "If that's your idea of kindness I hate to see what your version of cruelty looks like," he said tartly.

Cross's eyes did that creepy thing where they went completely black. "You know what I am. Never forget that. Kenntnis didn't."

Richard suppressed a shudder. Almost in a whisper he said, "I promised I wouldn't harm her."

Cross held out his right hand, palm up. "You saw those people at the Compound. Crazy as all fuck. Starving, attacking each other for our … the Old One's amusement and nourishment. There are multiple gates opening, so there will be thousands, maybe millions, of crazed dying fuckers. Versus …" He raised his left hand, palm up. "One girl."

"I have never been a fan of Utilitarianism, Mr. Spock and the *needs of the many* notwithstanding," Richard said.

Cross dropped his hands, slapping them against his thighs. "Easy for you to take the fucking high road when you're immune to what's happening. Kill her. Remember, Richard, there are worse things than death."

CHAPTER THIRTY-THREE
Promises Made, Promises Broken

RICHARD LAY IN the bed in the private cabana at the Beverly Hills Hotel listening to wild winds drive rain against the windows, and the fronds on the palm trees dotted around the property rattle like maddened castanets. The Lumina jet had touched down in LA at 1:00 AM, and he'd checked into the hotel for a few hours of sleep. Soon he would have to rise, shower, shave, and then have a car delivered. Sleep, however, was proving to be elusive.

During the flight he had read international news reports. As with the gate in Virginia, the madness was spreading worldwide, warping not only the minds of the humans caught up in the expanding wave, but the very land itself was shifting, changing. A monstrous army marched behind it.

When Richard retreated in fear and horror from the news, he found no peace as his mind kept replaying the past forty-eight hours—the fight with Weber, the toxic mix of anger and guilt he felt toward Rhiana. If he were honest with himself, the anger wasn't just over her betrayal of the human race, but because she used Richard's inability to control his emotions to destroy what could have remained a friendship and instead had become ... well, something ... distant and hard to define. And guilt because she was a girl who liked popcorn and ice cream, and he was going to … well, he didn't actually *know* what he was going to do.

His own father had rejected him. Weber had rejected him. Because of who he was. What he was. So, who was left? Well, Pamela. Their previously fraught relationship seemed to have taken a profound shift, but what if it shifted back? There were a plethora of Lumina officers—Dagmar, Kenzo, Gold—but he didn't know them well and ultimately they were employees looking to *him* to make the decisions. Eddie had a bad case of hero worship and would always defer. Grenier? Oh yeah, that would be like hugging an asp. He needed Kenntnis to guide him, to tell him what to do. And the only way to get Kenntnis was to do something *he did not want to do.*

I can't do this alone, he thought while the storm raged. *I'm not smart enough, strong enough … brave enough to continue this fight without his help.*

Then you know what you have to do.

I can't.

✧   ✧   ✧

WHEN THE PHONE rings at 3:32 AM you always assume the worst. *Mom? Dad? One of the sibs?* Angela bolted upright in bed and grabbed her cell phone off the bedside table. It was a 505 number, but not one for the family.

"This better not be a fucking spam call," she muttered to the darkened room. "Hello?"

"Angela," came the quiet tenor voice.

"Richard? What's wrong?"

He laughed, slightly hollow and with an edge of hysteria. "What's *not* might be the better question."

She sat up, resting her elbows on her knees. "Where are you?"

"Los Angeles."

"Okay. Do I want to know why?"

"Probably not."

Silence. She could hear him breathing on the other end of the line, too short, too shallow.

"Just needed to hear a voice?" she asked gently.

"Yeah. I guess so."

She had so many questions. What was the situation with Kenntnis? Was the government ever going to do anything other than the political parties blaming each other? And most important, *what had happened between him and Weber?* The lieutenant had returned to work battered and bruised, expression grim, but with sadness lingering in his brown eyes. All he had said when she asked what had happened was that he, Weber, had been a dumb ass, and Richard was an even bigger dumb ass. Since then, he seemed to have been avoiding her.

There were times when people wanted to bounce ideas, get things off their chest, find absolution. And then there were the times when they just needed to be grounded, held in the moment, have a chance to get out of their own heads. Angela sensed this was such a moment for Richard.

Filling her voice with brightness and a hint of laughter, she said, "Let me tell you about what my niece Consuela did.

So, she decided to take her cat, Rebotar, out for a walk in the snow. Needless to say, kitty hated the snow and looked for high ground, which happened to be the rump of my brother's prize bull. Rebo dug in. Bull broke through the gate and went romping through the village with the cat hanging on for dear life, thus making the bull run faster. Connie was screaming and crying and chasing after them. Eventually the entire village was in on the roundup with a combination of people on horseback and men in ATVs and pickup trucks. Once the bull and cat were belled everyone adjourned to my brother's and they had a *matanza*. Wish I had been there."

"Sounds wonderful. This was at the family ranch up north?"

"Yes. I'll have to take you up there sometime. It's beautiful. Nestled at the foot of the mountains."

"The ones where your grandfather would wrestle with demons?"

"Those'd be the ones."

There was another long silence, then Richard asked, "Tell me, did he win?"

"Every time." A faint ghost of a laugh came through. "Granddad did say that it was the demons inside that were the most difficult to tame," Angela added softly.

"I'll keep that in mind."

✧   ✧   ✧

THE GPS SYSTEM in Richard's phone had taken him right to the house in Van Nuys. After the cold and sleet of Washington and the storm last night, California was finally beginning to show itself as the land of milk and honey. The seventy-plus-degree weather felt like a caress. He had the windows rolled down, and the scent of star jasmine was carried on a soft wind.

Such peaceful beauty when he was on so dark an errand.

He was parked at the end of a cul-de-sac studying the small, one-story house. The winds from the night before had torn through this neighborhood as well, so palm fronds lay scattered across the road and postage-stamp front yards. They looked like wings torn from the bodies of gigantic alien insects.

Richard knew he was stalling. He glanced once more at the scrapbook resting on the seat next to him. Rhiana was only a few hundred feet away. It was time to do ...

Richard climbed out of the car, obsessively touching his coat pocket to make sure the sword was still there and in easy reach in case ...

He walked up the driveway toward the house. It was a small, boxy affair with white stucco stained from years of winter rains. Four hoary old palm trees swayed above the house. As Richard watched, another frond lost its battle with gravity, sailed down to land with a crash on the roof. There were no cars in the oil-stained driveway. Richard reminded himself that that didn't mean anything. Rhiana didn't need a car.

As he approached the front door, a chorus of barking welled up from the backyard. Richard could discern three distinct voices—a deep throaty *woof*, a high-pitched hysterical yapping, and the bell-like bay of a basset hound. Well, the element of surprise was definitely gone. He stepped to the side of the peephole, drew the sword, and knocked.

She just answered. Probably because she was home. Probably because she felt safe. Emotions flickered across her face like slides in an old-style carousel—joy, fear, relief, surprise, confusion, terror, and it ended on *guilt*. Richard tightened his jaw, feeling his own guilt welling up. He forced her back into the house and shut the door gently behind him.

Now that Richard was inside, he got a sense of the space. Piles of newspaper stood by the torn sofa. There was a giant fifty-two-inch TV on one wall. The picture had to be blurry in a room this small. There was the smell of toast and bacon grease and pet urine. There were large stains on the cheap green carpet.

She was staring at the sword. Richard berated himself; if he was going to do it, he should have just done it. Touched her the instant the door opened, done the deed, and gotten it over with.

"Are you … are you … are you?" She sounded like a lawn mower engine trying to catch.

"Why shouldn't I?"

She ran toward a wall. Richard leaped after her, thinking she was trying to escape, but she stopped and pointed at the frame hanging on the wall. On the floor beneath were the shards of a mirror.

"Look. See. I broke them all. I'm done with them. All of them. They used me. They tricked me. I can help you." The words emerged in a panicked rush and the green eyes fixed on his were filled with desperation.

"Little late for a Road to Damascus moment." Richard didn't recognize his own voice. It sounded far away and very cold.

"I didn't mean for anybody to get hurt," she cried.

"What part of evil invading aliens didn't you understand? Did you honestly think no one was going to get hurt? And you brought women to a psychopath *knowing* he would brutalize them. How many were killed because of you?"

"Doug did that. I didn't know. When I found out it made me sick. I didn't want to do it anymore, but they made—"

"That's sophistry, and you know it. It's the coward's excuse. You have enormous power. You could have brought Andresson to the authorities, to me, but you did nothing, and you *gave Damon to him*, and in rescuing him Rudi *died*."

She had no reaction to the death of a man she had known, who had protected her while she was living in the Lumina headquarters, and it was like a blow to Richard's chest. Was it a function of being eighteen and heedless? A flaw in her emotional makeup? The fact she wasn't truly human? Richard didn't know the answer, all he knew was that the growing anger he felt had a taste, like iron filings on the back of the tongue. It was becoming hard to breathe. He snapped out, "No pity? No sorrow? No shame? You knew him, Rhiana."

Her brow wrinkled. Cleary, she had no idea who Rudi had been. "I don't understand. None of them can help you the way I can. They're just ordinary. We're special." She gestured between them. "We're meant to be together. If we worked together, we could do anything—"

"There was *never* any *us*, Rhiana. And that's when a person's most dangerous, when they think they're special. When they think they are *better than*." He clutched at his hair with his free hand. "With every word you're saying you're showing me that …"

"What?"

"That I shouldn't trust you."

"How can I prove it to you? What can I do to show you?" She dropped to her knees looking up at him imploringly.

She looked so young and vulnerable, and Richard was once again seized by doubt.

We use Cross and he's one hundred percent alien. She's half-human, we can give her the chance for redemption, to return to humanity. And she could be useful.

Richard allowed the blade to vanish. "All right. You want to prove your sincerity, your desire to help? Free Kenntnis."

"I'm … I'm not sure I can. My father … Madoc made me tie a lot of myself into the spell." She pressed her hands against her chest. "I can feel it … *all* of it pulling at me." She gave him a desperate look. "Please, make it stop."

"I … I don't understand. The spin glass is pulling you?"

She gestured wildly. "*All* of it. It's like pictures on top of pictures. I see here and there and other places, even the *not* places."

And Richard realized with growing horror and sorrow that, just as he felt as if the weight of the human world was on his shoulders, she was the capstone of the Old Ones. Like him, her genetics had made her unique.

All of it—the glass prison, the gates—were linked to *her*.

Richard was suddenly back in the office on the Gulfstream V listening to Kenntnis saying, *"My guess is it would be similar to a lobotomy."*

And he remembered his response. *"I'll be on Rhiana's*

side. I won't harm her … or allow anyone else to."

Like Rhiana, he felt as if he were being torn apart.

You're breaking your word.

One girl against thousands, millions, potentially billions of lives.

It was Utilitarianism at its most brutal.

She seemed unaware of his turmoil. "Please, make it stop," she whispered. Those amazing green eyes were filled with tears. They spilled over and ran down her face.

"I'm sorry," Richard whispered.

He swept his hand away from the hilt and laid the sword on her shoulder.

He then called 911 because it was the worst reaction he'd ever seen and he feared she would die. During that call the phone beeped, indicating another call. Richard took it after providing the address to the dispatcher. It was Joseph, and he sounded like a man who'd just run a marathon.

"Richard! Sir. It's Kenntnis. He's back. He's here, but—"

"Tell him I can't talk right now." Richard had run into the kitchen for a butter knife to place between Rhiana's teeth.

"Sir—" Joseph began, but Richard hung up, and he turned off the phone because he didn't want to hear from Kenntnis about how he'd *done the right thing*. He didn't feel like he had done the right thing. He didn't *like* the person who had done this thing. Four minutes later the ambulance arrived.

It was forty minutes until the last seizure shook her body. Her mother was called away from the school where she worked in the cafeteria. Her father was just up the Ventura Freeway overseeing the loading of his rig with cantaloupes bound for market. In the chaos that was traffic in Los Angeles, he arrived only a few minutes after his wife.

Richard waited in the visitors' lounge. He wanted to leave, but he had to face her parents. He briefly wondered if Cross had sensed Rhiana's half-death and reported it to Kenntnis. Kenntnis would understand why he needed time and space to deal with what he'd done. Richard couldn't shake the memory of the blank-eyed creature that lay in the hospital bed and plucked mindlessly at the sheet. Richard had only been allowed to look through the window in the door. It had been more than enough. But Kenntnis was back. It was the reason he'd done what he'd done. It was for all of them. For all of humanity. It didn't help, guilt crawled through his gut begging him to vomit up his sin.

Richard was sitting in the waiting room, hands clasped between his knees, head bowed, when he heard footsteps and the voice of the neurologist saying, "It appears to have been a stroke."

They turned the corner, and Richard saw them for the first time. They might not have been related by blood to Rhiana, but there was no doubt they were her parents from their grief-stricken reaction. Tears coursed down Lottie Davinovitch's round face. In her haste to reach the hospital she was still wearing a hairnet and apron. Todd Davinovitch was a big man with a linebacker's shoulders and neck, and the big belly bestowed by middle age. He had his arm around his wife. Behind his beard his face was set in a rictus of anguish.

"But she was only eighteen," Todd said. Unshed tears roughened his voice.

"It doesn't matter the age if there's a flaw in the brain," the doctor said gently.

"If I'd just been there," Lottie said. "She seemed so upset. I should have called in sick—"

"Even if you'd been there, there was nothing you could have done," the doctor said, trying and probably failing to assuage their guilt. He then indicated Richard. "We're just lucky this gentleman found her, or she might have died."

Richard wondered if his guilt was etched on his face. He stood. "I'm Richard Oort. Rhiana was working on a project for my company."

"Physics?" Todd asked.

"Yes, my company specializes in high-tech projects. I was out here on business, and she'd told me she was coming home to see you. We met for an early breakfast, but she seemed disoriented and confused, so I stopped by your house to check on her." The lies flowed so easily. "The front door was open. I knocked, but nobody answered, so I went inside. I found her and called 911."

It was the hardest thing he'd ever done to stand there and accept their fervent thanks. Each word of gratitude struck like a blow. When they finally fell silent Richard said, "Since Rhiana was an employee, she's fully covered under our health plan. All the bills will be paid by Lumina."

He watched the wave of relief go across Lottie's face, followed by immediate shame that she had even been thinking about financial matters at a time like this.

"I'm very sorry, Mr. Davinovitch. Mrs. Davinovitch. If there's anything you need, don't hesitate to call." He gave them his Lumina business card and fled.

CHAPTER THIRTY-FOUR
DECISIONS AT A QUANTUM LEVEL

THE LUMINA JET was tucked among all the other private jets at the Van Nuys airport. Some bore the logos of their billionaire owners, others were painted black, or red, or gold depending upon their billionaire owner's ego and arrogance. The Lumina plane seemed nondescript by comparison.

The steps were down, the hatch open. Richard wearily climbed the stairs into the plane. Brook set aside his In-N-Out burger, washed down the bite with a sip from his can of Coke. He studied Richard's face.

"I have a flight plan filed, and I just kept pushing back our departure. We can leave in about forty minutes once I clear everything with the tower and FAA."

"Fine."

"Umm, we can share the fries …"

"I'm fine, really."

He thought he heard Brook mutter, *You don't look fine.*

"And boss, since you had your phone turned off, *my* phone has been blowing up. Everybody's trying to reach you. You might want to let them know … you know … that you're all right."

"Who?"

"Uhhh ... everybody. Your sister, Dagmar, Eddie, Angela, Kenzo ... you want me to go on?"

"Kenntnis?"

"Nope."

That was strange, Richard thought.

He hated himself for being unable to keep himself from asking, "Weber?"

"Yep, him, too." Richard felt a jolt of both joy and dread. "I think somebody else had called him to tell him they couldn't reach you."

"Is it awful if I wait to just tell everybody at once? I ... I don't think I can bear to repeat ... it ... over and over."

"Hey, you're in charge. You get to decide." Brook studied him for a moment. "Look, why don't you get some rest. I'll see if I can get wheels up sooner."

✧ ✧ ✧

"HE WAS JUST suddenly *here*," Joseph said as they left the underground parking lot and headed for the elevators.

They were starting the conversation for the third time since he'd picked Richard up at the airport. Richard understood his need for constant repetition; despite everything Joseph had seen and experienced in Virginia, it was clear he'd never *really* believed that Kenntnis wasn't human.

"It scared the crap out of Paulette. I was upstairs, and when I got down to the lobby, I could see right away that Mr. Kenntnis wasn't right." He shot Richard an anguished look. "He's smaller and his eyes are weird, and he won't talk to me, but you'll see."

The elevator deposited them at the penthouse, and Richard stepped out into a wash of dissonant sound. It was as if a maddened piano tuner was torturing the strings of the piano and a monster was clawing at the strings of the Celtic harp.

The living room was very full of people, all staring at Kenntnis.

Cross sat on the arm of the sofa eating chocolate cake. His expression was the most interesting. Grief and calculation were how Richard read it, and it made him nervous. Sorrow and devastation sagged the contours of Dagmar's face. Grenier's plump face held an expression Richard couldn't identify. Angela and Pamela looked confused. Eddie was completely fascinated.

Richard reluctantly turned his attention to the founder of Lumina Enterprises. In the past, whenever Kenntnis would enter a room where there was a musical instrument, the instrument would react. Almost like it was singing a greeting, and it was always melodic and beautiful. This cacophony told him more clearly than anything that Kenntnis was indeed *not right*.

Kenntnis was pacing up and down in front of the bookcases, trailing his fingers across the spines of the books. The man Richard met last year was a spectacular figure—six-foot-six, and massive. At first glance he appeared to be African-American, but as one studied his features it became clear they were an amalgamation of every human racial type. He was Everyman. And not human. Hints from their conversations led Richard to believe he was hundreds of thousands if not millions of years old.

Richard stepped in front of him, trying to halt the pacing.

The not-human became very clear when he looked into Kenntnis's eyes. Before, they had been dark pools that would occasionally flare with silver lights that were reminiscent of the nimbus that surrounded the sword. Now, they were filled with whirling lights both silver and gold. He was physically smaller, and the body seemed more like a hand puppet being imperfectly manipulated. It was a different emptiness than what had faced Richard in that California hospital bed, but the conclusion was the same. The essence, the spark, the soul, if you will, was gone.

Kenntnis frowned and stepped around him. Richard darted in front again.

This time Kenntnis froze, looking confused. "Sir," Richard said gently. Kenntnis shook his head, and the dissonance from the instruments grew louder.

"Maybe he'll recover," Dagmar said hopefully.

"I don't think so," Eddie said. He turned away from the glares from Joseph and Dagmar and looked at Richard. "The information on a light particle degrades the longer it's held in spin glass. I think that's what happened. He lost part of himself—whatever himself was … is. It's certainly fascinating proof of the theory. Shame I can't write a paper. But everybody would think I was nuts."

"If he's so degraded, then how did he get back here?" Pamela asked.

"Keep in mind that I've never met an alien light creature before," the physicist said. "But this is my guess. I think he was frozen at the exact moment he was preparing to escape. That decision was set at a quantum level. So, when he was suddenly freed, the last conscious action was completed. He ran and ended up here."

Angela shook her head. "Okay, I didn't get that at all."

"Doesn't matter," Richard said. "What's clear is that he's not going to be any help to us." *And I destroyed a girl for nothing.*

Richard pressed a hand against his forehead; the noise from the instruments was maddening. "Joseph, could you please take Mr. Kenntnis to the conference room? I can't take this noise any longer."

And Richard realized he'd said the wrong thing, or the right thing but at the wrong time. Joseph bridled. "This is Mr. Kenntnis's home."

Cross stood up. "Nope, it's not. He gave it to the kid here. And he's not Mr. Kenntnis anymore. Face it, whatever animated the meat suit he was wearing, well, it ain't home."

It was stark and cold and horrifically accurate.

✧　✧　✧

DAMON HELD HIS cell phone to his ear with one hand while he scrolled on his computer with the other. He could see what Franklin was describing from the drone images of the Virginia compound. The boiling clouds had been replaced with a normal-looking blue sky. And the gate itself was gone. Where Kenntnis's tomb had stood, there were just shards of glass glittering on the red sand.

"The opening to that other sun … star is also closed," Franklin was saying.

"Well, yay us … or, rather, you guys," Weber said. "All I did was get captured and rescued."

"Quit your bitching. You'd rather we left you?"

Yes.

"And it wasn't us," Franklin grunted. "All that shit was still in place when we pulled out. Must have been something the kid did." *Wonder how Richard would feel being called the kid?* "So maybe you could share with the class?"

"Haven't got a clue," Damon said. "I ... I've been busy ... work."

"So maybe find out? I've got the director on my ass, and he's got the President on *his*."

"Call Richard yourself," Damon said shortly.

"Don't you think I've been trying? That smooth secretary just keeps blowing me off in the most polite way possible."

"I'll see what I can do," Damon said, and hoped the lack of sincerity hadn't been too obvious.

THE APARTMENT FELT like it belonged to a different person. *It actually had,* Richard thought as he sat on the bench behind the Bösendorfer piano. He was pretty sure he didn't like the person he had become. The piano gave a discordant jangle as he rested his elbows on the keys and dropped his face into his hands. The sound made him think of Kenntnis, destroyed because of his failures. Rudi's burned and bloody body. The grotesque sounds Rhiana had made as she convulsed in his arms. Weber's face, twisted in anger.

Everyone kept asking him for his orders—Dagmar, Kenzo, Gold, Franklin, Jeannette, Joseph, Eddie, even Pamela. She had shown him her letter of resignation to the Newport

DA's office, asked if he wanted her to send it? He had given her the ultimate burden-shifting-weasel answer—*I can't make that choice for you.*

He looked around the room. Jeannette had removed his art, books, and clothing weeks ago. All that was left was his inexpensive furniture and the grand piano. Curious, he walked into the small kitchen and opened the refrigerator—empty—as were the cabinets. Why wouldn't they be? He wasn't supposed to live here any longer. He was supposed to live in a penthouse with a chef on call and security guards and a personal assistant. And the job of saving the world. Richard swallowed down nausea.

There was a sharp sound, a rap on glass. Richard whirled, left hand vibrating between pistol and sword, relaxed when he saw Cross standing outside the sliding glass doors to the patio. He crossed to the doors and opened them.

"I'm surprised you didn't just break through," Richard grumbled.

"You're not in any danger. Except from *this*," and Cross smacked the heel of his hand against Richard's forehead. The homeless god was looking grim.

"Going to be my shrink now?" Richard asked.

"Nope. Not my job. My job is to tell you the ugly truth. While it's great news the gates collapsed when Kenntnis went free, a whole shitload of my kind came through before they did, and they're all going to be working just as hard as they can to tear open the membranes between the universes. They have to be hunted down, and you're the only Paladin we've got, so you need to *get your shit together*," Cross hissed.

It was a situation he'd never foreseen or planned for.

Richard had assumed that once Kenntnis was freed, the burden, the expectations would be off of him.

"I can't—"

"Yeah, you can. Kenntnis wouldn't have put you in charge if he didn't think you could."

Richard shook his head. "No, it was an accident of genetics." He pulled the hilt out of its holster. "It's only because I can use this."

Cross leaned back and stared down at him. "I'm not a good person ... actually I'm not a person at all, but I've been molded and formed and changed by good people, so I know one when I see it. And you're a good person. You wouldn't be tearing yourself to pieces over that girl if you weren't. But there are a lot of people, good and bad, who need *you* to protect them now. Isn't that why you became a cop in the first place?" Richard felt his throat tighten. "And you don't have to do this alone. I don't know if this is more threat than solace, but you got *me*. You got your sis. And Eddie, well, everybody who works for Lumina. Okay, I've been empathetic for as long as I can stand, so sympathy time is over. We need you back in the fight. *Now!*"

Cross left through the front door. Richard returned to the piano. Played one minor chord. The notes hung shimmering in the air amplified by the weapon he carried.

CHAPTER THIRTY-FIVE

I Think This Is the Beginning ...

*B*EER IS FOOD, *right?* Damon raised the bottle to his lips and took a deep sip. He was sitting at the small dinette table in his furnished apartment staring at the divorce papers that had been delivered to him late that afternoon. It looked like him and Marge weren't going to try again after all.

And another one bites the dust, he thought, not entirely sure whether he meant the beer or the marriage or ... that other thing. He tossed the empty bottle in the general direction of the trash. With a weary groan he pushed to his feet and trudged into the postage-stamp kitchen to fish another beer out of the fridge. He was just popping off the cap when there was a knock at his door.

He returned to the table to pick up his pistol before moving to the door. It wasn't paranoid if you'd been kidnapped and tortured, right? He looked through the peephole and saw, to his surprise, Richard's sister. He opened the door.

"Hey," he said. "Come in." He turned away, headed for the kitchen. "What do ya need? Want a beer?"

"Yes, thank you."

That surprised him and he looked back over his shoulder at her as she closed the front door. "So, not a teetotaler like your brother?"

She paused pulling off her long fleece-lined coat. "No. *I* can hold my liquor."

"Ouch, you really don't like him, do you?" Damon said as he opened the bottle and handed her the beer.

"Sometimes no, and sometimes he drives me mad, but I do love him. Which is why I'm here."

"For which part? The driving you mad part or the loving part?"

She took a sip of the beer. "Can't it be both?"

"Yeah, I suppose." He gestured toward the couch and pulled around one of the dinette chairs. He sat down facing her, noticed the ashtray filled with cigarette butts and the ash strewn across the scarred top of the coffee table. He really ought to clean.

"I understand that his …" Her mouth worked for a moment as if tasting something unpleasant. "Affection … crush on you is awkward and uncomfortable for you. Honestly, I really didn't want to know these details about my brother's … proclivities either, but I want to assure you that if you were to … return, he will never make you uncomfortable by either word or action. He feels responsible for what happened to you."

"Okay, good to know. But I don't think that's the reason you came here tonight."

"No. Notwithstanding what I just said—he needs you. You give him confidence and courage. He's frozen right now, and we can't afford that. Humanity can't afford that."

"The gates are gone," Weber countered.

"But the monsters remain, and he's the only one who can fight them. He needs your support. And I'm worried about who might fill the void if you don't come back."

They measured looks. "Grenier," Damon finally said.

She nodded. "Yes."

Damon ran a hand through his disheveled hair. "He knows he can't trust that guy, right?"

"Yes, but Grenier spent thirty years convincing people *to* trust him, and Richard is vulnerable right now."

"Because of me?"

"You're part of it. Then there's the burden of managing Lumina. The knowledge he is the only Paladin, and Cross has been so helpful telling him how Paladins don't live long. And, finally, what he did to Rhiana."

"Is she dead?"

"No, permanent coma."

"He did what he had to do," Weber said heavily.

"We've all told him that. Maybe *you* can make him believe it." She stood, gathered up her purse and her coat. "I'm not expecting you to make a decision right now. Just think about it." She took one final swallow of her beer, slipped on the coat and left.

Weber stared at the two bottles, their condensation forming rings on the table. He finished off his beer, then for good measure he finished off hers. He definitely needed to be drunk to think about this.

✧　✧　✧

RICHARD WANDERED GHOSTLIKE through the building. 5:00 AM. None of the workers apart from security personnel were present. Even Franz wouldn't be in until six to start preparing breakfast. Pamela, Kenntnis, Grenier, and Eddie were still asleep upstairs. Well, maybe Kenntnis was sleeping. Every time Richard had checked on him the man ... alien ... he had been sitting quietly staring at nothing with those strange silver eyes. In desperation Richard had drawn the sword, and the cacophony from the musical instruments in the penthouse had ceased. Now Kenntnis just sat if you put him in a chair, or walked if you took his arm and guided him, and always with that thousand-yard stare.

Richard tried swimming, but after a couple of laps he realized what he really wanted was to get away from Lumina. *As if that's even possible,* he thought as he dried, dressed, and balanced the sword hilt on his palm. With a sigh of resignation, he holstered it.

So where to go? It really wasn't a question. Richard knew where he would go. Returning to the lobby he took the other elevator to the underground garage. One of the night guards, Richard tried to recall her name, but failed, approached.

"Would you like a driver, sir?"

"No. I've always wanted to try out some of these cars." He gestured at the line of muscle sports cars.

The young woman grinned. "Who wouldn't? I just love sports cars, and this is like sport car heaven." She pointed as she ticked them off. "Ferrari, Bugatti, Lamborghini, Aston Martin, Lucid, McClaren, and the vintage Mustang."

"And the armored SUV and the armored limo," Richard added. *Lest I ever forget that apparently there are a lot of people as well as monsters that want to kill me.*

She gave a small sigh. "But some of them have been adapted for electric; you don't get the roar, and I kind of liked the roar though I understand the reasoning for the switch out."

Richard nodded, then said, "I know you probably have to accompany me so pick your ride."

She gave him such a happy, joyful look that he almost felt guilty for resenting the fact that she had to follow him.

He leaned in and whispered, "And which ones still have the roar?"

"The Ferrari, Bugatti, and the Lamborghini Huracan."

"I'll take that one," Richard said.

"Then I'll take the Bugatti, and maybe I'll be able to keep up with you."

"What makes you think I won't be obeying all the speed limits?" Richard asked with a small smile.

"I'm sure you will, sir."

"Please forgive me, but I'm still learning all your names."

"I'm Ann Ridley."

"Nice to meet you, Ann." They shook hands. "Just in case we should get separated. I'm going to APD headquarters."

Richard slipped behind the wheel of the car, adjusted the seat and mirrors, and cautiously pulled out of the garage. The thunder from the powerful engine could be felt through his body, and the stick moved smoothly through the gears as he raced down Montgomery toward the freeway. Ann was good; she stayed with him.

Richard realized that Joseph needed to hire someone to replace Rudi. The reminder of Rudi, and how he died, had his eyes burning. He dashed away the tears before they could fall.

My fault, my fault, my fault.

He had told them to wait for him at the house. Get Damon ... Weber and *wait* for him.

There are going to be casualties. Grenier's words came back to him as Richard crested the ramp onto I-25 heading south.

But not my people. I should have kept my people safe. And then Richard thought about the people he'd cut down at the compound. They were casualties, too, and somewhere people were going to weep for them. Just as Lottie and Todd wept for their child.

No! Grief is a luxury I can't afford.

Richard focused on the road, while thinking about steps to be taken. They probably needed to hire a great deal more security. There was no longer just Kenntnis to protect. There was Kenntnis, Pamela, Amelia, Brent, and Paul, Angela, Grenier, Eddie ... and Weber. He hoped the lieutenant wouldn't resent it, but by his proximity to Richard he was also a target.

His arrival managed to coincide with shift change so there were a lot of cops in the parking lot to witness the arrival of the Lamborghini and the Bugatti.

When he entered the bullpen several of the cops rushed over to greet him. Lucile emerged from dispatch to give him a big hug.

"Oh, Rich, I'm so glad to see you." She held him at arm's length. "You look tired. You're too skinny, and how's the leg?"

Richard patted his thigh while sneaking a glance toward Weber's office. He wasn't in. It was a relief. "Almost healed," he answered. "I just wanted to check in. See if I had anything pending."

A large hand landed on his shoulder. "You need to hit the range and requalify," Captain Ortiz said. "Welcome back, Oort. Weber told me what happened back East. Said you saved his life."

Richard felt himself blushing. "I had a lot of help. The FBI—"

"Well, that'd be a fucking first," the captain snorted. "Look, you're still on medical leave, and don't think I missed that limp when you walked in. Lieutenant Gabaldon, our firearms instructor, is out at the West Mesa range today. I'll call and tell him to expect you. Go get qualified and we'll talk about how to structure your return. Assuming you want to come back."

Richard touched the badge clipped to his belt. "This means a lot to me, sir. Giving it up ... well, we can talk about this later. I'll go to the range now."

Even though it was a cold and windy day Richard was glad he would be under a New Mexico turquoise sky rather than in the dank confines of an indoor range. Also, driving to West Mesa would give both him and Ann more time in their fun cars.

When they reached the range there were a handful of cars in the lot. Ann climbed out of her car, and said to him, "I think I should come in with you, sir. Makes me nervous to have you around strangers with guns."

"Okay, the range is open to civilian shooters as well."

"Great. Joseph has us drill once a week at the Lumina range, but more practice never hurts."

The range he hadn't even known existed until a few short

weeks ago. But all he said was, "True that. In every aspect of life, I expect."

They went inside where a hard-bitten woman with too-bright, dyed-red hair sat behind the counter. She had a pistol on each hip, a package of Nicorette gum on the counter in front of her, and an open can of Red Bull. Richard hoped he hadn't just seen Sam in thirty years. They signed in, the woman provided them with targets, ear protectors, and waved them toward the range.

As they stepped out of the back door and onto the range there was the sharp report of gunfire followed by the Range Officer's amplified voice from the tower calling for *ceasefire.* Gabaldon was waiting, clipboard in hand. Richard gave a mental headshake. Paper and pen. Why not an iPad and just email the results back to the chief? *Let no one think police forces are progressive … in most ways, including the ones that really matter, as any black person in America can attest to,* he thought.

"Oort, we'll just run through your primary weapon today. Deal with backup weapons and phase two another day."

"Yes, sir."

They left Ann in the public shooting area and Gabaldon took Richard to the dedicated police range. Richard set his pistol on the table for inspection, Gabaldon checked out the weapon then gave Richard a nod of approval. Richard returned the weapon to its holster.

"My leg isn't fully healed so I may be a bit awkward going from standing to kneeling and switching sides," Richard said.

"Just do your best."

Richard nodded and took his place behind the barricade

at the twenty-five yard line. The commence fire order was given. He took his stance and double tapped out the eight shots from various sides and positions.

He had always been a good shot. Today was no exception. He had forty seconds to fire off eight shots. He did it in thirty-two, and all eight were grouped in the center mass of the targets.

Gabaldon made a notation on his clipboard. "Nice."

He had just finished the move-to-cover and walk-and-draw evaluations when a familiar baritone voice said, "Deadeye Dick."

Richard felt his heart leap with a mix of joy and dread. "Say that again and I'm going to punch you."

"Where? On the belt buckle?"

Richard turned to face Weber. "I'm not *that* short."

Gabaldon snorted. "Should I give you two a moment?" Weber stiffened and Richard felt his cheeks flaming.

Weber held out his hand. "How about I finish his evaluation?"

"Sure, that wind is colder than La Llorona's left tit. I'll be happy to get out of it." Gabaldon walked away.

"So, just one-handed-firing left to do?" Weber asked. Richard nodded, not trusting himself to speak. He finished the exercise, and Weber marked it down. "Okay, you're requalified. Take a walk with me?"

"Okay."

Richard holstered his pistol, dug his hands deep into his pockets, and shivered. The wind chilled his nose and cheeks, and his toes in the expensive Italian loafers were very cold. Ann gave him a questioning look, but he waved her off. They left the range and walked out onto the rolling expanse of the mesa. The extinct volcanoes were in front of them. Richard looked back to the east where the stark rock face of the Sandia Mountains blocked any further city growth. He narrowed his eyes when there was a gleam of white and silver at the north end of the mountains. The Lumina Building, or just his imagination? They made their way through clumps of sagebrush and chamisa. Weber paused and kicked at the dirt, bringing up streaks of black and an arrowhead.

"Firepit," he grunted as he bent and recovered the arrowhead. "Hunting party probably stopped here a thousand years ago." He laid the flint point gently in Richard's hand.

"How did you do that?" Richard marveled.

"Had a buddy who became an archeologist. We used to go camping and hunting together. He showed me how to spot these things."

"You don't see him any longer?"

"He passed away a few years back."

"I'm sorry."

Weber shrugged. "Eventually death comes for all of us." Richard studied the other man's profile, noting how his pock-marked jaw tightened. Weber suddenly turned to face him. "So, folks seem to think I can be of help to you. They also think you need help. Do you need help?"

For an instant Richard considered denying it, but he knew those wise, calculating brown eyes would see right through his denials. He nodded. "Yes. But my weakness doesn't have to be your problem. Shouldn't be your problem."

"Stop that shit right now." Richard flinched at the tone.

Weber looked briefly contrite. "Sorry, that came out a little strong. And just so you know, I'll never hit you again. Shouldn't have done it the first time. Christ knows you've been hurt enough." And his eyes drifted to Richard's right thigh.

He shrugged. "It's okay. Sometimes trauma needs to be expressed and sometimes it comes out in awkward and inappropriate ways."

Weber gave a short laugh and sat down on a rock outcropping near the firepit. Richard hated putting the material of his Xenia suit on the fine sand of the mesa, but it didn't look like Weber was preparing to move anytime soon. In fact, he was lighting a cigarette. Giving a mental sigh, Richard settled onto the ground, right leg stretched out in front of him. It was still sore enough that sitting cross-legged really wasn't an option for him.

Weber blew out a long trail of smoke and asked, "Is that a roundabout way of saying I was a giant asshole?"

"Maybe a little." Richard reached out and plucked one of the long sword-like leaves of the large yucca plant to his left.

"So, I'll ask again, are you in trouble?" Weber asked, and his tone was gentle in the way a man might try to calm a small, skittish, terrified animal.

✧ ✧ ✧

THAT SILVER-GILT HEAD was bent over the leaf as Richard began to nervously shred it. Damon studied the whorls of hair at his nape, the surprisingly broad shoulders tapering down to a slender waist. He waited.

Finally, Richard whispered, barely audible over the ever-present New Mexico winds, "I'm terrified."

"Of what? Getting hurt again? Dying?"

Richard shook his head. "No, making the wrong decision, doing the wrong thing. Letting more people die ... or ... or get hurt." He looked away and swallowed hard.

"You gotta stop beating yourself up over what happened to me. I should have been more on guard. I knew the bad guys were still out there. And you're not the only one with guilt. You all came to get me out and Rudi died doing that. We both got *woulda, shoulda, coulda* messing with our heads. And I'm sorry I took it out on you. I was angry, but with myself for ever putting you ... all of you in danger just to save my sorry ass." He held up an admonishing finger. "And do *not* say it."

"All right." The younger man stole a glance up at Weber from beneath those outrageous lashes. Richard muttered something that sounded suspiciously like, *"But you do have a nice ass."*

"What was that?"

"Nothing." A limpid look like butter wouldn't melt in his damn mouth.

Weber folded his arms across his chest and assumed a frown. "Goddamn it, I need you to respect my *authoritah!*" he huffed. That drew a small smile. "Seriously, Rhode Island, here's the thing; you *not* making a decision is going to lead to a whole lotta bad outcomes. Sure, you might be able to say, *not my fault, I didn't do anything that caused that*, but I think you're too smart and too honest with yourself to take the easy way out. And remember, *not* deciding is also a decision."

"So, Damon, of all the thousand things pending what should I do first?"

He noted the use of his first name. "Hire your sister. She's got your back and she'll kick your ass when you need it."

"I thought that was your job."

"Oh, trust me, I'll keep my foot and leg limber. Next, what's the most urgent thing *right now*?" And Damon realized this was just like talking a young, nervous cop through a tricky case. *Maybe I can actually help, and not just as emotional and moral support.*

"Tracking down the Old Ones that came through," Richard answered.

"Okay, and who you got who knows a shitload about Old Ones?" Weber asked.

"Well, Cross." Richard paused, then added, "And Grenier."

"And you're kinda stuck with the bastard, so why not let him make himself useful. What else?"

Richard pulled the hilt out of its holster. "We need more of these. And preferably not in sword form." He looked up at Weber with dawning realization. "I've got Eddie and apparently just whole boxcar loads of scientists that work for me."

"Good."

A frown marred the white brow. "But they're useless if we don't have people who can use them." Richard broke off suddenly. "Oh my, Cross can sense people with no magic."

"There you go, now you have something to keep the creepy alien bum busy."

Richard stood and dusted off the back of his trousers. "Thank you. I don't feel so frozen any longer. I'm still scared, but at least I can be scared while I do something."

"Good." Weber pinched the end of what remained of his cigarette and ground it into the sand. He put the cold butt into his coat pocket and stood. "So, what about me? You got a job for me?"

"I thought ... I assumed ... I—"

"I thought you'd absorbed that lesson about assuming, Rhode Island. I was planning on retiring when I hit forty-five. So, I do it three years early. Now how can I help?"

Richard stared at the ground while chewing on a hang-nail on his thumb. "After what happened to the Lumina facility in Indonesia, I think we need a far more robust security force." There was again that shy glance from beneath the lashes. "You were in the army, a police lieutenant. I think you'd be perfect ... for that."

Damon nodded. "In addition to beefing up security at the facilities, I think we need a rapid response force that we can send in as needed." He found himself already thinking about former army buddies who might be good prospects for the team. "So, am I in?" He gave Richard a wink. "We can discuss salary another time. Just don't hand it off to your sis, I bet she'd be tough as all fuck."

"You're right there. And I'd be a pushover, so we'll let you and Dagmar hash out the details."

He grinned down at Richard and draped his arm across the younger man's shoulders. "What was it Rick says to Louis at the end of Casablanca?"

Richard smiled up at him. "I think this is the beginning of a beautiful friendship."

If You Liked ...

If you liked *Morningstar's Heir* you might also enjoy:
Lucifer's War
One Fatal Tree
To Reign in Heaven

ABOUT THE AUTHOR

Melinda M. Snodgrass studied opera at the Conservatory of Vienna, graduated Magna cum Laude from U.N.M. with a degree in history, and went on to Law School. After 3 years as a lawyer she realized she hated lawyers and turned to writing.

In 1988 she accepted a job on Star Trek: The Next Generation and began her Hollywood career where she has worked on staff on numerous shows and has written television pilots and feature films. She currently has two television series in active development.

In the prose world she writes for and co-edits the shared world anthology series Wild Cards with George R. R. Martin.

In addition, she writes her own novels. She is working on a fourth novel in the Carolingian series and a fourth novel for her White Fang Law series.

For fun she rides her dressage horse, plays video games and spends a lot of time in the gym. (Or she did before there was a pandemic).

BOOK CLUB QUESTIONS

1. The author opens the books with a person in crises similar to a teaser in a television show before turning to the view point characters. Do you think this is an effective technique?

2. The author presented the main character firsts through the thoughts and eyes of others. did that work for you, or did it help ground you as a reader?

3. Can you think of other books or shows that have done this? Here is one example—the TV show House.

4. When you are writing a series it's important to give readers context for those who haven't read the first book. Do you think the author did a good job of summarizing what had happened in book 1?

5. Were you surprised when Synder tried to kill Richard or had you seen the foreshadowing?

6. Were Richard's father and sister right that he should have resigned from the police force?

7. Was Dagmar's reaction when being present with the sword realistic? Would you have run too?

8. Did Grenier's reason for coming to Richard make sense to you?

9. Were you surprised Richard allowed Grenier to stay?

10. Would you say this is a book about parental expectations that are reasonable, or are both Richard and Rhiana's fathers abusive?

11. How do you think the government would respond to a crises like the one in Morningstar's Heir. Do you think the parties would pull together or would they fall back on gridlock and politicizing the issue?

12. In the twenty-first century was it realistic to have a parent reject a child because they are queer?

13. Were you surprised that Pamela sided with Richard over her father?

14. Rhiana recognized that Richard was attracted to Weber and used that. Did the author raise questions for you about where Weber is coming from emotionally as regards Richard?

15. Was Rudi's death enough stakes or would you rather have had the author kill a more major character during the attack on the compound?

16. In the book Rhiana uses real science ie Slow Glass, and magic to craft a prison for Kenntnis. Did you enjoy the mixing science and fantasy in the book? Can you think of other novels that use that trope?

17. Are you interested in reading that section in the Jungle Book that was the inspiration for Richard's plan? You can read it here. https://www.sawanonlinebookstore.com/red-dog/

18. Did it feel right that Richard and Weber would have a physical confrontation?

19. Did Richard's reasoning for why he broke his promise to never hurt Rhiana make sense? Was Kenntnis more important than that promise?

20. Were you surprised when Kenntnis returned but was damaged? Why do you think the author made that choice?

21. Did the final scenes between Richard and Weber ring true for you?

22. Where do you think Richard and Weber's relationship will go in book three, Dawn's Despair?

OTHER TITLES BY
MELINDA M. SNODGRASS

Circuit series:
Circuit
Circuit Breaker
Final Circuit
Queen's Gambit Declined

The Edge series:
The Edge of Reason
The Edge of Ruin
The Edge of Dawn

The Imperials Saga:
The High Ground
In Evil Times
The Hidden World
The Currency of War
The Thucydides Trap

White Fang Law:
This Case is Gonna Kill Me, Book 1
Box Office Poison, Book 2
Publish and Perish, Book 3